PEREGRINATION SERIES
BOOK 3

FIRE

S.G. Boudreaux

curiosity, or he was truly interested was still a mystery. Perhaps she would take some time to find out during this peregrination.

Some of the other Dragoman and Peregrines were in relationships and seemed to make it work just fine. At least, so far it had worked. They probably hadn't had any problems since they had all only been reunited just a few days ago.

Zaccai looked up at the blazing sun. It was reaching well past noon and the summer sun was high in the sky with no cloud cover evident anywhere. It was stiflingly hot and dry with no relief to be seen for at least another hour. They were growing ever closer to the mountain ranges but still had several miles to go before they reached the base of Mount Timna. The entrances to Solomon's mines were an unsure thing since none of them had ever been here before. But current period maps placed them approximately sixteen miles southwest of Mount Timna.

Zaccai noticed some of the younger kids looking particularly hot and tired and rode forward to check on them.

"Dominic," she said, "are you drinking your water?"

"Yes ma'am, but it has been awhile since I had any."

"How long is a while?"

"Maybe an hour or so?

"Then I suggest you drink some. You need to slowly sip from your canteen regularly while out in this heat or you might dehydrate. At least every half hour, all right? Make sure that your body doesn't stop sweating." She rode off to check on the others.

"Wade, Bridget, are you two drinking enough water?"

Bridget shook her head as she answered. "Yes, but it's awfully hot."

Wade responded as well. "Too bad there isn't any shade." Sweat streaked the large boy's face.

"It won't be much longer now. I'll ride up and ask Ezekiel if he can do anything about some cloud cover." She rode off to speak with him, knowing full well that was probably a definite no. You can't to save her, transporting her to Malachi's safe house at Barrier's Edge. She awoke three days later to a new world and a new calling.

She hoped and prayed every day that her father, Viho, and the others had made it out of the fire in time. If he had survived, she knew her father thought her dead, burned up in the fire. That was eighteen years ago. She only prayed that God had given her parents, and Viho, comfort.

She and Viho had become very close. She wouldn't say she had been in love with him, but she had loved him. Zaccai had never allowed herself to experience real love towards a man. It was a luxury she couldn't afford in her youth and now it wasn't something she had time for. Not to mention there weren't many age-appropriate men around. Until lately that is.

Since the convergence of all the Dragoman and Peregrines on Reader's Island she realized there were more men closer to her age than she thought. Most of them were very attractive as well. One man in particular, Ezekiel Raphael Davis, known as Zeke to most, was just such a man.

Zaccai watched him as their slow-moving caravan of twenty made its way across the Araba Valley of the Negev Desert headed toward Timna. He was close to her in age, maybe a few years younger. He was also a man of color; strong, virile, and most of all, Godly. Viho had been all the above except for the Godly part. He had been determined to stick to the old beliefs and ways, and as his wife, Zaccai would have had to sacrifice her belief in God and follow the customs of her husband. Even though she had been a tribal princess it was the tribe's men who had been the ones to rule.

She shook herself from her reverie to scan the area around them. She had taken to riding the rear point of the caravan to keep a keen eye open. Zeke had agreed to ride mid-point which gave her the perfect vantage point to watch him. She hadn't really had much of a chance to speak to him while on the island but had noticed him looking at her on occasion. Whether it was purely coincidental, animals that had to make this journey, they would have to work as quickly as possible to not run short on the water supplies.

Zaccai Razi Wekesa was used to dry, arid climates. She had been born and raised in the African plains at the foot of the Kilimanjaro Mountains in Moshi. Her father had been a tribal chieftain of the Chaga Tribe. Thankfully she had been born during the colonial era when Christianity had been introduced to her people. Her father had already accepted Christ by the time she had been born, so therefore she had been saved from some of the more traditional customs of early tribal beliefs.

At the age of twelve her father had started grooming her to be a leader amongst her people. By the age of fourteen her father had made a pact with a neighboring tribe for peace and had bartered her hand in marriage to that village chieftain's son, Viho; also, of a Chaga Tribe. They had been thrown together almost daily for hunting, social events, anything really where they could spend time together before marriage, allowing them to get to know one another. Not that it mattered one way or the other, for if they ended up with a dislike for one another, the marriage would still have taken place, and Zaccai would have done as her father had asked and married him. It was her duty as a tribe royal. Whatever was needed from her to bring peace and prosperity to her people, she would have done it.

She and Viho were to be married on the eve of her eighteenth birthday, and she had found over the years that Viho would have made a good and honorable husband. But that was not the plan that God had for her life. When she was seventeen years of age, she, Viho, both of their fathers, and several other village warriors had been in the Serengeti plains when a brush fire had started and roared through the savannah at an alarming rate. The fire had burned so fast and hot she hadn't had time to escape. She had been tracking some game alone on one end of the plains when the fire had started, and the winds shifted in her direction. The heat was so intense that a portal had opened right where she had been kneeling and praying to God

One day the angels came to present themselves before the Lord, and Satan also came with them. The Lord said to Satan, "Where have you come from?" Satan answered the Lord, "From roaming the earth, going back and forth on it."

Job 1:6-7

Chapter 1

Timna Valley, Israel, Negev Desert, 1840 A.D.

Timna Valley was a horseshoe shaped area of mountains with layers of multiple colors of sand, and sparsely placed trees, flowering cactus, and shrubs. The large rock formations that could be seen off in the distance were the direction they were headed, and those formations sat on three sides of the valley which were the north, west, and south. They would travel the valley until they came upon King Solomon's Pillars which lay just southwest of Mount Timna where they would begin the search for Solomon's Copper Mines. The Mountain should provide adequate shade and hopefully a cave large enough to house all of them for however long they were going to be there. They had also brought along tents for just that purpose, but a cave would work much better. If they found one large enough then they could erect the tents inside, giving everyone more privacy.

They also understood, from what the Dragoman had told them, that this desert valley strangely enough had a small lake known as Wadi Nehushtan which was fed by one of the three stream beds that ran according to the seasons, giving a viable water source to animals native to the area, but only during rain run off which was during the winter months. Seeing as how they were in the mid-summer months water would be minimal during this time. With all the people and much-needed relationships formed while on the recent, month long furlough on Reader's Island.

The Dragoman have stayed on Reader's Island to try and open the five recently found ancient, archival books, and to translate the information found within the pages of the book known as the *Book of the Keepers*. The last book is yet to be opened since the recently found key disappeared before they could use it. Stolen away by a traitor of whom no one knows the identity. Several of the lead Peregrines have been charged with keeping the secret about the traitor to prevent mistrust amongst the entire group. They must also try and ferret out this traitor who could quite possibly prevent the saving of man and cause a mass slaughter of the Peregrines like the one that took place over thirteen years ago.

Now, on with the story.

Prologue

The earth is being plagued by violent storms that are growing stronger and more frequent. Cities are being devastated and people are dying. The storms are a result of man's ever-growing sin nature which has thrown the balance of nature off kilter. God has chosen certain people to travel throughout time and space by way of portals created during the strongest of storms to try and rectify the situation.

These special chosen few known as Peregrines are guided by people known as the Dragoman. The Peregrines are sent on missions to find artifacts, relics, and special armor that will aid in their abilities to save mankind from itself. The Peregrines must also battle demons that try to thwart their efforts and kill anyone they can in the process. The Dragoman are preparing the Peregrines for a long-awaited battle they refer to as the Final Battle. Unsure as to what with, when, or where they are to have this final battle, they follow Gods' leading in preparation for this great day.

This installment, Book 3: Fire, picks up where Book 2 left off. The Peregrines have just left Reader's Island in the heart of the Bermuda Triangle and have crossed over into Timna Valley in Israel, near the Copper Mines of King Solomon in the year 1840 AD in search of the first piece of the Armor of God. Its location was given to them from the *Book of Armor;* one of five recently found archives. They have been for-warned by the Dragoman that they must also face great trials that wage wars within themselves. During these trials, they must overcome their own battles that also line up with the Fruits of the Spirit. If they can overcome these personal battles, then God will reveal to them as to where to find the pieces of armor. If not, it could mean utter destruction for all of mankind.

They have also just recently discovered that they have a traitor in their midst. Trust in each other is crucial to the success of their missions, and this revelation could prove to be the undoing of the

Author's Note

First, welcome to any new readers who may be beginning with this third book in the series. I encourage you to go back and read books 1 and 2 to fully understand who the characters are and what the books are all about. Also, a big shout out to all my loyal fans who have returned to read the ongoing story entitled the Peregrination Series. I hope you've enjoyed the last two books, Earth and Wind, and that you will find even more fun, intrigue, and perhaps a few new favorite characters within these pages. The next in the series will be titled *Water*.

As per the first two books, I will introduce to you more on the characters that you have already been reading about. Book 3 will begin with an introduction to some of the backstories for the Dragoman known as Malachai Harel, and his Peregrine's who are Zaccai Wekesa, Uriah Mose, Gabriele Bailey, and Dominic Amando. Their stories both past and present are woven into the current situations, and are joined by all our past friends, and some new and forgotten characters. I hope you enjoy this, the third book entitled *Fire*, in this five book fictional series entitled the Peregrination Series

Glossary

Bold letters get the **long or hard** sound, while Capped letters get the annunciated sound.

Characters Names:
Zaccai Wekessa (za KI we kE sa) African Princess of the Chaga Tribe 1775
Ezekial Davis (**E** ze **k**i ul **Da** vis) New Zealand Aussie 1992
Uriah Mose Yer **I** ah **Mo**se) Ancient Hittite iron worker from 1400 BC
Memnah (Mem nah) Chief of her tribal clan, 1840 AD
Bartholome' (bar To lo may)
Rowthorn (ROW thorn)
Creature:
Tribhon (TRIb hun) a small animal bigger than a squirrel but smaller than a raccoon. Native to Zanchier and lives in the forest of Xantifal Mountains.

Peregrinate (v). Leaving one's homeland and wandering for the love of God; to travel especially on foot, to travel over or through something.

ISBN   978-1-960091-08-6 (Hardback Special Edition)
ISBN   978-1-7339636-2-6 (paperback)
ISBN   978-1-7339636-3-3 (digital)

www.zanchierpublications.com

sgb@sgboudreaux.com
www.SGBoudreaux.com

Peregrination Series Book 3

Fire

S.G. Boudreaux

make clouds without moisture and there was no moisture anywhere around them, save the little they had for drinking and they weren't wasting that for a little bit of shade.

"Ezekiel, is there any way you can conjure up a little shade to block some of the sun for a while?" She approached, falling into rhythm beside his horse.

"No way, not unless we find some water somewhere and I doubt that's likely to happen anytime soon," he apologized.

"I figured as much but, I told the kids I would ask." She grinned, nodding to her reference just behind them.

"By the way, you can call me Zeke for short if you like. Most everyone does." He flashed his bright smile at her. "How much longer do you think we have before we reach our destination?"

"All right, I shall do as you wish, Zeke." She smiled back at him before answering his next question. "We may have about an hour left before reaching the mountain's base, then another bit of time up the side of it. Hopefully we will find a cave at the base or on the side somewhere that will allow for more shade than camping on the top would."

"A cave would be a lot cooler than tents. Especially since there are probably no shade trees of any kind at the top."

"Yes. Let us hope that we find such a place. And one large enough for all of us. It is highly likely that we will. These mines were once very populated and housed many slaves to work them. The slaves likely lived in tents but the men in charge who ran the mining surely lived in the multiple caverns. Perhaps some of the caves located within the mines themselves are large enough for all of us," she stated, remembering the information that Malachai had given her to read about the area's history.

"Yes, but then we have the horses to worry about. We can't leave them in the hot sun all day with no shade, food, or water," he answered.

"I believe we will find a place large enough to house them as well. Surely our God will provide for us." She smiled again, turning to resume her place at the back of the line as Zeke watched her go.

They made it to the base of the mountain by two-thirty where they did indeed find a large cavern mid-way up where they could all fit, including the horses, with plenty of room to spare. Several of the women pitched the tents while others tended the animals. Some of the men gathered the wood they found along the way that Jason had insisted on picking up. Because of his foresight they had wood to make a fire to cook on for several days, allowing them to save the premade fire logs they had brought along as a latter provision. Not knowing how long they would be here, they had to ration appropriately.

The average temperature for the day was a scorching one-hundred degrees or higher and cooled substantially by nightfall with the temperature often reaching the low sixties. Burning the fire throughout the night for warmth might be needed but might also be a necessity just to keep any unwanted predators away from the camp and the horses. At the same time, they also didn't want to alert any traveling nomads to their presence. Of course, a group of twenty people and horses would be hard to hide anyway.

As everyone busied themselves with their chores, the group leaders, which consisted of Jason, Seth, Oz, Sofia, Zaccai, Zeke, and Nick, made their way to the top of Mount Timna to get a panoramic view of Timna Valley and where everything lay in perspective to the maps they had brought with them.

Seth stood upon the mountain top looking out over Timna Valley, marveling at the beautiful landscape before him. He had never seen so many natural sand colors all in one place. The shades ran from black, red, pink, yellow, white, gold, many shades of brown, and of course the green of the copper minerals that ran throughout the mountains. The stone pillars known as Solomon's Pillars were large and oval shaped, formed by the years of water runoff and winds slicing away at the rocks. There were many other large rock formations, such as one in particular that looked like a huge mushroom. Another was a large spiral mountain that twisted up towards them from below, and an area known as the arches which had large archways and holes within the rock. According to their information the mountains that surrounded the valley had large, cavernous areas throughout them. Hopefully they led inside the mines that lay buried deep beneath the valley floor.

Some other fascinating things to discover in the valley were the statues and the altars built by the people who once inhabited these lands thousands of years before. There was also a large sphinx statue guarding one area of the valley entrance along with several Egyptian statues standing out in the desert sands.

They were sure to find all other manner of things down in the mines as well. These mines hadn't been worked or inhabited for hundreds of years. Seth's curiosity and imagination were beginning to excite him. He had always had an adventurous side and was more than ready to climb down into the mines right now and have a look around. They still had to find the entrances to the copper mines and to see what they would need by way of ropes or ladders to venture down inside. The original plans were to explore the caves and tunnels early the next morning.

The maps they had brought with them showed many entrances to the mines. The shafts should be scattered throughout the valley at the base of several of the mountain ranges. Most of which seemed to be located due west by the Arches.

Also located around the base of Timna Mountain were smelting areas which consisted of bowl type structures in the ground which sat on the side of small stone fire pits, with bellows placed on the opposite sides to stoke the fires. Someone would stand upon the bellows rocking back and forth and stoke the fire pit, which in turn refined and separated the mined copper which was either placed in the bowls or ran into the bowls from inside the fire pits. Exactly how it was done was uncertain since archaeological sites from later time periods had not deduced the exact science of how all the ancient tools were used in the process.

Jason and several of the others pulled some binoculars from their packs and scanned the area surrounding the mountain.

Jason spoke as he slowly looked out over the vast desert lands. "Well, I can see several other formations more clearly, but we're too far away to see any mine entrances with the binoculars. Half of us can head west later this afternoon and see what we can find while the rest remain here to watch over the camp, at least until we know what we're dealing with. The mines are about sixteen miles from here, so depending on whether or not we can find some caves like the one we found below will decide whether or not we move camp."

"Sounds like a good idea to me," Seth stated.

"Yes, I agree," Zaccai spoke. "The cave below is very large and will provide good cover from the heat, but sixteen miles is very far by horseback. To make that daily or more than once a day will be difficult, especially on the animals. Now if we had Camels, it would be much easier."

"Yes, but there is nowhere to buy a camel, Zaccai," Zeke stated teasingly.

"True." She smiled at him.

Jason turned to look at his friends. "Let's get back to camp and have some dinner, rest, and pray. Let's also not forget that before God reveals the location of the Belt of Truth that someone, or several of us, has some trials to go through." An uncomfortable look crossed his features.

As they made their way back down the mountainside, they all became a bit more somber as they retreated mentally into their own thoughts and worries on the mention of the trials. Each of them wondering when and how God would begin to reveal their deepest secrets and biggest flaws, not only to themselves but quite possibly to the others as well.

"We also need ta' remember that we have a trait'r among us that we need ta' be lookin' out fer too," Oz chimed in.

Jason turned thoughtful. "Seems like we have a lot to pray about. Make sure not to slip and let on that we are searching for a traitor when in groups."

It was an hour or so past noon when camp set up was completed and everyone had eaten and rested. Jason, Seth, Zeke, and Oz set out in search of the mines, while Zaccai, Sofia, and Nick stayed behind to watch over the others who milled about doing whatever menial tasks they could find to occupy their time at the moment.

Gabriele Hannah Bailey, a young woman of 18 years of age and of Japanese and British descent, quietly sat on top of one of the large boulders that jutted out from the cavern floor with her ukulele in hand, strumming one of her favorite tunes and humming along. Her short pageboy-style haircut swinging around her oval shaped face as she swayed and plucked the strings to the rhythm of the music. Gabriele had always loved music and had been fortunate to have parents who believed in giving her a very well-rounded education. Her parents had enlisted private tutors for her who instructed her in the performing arts when she was very young. On top of that, her father who had been of an aristocratic birth, had a personal trainer from his childhood who was from Japan. He instructed her father in the art of Karate, and he had become a master black belt at a young age. Her father had seen to it that she also knew how to fight and how to wield a Katana, starting her training almost as soon as she could walk.

Her parents had met while her father had served as first mate on board a ship sailing around the continental coastlines in the year 1365 A.D. Her mother had been the product of a sailor's weekend furlough and had been born to a very young Japanese woman, Gabriele's grandmother. Her grandfather, by birth only, had been a sailor who, like so many, had cruelly taken advantage of a local girl. Her father on the other hand was a man of honor and had truly fallen in love with her mother upon seeing her. He married her very quickly and returned home shortly after, taking his new bride with him. Gabriele had been born a year later. Even though she was mostly of

British descent, her mother's genetics ran thickly through her blood. She appeared more oriental than British but had no accent, for she was born and raised in the British aristocratic circles.

She had found the ukulele on one of her missions to a futuristic time period and had purchased the instrument. It being small enough to carry in her pack enabled her to take it with her wherever she went. She had also experienced several different types and styles of music on her missions over the last two years and had discovered she liked a group known as the Beatles from the British era of the 1960s. The advances made by man over the years should have astounded her, but the things that she had discovered while traversing time and space for God far outweighed man's advances and was far more magnificent.

She looked around the cavern watching the different people going about different activities when her gaze stopped upon Sean Doran. He was helping Uriah Mose tend to some of the horses. She was very familiar with Uriah, as he was her travel partner over the last two years until six months ago when Dominic first peregrinated. After he arrived, she began traveling with Zaccai, who was like a much older, much wiser sister. Zaccai and Uriah were vastly different personalities. Uriah tended to fly off the handle and let his temper get the better of him, where nothing seemed to ruffle Zaccai's feathers. She watched everything and spoke little. But when she did, people tended to listen. Zaccai had a presence about her that seemed to overpower a room and gain her the attention of all present, whether she wanted it or not.

Sean Doran was a sort of enigma to Gabby. He was pompous at times, like many of the young men she had grown up around, but at the same time a very genuine person. She had watched him closely while they had been on the island, and he fascinated her. She was oddly attracted to him. She wasn't yet sure if it was romantically, but she often found herself watching him without realizing it. She would definitely like to get to know him better. She continued to watch him from beneath her lashes as he and Uriah watered and brushed down some of the horses.

Uriah Mose swiped at the sweat that was running off his forehead while tending to the animals. He was a man of 55 and had been a Hittite iron worker during 1400 BC before peregrination, which seemed like an eternity ago to him now. His first peregrination was in 1360 BC at the age of 40. He had lived this lifestyle for fifteen years now and had seen his fair share of death, war, greed, and betrayal. Hiram Burke had been his mentor back before he led most everyone to their death's, but he had also been his friend. One of the closest that Uriah had ever had. Uriah had also been like an uncle to Bridget before Hiram had taken her and disappeared all those years back. She surely wouldn't remember him now. Uriah watched the young girl along with Wade and Dominic, playing with some of the horses. Obviously using their Keeper abilities to train and communicate with the animals. He would have to try and speak to her later about her father and let her know that not everyone here held ill feelings toward the man. She had a friend and ally in him, and he would make sure she knew that.

Dominic Amando, who had been his peregrination partner for the last six months was a decent fighter. It had surprised Uriah to know that Dominic had been called to be a Keeper. He was an agile young man of fifteen who could handle himself quite well. He remembered Dominic's first peregrination very well. The young man had been terrified when he awoke from his PS sleep. He kept yelling and asking if someone had put something in his food or drink because he was having serious hallucinations. It had taken Malachai Harel, their Dragoman, several hours to calm him down and convince him that nothing of the sort had happened. Dominic was very Greek and spoke his mind and gave his opinion openly, even for one so young. He and Uriah had had it out more than once, and the young man defended himself and his views fiercely. Uriah respected him greatly for it, even if it was annoying at times. Uriah supposed he could understand being so young and trying to maneuver through this way of life. He himself had at least been a fully grown and capable man when he had first peregrinated. Some of these kids hadn't even finished puberty yet.

Uriah looked around the cavern at everyone doing little odd jobs or activities, killing time until they received their orders from the group leaders, when his gaze fell upon Zaccai, who also happened to have looked at him at that particular moment. They respectfully nodded to each other before he went back to grooming his horse.

Zaccai watched Uriah and Sean lightly conversing while they tended the animals. She had to remind herself that there was a traitor amongst them, and it could be any one of these people. She hadn't the faintest idea who it could be, but she would have to be very observant and extra cautious when trying to listen in on conversations. She never liked spying on people, it wasn't her nature. But she supposed she would have to learn to deal with it because the fate of everyone could very well depend upon it. She sat there on the large rock watching the different activities taking place around her. There were several newcomers to the group that she wasn't sure she could trust just yet. Of course, most of these people she had only met briefly over the last fifteen years or so. They never really got to know anyone other than the select few people that they peregrinated with, or the few Dragoman they chanced encounters with over the years. However, she did know most everyone because she had been at this for eighteen years. Most of the others were fairly new ranging from a few months to about ten years. Only a handful of them had lived this life for more than a decade. She would have to begin taking notes and plotting graphs to figure this one out. There were way too many people to try and remember all the little details that she was sure to uncover on this trip. She would however have to keep mental notes until she was alone. Making notes in front of everyone would surely draw quite a bit of curiosity as to what she was doing. Especially since she wasn't prone to keeping a diary or anything of the sort.

Zaccai had gotten to know the new-comer Caroline Jager while on the island. She liked her a lot but, liking someone doesn't mean you can trust them. She had also gotten familiar with Nadia, Dinah, and Odessa. She of course knew more of Odessa Megalos, being as she had been peregrinating for almost as long as Zaccai had. The other women, not so much. She would also have to figure out how to become acquainted with the younger crowd which included Sean, Kristen, Timothy, Bridget, and Wade. Of course, she had to remember that she wasn't the only one looking into the whole traitor thing. She just tended to over think everything. She liked a challenge and enjoyed puzzles, and this was just such an occasion to her.

Her thoughts drifted to the four men who had left over two hours ago to head to the mines on horseback. Until they got the exact coordinates for the copper mine entrance, they couldn't travel by the Portal Generators. But once they mapped it out traveling would be much simpler. Hopefully they would discover a cavern large enough at the mine entrance where the whole camp could move, making searching much easier and quicker. However, she didn't know how the searching would go until they dealt with the trials. When, how, and where that was going to start was a mystery to all of them. The anxiety of waiting was enough to drive a person mad. Unsure as to just what you were going to discover about yourself, or others. Human beings tended to judge others based on what we think we know or things we find out. How were these trials going to affect the friendships and relationships that were built over the years and the last few months on the island? Zaccai prayed that those friendships would withstand whatever was thrown at them, and that the betrayer wasn't one of her own.

Seth, Jason, Oz, and Zeke finally made the almost two-hour journey across the blazing hot sand in search of Solomon's Copper Mines. If it had not been for the immense beauty of the area and the striking colors of the differentiating sands, it would have been a miserable ride. But the carvings laid into the massive walls and surrounding rocks gave the eye plenty to look upon. Statues stood out amongst the flat sandy plains, lending light into man's history in this vast desert. Rocky mountains, void of little vegetation and shaped from the years of wind and water erosion stood out from almost every angle. If they didn't know any better they would have thought that the rocks had been carved by man, but their glimpses into the future and technology told them these formations came about by natural forces.

They came upon the mine entrances, southeast of Mount Timna where camp was being established in their absence. The opening to the mines were scattered across the floor of the Negev desert. Large holes were dug straight down. Some had ladders that still protruded up from the depths of the mining shaft. Whether or not those ladders could still hold weight was the question. With this in mind, Oz and Zeke decided to stay topside and keep watch over the horses and ropes, while Seth and Jason propelled themselves down into the mines on ropes tied to the horses' saddle horns. Neither willing to trust ladders that were built hundreds, possibly thousands of years before.

The first shaft they decided to explore was one that didn't appear to be too deep. Peering down into the hole, they could see a large floor area about fifty feet below. Taking their canteens and flashlights, Seth and Jason slid down the ropes to the flat ground beneath. The cavern was rather large, and light filtered into it from several different shafts that apparently led down into the same area. Possibly allowing large groups of people to enter and exit the area simultaneously, making quicker work of the mining. There were some ancient pickaxes, shovels, and other tools laying against the perimeter of the cavern, forgotten there by whatever civilization last inhabited the area. As their eyes adjusted to the dim light streaming into the cave, they realized they didn't need the flashlights just yet and stowed them at their sides as they walked around the cave floor, studying the carvings, tools, and multiple shafts that broke off from the center, snaking further down underground, twisting and turning into the darkness.

Seth spoke first. "I think we are going to need some more help with this. There are way too many caverns for just us to explore and this is just one entrance."

"Yeah, I do believe you are right," Jason answered. "Why don't we head back up the ropes, set the coordinates into the Portgens, and see if we can possibly find another cavern close to here large enough to house everyone and the horses. I don't want to continue making that trip across the desert and traveling by Portgen so frequently could get dangerous. If anyone is around, we could be seen."

"I agree. Let's get back up top and make a map of what we have here and the location coordinates. That way we aren't stumbling over ourselves exploring the same areas twice. I figure these caverns could all start looking alike once you start walking around down here for very long."

"Good idea, Seth."

The two men shimmied back up the ropes, vowing to have everyone back at camp to start work on several sturdy ladders to make climbing easier. After reaching topside, the four of them set out in search of large caverns and explored a few more shafts that were easily accessed by simply walking into them, making accurate marks in the Portgens for pinpoint coordinates.

They marveled at the large holes the sat within the center of some of the rock formations. As though someone or something had blasted a hole right into the center of it. Upon further searching, they did indeed find some caverns large enough to house all of them, allowing them quick access to the mine entrances for more searchable daylight time. Some of the caverns were cool and dark inside, the entrances carved back inside hollows and clefts in the rocks, hidden from view of the open plains.

The men decided to call it a day and set the Portgen's coordinates for Mount Timna. After taking stock of the area and making sure no one was around to see them, they walked the horses into one of the large caverns and opened a portal, walking through to the large cavern sixteen miles away at Mount Timna.

Not too far across the Araba Valley, on top of one of the vast mountains, someone lay watching the four men. They watched them through the long spyglass as they walked into the large cavern. These strangers had not yet exited the last cavern they explored. Were they still inside, bedding down for however long they were here for? Or had they found another shaft inside and continued down into the mines? What were they here for? There was only one way to find out and that was to go exploring, but not until the safety of nightfall.

Be still before the Lord and wait patiently on
Him; do not fret when people succeed in their ways, when
they carry out their wicked schemes.

Psalm 37:7

Chapter 2

It was late evening when the men returned to camp. They would spend the night in their current location, then pack up in the morning and return to the cavern they had found earlier and set up a more permanent camp there for the duration of the mission.

They spent the remainder of the evening making search plans and assigning duties to everyone for the next several days. They also decided to partner people up, three to a team to start, until they could see how dangerous the mines were. Then, they might possibly split up into smaller groups if it was deemed safe enough to do so. They decided to also assign one of the leaders to head up each group for decision making, and to keep an eye and ear open for any leads on the betrayer.

There were six groups of three, with Sofia and Bridget volunteering to stay behind to keep track of everyone, and to be map makers to track the explored shafts. A few of the Peregrines weren't too happy about how people were paired. Sean was particularly disturbed when Timothy jumped at the chance to be in a group with Kristen. He had spoken up before Sean had even had the chance to think about replying, assuming they would be paired with their peregrination partners.

Gabriele was happy to be placed with Sean. At least this way she might find some time to get to know him better without much interruption. She, Jason, and Sean were group one. Seth, Caroline, and Wade were group two. Oz, Dinah, and Dominic were group three. Zeke, Nadia, and Alec were group four. Zaccai, Uriah, and Odessa were group five, and Nick, Timothy, and Kristen were in group six. Gabriele noticed that Sean didn't appear too keen on Timothy and Kristen being in a group together. She was beginning to wonder if Sean had feelings for Kristen, or if he was just protective of his partner. She did notice that he seemed to hang around Nick the most during his free time, not Kristen. Maybe he just didn't like change all that much?

After dinner and some further discussions on the following days exploration plans, Jason instructed everyone to be up early and packed before dawn. He wanted to get started on the mine explorations as early as daylight would allow and suggested everyone get into bed early. This still left several hours for conversation, and Gabriele saw her chance to talk to Sean a bit. She walked over to where he was sitting at the cavern's entrance, gazing out over the vast desert landscape, taking in the moonlit bathed scenery that lay before him.

"Pretty, isn't it." Gabby walked up to where he was sitting.

"Yeah, it is." Sean was a little startled by her sudden appearance. "I never really paid attention to nature all that much. Not until that hike we all took back on the island."

"That was definitely a unique view. Quite breathtaking from the summit." Gabby leaned her back against the rock where Sean was sitting.

"That was the first time I had ever really been camping or hiking, for fun that is, you know, before all this peregrination stuff. I was never much of an outdoors kind of guy in my former lifestyle." He smiled at her. "What about you?"

"Well, we didn't have all the technological advancements where I come from so, I actually spent a lot of time outdoors. Mostly training with my dad. Still, I've experienced my fair share of nature. My dad was a sailor on a ship in his younger years, that's how he and my mother met. Anyhow, we had a sailboat of our own and he would take me and my mother out a few times a month to teach us how to operate the vessel. He used to say that I needed to know how to handle myself in any situation, and he made sure I received any and every kind of training possible." She smiled at the memory of her father. "He had no idea how much I would actually be using all of that."

Sean watched her face light up in animation and joy at the memory of her parents, then turn to sadness as she finished talking.

"You must miss them?"

"Yes. Quite a lot actually." She suddenly shook herself from her gloominess. "What about you? Did you get along with your parents?" She was glad that he seemed to be sharing so freely with her.

"Yeah, I did. It was just me and my dad. My mom passed away when I was about eight years old, so I don't have a whole lot of memories of her. My dad worked extremely hard all the time and wasn't around a whole lot, but I knew he loved me. He was a good man, you know. The kind that you could really watch and learn from." Different emotions flit across his features as memories of his family flooded his mind.

They sat there in companionable silence as they watched a lone animal streak across the desert sands. It was too far away to make out what it was.

Gabby spoke first. "So, you ready to go exploring tomorrow?"

"Yeah. I'm anxious to see what's down there." He turned to scan the encampment, possibly in search of someone. Gabby followed his gaze as it stopped on where Kristen and Timothy were sitting and talking by the campfire.

"So," she said as she watched his face, "do you have a thing for Kristen or are you just worried about something. It's kind of hard to tell."

Sean's head snapped around at her words, speechless as to what to say, a slight blush rushing to his neck and cheeks.

Gabby smiled at his reaction. "So, you do like her."

Sean grinned slightly at the very observant young woman. "Is it that obvious?"

"Well, like I said, I wasn't sure. I thought maybe you were just leery of Timothy." She noticed that Sean suddenly looked nervous. "Hey, don't worry. Your secret is safe with me." They smiled at one another

"Thanks Gabby. I'm just not sure how it will all work out, and with the trials ahead, I didn't want to cause any problems or distractions, you know? Besides, these feelings just sort of crept up since the missions to find the keys for the archive books. It's all still kind of new to me."

"Well, if you want my opinion, you best not wait too long or else you may be too late. Besides, I believe it's already become a distraction. At least for you." She adjusted her position to a sitting one next to Sean. They sat watching the desert nightlife and chatting about all manner of things until it was time to turn in for the night.

Kristen sat next to Timothy making small talk as she watched Gabby and Sean smiling and talking. *What about?* she wondered. She wasn't sure why Gabby's and Sean's new friendship bothered her so much. It wasn't like she and Sean were a couple. She thought that maybe Sean liked her with the way he was acting on the camping trip, but he had hardly spoken a word to her since leaving the island. Now, she was partnered with Timothy for the mine exploration and she and Sean wouldn't be spending as much time together. Sean and Gabby, however, would be. Kristen sat and pondered why this bothered her as she tried to concentrate on what Timothy was saying, all the while stealing glances at Sean and Gabby.

On the other side of the fire, Zaccai, Jason, Oz, and Nick, sat observing the others partaking in their various activities. They spoke in hushed tones to each other as they contemplated how to nonchalantly go about watching and questioning everyone. They decided that they would meet each night in the main tent to discuss the events of each day and start piecing together any unusual behavior or conversations that they overheard. Surely between the seven of them, they would be able to keep track of any and all information about the betrayer.

Oz asked quietly, "Either a' you heard anythin' strange as a' yet?" he gestured to Zaccai and Nick, the two leaders who stayed back at camp today to keep watch.

"No, not a thing," Zaccai answered him.

"Me either," Nick threw out. "Maybe we should ask Sofia? She was here as well and was helping set up a lot of areas today. She talked to a lot of people I'm sure."

"She always did have a' way with words. If'n anyone can finagle somethin' out' a' ya', without ya' knowin' it, she can," Oz said grinning mischievously, as memories of the past glistened in his eyes.

The others grinned at him and his expression. Oz called to Sofia to come sit with them at the fire, glancing all around them to make sure no one was sitting close enough to hear their conversation.

"Hey, what's up?" Sofia asked, approaching the fireside.

"Jus' wonderin' if ya' heard anythin' interestin' out a' anybody t'day?"

"No, not yet. Just still getting a feel for who everyone is. I've been at a great disadvantage for the last thirteen years I'm afraid. I know only Oz, Zaccai, and Uriah from before. It may take me a while to get a feel for people's characters." She looked around the cavern at the other sixteen people lounging about, chatting with each other, or beginning to pack the few things they could. "If I remember correctly, Uriah was somewhat of a hothead back in the day." She then looked at Zaccai.

"He still is." Zaccai smirked. "But I haven't seen anything over the last thirteen years that would give me suspicion as to him being a traitor. As a matter of fact, he was pretty torn up when Hiram disappeared all those years ago. They were pretty close if I remember correctly. He's never talked much about it. Even when we were peregrinating together."

"Well, that there is 'nough ta' give me suspicions," Oz seethed a bit between his clenched jaw. "'Sides, wasn' Hiram his Dragoman?"

Zaccai looked at Oz. "Yes, he was. But Hiram was also Clancy and Shannon's Dragoman as well, remember? There isn't anything suspicious about that. Hiram was also a friend and comrade to all of us. I don't think any of us would have expected him to do what he did. Basing it on who knew him the best won't help here, Oz, I'm sad to say."

Nick spoke next. "What about Bridget? None of us know much about her at all. Maybe she harbors some anger toward some, or all of us, because of her father?"

"Nope," Oz blurted out, "not that lass. She's as sweet an' innocent as anyone I ever knew. 'Sides, she didn't know anythin' about her pa's treachery till after I met 'em on Zanchier."

"Perhaps, Oz, but she had time to take the key while on the island," Nick stated.

"Maybe, if'n she had known about it. But, like most everyone else, she didn'. I'd stake my life on her innocence." Oz glared at him menacingly.

Sofia spoke in reply. "Well if we are basing it on who knew about the key, that only leaves Seth, Oz, and myself. It's not Seth since he is the one who found it in the first place. Oz wouldn't have led us to the waterfall where it was hidden if he had anything to do with it. And I could have simply lost it again before we left Zanchier. No one else knew of its existence until Oz mentioned it in passing conversation. At which time, Simon and I went to look for it and found it gone."

Zaccai pondered her statement for a moment, then answered her. "Yes, but you were the last person to see it. And, it did get 'lost again' as you said." She looked at Sofia with raised eyebrows.

"I know what you're thinking, Zaccai. I do look to be the guilty party. But I promise you here and now it wasn't me. I put that key in the drawer of the writing desk before I went to bed that night. It was very late too if you remember. Everyone was up and roaming the house until all hours of the night because of our return, and Seth's deadly injury," Sofia remarked in her defense. "The next morning, I went down to breakfast later than usual, about 8:30 and found about half the group there already."

Jason asked the next question. "Do you remember who all was in the kitchen when you arrived?"

"I'm not sure, why?"

"Well, whoever took the key would have had to have the opportunity to take it while you weren't in the room."

"Yes, but they also had an entire day to search for it. We all had the day to goof off on the island, remember? It could have been taken at any point by anyone. We didn't think about the key until the following day."

Everyone exhaled in frustration. Nick said what the others were thinking. "Well, that lead flew out the window didn't it?"

"Could it be someone who works on the island?" Sofia questioned. "A lot of the help at Reader's Island knew Hiram well and had access to my room. Especially the housekeepers."

"True," Oz stated. "I'm sure Simon an' the others will be investigatin' all them that are there."

Jason said to no one particular. "We'll just have to keep a trained eye and ear open at all times. I say we call it a night and start packing up and get ready to leave in the morning. I'll take watch tonight for the first two hours. I'm not sleepy and I need to have a very serious conversation with God tonight about all this. And, maybe see if He'll give me a heads up on the trials." Jason nervously grinned as he stood to retrieve his gun and head toward the cavern's opening.

"Good idea, goodnight Jason, everyone." Zaccai stood as well and walked to her tent to make notes of their discussions tonight. She would organize her journal to separate each person by a page for notations on each. Then she, like Jason, would pray about their situation.

Everyone said their goodnights, making plans for who would take next watch and went in separate directions, all of them with a lot to think about.

Nick considered his friends. It was going to be hard to be suspicious of them and his fellow Peregrines. After all, God had called them all to serve. But, if he remembered his Bible stories correctly, Judas Iscariot had been called to serve as well.

The next morning was a bustle of commotion as everyone busied themselves packing their meager belongings to prepare for the sixteen-mile trip across the desert. They decided to use the Portgens as little as possible to avoid being seen, deciding horseback to be the best option. With it being early, pre-dawn, the sun wouldn't beat down on them as before.

Jason wasn't too keen on making the long trip when the Portgen would have them there in a matter of minutes, but he sensed they were being watched yesterday. Maybe it had been his over sensitive military training, but his senses usually proved to be right. He just hoped it wasn't demonic forces. He could only sense them if they were close enough, and he was in no mood to do battle right from the get-go. Surely if that were the case, they would have attacked by now. No, it was probably just some traveling nomads or maybe even the local wildlife, curious about these new strangers in their valley.

The lead Peregrines had decided to pack themselves early and go about helping the others in hopes of spotting something in someone else's pack that didn't belong there or hope to hear something that may prove useful.

Seth, Caroline, and Odessa helped Bridget and the other younger boys such as Wade and Dominic with their packs and tents, while Sofia and Zaccai set about helping Nadia, Dinah , Kristen, and Gabriele. Nick and Zeke helped Uriah, Timothy, and Sean. And Oz, Jason, and Alec set about packing the food and equipment on the extra horses they had brought along as pack animals.

Thirty minutes later everyone was packed up, mounted on their horses, and ready to go. It was just past five-thirty when they exited the cave to make the journey across the Negev Desert once more, headed to their destination just two hours away.

Memnah had explored the cavern the night before just as darkness was settling over the valley. There had been no one inside the large cavern at that time. Even the horses were gone. Perhaps the strangers had traveled further into the deeper recesses of the cavern's tunnels? But the horses would not have fit down the tunnels located inside that particular cavern. Memnah lay there peering out over Timna Valley, hoping to get another glimpse of the men from yesterday. Just as the sun was beginning its ascent into the sky, a large caravan of people appeared, headed toward the same cavern. Were these people with the other men from yesterday? Were the men scouts, sent to find a place to camp within the mines? Unless they made the treacherous journey across the desert after dark last night they had to still be in the mine cavern somewhere, but where? And what was this large group of people doing here in Timna Valley at King Solomon's copper mines? What could they possibly want here? There was nothing of real value within the mines other than copper, to mine it would take a very long time with a small group of people such as this. Perhaps this group was only the first of many to come? Perhaps they were after the contents of the temple? Memnah thought that only her people knew of its location and existence. This did not bode well for Memnah's people. This would have to be reported to the tribal leaders. Memnah watched for a bit longer before retreating and heading for the tribe that had spent the last two-thousand years guarding Solomon's Temple and the copper mines from marauders.

Jason gazed out over the tops of the mountains that surrounded the valley. He felt it again, the sensation of being watched. If there was someone out there, they could be anywhere. This was a very large area, filled with places that someone, or a group of people could easily hide. They were approaching the cavern they discovered yesterday on the scouting trip. It was just a few hundred feet away. Jason scanned the ridgeline as best as he could. Seth approached him, sensing that his friend was out of sorts.

"Hey Jason, what's up?" Seth watched his friend's facial expressions for answers.

"I feel like we're being watched." Jason's eyes continually scanned the ridgelines.

"You really think there could be someone out here? Maybe demons?" Seth asked, a little on edge.

"Sure. I doubt its demonic though. There could be nomads traveling through here that could just be curious to our presence. Then again, it could be bandits as well." Jason gave him a warning glance. "We need to stay on our toes just in case. One of the men need to stay behind with Sofia and Bridget today just to keep watch. Bridget doesn't have any fighting skills, and Sofia may not be able to handle a group of bandits by herself."

"Perhaps the groups should all take turns. At least until we make sure it's safe."

"That's a good idea, Seth. We'll straighten that out once we get camp set up." Jason finished speaking as their caravan made the last several feet before entering the large cavern.

Just like the cavern they left sixteen miles back, this cavern was very large, but a bit more sheltered from the openness of the desert plains. The entrance was somewhat hidden in between two large, rocky, mountainsides, making it easier to conceal the large group, and to be able to post guards to keep watch at night. Jason's group would take first watch with Sofia and Bridget. They would comb through the cavern that was to be their home for however long it took them to find the Belt of Truth.

They set about unpacking the horses and setting up camp as quickly as possible. Caroline and Odessa made a schedule for everyone to tend to chores, such as cooking, cleaning, horses, tending the fire, and laundry, based on everyone's gifts, if it applied. This list also included the watch rounds schedule. Everyone was assigned a daily chore that they were responsible for while here. Bridget and Sofia agreed to do the daily cooking with Dominic's help. Bridget was used to taking care of Oz and Caroline in Zanchier, and Sofia was used to cooking for large groups while being held prisoner by the Scaithers. Dominic, who was very Italian, claimed he had been helping in the kitchen since he could barely walk. Everyone else conceded the job to them, saying they would help them when and if needed.

Dinah , Kristen, Odessa, and Caroline would tend to laundry, when and if the need arose. And they were sure it would. Nadia and Nick oversaw lighting and tending the fire for cooking and heating and gathering the necessary firewood. Everyone tended to their own messes and dishes, and the remainder of the group would tend to the needs of the horses.

It was just past 11 a.m. by the time camp was set up, the horses were in a makeshift corral, and lunch was being prepared. After a quick bite to eat, they walked the few hundred feet over to where the mine entrance they wanted to explore was located. Upon returning to camp the night before, Jason had instructed some of the Peregrines to make a few sturdy ladders to enter down into the cavern with. They had lashed them together with the rope and twine they brought with the supplies and used some of the still green wood Jason had insisted they pick up along the way. What they didn't have they cut off one of the desert trees just outside the cavern entrance.

After everyone climbed down into the spacious, underground cavern that led to several separate mine shafts, they sent each group down into separate tunnels with explicit instructions to stay together. Under no circumstances were they to go anywhere alone, or, leave anyone alone. They also had to drop thin rope lines to find their way out in case the tunnels branched off and snaked in separate directions. They were only to stay down no longer than two hours at a time until instructed differently. If something happened and they got lost or trapped, they were to stay by the ropes and pull on it to alert Bridget or Sofia that they needed help. The ends of the rope were tied to large eye bolts that were hammered into the furthest outer wall of the spacious cavern.

After the rules were explained and everyone was set up with the necessary equipment, each group picked a tunnel and stepped down into the darkness of the underground mining shafts. Bridget and Sofia made notes as to which tunnels were being explored and which group was where. The leaders of each group used the Portgens navigation system to mark how far they walked into the shaft so they could check off and mark the distance of each tunnel.

With Sean and Gabby monitoring the topside of the underground cavern, and everyone else in position and doing the jobs they were given, Jason walked the short distance back to the cavern that housed their camp to monitor things there and make sure they didn't have any surprise visitors. Whether they were human, demonic, or animal.

Memnah watched as the large group of people walked toward the mining entrance, hopefully leaving the cavern empty. She quickly scurried down the mountainside as carefully and quietly as possible and slipped inside the cavern. Unlike last night, it was filled to the brim with tents, cooking equipment, and horses. Fortunately, there was no one in the cavern from the odd caravan that had taken up residence here this morning. Memnah quickly looked through a few of the bags and clothing that was lying inside some of the tents. Some of the clothing was rather odd looking as well as some other items she had never seen before. As she walked deeper into the cavern, the horses began to neigh and prance about, alerting that someone was coming. Memnah darted behind the large group of horses trying to hug the cavern wall and not spook them too much.

Jason entered the large cavern and noticed that the horses were kicking up a bit of a fuss. He also sensed that something was not right. He stopped just inside the arched entryway and squinted into the dark interior of the cavern. He stood still just inside the cavern entrance until his eyes adjusted to the lack of sunlight. He slowly bent down to the floor pretending to tie his boot lace as he scanned the floor level of the cavern underneath the horses. There, just barely visible through the multitude of horse flesh was a pair of shoes, hidden almost completely by a long, sand-colored robe.

This must be the person I've been sensing watching us, he thought. He slowly stood back up and decided the best course of action would be just to call them out.

"You there. I know you're in here. I can see your feet beneath the horses. Come on out. No one is going to harm you." Jason cautiously watched where the hidden figure was standing.

Memnah hesitated for just a moment, grasping the knife handle at the small of her back that she always kept on her person. Slowly stepping out into the barely lit cavern, her face was still concealed by the hood and shroud she wore. She glanced at the opening of the cavern that was located just behind where the large, muscular, man still stood. Maybe she could make a run for it without being caught?

Jason watched the cloaked figure before him. The man wasn't very large. Actually, he was kind of small compared to most. This guy wasn't much larger than Dominic who was all of fifteen years old. He was probably a kid about the same age as well, if size were a determining factor. He watched as the young man's eyes darted between himself and the cavern entrance.

"You're welcome to leave, as soon as you tell me who you are and what you're doing snooping around in our stuff here?" Jason walked further inside the cavern but kept the exit behind him.

Memnah tried to disguise her voice to sound like that of a man. This stranger might not be as amiable if he knew she was a woman. She could speak English well since her tribe often traded with the British that were located in Eilat, the large seaport city just south of the Negev Desert. In her best English and thick Israeli accent, she answered him.

"I am no one of importance. I was only curious to who you were and what you were doing at the mines."

"Why the curiosity? Are we trespassing?" the man calmly asked her, watching her closely. He made her very nervous for some reason. She wasn't sure why.

"My tribe has protected these mines for thousands of years. They do not belong to us, but we are the appointed protectors by King Solomon himself. So, what you are doing here *is* my business." Memnah slowly made her way around the cavern edge, inching slowly toward the exit, hoping the stranger wouldn't notice the slow movement.

Jason stood with his arms crossed against his barrel chest watching the young man cunningly making his way toward the exit. Amusement played across his lips but only slightly. He himself slowly made his way toward the young man as he spoke.

"My colleagues and I are on a special expedition to find an important artifact believed to be located somewhere within the mines. That is why we are here. We will take nothing but that which we have come to find, I promise."

"Why should I take the word of a white devil? I have known your kind before. Men like you come here to our lands to steal whatever you can get your hands on. Including our young women and girls." Memnah's voice began to shake in anger at the remembrance of the white men she encountered years before as a young girl herself. She watched too, as the man moved closer to her. Her pulse began to race, and her adrenaline kicked into high gear. She ran at him, pulling the large, curved dagger from the sheath at her back. She lashed out at the stranger, but he was quicker than she thought.

Jason was taken by surprise at how quickly the young man moved. He ran at Jason full on with the large, curved dagger in his hand. Jason grabbed one of the shovels they had brought with them that was gratefully leaning against a nearby rock, and held it out in front of him. The large dagger sliced into the wood of the handle, sticking tightly into it. Jason threw the shovel and dagger to the side and grabbed the young man by the arm as he continued to flail, kick, scratch, and punch at him, landing several good blows to Jason's jaw, lip, and left eye. Jason managed to spin the boy around and pin both arms down against his side. He wrapped his arms around the boy to keep him from kicking him. Unfortunately, the boy's foot found a mark upon his shin. Jason picked the young man up to stop his kicking, and they both fell to the floor in the struggle. Jason managed to get the young man underneath him, straddling the boy with his legs and sitting on him while holding his arms down against the floor.

Much to Jason's surprise, during the struggle, the young man's hood and shroud had fallen away from his face to reveal a woman. Jason and Memnah sat staring at each other as their labored breathing made their chests rise and fall in rapid succession.

"You're a woman!" Jason gazed at the deep greenish-brown pools of her large eyes and the deep pink hue of her lips and flushed cheeks. The bone structure of her high cheekbones and the sharp but dainty, pointed nose and oval shaped face were stunning.

"Please remove yourself from my person sir!" she said forcefully through clenched teeth.

"I don't think so, lady. You just tried to kill me. If I let go of you, you just might try again." Amusement began to dance in his eyes as he licked the blood from his busted lip.

"Get off of me right this minute!" Memnah tried her hardest to get free of Jason's grasp.

"Just calm down, would you? I told you earlier that no one here is going to hurt you. Now, I'm going to slowly release you, understand? Just don't go getting all wild again." Jason began to stand up, pulling Memnah off the floor as he did. When they were both standing, he spoke again.

"What's your name?" He still held on to her wrists. He got no answer. She stood facing him, trying to avert her gaze. Jason followed her eyes with his head until he could get her to look at him once again. "I'm not letting go of you until you tell me your name." He gave a slightly crooked grin.

"Fine," she clicked out staring into his eyes. "My name is Memnah." A thick Arabic accent was evident in her voice, and she seemed to have calmed down and was breathing easier.

"Now, that wasn't so bad was it?" He began to relax his hold on her wrists.

"Hello, Memnah, my name is Jason. I'm going to release you now and we can discuss whatever this is like civilized human beings. Jason slowly let loose of her wrists, and when he realized she was calm he relaxed his stance. Just as he did, she kicked out at him, catching him in the groin and doubling him over onto the ground as she ran toward the exit. Jason lay there, waiting for the stars and blurry vision to subside, trying to catch his breath. He managed to squeak out, "Nice . . . to meet . . . you. . . Memnah," to her retreating back.

Memnah abruptly stopped at his words. Her brow furrowed in confusion at his response and the exchange she had with the stranger. She turned and looked at the man now withered upon the floor curled up in the fetal position. She felt one small pang of regret for nailing the poor man in the privates before turning and fleeing the cavern for the safety of her desert planes

When tempted, no one should say, "God is tempting me."
For God cannot be tempted by evil,
nor does he tempt anyone;

James 1:13

Chapter 3

Jason lay there on the cavern floor trying to catch his breath. He was shocked at being taken by surprise and miffed at himself for allowing the fact that she was a woman to make him let his guard down. His marine training had taught him better, especially since the Peregrines that are women are as tough as any man. Perhaps it was because she had been a desert woman from the current time period of 1840 AD that he didn't expect her to be so tough? Or, maybe it had been the mesmerizing depths of the brownish green pools of her eyes that had drawn him in? He had to admit; she was no raving beauty, but definitely attractive. And her fighting spirit and lack of fear to take on someone much larger than herself, and apparently win, also spoke volumes to him. His ego, along with his body, was a bit bruised at the moment, but at least the searing pain was beginning to ease enough for him to stand. He would have to make sure to keep his eyes open. He certainly didn't want to be taken by surprise by that little desert minx again. She might prove to be the death of him next time.

He thought about that last statement as he slowly walked to where he had cast the shovel with the large, curved, blade stuck in it. He picked it up and began tugging at the knife. Once he had freed the blade from its current bondage, he looked it over. It was extremely sharp, and the handle rather ornate. If that shovel handle hadn't been as thick, or if she had been any stronger, the blade might have sliced through the thick wood and possibly into him. He took the blade and stowed it away in his tent, then placed the damaged shovel against the back, cavern, wall. He was in no mood to relate this story to anyone just yet. But he would have to tell the leaders about it, leaving out certain information of course, so they could keep their eyes open for any future revisits. If she were a part of a desert tribe, it could mean serious trouble. Some of these clans ran large in numbers, especially if they were some sort of specially appointed guardians over Solomon's mines, as she had suggested.

He straightened his spine as best as he could, still feeling some small amount of the affliction imposed upon him by the young woman and walked back outside toward the mining entrances.

"Sean." Jason approached the young man standing guard. "I want you to keep a close eye on the ridgelines, watch for anything unusual, all right?"

"Sure thing, Jason. Any particular reason?" He looked at Jason sideways, squinting at the brightness of the sunlight.

"I'll explain why later, just keep a close watch and alert me to anything you see ASAP. And pass the information on to Gabby, will you?"

Sean nodded in reply and Jason strode past him, scurrying down the ladder to the open underground cavern.

"How are things going here ladies?" he asked Sofia and Bridget as he approached them.

"Fine so far. No mishaps to announce yet, but it's only been about thirty minutes or so. The ropes are all still wiggling from time to time and still lying loosely on the ground, so I take it that means good news," Sofia answered.

"What tunnels are everyone in?"

Bridget pointed to a large piece of canvas hanging on the wall.

"Well, group two, which is Seth's group, went down this tunnel here on the far left." She pointed at the map they were creating of the shafts as they were explored. "Group three, Oz's, is next to them. Four and Five have taken the third entrance there." She turned and pointed to one hole that had two distinct tunnels branching off in different directions. "The last group, Nicks, took the last opening. We won't know how deep they are or what they find along the way until they return."

"Well, I suppose all we have to do now is wait." Jason turned back to the ladder to return topside and go have another look around their cavern, just in case a certain woman decided to return for her dagger.

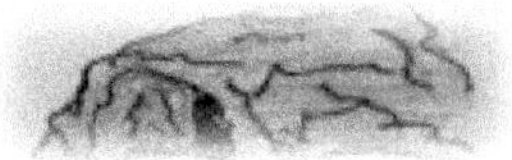

Nick, Timothy, and Kristen walked the long dark passage with relatively normal girth. The walls were approximately four feet apart, meaning that they at least didn't feel boxed in, and the light given off by their high lumen flashlights lit everything well. The sides of the tunnels were smooth, and lines of different colored rock streaked the surface in shades of tan, red, yellow, white, green, and copper.

They shined their flashlights into the sparsely placed holes in the walls that appeared every so often along the tunnel pathway. Some of the holes simply allowed a peek through to another adjacent cavern, while some were smaller rooms that led off the path. They explored the smaller rooms that branched off the pathway if it appeared that there was anything lying inside them on the floor or hanging on the walls. Nick walked a little ahead of Kristen, with Timothy pulling up the rear.

Timothy watched Kristen closely, maybe a little too closely? He really should be paying attention to the task at hand, but she kept drawing his attention away from where it should be. Not of her own fault of course, she was just walking and looking around like the rest of them, but he couldn't help watching her. She stopped at a sunken recession in the right side of the wall. She stepped into the small area to look around and noticed another pathway branching off from it, almost hidden by the way the rock camouflaged it.

She stepped into the new pathway just to see if it went anywhere, with Tim close behind her.

"Kristen, do you see anything?" Tim leaned in over her head a bit to get a better look, and to get closer to her.

Kristen, a bit startled by the sudden closeness, stepped left a bit to give him more room, looking at him from the corner of her eye.

"Just another pathway. We need to mark where it is on the Portgen so we can come back and explore it later." She turned to leave the small dark shaft where Nick was not. She didn't relish being alone with the tall, handsome man, especially since she found herself attracted to him. She didn't want to lead him on either since she wasn't even quite sure how she felt about Sean. Was she digging herself into a hole here? Two men, distinctly different in some ways and yet the same in others.

"We best step back out to the main shaft before Nick comes looking. You know the rules, no leaving anyone alone." She began to scoot past Timothy headed back to the almost hidden entrance.

Timothy put a handout to stop her. Kristen stared at him, unsure what his plans were.

"Kristen, can I speak to you for a second?"

"Tim, I hardly think this is the time or place for any conversations whatsoever. We can discuss whatever you want too back at camp later. We need to get back; Nick will surely have noticed us missing by now." She looked at his hand on her arm, then back to his face with a raised eyebrow.

He shrugged his shoulders as he sighed ever so softly, hesitantly dropping his hand from her right bicep. Just as he was lowering his hand Nick's head popped around the corner, catching the movement at the end. His eyebrows shot up as he glanced between the two of them.

"Did you two find something?" He was unsure what to make of the little bit of the exchange that he saw. "I missed this alcove earlier. The only way I saw it this time was because of your flashlights shining back through the entrance here."

"Yes, actually." Kristen straightened and moved past Tim toward Nick. She shined her light down the recently found pathway. "There's another shaft down that way. It appears to be a bit more narrow than the one we are currently on. What is the Portgen reading? I will make a note of where the entrance is on this map I've been sketching of the interior as we walk."

"About three miles. Which means we need to turn around and head back if we expect to return within the two-hour limit. We will have to amend the time for the next exploration trip. Two hours doesn't give us much time to look. Not to mention that it will take a lot longer to go any further down on the next trip."

"At least we know that this part of the mine is safe so far," she replied. "I'm curious to know how much deeper it goes."

Nick shrugged. "Well according to the maps and current data on this place, these mines could run for miles beneath and across the underbelly of the Negev Desert and Timna Valley. It was a sixteen-mile ride from Mount Timna remember? They could run that far back and snake in every direction."

"Wow," exclaimed Tim, "this search could literally take weeks, even a few months. With all the available technology, isn't there a better way to do this?"

"I'm not really sure," Nick replied. "We aren't sure what any of the others have found yet. Besides, what else do you have to do?" He looked at Tim with a questioning brow.

"Nothing I suppose." He shrugged.

Nick marked the coordinates given by the Portgen and they began making their way back to the entrance to rendezvous with the others, and find out what, if anything, they had found. So far, this shaft only revealed a few nooks and crannies, and another more hidden shaft they would have to wait to explore at another time. But, seeing as how sunset wouldn't be until about 7:45 at night during this time of year, and it was just around two in the afternoon, they may get a chance to head back down today.

As they were entering the dimly lit underground cavern, they met up with Oz's group which was emerging at the same time. While they stood there reporting on what they had or had not found, the other groups began appearing from the mining shafts.

Jason had returned earlier to be there when the groups emerged and to ask questions and make notes. Sean and Gabby stayed top side to keep watch while the groups all met below.

None of the groups reported anything fantastic as of yet, or anything that might resemble twelve belts lying around. On the next round of explorations, group two, Seth, Caroline, and Wade would take the next watch allowing Jason, Sean, and Gabby to explore the caverns in their place. After a quick water break and thorough explanation to Sofia and Bridget as to the details of the mining shafts, everyone excitedly took off again into their tunnels, hoping to travel faster this time since they already knew what the first several miles held. They also decided to extend the searching time by two more hours giving them a four-hour window, since the current two-hour time period would not allow for further exploration passed where they had stopped before.

Before the groups disappeared into the shafts once more, Sean watched as Kristen was gone once again followed by Timothy. How he wished to be able to be the one exploring the shafts with her. He only hoped and prayed that all this time spent with Timothy wouldn't cause himself any future heartache. He was beginning to realize just how much he truly cared for Kristen.

With all the groups retreating back inside the mine Jason instructed Seth what to watch for.

"Seth." Jason called him over for a bit of a private conversation. Speaking low so the others wouldn't hear what he said. "I had a little altercation with someone, a desert dweller, back at the camp-site. You may want to keep an eye on things there while Caroline and Wade monitor both sides of the underground cavern here. I'll explain a little more about what happened later when we have more time."

"All right, sure thing, Jason. Did they take anything or were they after anything particular?"

"I don't believe so. Perhaps it was just idle curiosity, but she left one heck of a knife behind in the struggle. And wounded my pride just a bit." Jason smirked and backhanded Seth in the chest, venturing off toward the shaft entrance where his team was waiting on him.

"She? Wounded pride?" Seth whispered loudly to his friend, a smile growing on his lips as he watched Jason's retreating back. After instructing Caroline and Wade of their duties without revealing too much, realizing Jason was speaking quietly to him for a reason, Seth set off toward the camp to make sure the horses were all still there. These desert people would value animals greatly. If they themselves couldn't use them, they could certainly sell or trade them for other needs. Seth certainly did not want to lose any of the horses.

After making a head count of the horses and a thorough check of camp and the surrounding area, Seth went back out toward the mines.

He approached Wade who was looking a bit overheated in the afternoon sun.

"Wade, are you all right?" Seth was a bit concerned for the young man.

"Yes sir. Just hot and thirsty." Wade wiped at the sweat glistening on his brow.

"Have you been drinking your water?"

Wade sheepishly looked at Seth, his face turning another shade of pink. "Well, I sort of ran out earlier when we were down in the tunnels."

"Why didn't you tell me or Caroline?" Seth's voice held a tinge of aggravation at the carelessness of the young man.

Wade shifted his weight nervously from foot to foot, staring down at the ground as he spoke.

"I know we have to be careful and ration our water. I just get so thirsty, so I drank my supply quickly without realizing it. I've always drank a lot. I guess I just got used to it when I was playing football in school. Being as big as I am, I sweat a lot." His embarrassment was evident.

Seth smiled at the young man. "Here's my canteen. Just sip slowly on it, all right?" Seth handed Wade his water supply.

"No sir, I can't take your water." Wade seemed even more embarrassed as he looked at Seth under hooded eyelashes.

"Yes, you can. I'll take yours back to the camp and refill it. You are going to have to learn to ration your supply a bit better though, understood?"

"Yes sir, I will certainly try," Wade said deflated.

"Trying is all I ask, Wade." Seth grinned at the young man. "Now, give me your canteen. After I refill it I'll bring it back to you." Seth took the item, slapped Wade on the shoulder with another grin and walked out to see how Caroline was doing.

Caroline was standing guard, her bow hanging down beside her in her right hand. He still had to catch his breath at times when he looked at her, especially now in this new environment and lifestyle they now led. Back home she had always been beautiful and delicate to him. He never thought she would have taken to this kind of life. He was very proud of her, yet still frightened for her at the same time. She had yet to experience a demon battle, and he was rather worried how she would fare. He would just have to keep a close eye on her to make sure she was safe.

"Hey Beautiful." He smiled broadly as he approached her.

Caroline brightly smiled in return. "Hey there handsome." She tiptoed to plant a quick kiss on his lips.

"Everything look all right out here so far?" He scanned the ridgelines.

"Yep. Quiet as a mouse, except for the occasional bird squawking overhead, or desert creature scampering across the sand."

"How are you doing on water?"

"Fine, I have about half a canteen left." She shook the bladder, the water sloshing around inside.

"Help me keep an eye on Wade, would you? He already emptied his daily supply and didn't tell me he needed more. I know these kids were called to this way of life by God, but I sometimes wonder what He was thinking?" Exasperation filled his voice and body language.

"Well, God does know better than us. His plans are far greater than we can possibly fathom, Seth. It seems a bit strange to me as well that God would call kids into this, but He has a plan. Kids are generally much more willing to listen to God's leading than adults are. Maybe their calling is far greater than ours and we are just here to protect them?" She glanced up at him, squinting against the sun.

Seth smiled at his wife. She always seemed to have the right answer to everything. "I best let you get on with guard duty. I'll see you later." He leaned down to give her a peck on the cheek. Turning to leave he had a sense of being watched. He slowed his steps and turned back to look at Caroline. She was looking out over the plains, not at him. Were his senses starting to peak like Jason had told him they would way back on their first mission to Israel? If so, did that mean they were being watched? He turned to walk back to Caroline to warn her to keep a close eye out.

"Back so soon?" She smiled at him as he approached once more.

"I have a feeling we are being watched. Jason told me once that my senses would kick in and I would sense people, mostly demons, watching me. If that's the case, I want you to be extra alert and careful, all right?"

"Certainly, I'll pay close attention." She gave him a small, reassuring smile before returning her attention to the plains and ridgelines that lay sprawled out all around them.

Seth left her once more and went to warn Wade to keep a closer eye out as well. He didn't know if it would really do much good since the young man really had no fighting skills whatsoever, but everyone had to do their part he supposed.

After talking to Wade again and telling him to closely watch the cavern entrance, Seth went back to camp and filled the canteen, taking stock of the cavern once more and the horses. He then left, exchanged canteens with Wade, and ventured back down to the underground cavern to check on the women and exploration teams.

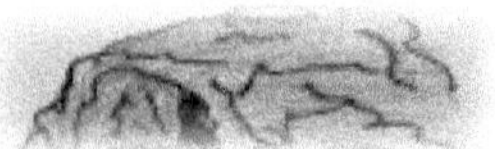

Nick, Kristen, and Tim made excellent time back down to the offset shaft they had found earlier in the day. Kristen was surprised at how quickly Nick could move with his prosthetic leg. His injury brought her back to the horrors she experienced in the front-line medic tents during World War One. The young men who survived that horrid time would never have had the opportunities of the medical advancements people do now. Sometimes her old life felt like a dream. One that wasn't real. Her nightmares about the war were finally beginning to fade. She only had them a few times a month now instead of nightly. She supposed that after a year of living a new life her dreams would change to some degree. She just wasn't sure what her dreams about Sean meant? The last few nights her dreams had been filled with memories of Sean. Their hike through the mountainside on Reader's Island, and the camaraderie they had been sharing as of late compared to their tumultuous relationship over the last year or so. But he had barely spoken a handful of words to her since they had left the island and she couldn't understand why. Maybe that was why she had been dreaming about him? Perhaps her concern over their blossoming friendship coming to a sudden halt just had her confused and was affecting her sleep habits.

She was lost in her thoughts about the morning of the hike when she had tried to wake him. She outwardly grinned at the remembrance of his big, goofy smile, and the sleepy, hazed look on his face, when he had wrapped his arm around her, nearly pulling her down on top of him. She also remembered the startled and embarrassed look on his face as well when she had yelled at him to snap out of it.

"Penny for your thoughts?" Tim's question shook her out of her reverie. "Something amusing you'd care to share?"

Kristen straightened her pack across her back and glanced at him only briefly, not willing to let him into her thoughts.

"No. Not really. Just old memories. Nothing that would interest you." She picked up her pace, walking faster to catch up with Nick. She hadn't realized she had fallen so far behind during her trip down memory lane. She would have to make sure she stayed more alert in the future. Tim had stayed behind her pulling up the rear. She supposed it was a good thing he had brought her back around, but it unnerved her to know that he watched her so closely. It kind of gave her the creeps. How often did he watch her? She was being ridiculous she told herself. He may like her, but surely he wasn't some sort of stalker.

Catching up with Nick, they were just getting to the shaft they had found before. Nick stopped and turned to them.

"All right, we have a decision to make. Do we continue on down the main path here, or do we see where the hidden one leads?"

Tim spoke first. "Well, I suppose it really doesn't matter. We have to explore them both anyway, eventually."

"Yes, but this path does seem to be sort of hidden. Maybe there is a reason someone made this one a little harder to find?" Kristen looked back and forth between the two men.

Nick nodded. "I believe you're right, Kristen. I say we take the hidden path first."

With that decision made, they turned into the small alcove to the hidden shaft and continued their journey down into the darkness of the smaller tunnel. Little did they know that the rope line they were laying down behind them to alert the others of trouble, had found its way underneath the sharp ledge of the bottom of the wall at floor level, and was pinned tightly where it lay. As they walked, dropping the line, it pulled a little more snuggly with each small tug of the rope.

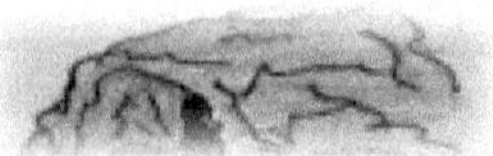

Deep within the mine, Jason, Sean, and Gabriele made their way through the shaft recently explored by Seth's group. With the meticulous notes and tracking made by Caroline, they easily and quickly found the point where they had stopped before. The coordinates on the Portgens helped, but they didn't show any obstructions or hazards like the drawn maps done by the others.

As they continued, twisting, and turning through the widening shafts they suddenly stepped out into a large underground cavern strewn with buckets, shovels, pickaxes, and loose copper minerals cascading down from where the walls had been dug out. The cavern was quite large with a few more tunnels leading off into other directions on the far side of the room.

The three of them walked silently through the cavern shining their flashlights all about. Located in the center of the room were some wheeled carts that were obviously used to pile the copper nuggets into, then pulled up the shafts toward the top cavern. Sean looked at the primitive devices, glad that he had not been part of the slave labor that was used to haul the certainly heavy carts back up to the surface. He could imagine men dragging or hauling copper in the buckets for miles out of the mine shafts. The tunnels were wide enough, but long, winding, and all uphill from here. He grimaced at the thought, grateful God had called him to a different sort of life.

"Jason," Gabriele called, "What exactly are we looking for?"

"Your guess is as good as mine." He scanned the area around him.

Sean replied with, "I would assume the belts to look like long straps, probably made of leather, very old and maybe even worn. They may or may not have a type of buckle."

"Obviously." Jason glanced at the young man whose description would have been obvious to just about anyone. "I doubt they are all just lying around somewhere down here in the mine. They could be stored in a chest of sorts. I believe that was what she was asking."

"Then why didn't you say that in the first place?" Sean said defensively.

Jason and Sean just glanced at each other and continued to survey their surroundings. They heard some noise coming out of another tunnel followed by a beam of light. Oz, Dinah , and Dominic emerged from the tunnel into the large area. It appeared that maybe all the other tunnels emptied into this cavern. Several other groups could be heard approaching them as well, as light bounced off the walls from different directions, and sounds could be heard amplifying and echoing off the cavern walls. Before long, all the groups, minus Nick's, were in the large cavern. They all chatted and walked around looking for anything that appeared useful.

Sean took stock of all the shafts that the other groups exited from. One tunnel remained to spit out its likely team of explorers. As the others, mainly the leaders, chatted about whether to head back topside, Sean caught himself holding his breath at times, watching the offending shaft while chewing on his lower lip, wondering why Nick and Kristen hadn't made an appearance yet.

"Jason, I think something might be wrong with Nick's group. They are the only ones who haven't shown up yet." Sean threw the words over his shoulder while his eyes remained on the dark hole.

"I'm sure they are fine, Sean. Besides, we don't know that all the shafts empty into this cavern," Jason nonchalantly replied, continuing his discussion with the other leaders.

"I just have a bad feeling about it is all." Sean tried to keep himself from running into the dark shaft that had yet to yield his friends.

"Sean, we have things in place to warn if anyone is in trouble, remember?" Jason was growing agitated at the young man.

"Yeah. And the only ones who would know if anyone else needs help would be the others topside, miles away from where we are now." Sean's agitation was growing as well, and he turned to look at the other groups in the center of the cavern.

Zaccai glanced at Jason. "He does have a valid point. I too find it strange that all groups have made an appearance except for Nick's."

"I understand your concern, but we have no idea how long all these tunnels are. There's no sense in getting all bent out of shape when we aren't sure anything is wrong," Jason said level-headedly.

"If we are done checking things out in here, I suggest we travel back up and a few of us take this tunnel here." Sean pointed to the shaft that held his concern.

"We can't do that, Sean." Jason was growing ever more frustrated with the young man.

"Why not?" Sean's voice escalated in pitch.

"Because of the rope system for one. Two, we have no idea if it even leads up to where they are. Just because it sits beside the others that everyone else exited from doesn't mean it is their tunnel. It could be any number of the other tunnels that sit on either side of this cavern. Three, Nick, Kristen, and Timothy are all capable of taking care of themselves. If you're all concerned about them, then I say we head back topside, and see where they might be. Besides, it is growing late, and this area is too large to explore much more tonight."

Uriah Mose spoke in aggravation next.

"This is a waste of time if we are just going to go up and down these mine shafts every day. We aren't going to get any real searching done unless we start staying down here to look around. We waste time going back up and retracing our steps; which doesn't lead to finding anything."

"That there be true, Uriah," Oz spoke next. "But, we don't know jus' how danger'us these ole' mines are. I worked in one back in Zanchier. They can be right treach'rous places unless ya' know what ta' look fer. Even then, they can throw some surprises at ya'. These here tunnels are lit'rally thousands a' years old." Oz forebodingly warned.

Zeke offered, "This would make a good camping spot. It has plenty of room for all of us too. And like Uriah said, we wouldn't waste hours going back up. At least stay down here for a day or two to explore the few shafts on the other side over there." He pointed to the few shafts disappearing into the far side of the cavern. "I really think it would expedite searching."

Jason conceded to the others. "All right, we'll have to discuss this with everyone else. Let's all head back up, get some dinner, and after that we will have a meeting and take a vote. See you all topside."

As Jason finished, everyone gathered back into their groups. He looked around the cavern, looking at Gabriele. "Gabby, where's Sean?"

"I'm not sure, but I bet I can guess." She pointed at the mine shaft that had him so concerned earlier.

"You have got to be kidding me?" Jason growled out in frustration. "Stupid kid! He's going to get himself killed or lost!"

Oz, who was close enough to detect the aggravation in his voice, asked, "What's goin' on Jason?"

"Doran decided to take off by himself to search for Nick's group." Jason was growing angrier by the minute.

"Well, we can't leave 'im down here, 'specially without a rope guide. Why don't we send the others back up tagether and a few a' us leaders can go a lookin' fer 'im?"

"I suppose we'll have to. Although I have a mind to leave him to his own decisions. When I get my hands on that kid, I'm going to wring his neck!"

"Jason," Gabby said timidly, "Don't be too hard on him. The other group has most of his friends in it. He's just worried about them. You'd most likely have done the same thing if it were Seth, Alec, or Odessa."

"You're right. But I wouldn't have just run off by myself putting other people in danger with them having to come look for me as well. I would have made a plan first." He stormed off to instruct the others.

"Listen up everyone! Sean has taken it upon himself to disappear into one of the shafts in search of Nick and the others. Oz, Zaccai, and I will go in search of Sean. The rest of you pair up and head up top. If you get there before we do, as I am certain you will, Odessa, I want you to let Seth know what happened. Does everyone understand?"

Dinah interjected amongst the mumbled answers. "I want to go with you. They are my friends as well."

"I want to go too!" Gabby also quickly insisted.

"Ladies, I understand your concern. But the more people we have, the more we have to worry about losing. Please, just head back with the others. I hope this won't take long." Jason was so aggravated with Sean and the ruckus he was causing that he entertained the thought of actually strangling the young man when he found him.

As everyone gathered into new groups for heading back out of the mine, Jason, Zaccai, and Oz, took some of the excess ropes from the others in case they ran out, tied their rope from topside off to a boulder, and then tied one of the new ropes off to a rock in the floor just outside the shaft entrance to help them find their way back. The trio then entered the unexplored shaft in search of one problem-causing, stubborn, young man named Sean Doran

I sought the Lord, and He answered me;
He delivered me from all my fears.

Psalm 34:4

Chapter 4

Nick, Kristen, and Tim traveled deeper into the mine within the hidden shaft. This shaft was much smaller than the one that led them to it. The ceiling wasn't quite as high, and the walls seemed closer together. They also didn't appear to be traveling downhill, but slightly uphill instead. Keeping their pace steady and checking the rope occasionally for supply length, they soon stumbled upon a room that opened at the end of the shaft. It was approximately a twenty-by-twenty area, laden with all sorts of pottery, metal ware, cisterns, baskets, chairs, and a small table. All of which were covered by centuries of mine dust.

They walked all around the room, exploring everything intently. Perhaps the belts were hidden in this area? Hidden within one of the many pots and baskets littering the floor at the wall's edge. The room appeared to possibly be some sort of storage. Kristen began removing lids off any baskets or pots, peering inside as she did so. Tim, following her example, picked up a lid from a large basket and peered down inside. As his light shone down into the depths of the basket, several large scorpions scampered out and over the edge of the basket opening.

"Ahhh! What the . . ."

"What is it?" Kristen asked quickly as she and Nick shined their light beams in his direction.

"Nothing," Timothy sheepishly stated. "Just startled by a few rather large scorpions."

"Watch out for those. They are poisonous here. Probably not enough to kill you, but certainly enough venom to make you very ill," Kristen answered with a warning.

"Kristen, how do you know so much about animals and nature?"

"My dad schooled me in camping and survival techniques." Not looking at him, she continued her light search as she moved across the floor. "Nick, I think I've found something over here in the side of the wall." As she leaned over the board fixed into the cavern wall, the board gave way and Kristen tumbled over down into the darkness.

Nick and Tim, startled by the scream, turned just in time to see her feet disappear into the hole.

"Kristen!!" They both yelled simultaneously, running toward the hole she disappeared into.

Nick shined his light down into the hole to see if he could spot her. "Kristen, are you all right?"

Dangling over the side in the dark depth of the hole, tightly gripping the thin rope they used for alerting the others to an emergency, was Kristen.

Nick sighed gratefully. "Thank God that you were the one laying that rope! Are you all right?"

"I think so!" Kristen yelled back up toward the two men peering down at her from above. She could hear the crackling of the rope as her weight pulled the woven strings taught. She held on tightly, silently whispering prayers to God to protect her. She grasped the rope even tighter as she tried to peer down below her, wondering where her flashlight had disappeared to. She couldn't see anything below her except utter darkness. If her flashlight hit the floor somewhere below her, it probably shattered into pieces. If not, it could still be falling into the depths of the mine. The thought of the possibilities of either of those scenarios happening made her grasp at the thin rope even tighter, her eyes tightly closed against the darkness surrounding her as she continued whispering prayers into the air.

Nick spoke to her with soothing yet quick words. "We're going to try to pull you up now, just hold on tight and let me know if you feel like the rope is giving way, all right?"

"All right!"

"Kristen, I want you to try and tie the rope around your waist if you can, then tie it to itself. With us pulling on the rope, I don't want the jarring motion to make you lose your grip."

"All right, I'll see if I can do it." She nervously inched her hand down the rope that also disappeared below her. The length of the remainder of the spool swallowed up by the blackness that stretched out beneath. She cautiously slid her hand down as far as she could and still maintain her grasp on it. She grabbed the rope below her and hauled as much of it up as she could. She awkwardly and carefully as possible slung it around her body underneath her backside, trying to tie it to itself just below her other hand, making as good a knot as she could manage one-handed. The extra movement on the thin rope made the threads creak and crackle with every little motion she made, making her wince in fear.

"All right, I'm finished knotting the rope. Nick, please hurry and get me out of here!" Her voice shook with fear.

Nick had walked back to the cavern entrance to check the integrity of the rope. He wanted to make sure that the pulling wasn't fraying the edges as it rubbed against the rock walls.

Tim answered Kristen's desperate plea.

"Okay. Kristen, we're going to start pulling you up. We'll be as easy as we can." Tim was nervous about the weight on the rope as well.

Kristen clung to the small rope as the two men above her pulled her up as gently and quickly as they could. She winced with each jerking motion made by the action, daring to glance up at the men every so often, praying harder than she ever had in her life.

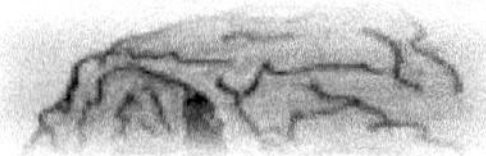

Sean moved as quickly as he could, following the light of his flashlight's beam, calling out to his friends and listening for any responses. As he moved along the shaft on the small inclining surface, he thought he heard someone yell. He stopped for just a minute as small undistinguishable sounds bounced along the passage, fading into nothing.

"Kristen! Nick!" Sean yelled into the darkness. He must have been nuts to take off by himself down in these mines. But he had a very bad feeling about them being the only ones not to appear in the large underground cavern with the rest of them. And, since Jason and the others didn't seem to feel he had a need to worry, he knew he couldn't count on them to be of any help, so taking off on his own was his only option. As he walked along the passage, staying near to the left-hand side wall, he nearly tripped over something. He shined his light down at the floor, spying one of the guide ropes they all used. *I knew I would find them!* He studied the rope, realizing that it was pulled extremely tight even though it was still against the floor of the shaft. It seemed to disappear around the corner of an alcove, back into the wall.

"I knew it! Something's very wrong here." Sean moved as quickly as he could, keeping an eye on the rope and following it to wherever it would take him.

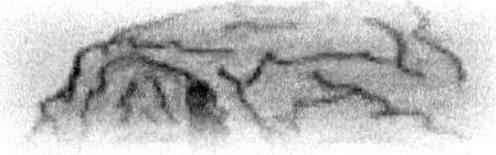

"Sean!" Jason yelled into the darkness as his, Zaccai, and Oz's light-beams illuminated the passage before them. "I am going to literally strangle that guy, if he isn't already dead or missing."

"Yes, yes, we know you are going to kill him," Zaccai repeated Jason's remark. "Let it go already. It isn't doing you or us any good to continue to hype over his poor decision to take off in search of his friends."

"Sorry." He turned to look at her. "I suppose it's my military training. You don't disobey a direct command."

"Perhaps YOU don't. But Sean is not military." She reminded him. "And, we are all adults here who are used to working with just a handful of people, and Sean was a leader in his peregrination group, so just remember that when we find him."

"I know that but, everyone was given strict rules to follow for a reason. We have to try to keep everyone safe, and if people start going off half-cocked and making their own rules and decisions, then we are going to have a mess on our hands."

"Sh...," Oz interjected. "You two be still a minute, will ya'? I thought I heard som'thin'." They all stopped moving, trying to home in on whatever sound Oz heard. "There," he softly stated, the sound echoing somewhere far ahead of them. "Sounds to me like someone yellin'."

Jason listened intently. "I'll bet that's Sean calling to Nick. We can't be too far behind him. Just keep a look out for any shafts that might branch off." They began to move a bit faster in hopes of catching up to the young man.

Continuing up the path, they too came to the tightly strung rope stuck underneath the bottom edge of the cavern wall, straining against its confines. They followed the rope as well into the alcove and along the small hidden pathway, also realizing that something was very wrong with the tightness of it, and its inability to alert those back at cavern headquarters due to its constraints underneath the rock ledge.

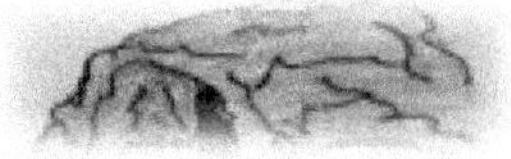

Nick and Timothy wrapped the thin rope around their hands, trying to grasp it as best as they could. Kristen's weight pulling the rope taught made it extremely hard to haul her up and out of the hole. With each feeble yank the rope frayed just a bit more as it slid against the side of the broken wood and rough rock wall. The only thing keeping them from dropping her was the fact that the rope was pulled tightly all the way back to the beginning of the cavern and looped into the outer wall ring they had installed for just this scenario.

The men tugged with all their might as the rope cut into Nick's hands. Timothy's gift of armored skin kept that from happening to him, so he wasn't experiencing what Nick was.

As they continued slowly pulling on the thin rope, they began to hear footsteps echoing behind them. They grew nervous as they looked at each other with growing concern over who, or what, could be approaching. Suddenly, a flashlight appeared around the corner of the cavern opening, and in ran Sean Doran.

Sean, realizing what was happening, quickly dropped everything, and grasped at the rope as well.

'Kristen!?" Sean yelled down to her but was unable to see anything.

"Sean!? What are you doing here?" she called back, confused.

"Never mind that, let's just get you out of there!"

"I sure am glad to see you." Nick grunted and strained against the thin rope.

"Me too." Sean grinned briefly at his friend and mentor.

"She fell further than we thought." Timothy glanced at Sean, struggling to talk. "Sean, pull easily, this rope is so thin, we're afraid it might snap."

"It's pulled pretty tight and its under stress back where y'all turned down this shaft. It's stuck underneath the wall ledge and it could be rubbing," Sean replied.

"Sean!" Another voice outside the small cavern entrance called.

"In here Jason! Hurry up!"

As Jason, Zaccai, and Oz rounded the corner, quickly assessing the situation at hand, they had just grabbed the rope when it snapped way back behind them at the place where it was stuck beneath the wall ledge. The constant weight and stress causing it to rub and fray completely in two beneath the rock.

Unprepared for the breaking rope, they all were pulled forward slightly by the motion, and Kristen, dangling on the other end dropped back down further into the dark, unknown, abyss below her, screaming out in utter fear.

"Sean!!" She panicked and began to audibly cry at the sudden motion and sense of falling. Thank goodness Nick had suggested she tie the rope around her, or she probably would have fallen.

"Hold on Kristen, we have plenty of help now. We should have you out soon," Timothy reassured her, uncomfortable with her unexpected plea to Sean and not him or Nick. Timothy was grateful for the extra help, just not overjoyed at who happened to show up.

Within a matter of minutes, they had Kristen out of the offending hole and safely planted upon the cavern floor. The rope she had tied around her body had tightened almost unbearably around her hips, and she had wrapped the rope around her left arm several times to make sure she could hold on, just before the unexpected jarring and drop, which shot painful sensations throughout her body.

"All right everyone, let's get out of here. Kristen, I'll look at your injuries when we get topside again. Can you walk?" Jason asked her.

"Yeah, I think so. I do hurt a little, but I'm pretty sure it's just cuts and bruising from the rope," she replied shakily.

"I can help you Kristen, if you need it," Timothy quickly interjected.

"She said she could do it," Sean said blatantly, staring the man down.

"I can, really, Tim. I'm all right to walk out." She quickly confirmed Sean's reply, watching the odd visible exchange that passed between the two men, unsure what to make of it.

"Good, let's go," Jason instructed everyone, not willing to discuss anything else at the moment. Emotions, nerves, and adrenaline were running high for everyone right now, and Jason did not want to get into a discussion about Sean taking off like he did. But he would talk to the young man, even though he had been right about Nick's group being in trouble, they still couldn't have disobedience in the ranks.

As they walked up the shafts that led them out of the mines, Kristen turned to Sean who was walking directly behind her.

"Sean?" She glanced over her shoulder as she walked.

"Yeah?"

"Thank you."

"Any time, Kris." He gave her a look so intense it almost made her dizzy. Or was that from the adrenaline still coursing through her body, making her shake as though she were chilled to the bone? Did he just call her Kris? He had never used a nickname for her before. She shrugged it off and tried to mentally disconnect for a bit from the whole ordeal, just praising the Lord that she was alive to fight and live another day.

It had taken them the better part of two-and-a-half-hours to walk the entire distance to the main cavern. Kristen's body ached and her hands were raw from catching and sliding down the rope when she first fell into the mining hole. Her hips and upper thighs were sore where the tightness of the rope pinched and bound her skin and muscles, and her left arm had rope burns and already visible bruises from where the rope cut into her arm after it had broken, and she had fallen once again. All these things were a nuisance at the moment but had it not been for those measures taken at the time, she may not be here right now.

Almost the entire group of Peregrines were there to welcome them out of the mines. Bridget, Sofia, Wade, and Dominic had gone back to the camp to start preparing dinner. It was now dark outside, with the moon beginning its climb into the night sky. By the time they all made it back to their campsite, dinner was well underway, and they were informed it would only be another ten minutes or so before they could eat.

Jason told everyone except Nick, Zaccai, Oz, and Sean, to go ahead and get their dinner so he could check Kristen over to assess her injuries and look over the other's hands to see if anyone had cuts that needed tending to. They all had a few cuts from the rope digging into them, especially Nick's. After tending to them and informing Sean he wanted to speak to him after he finished with Kristen, he turned his healing attentions to Kristen as the others went off to grab a plate of food. Sean looking back over his shoulder as he went.

"Your injuries are a little more substantial than the others. Let's go into my tent and I will take care of you there." Jason led her inside but left the flaps open. He pointed her toward a fold out camping chair where she sat down so he could begin.

Jason took Kristen's hands in his, looking them over. He released them and his hands just hovered slightly above hers as he concentrated and prayed over her injuries. Her hands slowly began to heal as he moved his hands up her left arm to tend to the broken and bruised skin there as well.

"All right Kristen, what next? Where else does it hurt?"

"My hips and outer thighs feel pretty bruised. I think there are some cuts as well. I can see some blood on my pants in a few spots."

"All right, do you want to stand up for me so that I can see where they are? Are long as you're comfortable with me checking you over?" He noticed her hesitation.

"Sure, I suppose so." She stood up slowly, wincing with pain.

"How about if I call Dinah in here with us, will that make you more comfortable?"

"It doesn't really matter, Jason. I was a nurse during World War One. I've both seen and had my share of medical emergencies."

Jason smiled slightly at the young woman, amazed at her gumption and spirit. He forgot that all these people came from lives he had no clue about before peregrinating. "All right, then let's get started, shall we? You'll need to remove your pants so that I can actually see the wounds."

Just then, Sean returned with two plates of food. He stepped into the tent and placed them on the empty obliging fold out chair, watching Kristen.

"I brought you a plate." He motioned to the chair. "I figured we could eat together."

"Thank you, Sean." She looked at him and grinned.

Jason looked at him. "Sean, you'll just need to step outside a minute while I examine Kristen."

"No, it's fine. He can stay." She looked at Sean who seemed a bit confused. "Jason has to see the wounds that are around my hip area, so I have to sort of disrobe. They are really around my upper thighs. I suppose I could go and put some shorts on. I'll be right back." She left the tent in search of her own.

This gave Jason and Sean the opportunity to talk, although Sean wasn't too keen on being left alone with the man since he disobeyed his orders earlier. He not only risked his life but the lives of those who had to come find him, and quite possibly the mission as well.

"Now that we have a moment to talk..."

"Look, Jason, I'm sorry I took off like that after you told me not to, but I knew something was wrong. I had to find out."

"I understand that Sean, but you can't go around disregarding what the leaders tell you. If you disobey orders again, I'm going to make you stay at camp and monitor things here. I won't let you near or back inside the mine again. Is that understood?"

"Yes, I understand. But if I hadn't gone looking, she could be dead right now."

"You don't know that Sean. Nick and Timothy probably could have gotten her out on their own. Even with the thinning rope."

"'Probably, but it isn't something I want to think about, Jason. You don't understand."

"I see." Jason pondered the young man's remark as realization set in. "Does she know how you feel?"

Sean's head jerked up to look Jason square in the eyes. "I'm obviously not very good at hiding my feelings, am I?" He watched an expression of understanding cross Jason's features.

Answering Jason's question, he said, "No, I don't think she knows anyway." Sean nervously looked out the opened tent flaps for Kristen's return. "And right now, I'm not sure I want her to. She has enough to think about as it is. I don't want to be a distraction for her in any way, so, please don't say anything."

"You have my word. As long as I have yours. No more stunts like today." The two men exchanged glances and nodded their acceptance of the terms just as Kristen reappeared wearing some loose-fitting shorts.

"I looked over my legs when I changed clothing. I found a few spots that I can show you." She began pointing to the general areas around the top outer part of her thighs.

Jason dropped the tent flaps to give her more privacy and began examining and healing the injured areas. The ropes had burned and pinched the skin through her clothing quite a bit. The worst of the injuries however was the bruising. She was already turning purple and green in most areas. It only took him about five minutes to finish the healing process, during which time Kristen and Sean exchanged some serious looks and a few words, chatting while Jason worked.

Kristen asked Sean the question that plagued her for the last four hours or so.

"Sean, what were you doing in our tunnel? I mean, where did you come from?"

"Well, all the other groups emptied into a large underground cavern about five miles or so down into the mine. When you and Nick didn't appear like the rest, I assumed something was wrong and went looking for you." He nervously shoved his hands into his pant pockets.

"What about the rest of you, Jason?" She glanced down at the man.

"We took off to find Sean who decided to disappear on his own." He sternly looked at the younger man.

She turned abruptly at his remark to look at Sean. "Are you crazy? You could have gotten lost down there or hurt and no one would have been able to find you."

"I didn't, did I," he said defensively. "Besides, they found me, and I found you and Nick. And . . . Timothy." He begrudgingly added the name.

Jason stood up and announced, "All done, Kristen. You may still experience some stiffness and soreness tomorrow, but the cuts and bruises are all healed. I'm going to go grab a bite to eat. You two are welcome to stay here to talk and eat if you'd like." With that, he left the tent.

Kristen and Sean took their plates and found a place to sit and eat. They were both ravenously hungry and spent the next several minutes in silence, shoveling the wonderful tasting food into their mouths. When the food caught up to their hunger, Kristen initiated the conversation again. Not talking about the incident, but just about what they had each been doing since they left the island for the desert.

Outside the tent, gathered around the fire, were some of the leaders and a few others, deep in conversation about the recent happenings since their arrival in Timna Valley. Seth and Jason sat next to each other talking lowly so others couldn't hear them, but not whispering so as to not attract attention. Seth was questioning Jason on the visitor they had earlier in camp.

"So, Jason, you said there was a woman with a rather large knife that attacked you earlier. I am assuming she got away. I'm just really curious as to how?" Seth's smile tugged at the sides of his mouth and eyes.

"Fine. You have to promise not to laugh." Jason sternly looked at Seth who simply shrugged his shoulders in reply. "Well, we had struggled some, after she came at me with that large, curved blade I told you about."

"Yeah, I saw that thing in your tent earlier when I came in to check things out. That's some knife."

Jason shook his head in agreement. "Anyway, I first thought she was a man, but when I pinned her to the floor, she lost her hood and shroud in the struggle. Obviously not a man." Appreciation laced his words. "I let her up, and she seemed to calm down, so I let her wrists go. That's when she kneed me in the groin. I went down like a wet rag." Jason slightly adjusted his seating position, wincing at the memory.

Seth cracked a small smile, trying not to laugh at his friend's obvious discomfort. "You think she'll be back then, since you have her blade?"

"Maybe. We'll just have to wait and see. What I'm most concerned with is she said she belongs to an ancient tribe appointed by King Solomon himself to guard the mines. If that is the case, we might just have more visitors. These desert tribes can run quite large, and if they've been around since the days of King Solomon and David, then we will be very outnumbered."

"Maybe, but we don't mean any harm. We only want the Belts."

"That's what I told her, we're only searching for one specific thing. I'm just not sure if she believed me or even cared. We will have to be more diligent during lookout. The last thing I want to do is get into a war with the locals." Jason picked up his plate to eat. Seth did the same, and they each lightly conversed with the rest of the group gathering around them and the fire.

Timothy sat and watched the two people who most held his interest at the moment, smiling and conversing in Jason's tent. Sean and Kristen seemed to hold some sort of special bond. Most Peregrine partners did. He would have to figure out how to get her to trust him the same way she apparently trusted Sean. Figuring out how to do that was the problem.

62

> But each person is tempted when they are
> dragged away by their own evil desire and enticed.
>
> James 1:14

Chapter 5

Dominic Abel Amando was a young man of fifteen from Greece, who had been called to peregrination about six months ago from his time period of 2001 AD. Although, if the ancient archival books that they recently found were correct, he was not a Peregrine. Instead he was what the book called a Beast Keeper, based on his recently discovered gift of communicating with animals. No one had questioned his Peregrine status before their convergence on the island because he had always been athletic and could handle himself well in a fight. He supposed that was from growing up in such a large family with seven older brothers and lots of male cousins who had tortured him regularly as the youngest in the family. His brothers and cousins may have been mean to him at times, but they would have beaten the life out of anyone outside of the family that chose to mess with him.

His childhood was riddled with good memories. His large family had taught him that he was part of something and that he belonged somewhere. Which is why, he supposed, he had taken to this lifestyle so well; he understood his calling here.

Dominic's parents had been devout Catholics and made sure they were all brought up in church. That was where he had first discovered a relationship with God. He seemed to take to it more seriously than most of his older brothers had. He often wondered if that was the reason God had chosen him for this life? He wasn't sure if all the other Keepers and Peregrines lives were similar to his, or if they were believers, but he wanted to find out. What would make him so special for such missions for God as what they were called to now? Why him, he often wondered? He truly could not think of anything else he would rather be doing other than what he currently was called to do. He truly felt special in the eyes of the Lord and was grateful for the chance to serve in such a noble way.

Dominic thought about Uriah Yousef Mose, his peregrination partner, who was another story altogether. Malachai, their Dragoman, had told Dominic about Uriah once. He said that Uriah had been a Hittite iron worker from the year 1360 BC. He had never been a believer, just a follower of whatever was the 'in thing' at the time, especially if he could make money at it. When Uriah had first peregrinated, he was angry at being taken from his life and homeland. He had refused to do anything that was expected of him for the first two months. His mentor at the time, Hiram Burke, had slowly earned the man's trust and he finally began to take to his new lifestyle very slowly. That was sixteen years ago. Uriah was still highly opinionated and brusque in certain ways, but he seemed sincere enough as a person, although no one was as close to him as he and Hiram had been. Hiram's betrayal had been very hard on Uriah, and he had closed off his emotions since that dreadful day thirteen years ago.

Dominic and Uriah had taken the last watch before dawn woke the remaining Peregrines and Keepers from their sleep. Another day of mine explorations would soon be underway. They sat and watched as the sun began its rise into the early morning sky, pushing the darkness away and replacing it with beams of light that broke across the mountain ridgelines, illuminating parts of the valley floor wherever a crack or crevice in the surrounding mountainside allowed.

The Peregrines began to stir in the dim light of the cavern where the fire had been kept burning by the night watchmen. Every few hours, as the men and women exchanged shifts, they would throw a few logs on the fire to keep the coldness of the desert night from creeping into the cavern. Learning to sleep in broken shifts was hard for some of them to get used to, but it was necessary on this journey.

Yesterday's adventures had taken them to the heart of the current mining shafts they were exploring. The central underground cavern was large, but there were only a handful of shafts leading off of it. Taking that into consideration, only two groups would return to the current shafts, while the other three would search some of the surrounding areas. The mines were extensive, and according to current information, there were literally thousands of entrances and shafts leading down into the mines. After last night's events, Jason and the others decided that Nick's group would stay topside and keep watch for today. They figured Kristen could do with a bit of a break from the mine searching seeing as how she came so close to death yesterday.

Jason's and Oz's groups would return to the current mine while the others would explore other areas and mines nearby. Since they really didn't need that many people to help with the old mines, Dominic was appointed to stay topside to help keep watch over the ropes for these two groups, taking Sofia and Bridget's place. Sofia and Bridget went with the remaining groups just a bit further over from their current location, to keep watch on the ropes and make maps of what was being explored next. This time, they were above ground in the heat and intensity of the desert sun. Jason had a tent constructed to help keep the sun off them while they worked, and had a table and chairs placed inside to make their jobs a bit easier. The Peregrines from Nick's group would switch off every hour or so to stay with the women in the tent and to get a reprieve from the intensity of the desert sun.

As Dominic settled into his new position, he thought about Bridget Burke, Hiram's long-lost daughter, also recently found. She was definitely a unique individual. He knew girls liked to talk, but Bridget talked more than anyone he had ever met before. Still, it was nice to have people around his own age here as well. He, Bridget,

Wade, and Gabriele were all teenagers. And, strangely enough, three of them were Beast Keepers. Gabby, however, was just a Peregrine as far as everyone else knew. He liked Gabby; she was a really cool girl. She had told him stories of growing up within a wealthy family, where her father had made sure she learned everything she could. She could fight with her Katana as well as anyone he had ever seen before. He had never seen people move the way Gabby could. He had gotten to know her over the last six months since they both were mentored by the same Dragoman, Malachai Harel; as were Zaccai and Uriah.

Malachai was an interesting man too. He reminded Dominic of one of his favorite uncles from back home. He had taken Dominic under his wing when he first peregrinated because of his age. It had shocked Malachai to see someone so young called to this lifestyle. He had said once that he had never known God to call anyone under the age of seventeen to peregrinating in all the years that he had been a Dragoman. He also told him that none of the other Dragoman had ever seen anyone so young called before either. Dominic wasn't sure if that was a good or a bad thing. All he knew was that he was happy to be called as an actual, demon-fighting, globe-trotting, time-jumping, soldier of God. He got to see and do things that very few others ever would. Sure, he missed his family at times, but he adapted well to his surroundings and made friends easily. He considered all the Peregrines, Dragoman, and other Beast Keepers his new family.

Dominic returned his attention to the thin rope that was jerking and wriggling occasionally, due to Jason's and Oz's groups deciding to make quick work of returning to the large cavern approximately five miles deep. They were apparently moving very quickly. They had said upon leaving, that they knew the tunnels quite well by now, and wanted to get started on exploring the shafts on the other side of the large cavern they all found yesterday.

Dominic sat down in the sand to continue his watch, pulling a sketch pad and some charcoal pencils from his pack. He might as well make some good use of just sitting, so he began making sketches of the desert landscapes that he could remember seeing, and the dawn he had observed that very morning.

Odessa Megalos climbed down the primitive, but sturdy ladder into the depths of the mine shaft. These new tunnels descended deeper by ladder than the last one they explored. It appeared she would never reach the bottom.

The sunlight was beginning to climb higher in the sky, affording them with more light. By the time the sun reached its highest point, it would filter through these shafts, hopefully providing much needed natural light.

She finally reached the bottom of the ladder which opened to a very small cavern that led off into one lone shaft. She stepped aside to allow the descent of Uriah and Zaccai, two other Peregrines she had known for quite some time. She knew them, but not like she knew her traveling group under Simon Lane's mentorship. Uriah and Zaccai were two of the oldest Peregrines she knew of. They had been doing this at least four or five years longer than Odessa had. Although they had never traveled together before this trip, they all had been living the same lifestyle for over thirteen years, and therefore shared a sort of kinship in that knowledge. They each knew what was expected from the other and there were no conflicting, or overprotective feelings to hinder their decision making.

She couldn't say the same thing for her current traveling partner, Alec Chevalier. That little Frenchman had wormed his way into her heart over the years. She loved him dearly and would give her life for his as would he for her, she knew that. He was closer to her than a big brother. However, she often wondered if he had feelings above brotherly love for her? Since the African expedition to retrieve the Goddelikheid crucible, she kept having a reoccurring dream about Alec and some of the things she thought she heard him say while she was on her death bed. Surely it had just been a dream.

They could never have a real relationship, could they? No, she was afraid it would ruin the amazing friendship they had built over the last ten years. That wasn't something she was willing to risk losing. However, he was a believer now since that very same incident in Africa, so there wouldn't be any conflict in their beliefs. What almost killed her had saved him. It amazed her at times what God used to get a person's attention to bring them to His saving grace. Odessa was suddenly shaken out of her reverie by Zaccai's voice just ahead of her.

"There is a series of smaller caverns just up here. They all seem to intertwine, like a small maze of sorts. Just watch where you step. We certainly don't need a recap of yesterday's events," Zaccai instructed over her shoulder.

As Odessa traveled throughout the small caverns, her light-beam bounced off the same sort of items, like cast off pots and baskets, as was in the last shafts and caverns.

Uriah slunk around the outer edges of the caverns, peering into the multiple, dusty, aged, pottery, and wooden buckets searching for something that might resemble a belt. "Surely the Belts of Truth aren't just lying around down in one of these forgotten caverns."

"Probably not," Zaccai answered him matter-of-factly. "More than likely, they are stored in something, like a chest of sorts. Or, whatever they used in those days as storage vessels. Like this one." She stopped walking, kneeling onto the stone floor to examine the box that was partially covered by old baskets.

Both Uriah and Odessa approached where Zaccai was. Pushing aside the baskets, she slowly and carefully opened the box, not wishing to disturb any creatures such as a desert snake or scorpions. Zaccai lifted open the lid as she peered inside with her light. There was only a handful of cobwebs located inside with some old coins and papers from days gone by. No belts to be seen anywhere. She closed the lid and they continued their search throughout the maze of caverns.

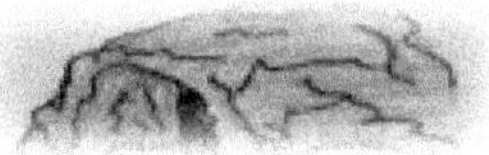

In an adjacent cavern, Seth, Caroline, and Wade searched through the dark mine shafts looking for anything other than rock and sand. The shaft was about a half-mile long, emptying into another mining cavern. This cavern however was completely empty. At least that's what they thought anyway until Caroline heard a faint rattle.

"Seth." She stopped abruptly. "Did you hear that?"

"Yeah, I did." He scanned the surrounding ground with his light.

Wade spoke up. "I see it."

"Where?" Caroline asked in a panic.

"Just in front of you and Seth, on the left against the wall, kind of underneath the cavern's edge in an indented area." Wade watched the rattlesnake carefully. "Don't worry, Caroline. Just back up slowly toward me. It doesn't want to harm anyone. It's scared of you just as much as you are of it. It just wants to be left alone."

"How," Seth began than stopped himself. "Never mind that question. I forget you can communicate with animals. I say let's do just that and go look somewhere else. There doesn't appear to be anything down here anyway."

They then left the area to explore another mine shaft, leaving the rattlesnake to his own business.

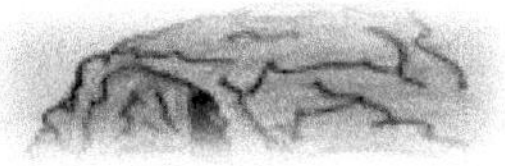

Zeke, Alec, and Nadia had ventured into one area where the shaft had caved in, so they had to turn around and head back to search another shaft that branched off from that one. They only hoped that the mines wouldn't have another cave in while they were searching through them. The tunnels through the mines in this area were narrow. Just wide enough to allow one person at a time in single file. The sunlight filtered through small openings above their heads. Occasionally, they would come across another opening with a ladder to the surface above. This was a large area where many openings connected the tunnels. This led them to believe there was a large mining cavern somewhere near to them. As they ventured further along, they walked past several other shafts leading off the one they were in. The tunnel they were in went straight, while the others snaked and turned in all directions. They only hoped they were just shafts leading to a larger cavern and not ones they would have to explore, because there appeared to be a lot of them.

They could hear sounds echoing around them, bouncing off the tunnel walls. It almost sounded like people talking. They must be converging with another group like yesterday. Sure enough, as they came upon a large cavern in the center, which was obviously where they drew the copper ore from, they could see flashes of light and sounds echoing from several of the other tunnels. They were soon met by Seth, Caroline, and Wade, and yet could still see flashes of light and hear mumbled sounds coming from other tunnels. Zaccai, Uriah, and Odessa appeared next.

They all looked at each other. Alec said what they were all thinking.

"It appears that most of these shafts are all linked together to empty into larger mining caverns. That at least may save us some time while looking."

"Perhaps," Odessa replied, "but, we did find a series of smaller caverns all linked together that were filled with things. Even an old chest which we searched. It didn't hold anything important, but there could be one somewhere that will."

Uriah spoke in his gruff, aggravated sort of way. "This is going to take us forever to search through all of these tunnels and caverns. Surely there is a better and faster way to do this?"

"I agree," came a voice from another tunnel. Exiting, oddly enough, was Jason, Gabby, Sean, Oz, and Dinah. The crews who went down into the other mines this morning that they had all explored yesterday.

"Well, it appears we found a shorter way into this cavern than you all did," Zeke said, looking at Jason and the others.

"Yeah, we pretty much jogged all the way down to the main cavern we found yesterday. This one here is even larger than the other one." Jason shined his light all around them. "We searched all the mining carts and anything else that looked like it might hold or hide something, but we didn't find anything."

Uriah looked at Jason. "So, what's the plan?"

"What do you mean, Uriah?"

"How can we make this searching go faster and easier?"

"Well, do you have any ideas?"

"You're the leader. Surely all of you who are 'in charge,'" Uriah used his hands to make quotation marks in the air, "can figure it out."

Jason watched Uriah's body language. He hadn't noticed before but, Uriah seemed a bit miffed about something. And it appeared it had to do with him not being in a leadership position.

"We'll see what we can come up with tonight back at camp." Jason watched Uriah's expression continue in disdain. "For now," he said looking pointedly at Uriah, "we do what we've been doing. Continue looking and pray God will lead us accordingly."

"Fine." Uriah gritted his teeth. "It's a little crowded in here. I'm going to search a few more tunnels." He began to walk off, but Jason stopped him.

"Not without your partners." Jason watched as Uriah's back stiffened in reaction to being told what to do.

Uriah turned to look at Zaccai and Odessa, raising his hands in question. The two women looked at each other and went with Uriah to search in a tunnel yet unexplored.

Once out of earshot of the larger cavern and the others gathered there, Zaccai questioned Uriah about his attitude.

"Uriah, what is going on with you?" Zaccai bluntly stated, never one to beat around the bush.

"What do you mean?" Agitation was still evident in his voice.

"You know exactly what I mean." She was growing short-tempered with him. "You are challenging the leaders and setting a very bad example for the rest of the group. Especially the younger ones. Why do you do this?"

"I've been peregrinating for fifteen years. Much longer than most of these "so called leaders". Why put them in charge instead of those of us who have way more experience?"

"I am one of those 'so called leaders', remember?" She sternly stared the man down. "The Dragoman selected those to be in charge. We did not appoint ourselves, Uriah. *And*, we are all in this together, on the same missions, doing the same amount of work. We make decisions together as best we can with what we are given. I suggest, you take your jealousy up with God." She stepped past him and walked on up the pathway, looking through the tunnels.

He glared at her back as she went, falling in line behind her. Zaccai was not someone he really wanted to get riled at him. He had peregrinated with her for more than 12 years before being paired with Dominic. He had seen her fight, and knew she stood up for what she believed to be true and right. She could make a fierce friend, or a deadly foe, so he preferred to stay on her good side. As for Odessa he wasn't sure yet. He peered back over his shoulder at the woman, then continued in the search like the rest of them.

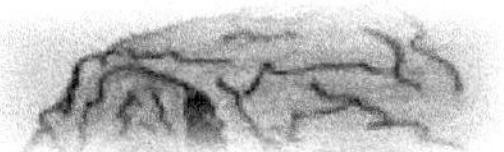

Day two of searching passed with nothing more to show for their efforts other than busted pottery, woven baskets, and several other unimpressive items they had found lying in the large, cavernous areas within the mines.

By dinnertime, tempers were short due to the excessive temperatures of the stifling hot sun that heated up the higher tunnels, and the dryness of the desert air which lacked any humidity at all, making them all feel like they were literally breathing hot, dry, dusty sand particles into their lungs, causing some to deal with some rather annoying coughing spurts. The miles and miles of walking, and some unpleasant, yet uneventful encounters with some of the desert wildlife had set some of them on edge even more. Never knowing what to expect or find with the lift of every lid or turn of every corner.

Some were also a little leery of stepping over any wood framing or doors in the floor of the shafts, for fear of plummeting to their death as Kristen almost had the day before. Even though she hadn't walked over anything but had rather leaned into it.

The cavern was quiet this evening, tension floating heavily in the air. There was hardly any conversation happening as everyone seemed determined to just clean up and rest instead of visiting, trying to recuperate from the abnormally higher temperatures of today's desert heat.

Bridget, ever the chatterbox, could be heard talking lowly to Sofia and Oz as they prepared the evening meal. Uriah watched the young girl. She always seemed to be excited or happy about everything she experienced. He supposed that was normal seeing as how she had never been allowed to do much of anything, and after her father's death years before, she had been alone for a long time. Apparently, Hiram had kept her away from everyone back in England because, she had said, he feared others would think them to be witches. So, her upbringing had been lonely and boring, which apparently made her love this lifestyle, no matter what sort of discomforts they were experiencing at the moment. Uriah turned to glance around the cave, his eyes landing on Tim. Uriah followed the direction his attention seemed to be drawn, shaking his head.

Timothy watched Kristen closely. She sat in her tent reading a novel and Tim waited for the opportunity to invade her space once again. Searching the mining tunnels hadn't been enough time spent in her company, and he wanted to cement a relationship with her quickly. The sounds of Gabby's Ukulele trickled through the semi-quiet cavern.

Gabby sat strumming her ukulele and humming lowly to herself, while Wade and Dominic sat in their shared tent. Dominic continuing his sketches, while Wade whittled small wooden animals out of sticks. Seth and Caroline were also in their tent with the flaps closed for privacy, as those who wished they had a significant other in their lives, felt pangs of jealousy once again over their ability to have a real relationship during this time in their lives. Sean sighed heavily as he glanced from their tent to Kristen's tent. Alec sat with Odessa, quietly enjoying their friendship, but still wanting more, lately it seemed on a daily basis. Nadia, Dinah , Jason, and Nick set about feeding and watering the horses, each of them only speaking whenever necessary for the chore at hand.

Zaccai sat by the fire, stoking the embers as the chill of the night began to settle into the cavern, her over-tired, over-heated, body succumbing to the chill quickly. Zeke noticed her shiver ever so slightly and watched as she slid a bit closer to the fire. He grabbed his light-weight jacket and walked over to where she sat, placing it across her shoulders. She startled only slightly, soon realizing what was happening and who the gentleman was. Zeke sat down beside her on the large log as she smiled at him, pulling the offered jacket tighter around her shoulders.

When dinner was served and everyone had been fed and the dishes cleaned, the mood in the cavern was a little more congenial with the aid of nourishment lending to the refreshing of their spirits and bodies.

Zeke and Zaccai continued in their earlier fashion of sitting by the fire to chat, now laughing and joking with each other. Although she was now considerably warmer, she relished in the fact that he had given her his jacket and continued to wear the item of clothing until it was time to turn in for the night.

Jason stepped outside to catch a breath of fresh air when he again felt someone watching him. Figuring it to be the woman, Memnah, whom he had encountered yesterday morning, he glanced in the direction that his senses were telling him she was, then saluted and bowed. He then waited to see if she would respond to his knowing she was there. She did indeed respond by standing and placing her hands on her hips in a defiant gesture. The motion made him smile ever so slightly to himself. She then turned on her heels, mounted her horse, and with one more look back, sped off across the darkening desert sands. Jason grinned even larger as he watched her for as long as he could make out her form. He then went back inside the cavern to talk to some of the others, joining Zaccai, Oz, Zeke, Sofia, Nick, and Seth around the campfire for their nightly leader's meeting to discuss the next day's searching plans, and the continued search for the betrayer.

Memnah rode away in frustration over the man named Jason. How he knew she was there was beyond her. And, he knew exactly where to look to find her. It was an eerie feeling but not enough to stop her curiosity. There was something different about him and she was going to find out what, if it was the last thing she ever did. She rode home, making her plans for tomorrow and how to watch these people without Jason knowing she was there.

Back at the cavern, Timothy had walked over to Kristen who was now sitting around the fire to warm herself. Sean had also noticed Timothy's approach and decided to go and have a seat with them, hopefully to ward off any unwanted conversation between the two of them. He still wasn't sure what their relationship was, but he did know that Timothy had the upper hand on him by spending all day, every day, in Kristen's company.

Dinah , Caroline, Nadia, Alec, and Odessa, all hung out playing some card games while Uriah, oddly enough, was in a congenial mood and entertained Bridget, Gabriele, Wade, and Dominic with stories from his youth.

The visiting and games went on for hours, with little mishap, except for the tension building up between Timothy and Sean as they each tried to outdo each other in an attempt to gain some sort of favor with Kristen.

She sat there listening to them banter back and forth with growing agitation, in an all-out competition over who was the better at anything and everything. After about fifteen minutes of the tiring exchange and ridiculous male testosterone battle, she rolled her eyes, stood up, unnoticed by either of them, and backed away from the barrage of, 'I did this', or 'I did that', and went to join in the card game with the others.

After a few minutes, Sean realized that Kristen had somehow disappeared. He and Timothy stopped their arguing and began looking around the cavern for her, finding her playing cards with the others. They both looked at each other, snarled, and grew quiet, both of them left with nothing to say to each other since their reason for comparisons had left. They sat there quietly for the next thirty minutes or so throwing sticks into the fire and poking at it, glancing sideways at each other every so often in an unfriendly like manner, while they watched Kristen enjoying the others company.

When the hour grew late, the two night-guards took up their first watch while the others bedded down, hoping to get a good night's rest.

The night air had grown exceptionally cold, a big difference from the heat of the day. Gabby stoked the fire as Sean added more wood to keep it burning through-out the night.

Sean liked Gabby and enjoyed spending time with her. She was a very interesting person and he was glad they had rounds together. He would prefer Kristin so that he could talk to her more, but at least he didn't have to serve guard duty with Timothy. Of course, he still hadn't been able to talk to Nick about his feelings for Kristin yet. He would be glad when they could get back to some kind of normal, where they were just in their own little groups. Then, maybe he could find time to talk with Nick and possibly get things sorted out.

Sean and Gabby stepped outside to walk the trails around the cavern. She went left while he started to go right but stopped for a minute, watching the massive number of stars twinkling in the big, desert sky when Kristin stepped out of the cavern.

"Hey," she said to Sean, who seemed a bit surprised by her presence.

"Hey," he answered, "what are you doing up?"

"I need to use the ladies' room." She smiled. "Too much water today. It was so hot; I think I drank nearly double what I did yesterday. Being on guard duty all day and standing in the sun just zapped me. I was afraid to get dehydrated."

"You want me to stand guard for you while you go?"

"No thanks. I'll be fine." She walked out into the dark night, the beam of her flashlight the only light to guide her.

Sean waited for a bit, hoping to get to talk to her some more. He soon decided that he had best get on with his rounds when he heard a slight rustle and Kristin give a little yell.

"Ouch!" Came her muffle yelp from somewhere in the desert.

"Kristen! Where are you?" Concern for her made him nervous.

"Over here!" She sighed, mumbling something in frustration.

He found her sitting on the ground, rubbing the same ankle she had injured on the Jog Falls dive a few months back.

Sean knelt down beside her. "Are you all right?"

"Yes, I think so. I tripped over something. I think it must be a rock hidden beneath the sand's surface." She was frustrated by her lack of ability to stay on her feet. "You'd think I was a total klutz lately with all the accidents I've had in the last few months. I'm normally not this accident prone."

"Your middle name wouldn't happen to be grace would it?" Sean half-smiled as he teased her.

"No." She smiled at his remark. "Actually, it's Shaina, after my grandmother."

Sean grinned, offering her his hand as he stood. Kristin took the offer and allowed him to pull her to a standing position.

"You've been awfully chivalrous as of late, Mr. Doran. Whatever has gotten into you?" She teased back. When she went to take a step her ankle gave out and she fell into Sean's arms. They stood there for just a minute, looking at each other. Sean cleared his throat, set her upright, and held out his arm for her to take as a gesture of support to help her back to the cavern.

"My lady, Wright, may I escort you in your journey back to the castle?" Sean stoically as possible, bowed ever so slightly, playing the chivalrous knight in shining armor.

"Certainly, my Lord," Kristin smiled, fanning herself with an imaginary fan, playing along. "And don't let that Lord thing go to your head," she quickly warned, knowing Sean all too well.

He slapped his hand over his chest with his free hand, feigning pain. "Ah, you wound me my lady."

Kristin giggled at his antics as he helped her hobble back toward the cavern. She missed this Sean. He was someone she had begun to get to know over the last few months. Somehow, when Tim was around, Sean changed into something else. She wasn't sure why, but she knew he didn't particularly care for Timothy, and for some reason, obviously felt like he needed to compete with him.

When they reached the entrance, she stopped to take a seat on a boulder outside the door. Not quite ready to go inside just yet.

Sean helped her sit down then looked at her. "Do you want me to wake Jason so he can heal your ankle?"

"No. It's late and everyone just got to sleep. Besides, I'm sure it will be fine in the morning. If not, maybe I'll have him look at it then. I've had so many incidents lately that I don't want everyone to think I'm frail or anything."

He settled in beside her on the boulder. "I'm sure they don't, and wouldn't, Kristin. I'd say everyone thinks you're rather tough. You did almost die yesterday. That would have scared most people off completely you know." He hoped to set her mind at ease.

She grinned at him. "Thank you, Sean. You know, you can be quite charming when you want to be."

Her words and expression were so serious and held such affection that he wasn't sure how to reply.

Sean just shrugged his shoulders and half smiled at her as he watched the moonlight play across her features, giving her an ethereal glow. He wanted so badly to reach over and kiss her but decided against it and fought back the urge. He really liked her and didn't want to mess things up by jumping into a relationship under their current circumstances. Especially with Timothy constantly hovering somewhere nearby, ready to pounce at any moment. He wanted her to decide who she liked without confusing her any more than she might already be.

Kristin shivered against the cool night air, not planning on being outside this long. Sean stood up and offered her his hand once again.

"We need to get you inside before you freeze or catch a cold to add to your many afflictions lately." His teasing voice returning once again.

Kristin giggled at his words, taking his hand. Leaning on his arm, she allowed him to help her to her tent. He helped her inside and down onto her cot. When he went to stand up and leave, Kristin placed her hand on his arm to stop him. She reached over and planted a kiss on his cheek, taking him utterly by surprise.

"Thank you, Sean. You are truly a gentleman."

"You are very welcome, Kristin." He tucked a stray strand of her hair behind an ear. He cleared his throat nervously and stood up to leave, playfully bowing again in role play.

"Goodnight, Lady Wright."

She smiled brightly.

"Sleep well." His voice held a more serious note of care this time.

"Goodnight, Sean." She called after him as he left her tent and headed back outside for night guard duty. *Since when did the once annoyingly cocky, careless, boy, Sean Doran become this charming, helpful, caring man?* she wondered. She thought she had a handle on her affections for these two men, but now, she wasn't so sure. Timothy was a little pushy with his intentions, not really coming out and saying how he felt, which was very obvious at times. But she always tried to avoid being alone with him for some reason, not feeling quite comfortable with the idea. With Sean it was different. She was used to being alone with him on peregrinations, but she also trusted him in a way she didn't trust anyone else. Still, she wasn't sure he was even interested in her at all. She knew he cared about her by the way he was always behaving. But was it just a blossoming friendship and nothing more? He hadn't given her any indication that he was romantically interested, but the way he acted when Timothy was around certainly made her believe he had feelings for her of a romantic nature.

"Lord, guide me according to your will." After her brief but earnest prayer, she fitfully fell asleep with Sean Doran on her mind and stealing his way into her dreams.

A hot-tempered person stirs up conflict,
but the one who is patient calms a quarrel.

Proverb 15:18

Chapter 6

The next morning the leaders divided all the groups into twos to make the searching go faster. Original peregrination partners were paired once more, making Sean, and Dinah , extremely happy. Sean would be back with Kristin, and Dinah with Nick.

Timothy looked rather miffed about the whole idea and asked, "Why are we switching back to just two people and our original partners?"

Zaccai answered him. "Groups of two will give us much faster searching abilities, and since we are only in pairs of two we decided that peregrination partners have already formed trust bonds and know each other best, allowing you all to anticipate each other's movements if any sort of trouble was to begin."

"Well, I don't know about that." Timothy said cockily beneath his breath, but loud enough for Sean and Kristin, who were standing near him, to hear.

Sean knew Timothy was referencing that day back on the island, when he and Kristen had fought about being partners for a whole year, and Sean not knowing anything about her.

Sean shot him a sideways look, wishing he could knock the smirk off of Timothy's face. *Why does that guy rile me so much?* he wondered.

"All right, everyone," Zaccai continued, "you have your searching assignments. Everyone is to meet topside by noon for lunch and hydration. With these temperatures, we certainly don't need anyone to overheat. I know the mines are cooler further down, but make sure and drink plenty of water, and watch for snakes and scorpions."

Everyone shook their head in agreement and went off in their separate directions. Seth and Jason were paired again, while Caroline, who had never had a peregrination partner other than Bridget had paired up with Oz, who also did not have a partner due to his thirteen-year confinement. They were happy to also be able to catch up, since they hadn't really had time to talk since Caroline and Bridget had left Zanchier. No one was aware of the figure who dropped down into the tunnels, just a few hundred feet or so away to covertly follow one Jason Marshal.

Zeke took this opportunity while they searched and walked, to talk with Tim about some concerning behavior he had noticed over the last several days. He and Timothy had been partners for about a year, which was when Timothy had been called to Peregrine status.

"Tim, now that we have a chance to chat, I wanted to talk to you about the amount of attention you're giving young Miss Kristin."

"So. What about it?"

"From the way you've been acting, I'm assuming you like her?"

"What if I do. What's wrong with that?"

"Nothing. As long as your intentions are honorable. But I don't think your timing or methods are optimal."

"My intentions are honorable, if it's any of your business, which it isn't. And as far as timing, we don't necessarily have 'perfect timing' for such things with this lifestyle. And, what's wrong with my methods?"

"Your overbearing and pushy, that's what. She looks like she wants to run the other direction any time you go near her."

"No she doesn't!" Timothy defended. "Look, I know how to handle women. I've never had a problem before getting a woman to go out with me."

"Is that right?" Zeke was a little perturbed by Timothy's cocky attitude. "Well, I don't know what kind of women you're used to dating, but I'm pretty sure this one is different. In a *whole* lot of ways." He shook his head in disbelief of Tim's arrogance.

"She's a woman. The same methods will work with her that worked with all the others." Timothy confidently brushed off Zeke's comment with a wave of a hand.

"Just don't say that I didn't warn you when she walks away, because I'm pretty sure that she will." Zeke smirked at the cocky, full-of-himself, Timothy Johnson.

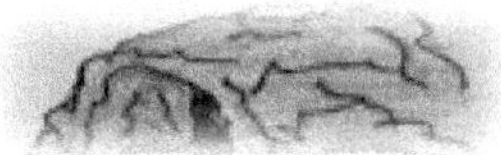

Jason and Seth walked the dark tunnels and mining caverns shining their lights through anything that looked like it might hold one, or twelve belts. As they did, they caught up on what had been happening since Seth had been stung by the water creature just a week or so back. Since Caroline and Seth had been reunited, he and Jason hadn't really talked much.

Seth inquired of Jason a little more on the details of his encounter with the woman who had gotten the better of him their first day here.

"So, Jason, have you seen that woman, Memnah, again since that first day?"

Memnah, listened from an adjoining tunnel as the two men talked. Her ears perking up at the mention of her name.

"Actually, I have." He didn't look at Seth but continued the search. "Just last night she was up on the ridge spying on us again."

"How do you know she was there? Did you see her?"

"No. I just have a keen ability to know when I'm being watched and where they are hiding. It's like our demon sensor, but mine works with humans as well apparently. I've never had it be this strong since the military. I actually didn't see her until I let her know that I knew she was there by waving and bowing in her direction. She stood up and stomped off like a spoiled little princess."

Memnah seethed at the unflattering picture he had painted of her. She had not stomped off! There was just no reason the stay since he had found her out. What was she to do, just stand there on the ridge, staring down at him? Wait, did he say something about demons?

"Bowed and waved, huh." Seth grinned. "That probably would have angered me as well if I thought I was being stealthy enough."

The men looked at each other and grinned.

"Looks like there is another tunnel down on the right." Jason turned to move in that direction. "Let's head in there and see what we can find. These here are pretty barren."

Oh no! Memnah thought, *that was no tunnel, it was the small, dark cavern in which she was hiding, and there was nowhere to go! Think Memnah, think!* She glanced around the room, trying to find somewhere to hide. On the far back wall was a large, woven, rattan basket that was large enough for her to crawl in. She scurried to it, pulled the lid off, and without even thinking, jumped inside in her haste to hide, without even looking inside it first. Just as she was about to pull the lid back over her head, something stung her on the neck..

"Ouch!" She jumped out of the basket, swiping at her clothing and hair, at the same time that Seth and Jason rounded the corner of the cavern entrance.

Jason ran over to her to help her swat at whatever it was that she thought was attacking her.

"Stop squirming will you. I don't see anything on you."

"Something stung me on the back of my neck. It may have been a scorpion."

"Let me look, all right?" Jason held his hands up in question.

She shook her head in agreement, fear of the deadlier ones' poison coursing through her veins making her more compliant than usual. How could she have been so stupid to do such a thing? She knew better than to jump into something like that. She was after-all born and raised here and knew the dangers of the desert better than most.

Jason pulled her hair back, and using his flashlight, found a small puncture wound on her neck. He took his thumb and rubbed the area to heal the wound quickly before the poison could work its way into her blood stream, as he pretended to check her over thoroughly.

"I don't see anything," he told her, unable and unwilling to try to explain his abilities.

"You must be mistaken. I felt it sting me right here." She reached back to see if she could feel a bite mark or puncture wound but found nothing. The stinging sensation was gone as well. Surely she hadn't imagined the sting?

"Maybe it was just a pinched nerve or something. Tension can cause those sorts of things you know?" A slight smile invaded his full lips.

Memnah scowled at him. "What do you mean by that? I am not tense, as you say."

"What are you doing down here anyway?"

"I believe that I could ask you the same question." She defended.

"I told you before, we are searching for an important artifact. Surely you aren't doing the same thing?" Jason looked at her in amusement. "You wouldn't be spying on me again would you, Memnah?"

"Do not flatter yourself, I only wish to keep the mines and its contents safe from pillagers such as yourselves. You are not the first to come here, and likely won't be the last. I am merely doing my job."

"Fine. Then why don't you walk with us instead of lurking around corners or trying to hide in scorpion filled baskets. You can be our guest each day we search if you wish. Perhaps you can even help us leave here sooner?"

Memnah steamed, trying to hide her embarrassment at him knowing she was trying to hide in the basket.

"I was not trying to hide inside, I only … tripped over it." She offered the explanation, hoping he would believe her. *What did she care if he didn't?* she thought. This man was nothing to her and would gratefully soon be gone once he found what he was looking for. His offer would allow her to keep a much closer eye on him, in a much safer way.

"All right, I accept your offer. But I will be watching you. And, I am quite capable of handling myself, so no funny business."

"Oh, don't worry about that, ma'am. I'm quite aware of your ability to handle yourself." Jason's tone was brusque, a bit put out himself at the memory of their last face-to-face meeting.

"What exactly are you all looking for anyway?"

"Some ancient belts rumored to be here in the mines." Jason gave a short answer, not wanting to reveal too much.

"What sort of candle is that you hold that shines like the sun?" She curiously leaned forward, just noticing their lights.

"Flashlights." How was he going to explain this? They hadn't even been invented yet. "Just a new invention where we come from."

"That is very interesting and useful. Where does the flame go, and how does it not catch on fire?" She tried to examine the light as Jason evaded her attempts.

"Can we do this later, outside the mines, after we are done searching?" Jason was ready to change the subject, hoping she would forget about it.

"Yes, I suppose so. Lead on." She gestured to him to take the lead and walked between he and Seth.

Seth watched the heated exchange with humored interest. If he didn't know any better, he'd think these two were attracted to each other. He decided that he had better keep a close eye on each of them. Neither one could afford to lose their heart to the other.

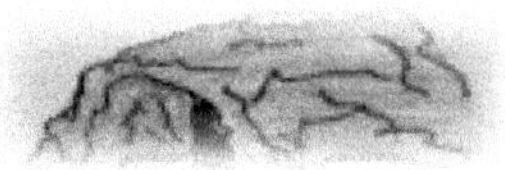

Kristin's ankle appeared to be working fine from her incident the night before. Sean watched her occasionally to make sure she wasn't limping from all the walking. He had really missed being around her. Of course, he hadn't been alone with her since he discovered he had serious feelings for her. This little revelation had hit him back in Samoa on the Jog Falls dive, and they had been with Nick and Dinah on that mission. After that they were on the island, and then here in Timna Valley.

This was the first time since discovering his feelings for her that they had been utterly and completely alone. Sean prayed silently in his own head that God would keep him from doing anything rash or stupid.

Kristin and Sean enjoyed companionable silence on and off between joking and picking with each other. She realized how much she had missed this. Even when her and Sean were at odds and at each other's throats she had always felt at ease around him, even if it was in irritation. Now that they got along and actually enjoyed each other's company, she could really get used to a relationship with him. Did that thought just enter her head? It didn't really matter anyway because he didn't appear to feel that way for her. He had never even tried to kiss her. Kristin sighed and continued in their work, stealing glances at him every so often, studying the lines of his face and the way it looked in the light of the flashlights beam.

They spent the morning searching the mines with no luck at finding anything that even remotely resembled a belt. Kristen didn't know how much longer she could stay emotionally detached from Sean. She may not be able to find the belts, but she had definitely found where her heart lies, and that was with Sean Doran. What was she going to do if he didn't feel the same way about her?

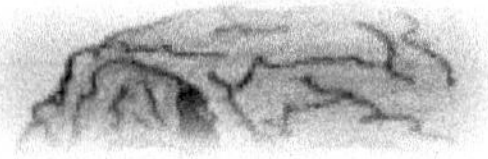

"It sure is nice to be back with my partner again," Dinah exclaimed, a big smile across her face.

"Yeah, I missed working with you too. It's hard switching when you're comfortable where you are." Nick not really thinking about what he was saying, didn't realize how it sounded to her.

Dinah smiled at his words. He was comfortable around her. She would take that, for now. She needed to make sure he wasn't *too* comfortable though. She really liked Nick and had been trying for months to think of a way to let him know without harming their partnership. Even though Nick was at least nine years her senior, he was a strong, rugged, good-looking man. His war-torn body only made him more appealing to her. She just needed to figure out how to get his attention. The *right* kind of attention.

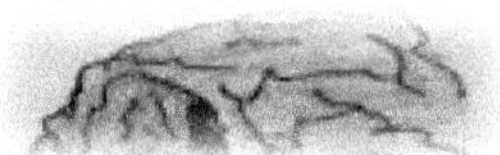

Uriah and Dominic walked through the dark cavern, emptying bowls, baskets, and crates, searching through everything that they could. Uriah started up a conversation with Dominic concerning Bridget Burke. He had been waiting for the proper time to talk to her about her father. He had been a personal friend of Uriah's after-all.

"So, Dominic, what can you tell me about your new friend Bridget?"

"I don't know, what do you want to know?"

"Just curious about her is all."

"Why?" Dominic was confused but he really didn't care why; like most fifteen-year-olds.

"Can't a man make civil conversation without getting the third degree?" Uriah barked.

"Yeah, I suppose so." Dominic weakly defended. "Just wondering what's with all the interest in Bridget all of a sudden."

"It isn't all of a sudden. I just knew her father is all. We were good friends. I just figure she might want to know a little about his life here."

"Maybe. She doesn't really say much about his life before."

"Because she doesn't know about it. Just, let her know that if she has questions, she can ask me."

"Why don't you tell her yourself?"

"She knows you better. It might sound better coming from you, okay?" Uriah turned to the boy with a questioning stare.

"Sure. I'll tell her." Dominic shrugged his shoulders in indifference.

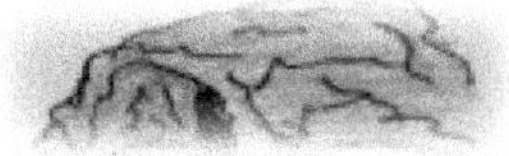

The teams spent the next several days searching the mines by day and waiting out the nights in the cavern. Tim glared at the now inseparable Kristin and Sean. Every time he thought he might get a moment alone with her someone else interfered with his plans, and that someone was usually Sean. Kristin seemed very happy about this too. Timothy felt that they just didn't seem to have the same rapport that he had with her before they reunited with their old partners.

Memnah questioned Jason and Seth daily about everything she didn't recognize or understand. They tried to explain as best as they could without telling her they were actually from another time period. Jason was worried she would probably think that they were both crazy and never return. Of course, maybe that wouldn't be such a bad thing after all. If she weren't around, they wouldn't have to be so careful about what they said. When she appeared daily for the mine expeditions, it was after they split up into their groups, and then she left before they finished each day. He assumed that no one else really ever saw her come or go because no one ever mentioned her or asked him questions about who she was. So, he and Seth decided to keep her existence a secret for now.

On the fifth day of searching, a large haboob had kicked up in the desert and they all had to retreat to some sort of cover until the storm was over. Seth had gone up earlier to grab his canteen he had accidentally left back at the cavern this morning when the haboob has struck. He was stuck back at the cavern and Jason was left in the mines with Memnah. Even though the desert sands blew strongly above them, some of the dust found its way beneath the surface, filling the tunnels with a light, hazy film that floated in the air. It resembled fog in that it made the use of searching impossible because the beams of light were unable to penetrate through the thick cloud. Jason began coughing a little, so Memnah, who had pulled her scarf up and over her nose and mouth, led him inside another cavern. She then took a scarf from around her waist and placed it around his head to cover his nose and mouth to give him some relief from breathing in the dust particles.

Jason watched her work staring into her eyes as she wrapped the scarf around his head. She did this without so much as a word to him. When she had finished, she sat down against the wall of the cavern, waiting for the dust storm to blow over. Jason joined her, sitting beside her. They would glance at each other occasionally while they waited in silence. Once the storm seemed to pass and the dust inside the cavern had settled, they stood back up and removed their scarves, Jason handing her back the one she had wrapped around his head.

"Thank you for the use of this. It helped a lot with the dust."

"You're welcome. Besides, we couldn't have you suffocating down here now could we." She wrapped the scarf back around her waist, glancing back up at his face while she tied it on.

"Jason, you said you were searching for belts. What kind of belts exactly?"

"Well, if you must know, the Belts of Truth, mentioned as a piece of the Armor of God in the Bible."

"But the Armor of God is representative only. It isn't really armor as you suggest. Not something that you can touch or wear."

"Perhaps not for you, but for me and those with me, it is very real."

Before their conversation could be finished, Seth had returned, and the hunting commenced. Memnah had excused herself for the remainder of the day and left.

The next morning, she hadn't shown back up either. Jason wondered why but left it at that.

The teams continued their search through more of the tunnels, all of them meeting back up once again in a central cavern. Jason and the others searched for another hour in the large underground mining cavern, which was proving to be quite a chore. Jason walked to the center of the cavern and called to the groups.

"All right everyone, let's take a break and head back up for some sunshine, water, and a bit of rest and regrouping. We need to give Sofia and Bridget the information we have on today's finds."

As they all emerged from the tunnels, Jason and Seth were the last two to exit. When Seth climbed out of the tunnel, he noticed the rest of the group just standing there. As Jason climbed up and out of the shaft, he looked around to see what the problem was that had everyone staring off in one direction across the desert sands. Surrounding their small makeshift tent with rifles, bows, and swords in hand, sat a tribe of desert nomads. Jason finished his ascent from the hole in the ground, standing tall and straight next to his friends. As he glanced around at the tribe of about twenty men on horseback, he recognized one lone figure.

He stared at her for just a moment before walking toward them and bravely speaking.

"Ma'am." He bowed his head yet continued to watch her at the same time.

Her horse pranced in place, picking up on her nervous body language as she tugged slightly at the reigns.

Memnah dismounted her horse, followed by several others. She walked toward Jason, past the others without fear or a care in the world. She stopped in front of him and dropped the cover over her face.

"Why didn't you come this morning?" he questioned lowly so the others could not hear him speak.

"What are you doing here? Truthfully?" she demanded.

Jason answered just as he had before.

"I told you what we are searching for. Nothing more." He watched her and the other twenty or so riders carefully.

"When you find your artifact, what then?"

"Then we will be on our way, hopefully never to return."

"I know of these items. They are sacred to my people. Part of what we were sworn to guard. What do you want with them?"

"Myself, and this rather large group of people here with me, are known as Peregrines. We were chosen by God to travel the earth in search of certain artifacts to help save mankind from destruction. The Belt of Truth is one of the pieces of the Armor of God that we have to acquire in order to fight in a battle to accomplish this." He answered her as honestly as he could. Knowing that if he tried to feed her anything but the truth, she would know.

"How do I know that what you say is true?" She searched his face.

"You'll just have to trust me." Jason looked deeply into her eyes.

"Fine. But my people will be watching you. And there will always be sentries standing guard to make sure that you take nothing but what you say you have come for."

"Memnah, I have found nothing of value in these mines as of yet, as you well know. But I assure you, that if we do, we do not need nor want any but what we have come for." Jason's gaze upon her face was unflinching.

"I wish to hold council with your leaders inside the large cavern where you camp. Four of my most trusted guards will accompany me." She turned to walk away, then stopped and turned to Jason once more, leaning in closer to him.

"And I want my knife back." She then turned away once more and headed toward their camp.

Jason grinned ever so slightly before turning to the others.

"Well, you all heard what she said. All the leaders follow me. The rest of you stay here. Alec, you and Odessa are in charge while we are gone."

Jason and the other leaders followed Memnah and her group of men to the cavern, unsure what else there was to discuss. As they entered the cavern behind Memnah's men, she stopped in front of Jason, holding her hand out in front of him.

Jason looked at her realizing what it was she wanted. He walked inside his tent, retrieved the sword, and returned to the center of the cavern, handing the knife over to her.

Memnah took the blade, returning it to its sheath at her back, then turned to sit upon one of the seats in the center of the cavern. Jason followed her lead, taking a seat across from her. Seth, Oz, Zeke, Sofia, Nick, and Zaccai joined them around the fire pit that now sat cold in the few hours before noon. Her guards stayed standing in the background behind Memnah, ever watchful, unmoving like stone statues.

Jason looked at Memnah and asked the next question.

"All right. All our current leaders are present. What did you wish to speak about?"

"If what you say is true, and all that you are searching for is the Belt of Truth, we may be able to help you with this." Memnah was still unsure that she wanted to reveal the location of Solomon's secret chambers. "I have mentioned on several occasions that my people were appointed by King Solomon himself to guard the mines. Well, as you have seen for yourselves, there isn't much there to guard other than the copper ore that laces the still viable mining shafts. I and my guards will take you and four others only, to a sacred place where very few have ever trod. It has only ever been seen by the most trusted amongst my people."

"Memnah, you cannot!" one of her guards stated strongly in their native tongue.

"I will do as the Lord commands me." She turned and reprimanded the guard. The man quickly held his tongue, his rigid form revealing the true state of his emotions as he glared at her. Jason and the others watched the exchange, curious as to what was spoken between the two of them.

"For some reason, I trust what you say is true. I have prayed to God, and He revealed you to me in a dream. Even before our first meeting." She looked confidently at Jason.

"Then why the friendly greeting the first time? And why haven't you mentioned this before now?" Jason replied irritably.

"I said God revealed you to me, I did not say that He portrayed you as a friend. That dream was why I was at the mines scouting that day and why I continued to return. God led me here. Your purpose was not clear, only that I would meet a man. You, precisely."

"Who can fathom the mysteries of God?" Jason quoted from Job 11:7.

"Truly. He is a God of many wonders and mysteries. That is why you can only bring your four most trusted leaders with you. You alone I have seen standing in the temple in my visions, so you must choose those among you who are worthy." She gestured to the others gathered around them.

"That will be difficult. All of these people were chosen by God to this lifestyle. I would trust them all with my life."

"Yes. But Judas Iscariot was called as well, was he not. And yet he betrayed the Lord for a few pieces of silver." She watched him carefully.

"True, but he was not the only betrayer amongst the Apostles. Was not Peter just as guilty in his own way?"

"Yes, proving that most cannot always be trusted. With that being said, know this, even though we are called to forgive, I will not hesitate to kill you and your friends if need be. Then I shall ask for my forgiveness. Guarding the treasures of the personal temple and chamber of Solomon was the task given to our people thousands of years ago. We have managed to keep that vow to this day, and we shall continue to do so at all costs." She made direct eye contact with Jason so that he did not mistake her words.

"Understood." Jason met her gaze directly, making Memnah squirm in her seat just a little. "My friends and I will discuss the terms." He stood and gestured to the others to join him in a private conversation to determine who will go.

"Listen everyone. I'm not so sure I trust these people, but she seems sincere. Maybe all this searching through the miles of shafts is leading us nowhere because the belts are not in the actual mines. If there *is* some sort of secret chamber of King Solomon, and the belts are there, then we apparently need these people to find it."

Zeke looked a bit nervous. "This could be a trap. She could be leading us all to our deaths."

Zaccai chimed in, "I do not believe that is the goal of this tribe. These people seem to be honorable to me. She reminds me of my own people from long ago. We always meant what we said. And her terms were discussed up front. If they had wished to kill us, I am certain they would have already done so. They had the element of surprise already this morning, yet we are all still alive."

"Well." Oz looked around the group. "How do we fig're on who goes an' who don't?"

"We can draw straws. Short ones stay behind," Sofia said.

"We don't have time for all of that. I'm just going to choose. The rest will stay here and watch camp. Especially with the other sixteen or so riders still out with the rest of our people." Jason had never had problems making decisions, feelings didn't come into such things.

"Seth, you, and Sofia will stay here. We may need your strength, Seth, if any conflict should arise amongst the others. The rest of you will come with me since you are the chosen leaders of the Dragoman from each group. Oz, you're a big man, and since I'm leaving Seth behind to head the group here, we just might need a man your size with us."

"Sure 'nough."

Jason turned back to Memnah and her men. "We have made our selections. Lead on, Memnah."

She nodded her head to him as she and her people filed out of the cavern. She stopped and turned back to Jason and spoke.

"You will need to saddle horses for the journey. It is across the valley to the Pillars of Solomon. It will be a several hour's ride."

This was one instance where Jason wished that others could see and travel by Portgen. It would make the sixteen-mile journey by horseback much quicker.

"All right everyone, you heard the lady. Saddle up." He turned to the makeshift corral to saddle his horse.

Memnah left the cavern with a small smile tugging at the corner of her lips. She wasn't sure what it was about Jason that intrigued her so, but he captured her attention and mind like no other man ever had before. The last several days spent in his company had shown her that she would need to be careful around this man. He was too much of a distraction in so many ways, and that made her very nervous.

Whoever is patient has great understanding,
but one who is quick-tempered displays folly.

Proverbs 14:29

Chapter 7

Reader's Island, Bermuda Triangle, 2018

Simon Lane looked through the ancient book they labeled the *Book of the Keepers* trying all that he could to unscramble whatever script had been used to write the book. Surely, somewhere, the Dragoman could find something that would enable them to break the code used in the ancient archival text.

The first of the ancient books opened was the *Book of Armor*, which explained the search and use for the Armor of God and gave them an ancient prophecy concerning the final battle, the Peregrines, and the Beast Keepers. It had afforded much needed knowledge and answers to many questions that had plagued them all as of late. It had first given them the knowledge as to what to do with a group of untrainable young people. These young people were found to be what the book revealed as Beast Keepers. Never in Peregrine or Dragoman history had such a group of people existed, and suddenly, they had three of them. They exhibited traits that no one else had. First, each one of them were very young in age. Second, they could all communicate and somewhat control animals of all kinds. Even creatures of the sea. One young woman, Bridget Burke, had the experience of dealing with creatures from another dimension in time, residing on a different plane altogether. A place known as Zanchier that did not show up on the Chip or Portgen's tracking systems. The chip trackers also do not work from this location, which Simon had discovered as of late. Zanchier was a world that thrived within the portals that were opened only by powerful storms, and it existed between two planes. They had no coordinates for this strange world and therefore could not set the Portgens to travel there. It was a world shrouded in mystery and one to which the Dragoman soon hoped to make a trip, curious about the undiscovered world and wanting to unravel some of its many secrets.

The third mystery surrounding the Beast Keepers was that Peregrination Sickness did not seem to affect them during their first peregrination, except for Dominic who had been sick the first time. All Peregrines and Dragoman alike, when first called by God to peregrinate, went through a period of extreme illness and unconsciousness upon their very first time-travel experience.

There were only two other people whom Simon could think of that Peregrination Sickness had not ever affected as well, Ryan Halloran and Safra Pilar Driscoll. Simon had a dream about Ryan and was instructed to fetch him, which he did with no issues. Safra, however, had none of the above-mentioned titles. She was what was known as a Seer and a Healer. She could not peregrinate without the aid of one of the Peregrines, Dragoman, or Keepers. She was the only human being, outside of their world and titles, that could travel the portals and not die. God had given Safra a great gift and she used it to bless them all and to further the work that God had called them all to. Her father had also been a friend to the Dragoman many years before, but Simon couldn't remember Sage Driscoll, Safra's father, ever walking between worlds as she did.

The fourth mystery surrounding them was what their purpose was concerning the Final Battle. According to the prophecy in the *Book of Armor*, they held a very important job but no explanation of what that job was. The Dragoman had been working tirelessly over the last 3 weeks or so to find something to translate the *Book of the Keepers,* which likely held the answers. Ryan Halloran had already run every computer search imaginable to find a match to the ancient language used in the book but had yet to find anything useful.

Ryan had also been working on an update for the Portgens. A device which allowed for time travel without the need of massive storms, which was not only safer for the Peregrines but also kept them much dryer. The updated chip that Ryan created allowed for the tracking of each Peregrine if separated from the group. It also allowed for a Walkie-Talkie type communication between devices. He hoped that this feature worked over time and space as the tracking chips did, but they would not know for sure until they were installed and put to the test.

Simon and Malachai were set to leave Reader's Island and venture to Timna Valley, Israel, in search of the Peregrines to install the new hardware into the devices. With the new hardware installation, Ryan hoped that he would be able to make any future updates from the main computer back on the island instead of having to physically install them. As soon as Ryan had all the update chips ready to go, he and Malachai would be ready to leave, but until then they decided to give the Keepers book a rest and focus on the other two books that they were able to open. The Dragoman hadn't focused too much on these other books since the prophecy and the aggravatingly, undecipherable, *Book of the Keepers*. But they weren't getting anywhere by just staring at the thing, so they grabbed one of the other books and began skimming through the pages, just to get a feel for what it contained within its covers. Several of the other Dragoman had already looked through the books sporadically, but Simon had been so focused on the other two he had not given the other books much thought until now.

The third of the ancient books seemed to be one of lineage. It held intricate, artistic, oil-painted portraits of Peregrine and Dragoman long passed. Simon had never met or heard of the people in this book, but they were no doubt past walkers of the same life they all currently shared. What he couldn't understand was why this book was hidden? The archival historical books that they currently use were set up much like this one, just not nearly as intricately and ornately designed. The script in this book looked like the books that monks from the earliest days of transcribing would have created. The first letter of each new biography was beautifully written in a different calligraphy style and finished with gold or silver leafing, or what appeared to be an abrasive, gritty, sand type material. Along the left edge of each page was a beautifully ornate scroll-type border decoration that matched each ornate letter. He knew that the first monks who began transcribing books, made them as decorative as possible. They often used gold leaf and crushed or ground gemstones to decorate the lettering and pages. They took great pride and care in their work. It made Simon wonder just how old this book was.

He closed the book to study the ancient, beautiful, leather-bound covering, stained with some sort of moss green dye. This book's cover was also deeply embossed, like the others. The embossing on it mirrored the inside pages almost identically. At the top left corner was one large P intricately drawn, and in the top right corner of the book was one large D, also intricately done. Between the two was an embossed illumination or artwork of the sun and the moon in an eclipse, and the bottom illumination was of a tempest at sea. This particular book was what was really known as a codex. It was a form of the earliest, ancient, handwritten, sequences of pages, bound together to make it portable.

This thought made Simon question his status as a Dragoman. He had thought that peregrination was something only visited within the last six to seven hundred years or so. The extensive archives they have now on the island in the archival library only dated back that far. Simon himself had never come across any book this old, or even close, that told of Dragoman or Peregrines that dated back possibly three thousand years or more. This was an astonishing discovery for the Dragoman. Simon would have to research and study this book carefully. There had to be some reason it was so special to have been kept with the other ancient books. He would certainly like to know who had placed them there and when. The legend of the Dragoman who first had the dream of Reader's Island and then discovered it, was believed to be only five generations old. Could it be much older than that? It seemed they had even more mysteries on their hands now. The list just kept getting longer, although some had been answered as of late with the finding of the ancient books.

The fourth ancient text appeared to be an instruction manual aiding them in battle against what appeared to be great beasts. It also mentioned how and where to call upon the "dry bones". If Simon remembered correctly, there was a passage in the Bible instructing on this very thing. He wasn't sure the passage instructed on calling them for war, but the ancient text seemed to be leading up to this. It also seemed to give instruction to the keepers to use beasts from other places or realms to help the champions fight in the Final Battle.

Simon thought about the fifth and final book that was yet to be opened. Since the recently found key had been stolen by an unknown traitor within their tightly knit group of Peregrines and Dragoman, its contents remained a mystery. Simon thought about the Peregrine leaders and wondered if they had found any clues yet as to who it might possibly be. The thought of another betrayer troubled Simon deeply. He certainly didn't want to have to deal with the circumstances that took place thirteen years before. So many permanent injuries and so many more deaths, friends and loved ones, gone forever. Some had disappeared to an unknown place, never to be seen or heard from again. One other Peregrine years ago had come back from somewhere, only to die days later. Only two returned alive after being gone for thirteen years and that was Oz and Sofia.

Simon shook himself from the dark memories. They would not be so blind this time, no matter what the cost. He would consider everyone as a suspect, if need be, until the traitor was found. He would also ask Safra to beseech the Lord in her special way for help in revealing the traitor to the leaders. The sooner the traitor was found the better, and the quicker they would be able to, hopefully, recover the stolen key.

Malachai entered the room, bringing Simon's attention back to the task at hand.

"Simon, are you ready to travel?" Malachai asked him, placing his backpack on the floor.

Simon laid the book down and turned to his friend.

"Yes, I just need to go upstairs and grab my bag. I'll meet you in the computer room in five minutes. We will get the updates and tools from Ryan, and head off to Timna Valley, Israel." Simon grinned. He was ready for a little adventure. As much as he loved Reader's Island and all the comforts it afforded them, he still missed the thrill of the search. That was what had made him take up the science of archaeology in his previous life. He loved searching for things and information about the past. Solomon's Mines should prove to be a great adventure indeed.

The two men met in the computer room with Ryan Halloran, the technologically brilliant, young, autistic man God had chosen for peregrination about twelve years ago, at the age of seventeen. Ryan's peregrination journey was as unique as he was. He had stayed in his charging station in the third dimension for the first eight years of his life, never leaving except for Dragoman council meetings here on the Island. Ryan was considered a Dragoman; he just did not mentor any Peregrines. He built and designed amazing technology that they all used to do the work God had called them to. Ryan liked to stay to himself and didn't take to change well. He also wasn't much on talking either, he was only just now adjusting to having to leave his home in Ireland two months back and move to Reader's Island for safety concerns.

Simon entered the computer/mapping room.

"Good morning Ryan. How are you doing today?"

Ryan answered in as few words as possible.

"Fine."

Simon smiled to himself at the young man's ways. Ryan didn't understand the concept of rudeness and none of them took anything he said or did as such.

"Malachai and I are about ready to go and install all of that new tech that you've developed. Anything else we need to know that you haven't already showed us?" Simon came to stand beside him at his computer desk.

"No," Ryan said. "J-just do what I showed you y-yesterday and they should work. Here are the coordinates for the m-majority of the Peregrines. The ch-chipping system is showing a few of the others t-traveling across the desert."

"We'll head to the majority then." Simon took the satchel with all the tech and tools from Ryan and turned to Malachai. "We shall be off. Thank you, Ryan. See you soon." Simon tossed the remark over his shoulder as they headed out of the room.

Ryan quickly waved to the two men and dipped his head in acknowledgement before turning back to the computer screen.

Simon and Malachai headed to the barn to take two of the horses with them. Unsure if they would be needed, but since all the others had ridden off on horseback a week ago, they decided it best if they did the same. The groundskeepers already had two of them saddled and ready to go, so Simon and Malachai thanked the men, mounted the horses, and opened a portal to the location of the team of Peregrines. They rode through the portal, unsure what to expect. This new way of portal travel was different to say the least, but Simon wasn't entirely sure it was better. While the storms gave them some cover from others that may see them, portal travel made them seem to just appear out of thin air. He hoped that they would not be spotted by any unsuspecting soul on the other side. He also wondered if people could see these unnatural portals opening, unlike the storm portals that were hidden from their view. He supposed they would one day find out.

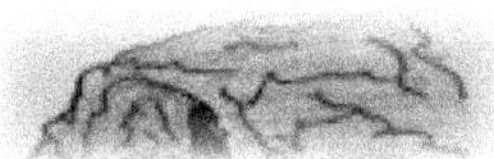

Seth watched Jason, Oz, Zaccai, Nick, and Zeke ride off across the desert with Memnah and four of her guards. The other guards, he assumed, were ordered back to their own camps. Memnah had told them something in her native tongue before she and the others headed out across the desert sands.

Seth felt a little pang of jealousy and resentment in being left behind with the others. He really wanted to go with the other leaders and get a look at the inside of Solomon's private temple. His roaming side had really kicked in on this trip and he wanted to see and do everything he could. He felt a restlessness and urgency he couldn't quite explain. Just sitting here in camp with the others was going to drive him absolutely mad.

Caroline watched her husband's body language from across the cavern. All the Peregrines had moved out of the noon-high sun, inside the coolness of the cavern. She had found Seth sitting on one of the boulders just outside the entryway, watching the others ride off across the sands. He seemed a bit irritable, so she had left him alone for a while to work out whatever was bothering him.

"Lunch time, everyone!" Bridget called out in her pleasant, cheerful voice, as Sofia and Dominic began passing out plates and utensils.

Seth sat unmoving, so Caroline grabbed a plate for herself and him, then headed out to speak with him. She seemed to have shaken him out of his thoughts when she approached. He glanced up at her, taking the plate she handed him and offered her a slight grin.

"Thanks." He returned his attention to the ever smaller-growing figures that were almost completely gone from his view.

"You're welcome." Caroline sat beside him on the rock ledge. "What's going on with you, Seth? Something seems to really be bothering you."

"Nothing, I just wanted to go with them and see Solomon's temple." He glanced at her briefly, returning his attention to the food on his plate.

"Well, this just gives us a little more time together. We haven't really gotten much alone time since we left the island. I miss you, ya' know." She smiled at him, jabbing him in the ribs with her elbow.

Seth turned to her, realizing he was being selfish. She was right of course. Just a week ago he was worried he would never see her again. Now, instead of relishing every minute he got to spend with her, he was mad over being left behind on a mission.

"You are absolutely right." He gazed into her deep sea-green eyes. "We probably have the rest of the day to kill until they return. We should make the most of it."

Sean Doran and a few others watched the exchange between Seth and Caroline. They were the lucky ones. They were the only married couple to ever get to peregrinate together. Why? No one knew the answer to that question. Not even the Dragoman. Sean glanced at Kristen, who again, was overshadowed by none other than Timothy. The man never seemed to leave her side when given the chance to be near her. Kristen was a pretty private person, and if Sean's guess was right, Timothy would, hopefully soon, get an earful about his constant presence. Sean had noticed she took her food inside her tent, said something curtly to Tim, and closed the flap, at the extreme irritation of Timothy. He just stood there staring at the closed tent flap for a few seconds before walking off to find a place to eat. Sean grinned at the exchange between the two. He hoped that her sudden and brief shunning of the man was a good sign. Of course, she did almost die less than a week ago. Perhaps she just needed some time alone. The thought made him frown just a bit. Should *he* be giving her more attention? The Kristen he knew from the last year would say no, but the Kristen he had come to know over the last several months ... he wasn't so sure. She was a confusing woman to say the least. Sean stopped at his last thought. That was the first time he had ever really thought of her as a woman. His thoughts unsettled him a bit. He knew that he had fallen in love with Kristen over the last month or so, but he didn't realize how much until lately. He really needed to have a talk with her, and soon. He glanced back out of the cavern opening at Seth and Caroline who sat next to each other on the rock ledge, arms wrapped around each other as they looked out over the desert, chatting and laughing. A pang of jealousy and longing settled into Sean's chest, wishing that he and Kristen could have what they had. He sat his unfinished plate of food down on the ground where he was sitting and got up to go for a walk.

Gabriele watched Sean. She noticed he seemed unnerved by Tim always being around Kristen. She also noticed the growing agitation Kristen seemed to have toward the constantly attentive Tim. Maybe she should go talk with Kristen on Sean's behalf? However, she would think long and hard before getting involved. Her father had always taught her to not get into people's personal business unless it was life-threatening. Gabby's attention was taken by the others as she glanced around the cavern at what everyone else was doing.

Wade and Dominic sat chatting about whatever young boys talk about, while Sofia, Nadia, and Dinah giggled about something Bridget was describing to them. Alec and Odessa had finished lunch and were walking outside to sit with Seth and Caroline, while Uriah seemed to stew over in a corner by himself. He seemed agitated a lot lately. Uriah had always been somewhat of a hothead, but lately it seemed different. Gabby could often sense when something wasn't right with someone. Something was bothering him in a big way. Maybe she should talk to him about it? They were, after-all, friends of sorts. They had traveled together for a while before Dominic had arrived. She stood up, deciding to do just that, and walked over to where Uriah was sitting.

She watched him stab at the food on his plate as though it were trying to get away from his fork. She also watched the expressions on Uriah's face change from anger to that of aggravation at her approach. He rolled his eyes as she continued in his direction, seemingly knowing that she was determined to talk to him.

"Uriah." She addressed him, taking a seat beside him.

"Gabby," he said around the food in his mouth, as he chewed and swallowed the last few bites on his plate, tossing the plate and fork to the ground haphazardly.

She settled in beside him, waiting for him to finish before she began her questions.

Uriah leaned forward, with his elbows on his knees, clasping his fingers together in front of him as he peered out at all the activity inside the large cavern. He waited on Gabby to begin whatever line of questioning with which she was going to start in on him. During the almost year of traveling with her, he came to know her as somewhat of a busy body in his opinion. She had a keen way of recognizing people's problems and then annoyingly trying to fix them.

"Uriah, I've noticed you seem really agitated lately." She cautiously searched for the right word.

"Nothing different from any other day. You know me, Gabriele, I'm just a grouchy curmudgeon." He gave an explanation, trying to avoid her questions.

"Yeah, you are, but lately you're more than just your normal grouchy self. You are fuming mad about something. Want to talk about it?" She knew full well she was right.

He looked sideways at the young girl. For one so young she was extremely wise and knowing, and he knew she was also just as persistent. She wouldn't leave him alone until he told her what was bothering him.

"Fine, you want to know what has me all riled up? It has to do with who the Dragoman put in charge of these missions. I have *much* more experience than any one of those so-called leaders, except for Zaccai of course. I just don't understand why I wasn't chosen as one of them. It's like the Dragoman don't trust me or something. And this mission with these people, wherever they are headed right now, I understand them better than anyone else due to being from around these parts. Even if there is a few thousand years between then and now. I would be the better choice on this mission." His agitation grew with each word.

"Well, Uriah, maybe it has to do with your attitude? You are always questioning everyone and everything, and yelling or fussing about something someone did, or does. You aren't very accepting of other people and you can be pretty sarcastic most of the time. Not really leadership material," she stated bluntly, knowing the man wouldn't except flowery answers. "And, as far as wherever they are going with these people, this woman Memnah seemed to single Jason out, no one else. Why, I don't know, but he didn't have much choice in the matter. They had to have met before somewhere because he knew her name. Obviously making him the better choice. It isn't about just you, Uriah. There are a lot of other things to take into consideration here."

"Way to support, Gabby," he said sarcastically.

"You want truth and answers; I'm just being as honest as possible, as I always am."

"Only problem is, I don't recall asking for your opinion or your answers. You came to me, remember?" Uriah stood up and stalked away from her across the cavern. He took his horse from the corral, grabbed his tack, and left the comfort of the cavern into the hot, noon, desert sun.

She watched him go, knowing that if he didn't get a handle on his jealousy and anger very soon, it was going to cause a major problem.

As Uriah saddled his horse, Seth questioned him. "Uriah, where are you headed? You know we aren't supposed to take off alone on missions." Seth watched him continue with the task of putting his tack on his horse, as he turned to Seth in irritation.

"I am a grown man, who has been leading these kinds of missions long before you came along. So, don't tell me what to do," Uriah spat back defensively.

"That may be so, but I was left in charge of the group while the others are gone, and for the safety of everyone, including you, you need to listen to orders. These are the rules that have been in place for years. Ever since the disappearances thirteen years ago." Seth's voice lent to the beginnings of agitation lacing his words as well.

"Exactly! A time when I was here! I experienced that very event! Did you?" Uriah angrily mounted his horse and raced off across the desert sands, the others watching him as he rode away.

Just as Uriah's retreating back sped away from the cavern, a portal opened just off to the right side of the cavern entrance and out rode Malachai and Simon. They noticed the sand and dust kicking up in the heat of the afternoon sun. Curious as to who or what was causing the disturbance and had the attention of the four Peregrines standing outside, Simon questioned them as they dismounted.

"Well, who was that?" Simon came to stand beside them as they continued to look and see which direction he was headed just in case they needed to go and find him later.

"That," Seth said in an aggravated voice, "is Uriah. He seems to be having a problem with authority lately."

Malachai stated, "Uriah has always had a problem with authority, and a temper. Just give him some time, he'll cool down." Malachai certainly knew Uriah's temper. He had been his Dragoman for the last thirteen years.

"Maybe," Seth said warily, "he seems more riled up than usual. We certainly don't need dissention in the ranks." Seth turned to the two men who had just arrived. "What are you two doing here?" He shook their hands.

Simon replied to his question. "We've come to update the Portgens. Ryan has created some knew, useful technology that has to be physically installed."

"Well, you couldn't have picked a better time. Most everyone is here right now and have nothing useful to occupy their time. This will be a pleasant distraction. And everyone else can help install them and make quick work of it."

Simon asked, "Who are the desert people standing outside the cavern over there?"

"I'll explain inside."

The six of them walked inside the cavern, handing the horses over to Wade and Dominic, as everyone stood and approached them to welcome the two men.

They explained what they were there for and everyone gathered around a table to help them with the task of installing the tech.

Simon asked Seth the next question while they worked.

"We noticed on the computer screen back on the island that five of you rode out across the desert. Why and where did they go?"

Seth glanced around the table, choosing his words carefully when referencing the situation with Jason and Memnah. He explained about the men Simon saw outside belonging to the tribe of locals who had been waiting for them to surface when they came out of the mines this morning, and how they took Jason and the other leaders to Solomon's Pillars to a private chamber of the king to search for the Belt of Truth.

"You trust that these people are telling the truth?" Simon asked.

"We really don't have much of a choice. We haven't found anything in the mines yet. We've only searched through about a hundred tunnels so far and there are literally thousands to go, but this woman, Memnah, said she knew of the armor and where it was kept and guarded. That her tribe were special guards over the mines and temple of Solomon, appointed by him thousands of years ago."

"Why did she choose Jason to speak with if you two were the last ones out of the mines this morning?"

"They kind of have a little history." Seth gave him a slight smile. As quietly as possible, so as not to betray the details of Jason's story to everyone, he began telling Simon the story behind Jason and Memnah's first meeting.

Simon laughed out loud, gathering some curious glances from the others.

"Well, it appears that Jason Marshal has met his match when it comes to women."

Seth looked a bit concerned when he spoke his next words.

"Yes. But I'm more afraid of what could happen to his heart, Simon. I think he might be falling for this woman, and you and I both know it can never happen."

"Yes, as does Jason, but we have no control over who captures our hearts. Only what we do about it. Jason has never been in love before. I only pray he uses his good sense and judgment to establish some self-control where it concerns this woman." Simon glanced at Seth, the humor of the moment now replaced with the knowing pain and regret that can accompany just such a situation.

"She has also been exploring the mines with us the last several days, so she and Jason have spent quite a bit of time together. I thought they seemed to be forming an attachment, and when I watched them this morning during the meeting, and before when we came out of the mines when she and her tribe were waiting on us, I noticed some definite sparks flying between those two. I have a distinct feeling that she feels the same way about him. If she is just as interested in a relationship as he might be, then we are going to be hard-pressed to keep them apart. Especially since they are sixteen miles across the desert from us at this moment."

"Yes, but the others with them will certainly see any connections forming between the two of them and remind Jason of the impossibilities of a relationship with this woman. Zaccai, Nick, and Oz are all extremely observant people and are in tune to human suffering unlike others are. We must trust them to take care of and guide Jason accordingly. Besides, Jason is a very strong man physically, mentally, and emotionally. His military training has afforded him that. He will surely make the right decision concerning the situation." Simon hoped that his faith and trust in Jason's decision making was spot on.

He remembered trusting that Hiram would make the right decisions years ago as well. Too late did they discover that he had chosen his own selfish wants and needs above the things of God, and the people whom he had called friends and family for almost ten years.

God gave Solomon wisdom and very great insight,
and a breadth of understanding as measureless
as the sand on the seashore.

1 Kings 4:29

Chapter 8

Timna Valley, Solomon's Pillars, 1840

Jason, Zaccai, Nick, Zeke, and Oz followed Memnah and her men across the Negev Desert toward Solomon's Pillars. From the information the Dragoman had given them before heading out on this trip, Solomon's Pillars was a naturally formed rock formation where the sand, wind, and rain had caused so much erosion over the years that the pillars looked to be separate, cylindrical-shaped, rocks, joined together near the back of the long crevices that extended from the top of each to the base of the mountain on which they sat.

Jason could see the mountain growing ever closer for the last thirty minutes or so of their trek across the desert. It wasn't much longer until they finally reached the large structure. It was quite impressive looking in person, and it did look as though some craftsman or master carver spent years chiseling the rock away to create this unique structure. Knowing it was formed by God himself made it even more impressive to look at. The handy work of God never failed to impress him. Creation often amazed and astounded him, especially since peregrinating.

Jason and the others dismounted, tying their horses off to some tree branches sticking out of the mountainside. Jason made sure the horses were able to be shaded from the sun as much as possible while they were exploring inside Solomon's Pillars.

Without a word in their direction, Memnah and her men began to climb up the steep, rocky mountainside, apparently expecting Jason and the others to follow them. Taking the unspoken hint, they followed them up the steep incline, finding foot and handholds to aid them. Once up the bottom third of the mountain, it leveled out a bit, allowing them to at least stand on flatter ground.

Memnah stopped, almost like she was rethinking what she was about to do. She turned to look at Jason.

"Follow me; but let me remind you that this is a sacred temple. We are here only for the Belts of Truth, nothing else. If anything else should be found to have been removed, I and my people will not hesitate to kill all of you."

Jason watched the expressionless warning that graced her features. He answered her with all the seriousness that she warned him with.

"We understand. We only need the belts, nothing more. You have my word and the word of my people." Jason gestured to his friends standing just behind him.

Memnah looked at him, then at the others. Seemingly satisfied with what Jason said, she turned and walked between one of the cylindrical, curved, surfaces of the large rock. It was shady, cool, and dark the further back they walked. When they came to where the rock's erosion ceased and melded into the rest of the mountain, Memnah took an emblem from around her neck which was tied to a thick string. It was round and flat, and the Star of David graced the center of the medallion. It was rather large, almost the size of her hand. She reached out to remove a small flat stone which lay inside the mountain. She then took the medallion, laid it into the carved section, sitting it perfectly into place in an exact cutout for the necklace, turned it to the left and then pressed down. There was a click and a slight rumbling sound, after which a stone door, about six foot in height, popped slightly open inward into the mountain.

The look on Jason's and the other's faces was one of surprise as they all made their way into the mountain behind Memnah. She picked up some torches wrapped in rags and oil lying on the floor just inside the door. She handed it to Jason and removed a flint from her pocket to light it with. Once lit, she handed more out to the others, lighting them with her own torch, until everyone had one, including her own guards, minus the one who stayed outside to guard the now open entrance to the temple.

As they followed Memnah through the narrow passage into the belly of the mountain, Jason could see carvings laid into the walls, much like those that graced the temple in Jerusalem on the mission he and Seth had taken to acquire the Staff of Moses. Every so many feet there was a carving of a cherubim, palm trees, and flowers. These however seemed to be painted with the colors of the twelve tribes of Israel. Not inlaid with gold as the temple had been.

They walked about a hundred feet or so into the mountain when they came to another door. Like the first time, Memnah took the medallion she wore around her neck, and placed it into the same design engraved into the stone door that lay before them. Turning it to the right this time she pushed once again as the door gave way swinging open. As they all stepped inside, Memnah lit a trough of oil that lay within the wall about five foot up. The fire chased the oil all the way around the inside of the cavern walls, branching off midway, and streaking across elevated stone troughs that ran across an elevated platform, and behind a throne seat, to the other wall, illuminating everything around it as it went. The fire burned brightly upon the oil, and bathed the large space in flickering light, bouncing off the ornately decorated area which held all manner of things.

Gold, silver, copper, and precious stones, all graced pottery, statuettes, cups, goblets, and serving trays. Chests of jewels and gold sat upon the floor, and fine linens and fabrics graced the wall behind a large, stone throne. The seat was inlaid with 12 precious gemstones, again representing the twelve tribes of Israel. Golden cherubim sat upon the elevated floor of the throne seat, facing outward toward them. They stood there staring at the intricately designed, ornate beauty of the large chair where King Solomon himself had once sat when he came to visit the mines. Behind the throne, off to each side were two archways. The one on the right was lined with fabric on the opposite side which served as a door of sorts, offering privacy. The one on the left had a large wooden and iron door.

Along the back wall, fine linens hung from the ceiling of the large cavern and ran all the way to the floor. Each piece of colorful decorative fabric representing one of the twelve tribes of Israel. Behind the fabric pieces, acacia wood stood against the walls of the cavern from floor to ceiling, blocking out the cold stone of the mountain and bringing a warm, majestic feel into the room.

Memnah and her men stood and watched as Jason and the others quietly took in the spectacular view of the massive room that barely resembled the inside of a cave. Jason ventured up the platform, pulling back the curtained entrance to reveal a sleeping chamber for the King himself. A large four-poster bed stood in the center of the room graced by yet another set of fine linen fabric that wrapped the bed canopy. Chairs, settees, dressers, and empty pots that probably once housed living plants sat around the large room's perimeter. Jason noticed that it was astonishingly well kept and clean. Memnah's people must tend to the chambers regularly.

Memnah's voice broke through the silent wonder in the room capturing everyone's attention.

"The Belts are this way." She stepped up onto the platform and went through the massive wooden doorway. They all followed her as she led them down another corridor which had many areas that branched off the main passageway. A kitchen, servant's quarters, eating area, and other living spaces were visible through the light of their torches; the trough of oil not extending past the throne room. This area was not as well tended as Solomon's throne room and private chambers. It appeared forgotten and dusty, although there weren't any cobwebs so someone must at least tend to it in some fashion. They continued the long passage, passing room after room, coming to a stone staircase that twisted upwards through the mountain. Its steps carved and chiseled out of the mountain's own rock. They ventured upward about fifty feet, coming to a large landing that held two doors. Memnah used the medallion again in the same manner as before, opening one of the doors. She walked to the center of the room and lit a circular bowl of oil which sat upon an intricately carved stone base. The fire, once again, illuminated the contents of the area. Against the wall, on one side, were twelve empty mannequin forms. The only thing that remained upon them were the Belts of Truth. Jason and the others looked at each other and smiled.

Jason looked at Memnah with a questioning expression.

"May we take them?" He motioned toward the belts.

"That is what you came for, is it not?"

"Just making sure. I don't want to make you live up to your word, ma'am." He gave her a small, crooked, grin.

Memnah tried her best to hide the small smile that formed on her lips at his teasing, but she wasn't quick enough. Jason's raised eyebrows and wider grin at her slight smirk gave her away.

He and the others stepped forth to remove the belts from the iron mannequins with the help of Memnah's men. They looked at the belts in their hands. They were made of strong, thick, brown leather, with engravings and words in Hebrew inlaid into it. The polished brass buckles had the gem imbedded into it that represented that particular tribe. The belts appeared to have been oiled and polished over the centuries, for they looked to be brand new. Jason wasn't sure if they had ever been worn. Nothing in history had ever mentioned anyone ever wearing the Armor of God. In his time and realm, they were only figuratively used, referring to the word of God as the armor. He supposed that if God wanted real armor, then He could, and apparently did, make it so. Or, instructed someone, perhaps King Solomon himself, to fashion the armor for such a day as this.

They made short work of removing and storing the belts in their packs and were soon on their way out of the mountain to head back across the desert. Memnah instructed that the fire would burn out once the doors were closed and the oxygen in the room was used up.

Jason and Memnah rode side by side as they made the two-hour journey back to the Arches and the mining area.

"So, I see you aren't completely void of humor." Jason grinned at her slight, obvious, discomfort. "I saw that smile back in the cavern."

Memnah grinned, laughing slightly at Jason as he grinned and chuckled back.

"Fine," she stated exasperatedly around her laughter. "You are different, Jason. I must admit that. You are not like most other foreigners we have encountered. You are true to your word. The treasures of Solomon's throne room did not seem to move you, other than the overwhelming awe of it. What makes you so different from the treasure hunters who have plagued our people and this area for centuries?"

"Earthly treasures mean nothing to me. My way of life is different than most peoples. Even yours, Memnah. I can't really explain what it is I do in detail because you wouldn't understand it. Let's just say that God guides my steps and my path, as he does for the rest of those whom I travel with. We are all soldiers working toward God's plan. And His plan apparently is for us to try and stop the destruction of the earth."

"How are you to do this?"

"We travel from place to place on missions that our leaders, known as Dragoman, send us on. We look for and acquire certain artifacts and complete missions that will hopefully aid us in stopping man from destroying the world."

"How does God choose you for this work?"

"I'm not sure. We all just sort of woke up in a new world one day after going through a massive storm system of some kind. All from different places. None of us knew each other before that." He tried explaining as best as he could without getting to much into detail. Would she believe him if he told her they traveled through time?

"And where is it exactly that you come from, Jason . . .? Sorry, I did not get your last name."

He looked at her at this question. Her greenish brown eyes sparkled with curiosity amidst the glaring light of the afternoon sun. The look on her face almost stole his breath for a moment. *Was she flirting with him?* he wondered. He grinned to himself, hopeful of the thought, and answered her question.

"Marshal. My last name's Marshal. I come from a place called Montana, in a country known as America." Jason knew she had probably never heard of America in this corner of the world, not in the year 1840 anyway. He wasn't about to tell her what year he came from.

"I have heard of this America. Traders who come to Eilat have made mention of it. What is it that you did before you became a soldier of God?"

"I was an animal doctor." He smiled at her. "What about you, Memnah? What is it you do, other than guarding the mines and temple?"

"We are a simple people. We live off the land from day to day, tend the herds, harvest our fields, protect and take care of our families. There is not much more to tell."

"Are you married; do you have any children?" Jason wasn't sure why he asked that question. It wasn't like he could act on any feelings he might have for her.

"No. I have neither. My father wished to see me marry before he passed on, but I am stubborn and strong willed. Not exactly marriage material for the men in my tribe. Besides, I believe in marrying for love, not position or duty." She adjusted herself in her saddle and sat up taller. "What about you?"

"Nope. Never married. I didn't have the time before I came to live this life of a warrior for God. And now, there's no point. My lifestyle doesn't exactly leave room for relationships." He suddenly felt regretful about this for the first time in his life. He needed to watch himself carefully and put space between him and this woman. He feared he was falling for her and that was *not* a possibility.

They rode in silence for the remainder of the journey back. When they arrived around six that evening, Jason was surprised by his own invite for Memnah and her men to join them for dinner. He was just telling himself to put some distance between himself and her, and here he was offering to spend more time in her presence. She and her men accepted the offer and tended to their horses, while Jason went in to let the cooks know they would have another twenty guests for dinner. Hopefully Sofia wouldn't throw one of the pans at him, but he did feel the need to thank her and her people for their help in finding and acquiring the belts.

He was surprised to find Simon and Malachai in the cavern with the others, greeting the two men as he entered. The cooks, Sofia and Bridget, had already prepared extra food since most of Memnah's men were still at the cavern with them. They knew Jason and the others would be back soon since Simon could now track him on the Portgen with the new updates which showed they were returning.

Simon explained to him that, before the updates, the Peregrines and Dragoman could only be tracked from the main computers. Now anyone could be tracked from any Portgen, connecting them all together at all times. No more worrying or wondering where someone was or if they were all right. You just had to press a certain function button on the Portgen to see everyone or give a voice command for locating just one person. They also installed home locators on the Portgens which would allow them to speak preprogrammed locations into the Portgen, such as the Island or the Dragoman safe house, and an emergency portal would open taking them straight there. But for safety and precautionary measures, it would only remain open for five seconds.

Introductions were made all around as Memnah and her men entered the cavern. When finished, they commenced to eating dinner, after which, Simon, Malachai, and a few others took the Portgens from the Peregrines that were out on the mission to finish the updated installs. The cavern inside and out was a bustle of activity. The Peregrines were engaged in lively conversations, Gabby was playing her ukulele and singing around the campfire with several other people, many who were from Memnah's tribe, as others gathered around the edges of the cavern watching the activity and laughing and conversing amongst themselves. Uriah sat brooding as usual in a corner, but at least he was having what appeared to be congenial conversation with a few other people.

Jason ventured outside into the cool temperatures of the moonlit night. The half-moon shone brightly over the desert landscape, illuminating creatures of the night that would scamper and scurry across the sands from one shrub to another. He took a seat upon one of the rock out-groupings to ponder what was happening to him lately, but before he could get very far, the source of his turmoil appeared from somewhere out of the desert, walking out from behind one of the rocks.

"Memnah?" Jason was a little startled at her sudden appearance.

"Jason?" she replied, seemingly surprised herself. "What are you doing out here all alone?" She slowly made her way toward him.

"Just needing a little quiet time to think. What about you? What are *you* doing out here?"

"I went to check on the horses we have tied up and take the night guard some food." She was unsure if she should just excuse herself and go inside. But instead she asked, "So, what's on your mind. Maybe I can help with whatever seems to be troubling you?"

Jason squirmed in his seat and cleared his throat before answering. "I highly doubt that."

"Oh, come now, Jason. Surely you're not one of those quiet, brooding, self-suffering type of men who never discuss their true feelings, are you?" She jokingly spoke, determined to weasel out of him what was so troubling.

"All right, Memnah, since you're so interested in my problems." He jumped down from the rock to stand face to face with her. "You're my problem." His words sounded a bit too harsh.

"Me! What on earth did I do to you?" She asked defensively. "Are you still angry over our first meeting when I got the better of you?" She placed her hands on her hips and squinted up at him.

"No!" He nearly yelled in defense. Realizing his voice was escalating, and not wishing to draw unwanted attention to their private conversation, he glanced at the cavern to make sure no one was coming outside. "That is not what I'm having trouble with, besides you caught me off guard. That was an underhanded move and you know it!" He clenched his jaw, his teeth grinding together.

"Oh please, a woman defends herself against a brute who is taking advantage of her and *she* is seen as underhanded." She was determined to not back down from his towering, broad, physique.

"I had already let go of you. You knew perfectly well I didn't have to be a gentleman. If I had wanted to take advantage of you, why would I have let you get up and release my hold on you?" He stared her down, taking a step closer to her. "Besides, you're the one who came at me first, remember?"

"So that you could not take me by surprise!" She stammered to find an excuse or defense. "Besides, if I had tried to run without your being incapacitated, you probably would have caught me and then who knows what you could have done." She threw her hands in the air like a wild woman.

Jason grinned at her weak attempt at rationalization and her temper filled argument. He reached out, grabbed her around the waist and pulled her to him, planting a kiss on her lips that made her stand stock still. He released her, took one small step back and watched her face for a reaction. She stood there for a few seconds just staring at him, breathing heavily either from the argument or from the kiss, he wasn't sure. Just as he was about to step back, thinking the kiss was unwelcomed or ineffective, she stepped up and wrapped her arms around his neck, planting a kiss on his lips this time. They clung to each other for a few seconds, locked in a kiss they both knew was illogical. When she broke the connection of the fierce passionate kiss and stepped back, they both were reluctant to let go of each other.

"Memnah," Jason whispered, standing there as his forehead leaned into hers. A guttural moan escaped his lips. "What am I doing? I … can't …," he rasped out through his emotions, sighing heavily. "I'm sorry." He stroked the smooth skin of her cheek and neck, reluctantly walking away into the desert night and out of sight.

Memnah stood there, confused by what just happened. Didn't he kiss her first? She began to get a little angry, as well as more and more confused. Was it just their different backgrounds? They were definitely from different worlds, but surely if they wanted to, they could make a relationship work. Maybe he just wasn't as attracted to her as she was to him. She watched the direction he had gone, waiting for just a few minutes to see if he would return. When he didn't make an appearance, she turned and went inside the cavern to gather her men, thank the others for their hospitality, and head home for the evening. She would return tomorrow to say goodbye to her new group of friends and acquaintances, and to see Jason for one last time. They returned to where they had their horses tied off and mounted the animals.

The riders took off at a canter across the desert sands. Memnah turned to take one last look back at the camp. When she did, she spotted Jason standing on top of one of the outer rock-groupings watching her. They locked gazes once more before she turned her horse to follow the others, kicking the animal in the sides to make it speed off across the desert into the darkness.

Jason just stood there, watching her go. The turmoil inside him was enough to make him want to scream. He wanted so badly to go after her. To bring her back and make her stay with him, but he knew it was an impossibility. She could never go with him and he would never be able to stay. His heart felt like it was going to break in two. How could he explain to her why they could not be together? How in the world did he fall in love with a woman from another time period in the matter of just a week? The incredulity of the situation weighed heavily on his mind.

"God," he spoke into the night sky, "why did you let this happen to me? Why, with this woman? Why give me such strong feelings for someone I cannot have and will never be able to be with?"

He spent the better part of the next hour, sitting and praying that God would take this burden from him. He didn't want these feelings if he couldn't act on them.

Back in the cavern, Seth and Simon both began wondering where Jason had gotten off to. Memnah and her people had left almost an hour ago. Jason had disappeared after dinner and had yet to reappear.

"Simon, I think I'm going to go look for Jason."

Seth stood up. "Caroline, I'll be right back." He leaned down, kissing her on the cheek.

"All right."

"I hope everything is all right," Simon stated, a wary tone in his voice.

"I'm sure it is. I'm certain we'll both return soon." Seth turned and walked out of the cavern into the moonlit desert, walking the half-perimeter of the outside of the cavern and the surrounding rock-groupings. It hadn't taken him long to find Jason, sitting out on top of the rocks, peering up at the moonlit sky. Seth made the short climb up the rocks and sat down beside him.

"Hey, we were wondering where you had gotten off to."

"Just sitting here thinking things over."

"You want to talk about it?"

"Not particularly," Jason answered irritably.

"What's bothering you has to do with Memnah, doesn't it?"

"Didn't I just say that I did *not* want to discuss it?"

"It might help to talk about it?" Seth pressured him.

"No, Seth, it won't help. Nothing, will help!" Jason jumped down from the rock and stalked toward the cavern.

Seth shrugged his shoulders, sighed heavily, and followed his friend inside, deciding he had best leave him alone until another day.

Seth watched as Jason went inside his tent and closed the flaps, signaling an end to any further conversation on the subject.

Seth could only hope that Jason would get over his feelings for Memnah eventually. They had only known each other for less than a week for crying out loud. Surely their feelings could not have grown that strongly for one another in that short amount of time.

Seth looked at Caroline who sat around the fire, laughing, and talking with the others. He remembered how he had felt the first time he had seen her, and the life changing decision he had made, all in less than a week. He suddenly felt for his friend, understanding the depth of his feelings.

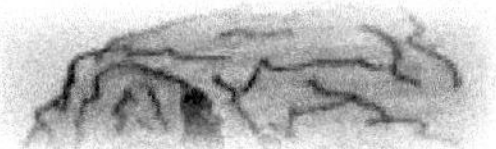

The leaders had all decided to wait until the next morning to move camp to search for the next piece of armor. They really had no idea where God would send them next since the location of the next piece had not yet been revealed to them.

The night hour grew late and they all settled down for bed, except for the two night-guards. Dinah and Nick were the first two on duty, and Dinah was expressly happy about getting the chance to talk with Nick. She hadn't really had the opportunity to talk with her peregrination partner since they had gone to Reader's Island for training over a month ago. Dinah really liked Nick and hoped to one day have a real relationship with him, but often times Nick was distant. It was painfully obvious he did not want any relationship at the present moment. Still, she could hope that maybe one day it would be possible. She walked around outside the cavern entrance, the chilly desert night temperatures making her shiver. She should have grabbed her jacket before rounds started. She was rubbing her arms with her hands to keep them warm when Nick noticed her discomfort.

" Dinah , you look like your freezing. Here, take my coat." Nick walked up to her and threw it around her shoulders.

"No, Nick, I'll be fine. " She objected, trying to hand the coat back to him.

"Look, I'm near twice your size. I can handle a little bit of cool weather. Besides, I've dealt with worse than this in Vietnam." He smiled down at her. They walked in companionable silence around the camp.

"Thank you, Nick." She pulled the coat tighter around her shoulders before she spoke again. "This is nice."

"What do you mean?"

"This. Us. Out here pulling guard duty together." She smiled at him. "We haven't really spent any time together since before we were all searching for Bridget Burke."

"You're right. It has been a while since we've been able to just visit with each other without interruption."

"Yes. I've missed talking with you, Nick. I've just missed, you." She braved the words as she watched his expression. Nick was tough to read; he had an excellent poker face.

Nick chose his next words carefully. He knew Dinah had a thing for him, but he didn't feel the same and didn't want to encourage her in any way. At the same time, he also didn't wish to hurt her. He cared for her deeply, just not in a romantic way.

"Dinah , you are by far one of my all-time favorite people. But you know I only love you like a sister, right? I don't want a relationship with anyone right now. Probably never will." He quickly added. "It's nothing personal against you. You are an amazing woman ..."

"Yeah, yeah. I know. It's just you, right?"

"Yes, actually." Nick stopped walking and exhaled slowly before he began. He felt he owed her an explanation and turned to look directly at her. " Dinah , I've never told another living soul about my past, and I'm going to hold your feet to the fire and make you swear to never mention it to anyone else. Understand?"

Her curiosity was now piqued, even with his rejection pulling at her heart strings. She shook her head in agreement and watched his expression, that was often unreadable, turn to one of sheer pain.

"I was married once, long ago. I was young, just back from the war. I had lost my leg and wasn't sure what kind of future I faced. After a few months of self-pity, I decided to go back to school for a teaching degree at the local community college near my parent's home. I met Jenny there; she was my wife." He clarified so she would understand. "We fell in love and were married within the year. She didn't care about my missing leg. She always called me her hero. We had a very strong relationship at first. About a year later, we had a daughter, Cassie. She was our whole world. Jenny never got pregnant again so, Cassie was an only child. We spoiled her rotten, but in a good way." He smiled sadly before his demeanor turned somber. "When she turned seven years old, she contracted an incurable disease. The doctors told me it was a genetic deformity on my side that didn't take to being paired with Jenny's genes. Cassie died a year later." He stopped for a moment to gather his composure.

Dinah began to comment, and he stopped her, needing to finish the story.

"Cassie's death ripped my wife and I apart over the next few years and she eventually divorced me. It was all my fault. I wouldn't talk to her, look at her, or even touch her. I was afraid of the same thing happening again to another child. I felt guilty because it was from my genetics, and I couldn't deal with it. I became an alcoholic. I was mean and thoughtless toward Jenny. I never even consider her pain upon losing Cassie, just my own. So, you see, I'm no good for anyone. I have no desire to ever have a relationship again."

"Wow, Nick. I'm so sorry for everything that you've suffered and lost. And I even understand that you don't feel that way toward me at all and that's okay. But you shouldn't let it turn you bitter toward finding love again. The odds of that happening again are astronomical. Just, don't close off your heart forever, Nick. It can be awfully lonely." She stood on her tiptoes, kissed him on his cheek, pulled the jacket closer to her, then walked away to check the camp's borders once again. Nick watched her go, thankful for her friendship and understanding. He felt a small sense of relief at telling his story to someone. Dinah was a good friend, he just hoped that one day she could get over him and find someone truly deserving of her. He turned and walked off in the opposite direction.

By the time they met back up in the middle by the cavern entrance, Alec and Odessa were walking out to relieve them of watch duty.

Alec too was happy to be able to spend some alone time with Dee. The two of them sat upon one of the higher rocks overlooking the area in all directions. They chatted about all the things that had taken place over the last few days while they partnered with other people. While in the middle of conversation, Dee suddenly stopped talking and went into a trance like state.

Alec watched her closely. She was eerily still, staring off into the night air. Could she be having a vision? Dee's powers didn't normally manifest in this manner. It usually happened when she was asleep. He wasn't sure what would happen if he disturbed her, so he decided to give it a few more minutes. When another minute had passed, and she had begun to mumble and become growingly distressed, he decided to see if he could make her snap out of it.

"Dee, are you alright. Dee!" He shook her, trying to gain her attention. She suddenly stopped ranting and came out of her trance-like state.

"Alec, we need to wake Simon. I just had a vision of a massive demon war. And I think it's going to take place today, right here in Timna Valley."

No temptation has overtaken you except what is common to mankind. And God is faithful; He will not let you be tempted beyond what you can bear. But when you are tempted, He will also provide a way out so that you can endure it.

1 Corinthians 10:13

Chapter 9

"Odessa," Simon began, still uncertain about her dream, "are you sure about what you saw in your vision?" He stood up from his cot, now fully awake.

"Yes, Simon, positive. We will battle demons soon, just after dawn when first light illuminates the valley."

"How many did you see?"

"Hundreds, I'm afraid."

"Those are very steep odds. That could be ten or fifteen to one if you're right. We only have three or four hours before sunrise. We'll let the others sleep for another hour or two. They may need their energy and strength if we are to battle that many. I'm going outside to find a remote place to pray, but I won't stray too far, I promise." He added the last statement at their looks of concern.

"We need to get back to watch duty." Alec glanced at Odessa for confirmation.

"Yes, I agree. Especially in lieu of what is about to happen."

Simon looked at them before leaving the cavern. "All right, see you two in an hour."

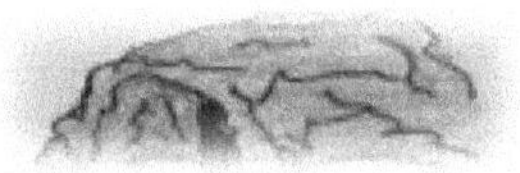

The guards stationed around the camp came running to inform Memnah of the large dust cloud being kicked up by an army of men marching across the Negev toward the Arches and Solomon's Mines.

"Arc you certain that was what was causing the dust and not a haboob?" she questioned the guard.

"Absolutely. The sun is beginning to crest over the valley, and using the spyglass afforded a clear view. There are hundreds, Memnah."

She thought a moment and remembered something she had overheard Seth and Jason speaking about one day in the mines. They said they battled demons and others in their line of work. She wasn't sure who these invaders were, but she had to help Jason and his friends.

"Tell every available warrior in the village to saddle up. We ride to do battle today. I will leave out as soon as I get my horse saddled. The rest of you meet me at the cavern where the foreigners are camped. We need to leave fast; they may not know about this army yet." Memnah left to gather her weapons and to saddle her own horse, stopping only briefly to offer up a prayer to God in heaven for their victory, and the safety of her people, and Jason's.

She set out at as fast a pace as her horse could run across the desert sands, slapping the reins from side to side to urge him on even faster.

When she reached the cavern, just as the sun began to spread its light across the desert floor, the Peregrines were all up and moving around, donning their weapons.

Memnah reached the entrance, jumped down from her slowing steed, and ran into the cavern in search of Jason. She spotted him talking to some of the others.

Jason saw her coming toward him, surprised to see her here at all, especially so early in the morning. He didn't have time for another confrontation.

When she reached him, he realized by the look on her face she knew something was wrong.

"Jason, from the looks of everyone in here, I assume you know about the advancing army of several hundred men coming your way?" She stopped just a few steps in front of him.

"Yes, Memnah, we do. This really isn't a good time for you to be here. You need to leave. These are demons that we are about to go into battle with. It isn't like fighting regular men. You could get hurt if you stay." He urged.

"I have come to aid in the battle, Jason. Others from my tribe are on their way here as well."

"Memnah, I can't ask you to sacrifice yourself and your people for us..."

"You did not ask, Jason. We are freely offering our weapons, strength, and skills to aid you and your people. Our tribe has sworn to protect this valley, we have always defended it and we shall do so now, whether you fight or not."

"There are a lot of them, Memnah, and the outcome is not guaranteed."

"I know this. I have hundreds of people, ready to fight by your side. It will at least make the odds more agreeable."

"All right then. Thank you, Memnah. Just, please be careful." He stared into her eyes with so much emotion that she felt her knees go weak. "Oh, and one more thing. Remember when I said we were hand-picked by God for this?"

She shook her head as she replied. "Yes."

"You will probably see my people do some very strange and miraculous things today. We have all been given remarkable gifts for times like this. Just remember we are on the same side."

She watched him with an odd expression as he walked away to organize a few others. She pondered what he told her while she headed back outside to greet the approaching tribe of her people.

The other Peregrines who were already outside waiting to do battle, were slightly startled by the sound of hoof-beats rumbling across the desert and the cloud of dust that followed. A few of them even readied their weapons in preparation of an eminent attack.

Memnah threw her hands up into the air and yelled to them that it was her tribe approaching. As the army of riders slowly came to a stop just outside the cavern entrance, everyone turned their attention to Jason, who had jumped up onto an obliging rock which overshadowed everyone else below, so that they all could hear him well.

Memnah did the same to talk to her tribe and translate. As she listened to Jason instruct his people, she relayed to her people what Jason had told her earlier about their gifts as he had called them. Then they all listened to Jason give instruction.

Jason looked at the younger kids without any known fighting skills, hoping beyond hope that they would be all right. He instructed some of the others to keep an eye out on them as much as possible.

Oz and Sofia both agreed to cover Bridget, Nick and Sean said they would keep an eye out for Wade, and Zaccai and Uriah agreed to help protect Dominic, even though he could handle himself quite well.

Jason paced the rock. Looking out across Timna Valley he could see the cloud of dust growing closer. He calmly addressed the group looking to him for direction.

"All right, people. We all know what to do and what to expect, even though we've never taken on this many demons at once. Thankfully, Memnah and her people are here to help. Memnah, let your people know that in order to kill a demon, they must strike them in the head or the heart. Nothing else will stop or even slow them down. Now," he said turning back to address his group, "this is the time to remember the gifts God has given you and use them wisely. God has prepared us for this fight. He has even given us an army to help us in battle. God speed to each and every one of you." Jason finished, leaped down from the rock, and mounted his horse.

Memnah scanned the area as the large group of riders set out across the desert in the direction from which the demons were coming. They needed to get into a good position where their powers would be useable, and possibly up higher with a vantage point from which to shoot. She found just such an area, sending about ten of her best shooters up top on the ridge.

Jason noticed some of her people ride up the side of the hill while he and the rest of the Peregrines and Dragoman took their place in front of the ridge, just slightly behind where Memnah's men were taking their place up top. The men on the ridge would be able to begin shooting at the demon hoards before they even reached the rest of the army, hopefully picking off a lot of them before they could even get close.

All seventeen Peregrines, three keepers, and the two Dragoman, Simon, and Malachai, plus the one-hundred and ninety or so warriors from Memnah's tribe stretched out side by side along the desert floor, the mountain ridge to their right flank. The leaders glanced up to see some of the tribal men that had taken higher ground and had settled into their places for shooting.

They all sat there on their mounts in nervous anticipation of the advancing army of demons. Their horses pranced anxiously, feeding off the tension in the air.

The young Keepers stayed directly behind the Peregrines who were to keep watch over them. Bridget, Dominic, and Wade held semi-automatic pistols given to them this morning by Alec. He had decided early-on, that since the kids had no discernable fighting skills, he should teach them to handle a gun. Since their arrival here in Timna Valley, whenever they had any down time, Alec had taken Bridget, Wade, and Dominic out to learn to shoot, just in case a situation ever arose for them to need a weapon. His forethought had afforded them some defense in this fight.

The peregrines all took stock of their surroundings, homing in on what they could use with their powers. Fortunately, as it was early morning, there was still some cloud cover to aid them from a moisture standpoint. Some plants and trees spotted the landscape, and a few animals stood watching over the scene playing out before them, nervousness making them prance, ready to take flight and hide for protection.

Jason being a marine, took the lead in the battle, the other leaders all stretched out on either side of him, with Memnah just to his right.

"Once the first line of defense is visible, you all need to wait. Give the sharpshooters time to pick off as many as possible. Unless the demons shed their human forms, they will be unable to take flight of any kind. If we can kill them before they change it will be an easier battle. Wait for my signal before advancing." He spoke as loudly as possible, looking around him so that everyone could hear what he was saying. They couldn't afford any mistakes today, not against this many.

Memnah looked at Jason as he spoke about the changing the demons might make. She had never seen a demon, at least not that she could remember. She hoped she was prepared for the possibility of whatever it was that they could change into. She wasn't sure she wanted to find out.

The hoard of demons marched across the valley, growing ever closer, their battle cries and deep, vibrating, trumpeted horns making the very air around them seem to shake. They could feel the soundwaves penetrate their skin, sinking into their bones, making them and their horses even more anxious.

The men on the ridges began firing their rifles, dropping demon after demon, taking out as many as possible. They shot arrows with flaming tips at the army just a thousand or so feet away, most finding their marks either between the eyes or through the chest. When the advancing army started to grow closer, Jason gave them the signal to advance. The men on the ridge continuing their barrage of bullets and arrows, careful not to strike their comrades in arms.

Memnah's tribe all let out a loud, tongue-rolling cry, as their horses took off at top speeds out in front.

As the Peregrines got close enough for their gifts to be useful, Kristin set the ground in front of her about twenty feet in all directions to shaking and caused a crevice to open up beneath the demon hoard, dropping many beneath the ground's surface. Zaccai, on the other side of the battle had caused several of the larger trees to grow branches that vined out and grabbed at some of the demons, pinning them to the ground as the warriors decapitated or pierced them through the heart, striking them dead.

The Keepers kept to the rear of the battlefield, keeping plenty of distance between them and the demon hoard. They only ventured close enough to get in a shot from the guns Alec had given them.

The Peregrines fought bravely with their new powers, each of them taking to the battlefield with confidence. Timothy grinned broadly as he turned and twisted, laying blow after blow to the enemy whose weapons landed unaffectedly against him. Their spears and blades shattering against the armor of his thick skin.

Nadia was uncertain how her gift of turning water to ice or snow would benefit her in the arid, dry desert climate, but when one of the demons stepped close enough, the near contact with the unnatural creature enabled her to turn its body fluids to ice within its veins. Changing it to a solid, frozen, white form standing stock still in the desert sun. She then laid her blade to its head, severing it from its body, leaving nothing to chance.

Caroline twisted and flipped through the air, slashing at, and slaying the beasts around her. She sailed through the air almost as if she had invisible wings which hurled her across the battlefield in leaps and bounds with incredible speed and accuracy.

Seth's brute strength and agility was something to behold as he took on more demons than most, landing them flat with one punch, kick, or slice of his blade. The demons dropped around him like an army of boneless rag dolls.

Ezekial transformed the few sparse clouds into a large, dark mass, which rumbled with thunder and flashed with lightning, hanging above the vast demon army.

Dinah then used her wind power, which formed small encompassing whirlwinds that snatched the demons up and hurdled them across the desert, throwing them against the massive rock of the mountainside. The small tornadic forces also trapped the demons in place, allowing one of the Peregrines or tribesmen to strike them down.

Uriah pulled the electricity from the clouds and air, throwing out bolts of lightning, striking his opponents through the heart.

Alec transported himself telepathically in and out of different places, shooting with deadly precision at the enemy before they even knew he had been there. Here and gone in a blink of the eye. He was impossible to track or keep tabs on.

Nicholas shot balls of fire from one hand, setting them ablaze while he struck them with deadly blows. While Oz, who hadn't used his gift in over thirteen years, was surprised to find that he could still manipulate a bodies molecular structure, turning the creatures into piles of liquid, pulpy, mush on the desert sand.

Gabriele's force shield protected not only herself, but anyone else that was near to her that she wished to cover, making a large, impenetrable barrier through which they could strike out but not be struck themselves.

Odessa was still powerful and agile, aiding in her success on the battlefield. She was also able to use her gift to foresee what was about to happen several seconds before, giving her an advantage over her adversaries.

Sean's abilities had no real bearing on this battle since his gift was water manipulation. But his years of experience as a skilled warrior gave him the ability to overcome on the battlefield.

Sofia's gift, also unused for over thirteen years, was the gift of invisibility. She could vanish and reappear at will, making her impossible to strike in battle.

Simon and Malachai fought as well, using their Dragoman powers. Simon was a magus of old and struck the demons down with his powers or disintegrated them using both the powers of his staff and the thin sword hidden in its tip. Malachai was an apprenticing magus as well, training under Simon during their confinement on the island. His powers were nowhere near those of Simon's, but Malachai was a trained warrior of old.

If anyone did happen to get struck by a demon blade, they called out to Jason for his aid. His healing touch quickly sealing the wounds in between battling with the demons himself.

Memnah and her men were overtaken with shock at the scene playing out around them. These warriors of God had powers like nothing she could have ever imagined. She fought as well as she could amongst all the distractions, wanting to take in all that these people were capable of. She gasped in confusion along with her people as they watched and fought alongside these God warriors. Some of her own people being the recipients of Jason's healing abilities.

The war waged on for half an hour, demons falling quickly, unable to match the equal size of the army they fought against and the supernatural powers of the Peregrines and Dragoman. When the last of the demons had fallen, the chaos of the battle was over, and the last of the dissipating demon remains had vanished upon the slight desert breeze which lifted them and blew them across the Negev and out of sight. The Peregrines and tribal men still standing began taking stock of what and who lay on the desert ground. There were around ten men from Memnah's tribe who had fallen and were mortally wounded, along with one of their very own, Dinah Peters.

Nick, Sean, and Kristen all ran as quickly as possible to her side, realizing too late that she was gone. A demon's pitchforked weapon had found it's mark in her chest and had pierced not only her lungs, but her heart as well. Nick yelled for Jason.

Jason and the others ran toward them, hoping that she was still alive. When Jason reached them, he knelt down beside them to assess her wounds.

"Jason, please tell me she's not gone. You can heal her, can't you?" Nick begged him as he sat on the ground, holding his partner of the last year against his chest, begging her to wake up.

Jason felt for a pulse, not finding any signs of her still being alive.

"Nick, I can't heal this. I'm afraid she's gone."

"No, you have to try, Jason! Please!"

"Nick, my powers to heal doesn't include bringing someone back from the dead. I'm afraid that's impossible." Jason felt terribly guilty that he had not seen her fall and wasn't able to get to her in time.

Kristen, Sean, and Nick sat there on the ground, weeping for their fallen friend. Everyone took a few minutes to mourn and say their goodbyes to the friendly and very likeable young woman who now was in the bosom of her maker.

Nick and Sean picked Dinah's body up, laying her across one of the horses.

"Jason," Memnah said, "we will bury Dinah amongst our people, in a place of honor amongst our warriors. Her grave will be tended with the utmost respect of my people, just as we tend to our own."

"Thank you Memnah, that is very kind. But I believe Simon and Malachai will take her body back home with them when they leave."

"Would that not be a hard and long journey across the desert? Her body would not withstand the trip." Memnah's brows knit together in confusion.

"I will explain when we get back to the cavern. Memnah, I'm sorry you lost people today as well."

"It is the inevitability of war, Jason." She sadly looked around at the bodies of her people.

The Peregrines and tribesmen set about claiming the bodies of the fallen warriors, placing them across some of the horses and taking them back to their people to resume with burial rituals. The entire group of Peregrines went to the village with them as Dinah was included in the ceremony.

The village welcomed the Peregrines as they all mourned the fallen men and women. The rituals took the better part of the afternoon as the village women set about preparing the bodies for burial, while others prepared the gravesites.

When the ceremonies were over, the Peregrines took Dinah's body back to the cavern with them, so that Simon and Malachai could take her to Reader's Island and lay her to rest amongst the tranquility of their homeland.

Nick was still in shock and now even more angry with God for taking another person from him. He may not have been in love with Dinah, but he had loved her as a sister. She had become more important to him than he had realized.

The mood in the cavern was a dark one for the rest of the afternoon. The group took turns cleaning up and grabbing a bite to eat in between packing their belongings to prepare for the next journey. God had not yet revealed the next armor piece to them, so Simon and Malachai suggested they all return to the island for Dinah's funeral while they wait on God's leading.

Memnah had returned to the cavern that evening, knowing that Jason would soon be leaving. She had some questions she needed answers to, and knew that once he was gone, she would never get those answers. She found him packing up his tent. He stopped when he saw her enter the cavern and head in his direction. He watched her move methodically and gracefully through the packed equipment strewn across the cavern floor. How he wanted to grab her and plant another kiss on her lips. She stopped just a few small steps in front of him, the scent of flowers wafting in the air from her freshly washed hair, and clean, silken linens in shades of the sea. She was a beautiful woman, one who had invaded every recess of his mind and soul.

"Jason, may I speak privately with you?" She stood staring up into his eyes.

He knew it probably wasn't a good idea to be alone with this woman, but after what she and her people had done for them today, he at least owed her an explanation, and answers to whatever questions she might have. Jason looked around the cavern and out the opening to the darkening sky.

"Let's go outside." He motioned for her to go ahead of him. He started to place his hand on the small of her back to lead her, then thought better about touching her. He quickly withdrew his hand and stuck it inside his jacket pocket.

Simon and Seth watched the exchange with interest, knowing that Jason would, without a doubt, make the right decision. He was after all packing up like the rest of them. After today, the threat of demon attacks as a constant and never-ending event, plaguing the earth for eternity, was something that weighed heavily upon all of them. They must win the final battle for the whole of the earth to live in peace, and they couldn't do that without the pieces of armor and the Final Twelve, and Jason was one of the Twelve. He knew his place, as did they all.

Memnah stepped out of the cavern into the cooling evening air, the trials of the day, the tiredness of her weary body, and the weight of the loss of her people and the newly widowed and orphaned in her tribe making her mind a foggy mess. On top of that, the only man she had ever fallen in love with was about to vanish from her life, probably forever, and she could do nothing to stop it.

She and Jason walked away from the cavern and the bustle of activity, no matter how somber the moods, to find a quiet place to talk.

Memnah finally stopped when they had gone far enough to not be disturbed by anyone. She turned to Jason, motioning to a group of small rocks for them to sort of sit or lean on while they talked. Memnah settle down onto the rock, while Jason sat down next her trying to keep some distance between them, but not doing very well.

Jason started the conversation.

"So, I'm sure you have a lot of questions, Memnah, and understandably so."

"Yes, I do have a few." She sighed just a little at the weight of it all. Still a little overwhelmed by what she had witnessed earlier that day.

"First, I'm still not sure that everything that I witnessed today was real. Although I'm also certain I couldn't have imagined it. How is it possible that you can all do the things that you do?"

"Remember I told you that God has given us all gifts? That's what you saw today. Each of us has been gifted with a different ability to aid us in battle against the demons."

"Isn't that dangerous? I mean, people are a fickle lot. Couldn't you set someone on fire, or turn someone into a puddle of liquid if they made you angry? Seems like a very dangerous responsibility to keep."

"No. Our powers are only useful against the demons. We aren't allowed to use them on other human beings."

"So, it's a choice you have to make?"

"Not really. Our powers don't work on regular people."

"But those demons looked like normal people to me before they turned into beasts on the field once the battle started."

"Yes, but we also have a *sense* of sorts, to alert us of demon activity nearby. We get a feeling, letting us know that there are demons around us. We can pick them out of a crowd if we can see them. I'm not sure how it works."

"But your gift of healing was used on my men."

"Yes, but it was to help, not to harm. I can only assume that is why it worked for them."

"All right. Next question. How are you going to take your friend's body back before it is too late?"

"We are from another place, Memnah. A completely different time era than this one. I know this is hard to understand, but we are time travelers." He pulled the Portgen from its pouch at his left side.

"Do you see this device?" He turned it over in his hands as she looked closely at it.

"Yes. What is it?"

"This is called a Portgen. Its short for Portal Generator. A man back where I am from created this device to help us travel easier. When I first started time-jumping we had to travel by really strong storms that generate enough power to open time-portals; really bright lights in the center of the storm's strength that leads to another dimension or time period."

"I have seen many storms in my day, and I have never seen such a thing as what you are describing," Memnah said, a little in disbelief.

"It isn't something you can see. Only we Peregrines and Dragoman, and the Keepers of course, can see them. Another provision of God I suppose."

"Can you show me this portal with your device?"

"I can try, but I'm not certain you will be able to see it open." Jason stood and pushed the new home button recently installed to take him directly to the Island.

The portal opened before her eyes, showing her a beautiful paradise on the other side.

"How is this possible?" she exclaimed in amazement. "How do you travel this way?"

"We just walk through to the other side."

"Can I also walk through as well?" she asked curiously, inching her way toward the portal.

Jason quickly shut the portal opening down, startling her, making her turn to him quickly with a questioning look.

Jason swallowed hard, knowing that it might come to this.

"Memnah, as much as I would like to take you with me, I'm afraid I can't."

"Why not, if I am willing? I have proved useful in battle, have I not?"

"Regular human beings can't time travel."

"How do you know that I can't! Could we not try it?"

"No!" Jason's voice suddenly elevated and he abruptly stood. Jason huffed, controlling his voice and nerves. "Many people who have tried before without God's blessing, have died doing so. It's not a chance I'm willing to take with your life."

"Oh. I see." She walked back toward him, confusion written across her face.

"Memnah, if I could stay here with you I would, without a second thought. I don't know how, but I have fallen for you in the very brief amount of time that I have known you."

"Well, why could you not stay?"

"I have missions that I must complete, or the world's fate will be like it was today, but much worse. I am one of a few specially chosen people to fight in a battle that is supposed to free man from the destruction of the world. If I choose not to return, then the world will never be free. I must do my part, just like everyone else with me must. Think about what your tribe represents here Memnah. You have guarded the ancient mines and chambers of King Solomon with your lives. I must do the same for the entirety of the earth. I can't just turn my back on my mission. You have no idea how badly I want to stay here with you or be able to take you with me. I've never felt for anyone the way I feel about you. You do things to me that I never thought possible." He gently grasped her behind the head and leaned down to kiss her.

Memnah kissed him back, wrapping her arms around his waist. They stood there holding each other for several minutes, relishing in the feel of it, knowing that they may never see or touch one another again.

"I must get back to the others. We need to get Dinah back to the island. But I promise you this, Memnah. If there is any way to come back here for you, I will. I'm not sure how long it will take, it could be years. But I will come back if I can."

"I will wait for you, Jason. You are the first man I have ever wanted to give my heart to, and you certainly have it. I will wait for you for as long as God gives me breath."

They walked slowly back to the cavern, hand in hand. Everyone was ready to go. Seth and Caroline had packed his camp up and saddled his horse for him. Everyone was waiting on him to return, and when they saw him coming, mounted their horses. They had made a gurney to take Dinah's body back to the island, pulled behind her horse for the brief journey through the portal.

Seth handed him the reins to his horse, and everyone said their thankyous and goodbyes to Memnah as they rode through the portal.

Jason turned to her one last time and leaned his forehead against hers for a brief moment. She pulled a small, jeweled knife from her robes and handed it to him.

"To remember me by." She placed the small dagger in his hand. "May it bring you good fortune and safety.

Jason reached up, pulling off the cross necklace he often wore around his neck and handed it to her.

They looked at each other longingly one last time before Jason mounted his horse and rode through the portal. He turned back to take one last look at her as she lifted her hand in one small, motionless, goodbye, just before the portal closed.

Jason turned his attention back to the island he once loved. It held very little appeal for him now. His heart ached like it had never done before. Hundreds of years separated he and Memnah, and yet the simple push of a button and a matter of only seconds could reunite them as well. How was he going to manage staying away from her when it would be so easy to see her again?

"Lord," he said audibly, "please give me strength."

Be completely humble and gentle; be patient,
bearing with one another in love.

Ephesians 4:2 NIV

Chapter 10

Reader's Island, 2018

Memnah's people had dressed Dinah in the best fabrics they had to offer, rimmed her body with fragrant flowers, and placed a wreath of green about her head. The groundskeepers had never dug a grave on Reader's Island before, so Nuncio instructed them to find a place near the prayer gardens to lay her to rest.

The mood on the island was a somber one for the rest of the evening. Most everyone took to the quiet of their own rooms to think about whatever emotions or deep thoughts the events of the day brought out for each of them. Some of them realized that even though they served God and were chosen for this life, they were not guaranteed a tomorrow. Dinah had been one of them. She served as they do, had special powers as they do, yet she still fell fatally in battle.

Nick took to walking the island's perimeter to think, unable to sit still, even more angry at God, wondering why He seemed to take those he cared for most.

Sean and Kristin sat by Dinah's graveside late into the night, remembering stories about their brief year together, getting to know her and her unique slang and culture from her days out of 1940s America. She had always been upbeat and positive, and made them laugh with her quirky personality.

"Sean," Kristin sniffed as she wiped at the tears and her running nose with the inside of her long-sleeved hooded shirt. "Dinah was the best friend that I've ever really had as an adult. I didn't have time to make lasting friendships on the German war front before I peregrinated. Dinah was like the big sister that I never had. What am I going to do without her? She was my confidant?" Kristin's eyes welled with tears once again. Sean slid closer to her, reached out and pulled her into his arms as she fell into him, wrapping her arms around his waist and leaning her head into his collarbone under his chin.

"I'm sorry, Kristin." He consoled the grieving young woman. He smoothed the silky strands of her straight dark hair and rubbed her back. Losing Dinah was hard on most everyone, and he would miss her as well, but Sean wouldn't trade this moment of holding Kristin for anything in the world. It felt as natural to him as breathing. As long as she needed him, he would be there for her.

"You'll always have me, Kris. Like it or not. You can't get rid of me, we're peregrination partners." Sean grinned down at her.

She giggled ever so slightly at his attempt at a joke. "I don't think that I will ever, *not* like having you around." She smiled weakly up at him. "Thank you, Sean, for your friendship. It's nice that we can get along now." She grinned and then leaned her head back against his strong shoulder, her forehead resting against his cheek.

"Good, because I don't plan on going anywhere for a long time. And I agree, it's nice getting along with you too, Kris. Let's keep it that way, okay? Let's make a pact. If either of us do or say something stupid or inconsiderate we will tell each other immediately and work it out."

"Agreed." She smiled at his words, content to not move from the protection of his arms.

They sat in companionable silence for a while longer before walking back toward the house and bidding each other good night, retiring to their rooms for some much-needed rest.

Everyone else's moods were grim, but Timothy's was one of invincibility. He felt as though nothing could hurt him. No matter what the demons hit him with this morning in battle nothing could penetrate his skin. The thought made him wonder what he was capable of. It also gave him renewed confidence in other areas as well, mainly the one concerning Kristin. He sat watching them, his agitation rising at the seemingly budding relationship between the two of them. He first thought that they didn't get along very well at all from the way they bickered when they all hiked the mountain peaks of the island together a few weeks back. Now they almost seemed inseparable. Sean seemed to hang around Kristin every chance he got. Timothy was going to have to figure out how to get her alone to let her know his feelings and intentions. He decided the next opportunity he had he would tell her how he felt about her. Besides, Dinah's death had taught him that waiting could mean he could be too late.

Seth and Caroline clung to each other, both knowing how fortunate they were to still have one another, as did Prisca and Oz. Prisca was broken up by the loss of a dear friend whom she had mentored for the past year and a half, this being the first loss she had under her mentorship in thirteen years.

Jason took to the prayer garden to ponder losing Memnah. Was it all worth it? Dinah's life had been a short one. Would it not be better to spend what life he had left with the one person he loved most than to toil away at what could be a lost cause? Would they even be able to save the Earth? If so, how long would it take? His mind had never been plagued with these questions before and it was becoming a constant thought for him. Perhaps with time, the questions would fade, as well as Memnah's memory. Jason rubbed the tiredness and anguish from his face as he prayed fervently that God would ease the torment within him.

Simon and Nuncio were concerned about everyone's current mood and hoped that the cloud that had settled over Reader's Island would soon lift. Perhaps tomorrow would reveal a new day and renewed strength to all. Hopefully before the next piece of armor was revealed to them, and they would again leave the island on another mission. They certainly didn't want to send them all out on another mission in the frame of mind they were in at the moment. However, death was a part of this lifestyle and Dinah was not the first to die, and she probably wouldn't be the last.

Simon had walked to the prayer garden to speak privately with Jason. He stood still a moment and watched the man he had spent the last eight years mentoring. He had never seen him so distraught over another person. He remembered how Jason had been saddened and angry by Phoebe's death last year, but it had been different then. Jason had felt responsible for her death and that ate at his soul. These feelings he seemed to have for the woman, Memnah, were new to him apparently. Simon figured that Jason had truly fallen in love with her, and she seemed to feel the same way from what Simon could tell from watching them over the last several days. It was times like this that Simon wished things could be different. Watching Jason's demeanor brought back memories of how Hiram had acted the first time he mentioned Mary to him. He had been distraught too, and those feelings had led to a disastrous situation. Simon had let Hiram work out the details alone as he had asked, but he would not make the same mistake with Jason.

Simon cleared his throat to let Jason know he was there, but he made no movement to show he heard Simon's approach.

"Jason, may I speak with you?" Simon stood just beside the bench where Jason was sitting staring at the ground, his bent arms on his knees and his hands clasped in front of him.

Jason barely nodded a yes to Simon's request without looking at him or moving. Simon could see Jason swallow hard, the sadness written across his face. He took a seat beside the man on the bench and just sat for a moment with him in silence.

Simon tried to choose his words carefully. The last thing he wanted to do was make Jason feel as though he were lecturing him.

"You know, I love this garden. There is just a sense of peace and communing with God here. I can feel his presence all around. Of course, we can talk with Him anywhere, but I've always just felt closer to Him here." Simon chose his next words carefully. "Jason, I understand what you're going through more than you know. I too lost someone once, many years ago."

Jason turned to look at him as he continued.

"Her name was Lilith. I called her, My Lilly. I met her on an archaeological dig in Cairo, Egypt many years ago. Her recently deceased father had been one of the financial backers on the dig, and she had taken over in his interests upon his death. I took one look at her and my heart felt as though it would beat out of my chest. She was the most striking woman I had ever seen, with a beautiful heart and soul to match. We formed an instant attachment; both young, impetuous, and head-over-heels in love with one another. It had been a whirlwind romance over the next several months. One morning, we made an astonishing find at the dig site beneath one of the pyramids. It was a day to remember. I was going to propose to Lilly that evening at the dig celebration. I had gone down into the pyramid one last time before dinner when an earthquake struck the area. The cavern gave in and I thought I was dead for certain. I woke up days later in a strange place, with a whole new life. Lilly was gone to me forever." A wistful look and sadness filled Simon's eyes as he recalled the painful memory from his past.

"I'm sorry to hear that, Simon."

"I spent the first few years angry at God. Yes, you heard correctly, I said years." Simon repeated it due to the look on Jason's face. "Got myself into a bit of trouble for it too. It took me quite a while to get over her and understand that life isn't just about what I want. It's what God wants from and for me."

"I understand that Simon, and I was perfectly fine doing God's work. I was happy with my life, content with what He had given me. So, why bring this woman into my life now, knowing that we can never be together?" Jason's anger and hurt was evident in his voice.

"Perhaps she was your trial, Jason. Maybe you needed to learn something from it, I'm not sure. Just, please remember not to let it turn you from your destiny. Hiram did, and it destroyed so many lives. I see the pain you're in, and I just want you to know that I'm here if you want to talk, and I truly do understand how you feel."

"Thanks, Simon. I just wonder if it is all worth it, you know? I've never had to let go of something that I wanted so badly. I've never *wanted* anything or anyone as badly as I do Memnah."

"Yes, I understand all of what you are saying. But I am certain that in the end, we will all see the value in this way of life. There is pain in everything we do, no matter where we are or what we are doing with our lives. This life is no different. We may experience more pain here than most ever will, but I truly believe that in the end, we will also experience true joy like no one else could."

"I only pray you're right about that, Simon."

The two men sat in companionable silence for a while, staring out into the approaching night sky, contemplating their own lives against what was truly in their hearts.

Nadia struck out across the grassy, sea-oat laden dunes, headed in the direction of Nicholas. She had gone in search of him about thirty minutes before and finally found him. He sat upon one of the wooden lounges by the ocean's rolling surf, staring out across the sea. She needed to speak to the man. She felt like God was pushing her in his direction. She had never really spoken to him much before, except for a few group conversations while training on the island, and tending fire duty in Timna Valley. He seemed to be taking the death of his peregrination partner very hard. Not that the death of a friend would be easy, but perhaps they had been more than just partners? She had noticed the camaraderie they had shared, and the way Dinah had often looked at Nick when she didn't think anyone was watching.

"May I join you?" she asked in her thick German accent as she approached him, noticing that she had startled him a bit.

"Sure." Nick motioned to an adjacent chair.

Nadia sat upon the weather-beaten, wooden chair, unsure how to start a conversation with the grief-stricken man.

"Are you all right?"

"Yes and No." Nick honestly replied.

"Nicholas, I wanted you to know that if you wish to talk, I am here. I know we do not know each other very well, but I feel as though God wishes for us to be friends."

Nick looked at Nadia, unsure how he was to react to her statement or what he was supposed to say.

"Nadia," he began. "I doubt very seriously that you want to get close to me. It appears that everyone I have ever gotten close to, dies or disappears from my life. Do yourself a favor and stay as far away from me as you can."

"You and Dinah , then? You were much more than friends?"

Nick turned to her quickly at the statement, then turned to throw washed up shells back out into the gently lapping waves. "No. But she was like a sister to me. We were close in that way."

"I see. Then there is someone else that you mourn along with Dinah I think?"

Nick stopped and abruptly looked at the woman who seemed to see into his very soul. "Why do you ask?"

She leaned close and stared directly into his eyes. "I have seen the pain in you, and I know it well. I too have lost many loved ones."

"Why do you think that is? Why do some of us seem to lose so much more than others?"

"I do not know. I only know that if I did not have God in my life, I would not have been able to bear it. I do not know your story Nicholas, but I imagine it is much like my own. I recognize your pain, and I truly feel for you and understand it. If you ever wish to talk about it or share with me, I will be here." She sat back into the chair, closing her eyes and lifting her head into the breeze that whipped around them.

Nicholas watched the woman beside him and felt the earnestness of what she was saying. The pain in her eyes had mirrored his own. Perhaps not because of Dinah's death, but from something that ran much deeper. The silent exchange between them was like a tightly knitted thread that had swiftly woven a connection. He had never really spoken to her much, or anyone else for that matter. Not about what really haunted his nights and days. He suddenly realized that others around him may have just as many haunts to deal with as he did. Feeling slightly selfish, as though he held the corner market on pain, he sat back against the chair lifting his head into the wind, silently stealing glances at the woman who sat quiet and unmoving beside him.

Uriah watched his old friends and the torment that they were going through over Dinah's death, especially Prisca. It had been years since the old gang had ran together. The last time they had been around each other was a sad moment as well. Most of their friends had died, disappeared, or been badly wounded in the war thirteen years ago. Uriah, Hiram, Simon, Oz, Zaccai, Prisca, Sofia, Safra, Nuncio, and most of the island staff, had all been a tight knit group of friends back in those days. Between the deaths, disappearances, and Hiram's betrayal, it had ripped them all apart. They each had to deal with their own pain and loss. No one had been exempt from the horrors of that day. He and Prisca had been close friends once. She was a woman with a giant heart. She truly cared deeply for everyone she mentored and seemed to be taking Dinah's death very hard. Uriah heard Oz ask Prisca if she wanted a hot cup of tea. She replied yes and Oz left the room headed for the kitchen. Uriah went up to his old friend to offer his condolences.

"Prisca, are you all right?"

"Uriah." She patted her puffy, red, eyes, and tear-stained cheeks. "Yes, I will be fine. It is never easy losing one of my Peregrines. I always seem to take it so personally." She sniffed, sitting up straighter to speak with him.

"I always said that you had too big of a heart, Prisca. You always feel everyone else's pain on top of your own." Uriah sat beside her on the edge of an overstuffed armchair.

"Perhaps, but it is better to feel the pain and deal with it Uriah, than to bottle it all up and let it one day explode." She looked pointedly at him. He knew she understood him well enough to know that was exactly how he dealt with all of his emotions. He wasn't one to show pain. Anger yes, but not pain. Perhaps he could learn a few things from her. She seemed to wear her emotions on her sleeves, and she told you what she thought without holding back, but never in a mean way. Prisca had been a good friend to him at one time. After Hiram's coo, Uriah withdrew from everyone. But then again everyone pretty much withdrew from everyone else. Things were never the same again in their little group. Trust had become a huge issue, on top of all the pain it had caused, and everyone went their own separate ways, even though they all still worked together, they didn't see each other as much as they used to.

"Well, I'm sorry for your loss, Prisca. I just wanted to let you know that. You have always been kind to me, no matter what. I just wanted to let you know that I appreciate you for that. Even when I was wrong about Hiram all those years ago."

"Thank you, Uriah. It appears that you have learned to have compassion for others. That is a good thing, Uriah, whether or not you believe it."

"Perhaps, but compassion has never been a strong suit of mine." Uriah smiled slightly, stood, and left the room just as Oz was returning with her cup of steaming tea. Uriah walked out of the living room and out of the door onto the veranda to sit and think in the warm night air.

Alec and Odessa watched as Uriah took a seat underneath the covered pergola. They too were perched in two of the large porch chairs underneath the pergola on the other side, just out of earshot of Uriah. Alec sat and watched as Odessa breathed deeply of the flower-scented air as the breeze blew loose, curly, strands of her hair across her face. The somber mood of the evening along with the intense demon battle from this morning had everyone completely worn out, mentally, physically, and emotionally. Dinah's death had given Alec renewed confidence about finally revealing his feelings for Dee. He had held his tongue for more than seven years now. Why? He wasn't exactly sure except their way of life had never been ideal for relationships. But now, Seth had Caroline, Oz had Prisca, so why couldn't he and Dee make a go of it? Jason and Memnah were a different story all together. Jason had known to not get involved with a woman who wasn't part of their world. He and Dee however were both Peregrines and could make a relationship work.

"Dee, this whole thing with Dinah has really started me thinking." Alec started slowly, trying to find the right words.

"About what, Alec?" Dee sighed heavily; her eyes still closed to the world.

"About life in general, and how it could end so abruptly."

"Yes, I know what you mean."

"Well, since you agree on that then I have something important to say to you." He sat up and leaned toward her chair as she took the hint and opened her eyes to look at him.

"You sound awfully serious, partner. What's up?" Odessa sat up straighter in her chair.

"We have been partners for what, about eight years now, yes?"

"Yes, somewhere around there."

"Dee, I have never said any of this before because our life-styles did not permit it, but things are changing."

"Alec, what are you talking about?"

"Just . . . let me finish before I lose my nerve."

"Now you have me worried."

Alec raised his hand to silence her. Dee's eyebrows raised in curious question.

"Odessa Megalos, I have been madly in love with you for the past seven years."

"Alec…"

"Cht…I am not finished. Please do not interrupt me yet. I watch Seth and Caroline, and Oz and Prisca, and think to myself, why can we not have that as well. Today has taught me that life is very short, and we should make the most of it. Dee, I love you with my whole heart and soul."

"Alec, I understand what you're saying, but now is not the time to discuss something like this."

"It is most definitely the time. Life is too short to wait, Dee. Do you not love me as I love you?"

"Alec, you know I love you; I just don't think that I am *in* love with you."

"So, let's give this relationship thing a try to find out."

"No, Alec, that isn't the way to do things. What happens if it doesn't work? It would put a strain on our working relationship and our friendship, and you mean too much to me to risk it. Not to mention the distractions it could cause during battles."

"I have already been dealing with that since Africa, and I have a handle on it. I understand that we both have the same exact job, and I can manage my emotions. I just want to make the most of our time together."

"Alec, this is too much for me to think about right now. I just can't start a relationship at this point in my life."

"Then when, Dee?" he asked in frustration. "This life we have could go on for years and years. Look how long Simon and Prisca and the others have been doing this. Nuncio has been at it for forty years! Do we really have to wait that long?"

"Just, give me some time, Alec, all right? I can't even wrap my brain around this tonight. Not after the day we've all had."

"Fine, Dee. If you don't care for me as I do you, then just say so. If you loved me the same way you wouldn't have to think about it." Alec abruptly stood and walked away from her and into the house.

"Alec!" She called to his retreating back. He did not stop or turn around. She knew Alec well, and if he thought that she did not feel the same for him then he would not bother her about it again. She knew that she would have to broach the subject again should she wish to revisit the conversation.

Alec stomped his way upstairs to his room. Hurt and anger fueling his motions. He had bared his heart and soul to Dee and she had thrown it right back in his face. Now, the ball was in her court.

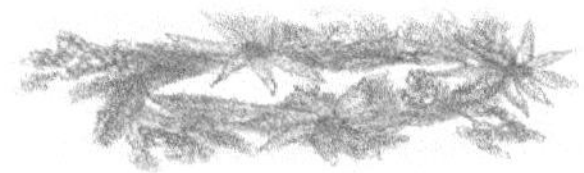

The next morning, everyone slept in as late as their exhausted bodies and minds allowed. All except for a few.

Jason had risen early as sleep did not come easily to him. He sat in the large wicker patio chair on the balcony outside his room. His feet propped up on the cool bamboo railing as the chilled early morning air ruffled his hair and clothing. He sat and watched as the sunrise began to streak colors across the sky, bathing the dark parts of the earth in brilliant golds, yellows, oranges, and pinks. It reminded him of the sunrises across Timna Valley as his thoughts once again returned to Memnah. He sighed heavily, rubbing his tired eyes and face with the palms of his hands, which continued up through his hair in frustration at the fact that he couldn't seem to control the wanderings of his mind. He stood and went back into his room, grabbed a change of clothes, and headed for the showers. Afterwards he would head downstairs for breakfast and see if he could find something to keep his mind busy. They needed to get back out there and find the next piece of armor. The sooner they got back to the search the better. Hopefully others would be up and about, and they could begin making plans to leave within the next few hours. Sitting around on the island wasn't doing anyone any good.

Jason met an equally tired looking Alec in the hall on the way to the showers as well.

"You're up early, Alec. Couldn't sleep either?"

"No. I'm not sure I will be able to for a while to come."

"Yeah, I know what you mean. I'll meet you downstairs for breakfast in say, ten minutes?"

"Will do my friend." Alec disappeared behind one of the many bathroom doors.

When they made their appearances in the kitchen, the only ones awake were Clancy and Henry the two kitchen chefs. They had been cooking up a huge mess of pancakes, eggs in various forms, hollandaise sauce, bacon, hash-browns, and sausage. The table had been set with orange juice, milk, coffee, and tea.

"Clancy," Jason began, "If I didn't know any better, I'd say you missed all of us."

Clancy smiled at him. "You're right about that. I really enjoy cooking large breakfasts. I don't get to do it that often."

"Thanks, it all looks great." Jason and Alec each grabbed a plateful and went out to sit on the pergola covered veranda and enjoy the island weather.

It wasn't long before other stragglers made an appearance downstairs for breakfast. Soon the entire patio area and veranda were filled with people eating and making light conversation. However, people still weren't in jovial moods.

Simon and Nuncio watched everyone, both hoping that the Peregrines would soon be off again on another mission which would at least keep them busy. That is unless they were attacked by demons again which could cause some fear to creep in, especially amongst the newer Peregrines and the non-battle-trained, teenaged, Keepers.

Simon sat watching the group of people making slight conversation between yawns when Odessa approached him.

"Good morning, Simon."

"Good morning, Odessa. Did you sleep well?"

"As well as can be expected under the circumstances. Simon, I had another dream last night. I think it concerns the next piece of armor. Would it by chance be the Breastplates of Righteousness?"

"Well, if we are to search for the pieces in the order that they are mentioned in the Bible, then yes."

"I had a vision, or dream, whatever you want to call it, of knights jousting in full armor. People were yelling 'hail King Arthur' and I could see that the name on the King's sword read Excalibur. Wasn't King Arthur just a legend?"

"Well, it was never proven that he actually lived, but it was also never proven that he didn't. Perhaps this clue is only meant to give us an estimated time in which to look for the next piece. Some historians speculated that King Arthur ruled in the late fifth and early sixth centuries. That could still be an extensive time period to search through. Let's go over your dream or vision slowly, considering everything that you saw. It may narrow the search field down quite a bit."

"All right, shall I get Safra?"

"That would be a good idea. I believe I last saw her in the kitchen. Oh, and Odessa, can you bring this year's archive book with you so that I may record the information as well?"

"Sure thing, Simon. I'll be right back." Odessa left to go inside to search for the woman and the book.

"Simon." Jason called as he approached the table. "I wanted to thank you for the talk yesterday. It did help, even if just a little." He sat next to his mentor.

"You're welcome, my boy, any time." Simon smiled at him over his glasses, as usual. "By the way, what is Memnah's tribe and does she have a last name?"

"I don't think she ever mentioned either. Why do you ask?"

"Oh, no reason in particular. Just 'name meanings' are a thing of mine. All of us Dragoman research and record the meanings of the names of every Peregrine, Dragoman, and now Keepers, that ever served. In ancient times, people often named their children according to traits or features that were obvious at birth. Do you know what Memnah means?"

"No. Should I?" Jason was intrigued by the smirk on Simon's face.

"Well, Seth mentioned your first encounter with her. I find it fascinating that her name means 'to strike'. Don't you?"

Jason grimaced ever so slightly, then smiled at the thought. "Makes perfect sense." He gave Simon a large toothy grin.

Odessa returned to the table at that time, followed by Safra who had her sketch pad and pencils in hand.

"Okay, we're ready to get to work if you are?" Odessa handed Simon his archive book as she and Safra pulled up chairs alongside Simon, Nuncio, and Jason.

"What's going on?" Jason asked.

"Odessa has had another dream about the next piece of armor. We are trying to pinpoint an exact time in history by having Safra draw and record everything that Odessa says while I make the historical notes."

"Really, already! So, where are we headed next?"

Simon smiled over his glasses at Jason. "Ever hear of King Arthur and the Knights of the Round Table?"

"Who hasn't? But isn't that all just Celtic legend and myth?"

"Perhaps, but I suppose you are all about to find out. Like I was telling Odessa, it could just be a simple reference to the time era in which to look. I can't say that you will actually be meeting King Arthur himself, however, I may just have to come along with you on this one. I have to say, if it is true, I would love to have a conversation with Merlin."

"Perhaps we should spend the rest of the day researching the time period and area to try and narrow down exactly to where it is that we need to travel."

"As soon as Safra and I finish with recording Odessa's dream, we will hopefully have a better idea of that anyway. The information concerning Arthurian legend isn't very precise. The era in which he supposedly reigned was very vague, over 700 years or more, so we may have our work cut out for us there."

"Surely Ryan's computer programs could make short work of the search?"

"Yes, if there were actual proof of Arthur's reign, but as I said, there is no definitive proof either way. Computer searches may reveal some more closely-knit legends and eras, but there are so many different ideas out there about when he may have ruled, that it might not be of any help at all. Medieval times were barely recorded, and the little that was is vague to say the least. There is very little information about those times in history. The Renaissance era was the age of enlightenment and when people really began to write things down."

"I guess it's up to God to guide us then," Odessa chimed in.

"Safra, I believe that is your specialty." Simon smiled at her.

"I shall don my prayer robes and head to the temple when we are done here," Safra said with a small bow and a smile.

Folly brings joy to one who has no understanding,
But whoever has understanding keeps a straight course.
                                        Proverbs 15:21 NIV

Chapter 11

After returning from the prayer temple, Safra soon emerged from her room with a few of her own drawings. Her hour-long prayer vigil had revealed a few more images for her relating to the middle ages, however her images also revealed knights wearing a white tunic with a red cross embellished on the front. This one image was very distinct in her revelations, and so she had the forethought to have Ryan run a computer scan before going to speak with Simon and the others about her findings.

Ryan was able to find information pointing to a particular nobility that reigned during the late medieval era into the renaissance age.

"Simon," Safra called, waving the drawn images in front of her as she entered the archival library where Simon was once again going through the recently found ancient texts. "I have good news."

"Praise the Lord for that!" Simon smiled in return.

"I had Ryan do a computer search on an image I received during my prayer vigil, and he found some interesting information."

Simon took the images and computer printouts from Safra and scanned the information. He smiled at her once again.

"Thank you, Safra. This is very helpful indeed."

Simon called a meeting for just after lunch with the other Dragoman and the Peregrine leaders in the larger conference room to discuss the findings.

Everyone gathered around the large, heavy, wooden table that was rectangular in shape with rounded corners. The shade of the highly polished wood was that of a light oak, lending brightness to the large piece, and reflecting the light from the windows at the far end of the room. The center of the table was laden with a spray of tropical flowers that stretched out across the center of the table in all directions and gave off a pleasing scent that permeated the air. The large, high backed, oak chairs were stained to match, and were upholstered with a bright, ocean blue fabric that matched the thin, vertical striped, white, gray, and blue curtains that danced in the slight breeze of the large, opened windows.

Simon waited until everyone was seated before he began.

"Safra has found something very distinct about the time period in which Odessa had her premonition." He passed out copies of the drawings and information, and as they made their way along from one person to the next, he continued.

"The image of the knight in the white tunic and red cross on the front is of warriors known as the Knights Templar. Some of you may have heard of them and for what they stood. A brief history is this, they were a band of knights, who around the year 1095 AD, swore to protect Christians who were traveling to the temple to worship from the Seljuk Turks who sought after them to kill them and to keep them from making the journey. I'm not sure why Odessa's dream was about King Arthur and Excalibur when Safra saw the Knights Templar. Both of these could have resided around the same time period, but King Arthur's legend was placed earlier than that of the Templars. Any thoughts?"

Nuncio spoke first. "Perhaps the two legends are somehow connected?"

Simon replied, "Perhaps? I intend to go along with the group on this mission to find the breastplates. I am curious about a few things and hope to have a few of my own questions answered."

Malachai chimed in, "I believe I'll go along as well. It's been many years since I've gone out on a field mission. Our little stint to Timna Valley has made me yearn for a few more adventures."

"Anyone else?" Simon questioned the group around the table.

"Oh, that I *could* go," Nuncio expressed wistfully, patting his bum hip.

Simon felt for the once proud and strong man. Nuncio was quite the warrior back in the day. Simon used to stand in awe of his battle strategies and strength.

"I believe that I will stay here and try to decipher the Book of the Keepers," Vashti chimed in.

"Me as well," Prisca replied. "I have no desire to sit in a saddle for days on end, battle demons, and be tried by God in my indiscretions. I will stay with Vashti and Nuncio and sort through the books."

"Safra, would you care for a bit of adventure?" Simon grinned questioningly over the rim of his glasses at his older, yet still agile friend.

"Perhaps," she returned with a grin herself. "I too would fashion a possible visit with the great Merlin himself. That is, *if* he is real and not just myth or legend."

"Well, it seems that we have our riding party. Now, we just need to determine what time period to return to."

Nuncio cleared his throat and spoke. "Simon, might I suggest a middle ground approach to begin. Perhaps directly between the two periods. Since Arthurian legend places him around the late fifth and early sixth centuries, and the Knights Templar were said to begin around the end of the tenth century, then why not return around the 800-900s era?"

"That is as good a place as any, now we just need to research where the Kingdom of Camelot was said to have existed and we are off!" Simon announced excitedly.

The group of thirteen left the room and each went in different directions to give orders to their groups. Nuncio instructed the groundskeepers to saddle three extra horses for the journey to accommodate Simon, Malachai, and Safra. Prisca informed Clancy to pack more rations to include the extra three people, and Simon instructed Shannon to search for some extra camping gear.

Safra went to pack for the journey ahead, always packing her herbal medicines and tonics just in case the need should arise. With Jason's ability to heal, her talents weren't needed nearly as much if at all, but she still liked to be prepared.

Jason, Seth, Oz, and Sofia went in search of their friends to inform them of the new mission and share some of the details. Jason scanned the area around them to make sure no one was within earshot.

"You all do remember that we still have a thief among us?"

Oz looked at him with a side-ways glance. "Sure do. Any a' ya' have any clue as ta who it might be yet?"

Sofia shrugged her shoulders. "None. Of course, I'm not as familiar with everyone as you and Seth are, Jason. Perhaps Zaccai, Nick, or Zeke have had a breakthrough."

Seth replied, "I'm not particularly familiar with a lot of these people either. It hasn't been that long ago that I met most of them. But I have a few suspicions. I'm not ready to voice them yet, not until I'm more certain. I don't wish to sway anyone else's opinion with my own."

Jason shook his head in agreement with Seth's comment. "We need to call a meeting with the other Peregrine leaders before we get under-way. We need to devise a plan to fetter the thief out. The longer it takes to retrieve that key the more chance he or she has to make it disappear for good. If whoever has it is one of us on the mission trips, then the key could again be easily left in another time period."

"Perhaps, but God could lead us to it again if He chooses," Sofia replied.

"Yes, but when? We had it, but it disappeared. Who's to say He will give us another opportunity. We need to be more careful with our findings from now on," Jason answered her.

"Speaking of which, does anyone know where they put the Belts?" Seth looked around at the other three.

"Sure do, sort a'," Oz stated. "Simon an' Malachai took 'em an' hid 'em somewhere. Said they weren't takin' any chances either. Probl'y the same place they hid the other archive books."

Everyone looked at him questioningly.

"I noticed they were missin' b'fore we left fer Timna Valley. Guess they don't trust some a' the others in the house neither."

"Or they're just being extra careful," Sofia stated.

Just then, they came upon most of the others sitting on the covered veranda awaiting orders. No one had ventured too far off, knowing that very soon they would all be leaving again on another mission.

Jason informed them all of the mission details, and everyone departed shortly after to pack and get ready to leave. The plan was to meet at the stables and head out in about an hour. Seth, Jason, and Oz each went in search of the other Peregrine leaders for a brief meeting before leaving, agreeing to meet in the small conference room at the back of the house in fifteen minutes.

Seth, Jason, Nicholas, Ezekial, Zaccai, Oz, and Sofia, all gathered around the small table in the middle of the room. They closed the door and locked it to avoid anyone stumbling into the meeting at an inopportune moment and began the discussion with Jason's lead.

"We need to devise a plan to maximize our search for this betrayer. I feel like we aren't making much, if any headway with this problem. Have any of you found out anything or have any clues yet?"

Zaccai answered, "I agree. We all need to take a more active approach to finding them and the key. There could be important information in the unopened book that could benefit us now. However, I still have no clue as to who it might be."

"Nor do I," Zeke answered.

Nick spoke next. "I've been trying to watch others for suspicious or unusual behavior but have seen nothing. Whoever it is, either is not one of us on the missions, or they are a very good actor. I usually have a gift for discerning people's motives or intentions, but I have no clue on this one."

"Do you think it could be someone staying here on the island? There are a lot of people still here. About twenty or so to be exact. It could very well be one of them," Zeke offered.

"Yes," Zaccai answered. "Malachai said they have thought of that and the Dragoman are watching here as well."

Seth listened to the conversations and answered, "I suggest that we each take more time on this next mission and get to know some of the others. Perhaps those of you who have been traveling with people for a long time may be too close to them to be suspicious of them. Maybe everyone should pick someone outside our own groups to get to know better. We can all still keep our eyes open around everyone else as well."

"Sounds like a plan ta me," Oz interjected. "We also need ta maybe take turns stayin' up after bedtime, without the other's knowledge, to watch fer any suspicious activity. The thief ain't likely gonna' do anythin' durin' daylight hours."

"Good idea, Oz," Jason offered. "I'll take first watch tonight. Then later, we'll decide who will take the next night and so forth. All right, everyone, let's catch us a thief and find the next piece of armor."

They left the office and went to pack their things for the long journey. Unfortunately, not one of them noticed the dark figure that darted into the linen closet just before the door opened. The hooded figure clung tightly to the note that they had quickly scribbled out. They threw the robe off, stuffing it beneath some of the extra sheets in the closet, then ventured upstairs to the bedrooms. They knocked on the door with no answer and went into the room to leave the note in the agreed upon place for their correspondence.

Stopping to think for just a brief moment, reconsidering their role in all of this, they placed the note in the usual spot in the hidden drawer in the bedside table. Then, left the room and went about their normal duties.

They headed downstairs in search of the intended recipient, found them, and nodded ever so slightly to let them know of the exchange.

The intended recipient climbed the large set of steps, entered their room, pulled out the secret drawer and retrieved the note. Just as they were about to read it, a knock was heard on the bedroom door and a voice called out.

"Hey, did you forget something in your room? We're just about to leave. Everyone is mounting up. Malachai sent me to find you," Dominic yelled against the closed door.

They quickly stuffed the unread note into a pocket, opened the door and greeted the young boy.

"Yes, just coming. I had left my weapon on the foot of the bed," they replied, patting the side of the hilt where the sword hung.

The two ventured outside, mounted their horses, and rode out with the others into the opened portal to the year 835 AD, in Cornwall, England.

Simon pulled the reins of his horse to turn and address the large group of riders that were gathering around him. They had just exited the portal into the cover of the lush, thick forest of northern Cornwall, and were pulling to a stop to get their bearings on which direction to head next.

"I suggest you all be very careful about using your powers, no matter what happens. We can't chance having any of the locals see any of your abilities or you could be labeled witches. These are times of little to no education, and they are heaped with superstitions."

"Simon." Oz pulled up beside him. "I suggest we find a place ta go ahead an' make camp. We only got a few hours b'fore dark sets in, and with this many people it'll take us a few hours to set'le in."

"Good suggestion, Oz. All right everyone, let's find a large enough clearing to make camp."

They traveled through the forest for about another half an hour before finding an adequate area to use. The leaders set out in different directions to scout the area surrounding the camp to make sure it was secure, while the others set about making camp. They were so used to traveling that they worked as a well-oiled machine, having the tents up, fire built, and dinner on before the scouts returned.

"All secure on all fronts," Jason called from horseback as the riders returned together after meeting up in the forest. After dismounting, they gathered with the rest of the group around the fire, keeping their steeds' reigns in hand until they could unsaddle them and corral them for the night.

"How close to civilization are we?" Simon questioned.

Seth answered. "About five miles due north there is a small village just on the edge of the forest. I didn't catch a name."

"Perhaps the Portgen can identify it for us?" Caroline answered.

"Good thinking, Caroline." Simon praised her quick thought.

Putting in the approximate coordinates of the village that Seth found, Seth did indeed find its name. "It says here that it's called Tintagel." He read from the digital screen of the Portgen.

"Well, looks like we came out at just the right spot," Simon said grinning.

"Why is that?" questioned Zaccai.

"King Arthur supposedly reigned from Tintagel Castle," Caroline answered.

"Ah, you know British history, Caroline," Simon said.

"Yes. Actually, I know a lot of history from just about anywhere. My father was head librarian at the San Francisco library for years. I grew up around books, devouring anything I could get my hands on to read." She grinned.

"I read about King Arthur and Merlin in school, but I don't remember ever being taught where they supposedly lived except for Camelot," Nick said.

"Well, unless you studied British history extensively, you wouldn't have known about Tintagel being the suspected place of Camelot. The castle sets on the edge of the sea, above a cave known as Merlin's Cave. They say that he lived there beneath the castle from which Arthur reigned."

"That sounds awfully exciting. King Arthur is legendary where I'm from." Bridget wiggled in her seat, clapping her hands together in anticipation of seeing it.

Several others giggled at her excitement as well.

Dominic rolled his eyes at her silly, little girl attitude. She was sixteen after-all. You'd think by now she would act her age. He liked her as a person, but good grief, her personality sometimes grated on his nerves. She was a year older than him, yet sometimes seemed like she was twelve, like his irritating younger cousin Gina back home.

He looked at all the people around the fire, studying them. Being an artistic type of person, he studied everything. People were so different, and he noticed things about others that most people tended to miss. For example, he could tell who liked who, who was hiding something, who thought a lot about themselves, and who the honest and down to earth people were. Not that everyone didn't have something to hide or some dark secrets of their own, but for the most part, there was a complete difference in demeanor and mannerisms between the different personalities. Such as, he could tell that Wade liked Gabriele, but she wasn't interested. Alec and Odessa, usually chummy and getting along great, were fighting about something, and that Alec was the one who was angry. He knew that Uriah was more on edge since the Peregrines all joined forces, but that could just be his personality as usual; he always seemed to be on edge. Timothy had grown more cockier than usual since the demon battle yesterday, walking around every once in a while, puffing out his chest. Sean liked Kristin and maybe she liked him back, but Timothy also liked Kristin. Dominic couldn't tell if she liked Tim in that way or not. Sean and Timothy barely tolerated each other because of their mutual feelings for Kristin. Oz and Sofia were pretty laid back. Oz was someone that Dominic wanted to get to know better. He seemed like he had a lot of interesting stories of past adventures to tell. Seth was a giant, gentle bear, but fierce if needed. He saw things as matter of fact, no grey areas. Caroline was extremely intelligent, with a gentle heart as well. Jason was very military minded from being a marine. He expected order, timeliness, truthfulness, and loyalty. He was a man of great honor and wisdom. Zaccai was a fierce warrior with dignity, integrity, and honor. She told you what was on her mind whether you liked it or not. Ezekial seemed to be a crazy Australian. He liked to joke around and have fun, but when it was time to get down to business, he took charge. Nick was interesting to Dominic and perhaps the hardest to draw. The fact that he could fight like he does with an artificial limb was really cool, but there always seemed to be something lurking behind his demeanor. He wasn't sure what it was, but Nick seemed to be hiding a lot from his past. Nadia was beautiful, graceful, and kindhearted, and also noticed people's personalities and pain. He noticed *her* watching people, and she noticed *him* watching people. They've had several shared moments smiling at each other's knowing.

Dominic spent most of his evenings, drawing and sketching his fellow Peregrines and Keepers in their everyday settings. Maybe even one day, he could catch some glimpses of everyone in battle and commit those images to memory. The first, and last demon battle had been too scary to even try. It was all he could do just to stay alive, much less remember anything significant, other than Dinah's death. He had drawn her adorned body and the emotions of the funeral proceedings. He supposed that was how he dealt with his own pain, by committing them to paper, looking at them, and then putting them away.

Gabriele approached him as he was lost in thought, scribbling away almost robotic like on his paper, sketching the scene in front of him, and the emotions tied into it.

"Hey, Dom, what are you drawing now?" Gabriele was under the same mentor as Dominic and was used to his constant sketching.

He was extremely talented and captured people's likenesses and moods very well. She glanced down at his pad, looking back and forth between reality and the sketch. She grinned at some of what she saw. Especially the pining-look on poor Wade's face as he stared at her across the low-lit fire.

"You're really good, you do know that right?" she said to him in awe.

"Yeah," he cockily stated, then grinned at her pretended look of shock at his brazen answer.

"What are you going to do with all of these?" she asked, motioning to his stacks of sketch pads.

"I don't know. Maybe Malachai and the other Dragoman would want them for the archival library. After all, they are historical representations of our travels and missions."

"I think that would be a really great use for all of them." She stood up offering her hand to her young friend. "Come on, let's go get something to eat before you get lost in these and forget to actually put food in your stomach."

Dominic grinned up at her, placed his pad and pencil in his backpack, and took the offered hand-up.

Darkness soon descended on the camp; the low burning fire crackled occasionally as it slowly died out. The moonlight barely made its way through the thick upper canopy lending little light to the night sentries. Everyone had bedded down an hour or so before and the camp was quiet except for the occasional snoring or dream-talkers. Jason watched the camp as closely as possible, trying to keep an eye open for any strange activity coming from the tents. The two night-guards on watch tonight were Timothy and Nadia, and Jason tried to remember where everyone else was, and who shared accommodations with whom. Most were divided up into groups of two or three per tent.

Jason squatted at the opening of his own tent and scanned the perimeter of the camp once more, stopping briefly when he thought he saw a dim light, perhaps from a flashlight, coming from one of the tents. It was so brief that he wasn't sure that what he actually saw was real or just imagined. He couldn't get a very good vantage point having to stay in his tent. Maybe he would take a little walk. If anyone asked, he would just tell them he had to go to the bathroom.

Climbing out of the tent that he shared with Oz and Simon, he slunk his way as quietly as possible around the camp, checking for any signs of movement.

Now that everyone was basically asleep and without the worry of prying, questioning eyes, they removed the folded paper from their pocket, took the tiny flashlight and placed it beneath the covers of the sleeping bag so as not to wake the others who shared the tent. The note read:

You need to be careful. I believe the peregrination leaders are searching for something or someone. It was hard to hear through the thickness of the locked door. Watch your step. Something is going on, and I'm not sure what.

They folded the note back up, shoved it back into their shirt pocket, and quickly shut off the flashlight. They lay there for the next several minutes, wondering if the message meant that the Dragoman realized that the key was missing. They wondered themselves as to whether or not it was the right key. They hadn't had time to check it before leaving. They reached into their bag to the padded, hidden, zippered compartment near the bottom, unzipped it and felt for the key. It was still there. What to do with it? Maybe it wasn't the right key after all. Maybe the secrets hidden within the book are no more than actual historical facts or instructions like much of the others. If the information that is in that last book will do what Hiram Burke thought it would, then getting their hands on that book could be the game changer for their future and for the world. They needed to get a good look at that book before the others did. Placing the key back into its hiding place, they hunkered down and drifted off to sleep.

Jason was certain he saw a small flash of light, but several of the tents overlapped somewhat from the directional view of his tent opening. In the morning, he would see who all slept in the three tents that could have held the light he saw. It could be nothing at all, but they would have to follow any and all leads if they were going to come up with anything useful.

The camp was quiet and dark, and Nadia had already found him and had asked why he was out wandering about the camp, so he decided to call it a night and get the few precious hours of sleep that he had left. If anyone else emerged, or anything else seemed out of place, he would ask the night guards in the morning.

For our light and momentary troubles are achieving for us
an eternal glory that far outweighs them all.

2 Corinthians 4:17

Chapter 12

Tintagel Forest, England 835 AD

Jason woke just a few hours later, hoping that he would be the first person up moving around to try and watch who emerged from the tents in question. However, when he opened his tent flaps, he noticed about eight or so people already out and about. Perhaps he could get with the other leaders later on and see if they could flesh out who was bunking with who. The only problem with this theory was, if they moved camp today then he would never know what he saw and be unable to possibly narrow their suspects down. He noticed Seth sitting by the campfire with a cup of coffee in hand, so he walked over, grabbed himself a steaming cup from the fire-stand pot, and joined his friend on an obliging log.

"Morning, Seth."

"Good morning, Jason. Get any ideas last night?" Seth asked as cryptically as possible in case they were overheard by anyone.

"I did see something, but I'm not sure what exactly." Jason blew the steam from his cup before sipping from it.

"Where?" Seth followed his friends' example.

Jason nodded to the areas where the tents sat. "I saw a flash of light in the early morning hours in one of those three tents over there. It was brief, but I'm hoping it meant something." He glanced around them to make sure no one was standing too close.

"You're not sure which one it was?"

"No. My angle of observation was off. By the time I stood up to see better the light had been turned off. It could be nothing, but it's worth looking into. We need to see who all is sharing those three tents that line up with my tent front. You didn't happen to see who came out of those did you?" Jason gestured slightly with his head.

Seth studied the area and angle of Jason's tent front from his seat by the fire, trying to gauge which three tents he would have seen.

"I did see Timothy and Uriah come out of one. Sean came out of another. I think the other one belongs to some of the women, but I'm not sure who all is in there or if anyone came out. Some people were already up when I woke up."

"Well, let's just sit and drink our coffee and see if anyone else comes out. Hopefully camp will stay put for another night and we can get a good idea about who's sleeping where."

The two men sat inconspicuously watching the tents, chatting with the others who made their way to the fireside to visit with them. They did notice Sofia and Nadia come out of one of the women's tents. Dominic appeared out of one of the others, but that was all they saw. So far their suspects for the mysterious nightlight was, Timothy, Uriah, Dominic, and Sean. Sofia was one of the leaders looking for the betrayer, and Nadia had been on night-watch duty when the event took place, so neither of them were under suspicion.

When Sofia joined them by the fire, Jason leaned over and quietly whispered in her ear with a question of who her tent-mates were.

"Well, in our tent is me, Nadia, Kristin, and Bridget. I think Gabriele, Zaccai, Odessa, and Safra share the other women's tent."

Seth leaned forward. "Did you happen to see who else was in the other two tents that are near yours?"

"No, sorry. I went to bed early last night due to a beginning headache."

Finishing off their coffee and a quick bite to eat, they stood to get on with the mission ahead of them.

The leaders decided that four of them, Jason, Seth, Zaccai, and Oz would go to the village, including Simon, while the other three leaders Nicholas, Zeke, and Sofia, would stay in camp to continue the search for the betrayer.

The five of them set out for the village located near Tintagel Castle just to have a look around. After giving everyone explicit instructions and duties concerning hunting for dinner, prepping the meals, gathering firewood, and taking turns keeping watch for any travelers who might stumble upon their camp, they headed out. Tintagel was only a forty-five-minute ride, and once they arrived, they were surprised by how large the bustling village was and what it had to offer.

Seth watched as people milled about the streets, beginning their workday. Some tended to the village market booths while others led horses and oxen hitched to carts out of town, possibly to some field somewhere to either plow or harvest their crops. Carts loaded with produce, wood, animal pelts, barrels of ale, water, and salted curing meats passed by them in the streets, along with some curious people who watched them. He especially noted they watched Zaccai. He assumed it was because she was dressed a bit differently than the other women from this period; her weapons strapped to her back and hanging from her side like a man. She also wore pants and a shirt, not a dress. Apparently, a woman wearing these clothes and brandishing a weapon was a rare sight in these days. That is, if that was why people were looking. Zaccai was a very attractive woman who commanded attention with the way she carried herself. Now that he thought about it, practically all the women who were Peregrines seemed to stand tall and command respect. He supposed it was their way of life that gave them that quality. They had to fight along-side men. To kill or be killed. These women saw and experienced things regularly that most normal men would never encounter in a lifetime.

The thought gave him a greater respect for his female friends, especially his sweet, loving, Caroline. He would have never imagined her doing the things that were required of her now, and yet she handled it brilliantly, as if she were born to it. He supposed that she *was* in a way. God did choose them for it after all. Set them all apart at an early age for peregrinating. His mind turned to the younger kids; the barely teenagers. Of course, it isn't much different than what he had learned to deal with when he was fourteen and boarded a boat headed anywhere to live the life of a sailor. He had learned at a young age that life was hard, but one thing that had been different for him was that he hadn't had to deal with demons. That was quite disturbing to him the first time he saw one in its true form. He wondered how they had handled that being so young? Wade, Dominic, Bridget, and Gabriele have handled this life with understanding and grace, as if it was just the way things were supposed to be. It made him curious as to the sort of lives they may have left behind to be able to take to this one with such ease. Of course, several had been living this way much longer than he had. Bridget was another story all together. Caroline had told him of her lonely existence and the daily fear of the witch hunts that she had lived with. Her new life must seem like an answer to a long-awaited prayer.

Seth turned to look at the older man he had come to respect and appreciate as a father figure, and the look on Simon's face brought a smile to his own.

Simon grinned broadly at his new adventure as the five of them rode through the dirt-packed streets. The road turned north and when they rounded the corner near some very tall buildings Tintagel Castle came into view. It sat off in the distance on the outskirts of the village, commanding the eastern point of the land near the rocky water's edge of the Atlantic Ocean. Simon noticed the castle sat high up on the cliffs, and he figured it must have a spectacular view of the ocean that stretched out far beneath it. The anticipation to see it up close welled up inside Simon and was enough to make him want to spur his horse on at full speed, but he held back, reigning in his own excitement.

Everyone was in awe of the breathtaking views, making the ride up to the castle a quiet one except for the cry of seagulls riding on the ocean's salty breeze, and the muffled sound of crashing waves emanating up from far below. They quietly took in the massive dwelling and the spectacular scenery around them. The large, towering, slate-stone castle sat on the cliff's edge overlooking a small inlet. The road leading up to it sat between rising, wind-swept, grasses to the left, and to the right it stretched along the steep cliffs that lent a remarkable view of the sea far below. The coastline, which was mostly craggy rocks, gave way to a small, sandy, beach where one of the entrances to the cave of Merlin was most likely located.

Simon had inquired as to the castle's occupants while in the village, receiving the same answer from all. Its current resident was a Lord Percival Cumbrey. He had been the village overseer for the last thirty years or more. King Arthur was not mentioned by any of the villagers nor was Merlin, but that did not dampen Simon's spirits. If Arthur had reigned within the last sixty or seventy years, he was certain he would hear about his deeds from someone. Maybe later that evening in the village tavern they would have some luck. If that proved ineffectual, they would just go further into the future or back into the past. But he felt certain he would likely meet one of them. Odessa's vision had specifically named Arthur and Excalibur. But then there was Safra's vision of the Knights Templar which was a bit confusing to him. Simon's research had placed the Knights Templar much later nearer the Renaissance age, beginning in the early 1100s.

The castle's open courtyard was accessible to everyone who passed the guard's checkpoint. Jason noticed the guards were making people remove their weapons at the gate.

"Simon," Jason stated turning in his saddle to address the man. "Since there is no real need to enter the castle, I suggest we head straight down to the water's edge. Now would be a good time to get a look at the cave below while the tide is out."

"You're right. We know that Arthur or Merlin are not here so the cave sounds like a good idea to me."

"I'll ask the guard how to get down there." Jason turned and headed toward the gate.

"Excuse me sir," he said to the man, "my uncle is ill and wishes to see the coastline up close before his time is up. Is there a road down to the water below the castle?"

"Yeah, just a bit further up the main road there is a side pass that leads down there."

"Thank you kindly. I don't want to deny a dying man his last wish." Jason's slightly anguished tone lending validity to the situation, as Simon coughed and sputtered a bit to sell the tall-tale. Jason returned to his party who had already began to ride out.

"Dying man? Do I look that feeble?" Simon asked.

"Of course not, Simon. I just didn't want to raise any suspicion with all of us heading down the path for no obvious reason." Jason grinned mischievously at Simon's obvious discomfort.

Simon cleared his throat and sat taller in his saddle.

The ride down the cliffside road took another twenty minutes before they reached the small sandy shoreline. The beach was a small one and finding the cave was very easy indeed. From the dampness of the sand and rock inside the cave it was obvious that the cavern filled with water at high tide.

Seth and Jason lit the few torches they brought to stay in keeping with the era while everyone else carried flashlights. They didn't want to be caught with the new devices in this era for certain. If anyone happened down behind them, they would quickly hide the flashlights leaving only the flaming torches visible, and no one would be the wiser.

The cave was dark and damp, and according to the information they had, it was three-hundred and thirty feet in length, passing through the entire island from the east side to the west. Since it was so long and may take them a while to explore it, they decided to take the horses in with them and exit the other side instead of returning the way they came. Besides, they didn't want to get caught inside during high tides and possibly lose the animals.

"What exactly should we be lookin' fer, Simon?" Oz stated, scanning the area.

"I'm not sure, Oz, anything out of the ordinary. If this is the cave that Merlin was rumored to live in there must be something else to it, such as a hidden passage of sorts. I doubt he moved somewhere else every time the tide came in."

"Not likely. He prob'ly has a hidden area down here somewhere. He was supposed ta have been a wizard after all. Kinda' like the hidden rooms you have back at yer place, Simon."

"Yes, Oz, you're correct. Very good point." Simon closed his eyes and raised his hands and staff in the air as he spoke a revealing spell into the large passage's interior. Nothing came of it.

"Well, there doesn't appear to be anything in this area. The spell only reveals what is in proximity of my vision. I will continue to speak it as we walk. It may take some time to get through the cave but, this is what we are here for after-all."

"Simon," Zaccai stated, "shouldn't the others be here as well? The rules clearly state that all of "The Twelve" must be present to locate the pieces."

"Perhaps, but not all "Twelve" went with Jason to find the belts. I assume since they are all here on the present mission that that is enough."

Seth looked back at the cavern opening at the waves that began to pound the shoreline. "I think there might be a storm coming on, Simon. The waves are getting fiercer, meaning that the cave could fill even without high tide. I suggest we quickly ride through to the other side and come back tomorrow."

"Yes, I believe you are right, Seth. All right everyone, mount up and let's get out of here as quickly as possible."

They galloped the horses as quickly as they could in the dim light of the passageway. The tide had already crept into the caves opening up to the horse's ankles which made them a tad bit skittish.

They exited the western side just as the rains began to pound the earth.

They rode up the side of the grassy cliffs headed in the direction of camp. The rain's intensity was increasing as the wind began to die down, dropping heavy droplets of rain straight down upon their drenched bodies. The ride back to camp was quicker since they had exited several miles past the edge of town. When they arrived back at camp the rain had slowed to a steady drizzle, and the party of five was met by some of the others who took the horses reigns to unsaddle and corral them, while Simon and the others headed to their tents for a dry change of clothing.

Everyone met in the camp center where a larger twenty by twenty meeting tent had been erected for such occasions as today's rain. All twenty-two of them piled into the tent, some carrying steaming plates of food to Simon and the others who had recently returned from the scouting trip. Everyone conversed amongst themselves while they awaited the others to finish off their meal and warm up.

Simon placed his empty plate on the small table at the back of the tent and began to speak.

"Well, I'm sure you're all anxious to hear of our findings today so let's get started, shall we?" The talking hushed as everyone gave him their full attention. "We did find the cave of Merlin but was unable to truly explore it as we had hoped. The storm surge literally ran us from the cave just in time before it filled any further. With today's rain and the late afternoon hour, we shall wait and all head into town tomorrow to see what else we can find out. You will all split into groups of four and spread out, all taking different areas of the town. Talk to the people about their local legends and see if anyone mentions King Arthur or Merlin, the Knights of the Round Table, anything that has to do with Arthurian legend. I, Malachai, Jason, and Oz, will head back down to the cavern to see if we can find any hidden passages. We'll all meet back here before nightfall. I warn you all, do not use your powers here. You will be found as witches for certain and burned at the stake. Many a person has died for far less than what you are all capable of doing. Safra, I will need you to make a sketch of the town so that everyone can see where they are to search."

"I can help with that Simon if you like?" Dominic chimed in. "We could make copies for everyone to take with them."

"All right, thank you, Dominic. Everyone has a little down time this evening. We'll present the maps and search areas after dinner."

Everyone continued with their light conversations while the rain continued outside. Dominic rushed to his tent to retrieve his sketch pad and pencils for the mapping.

Timothy watched Kristen leave the tent and head outside. He followed her, hoping this would be the moment he had been waiting for to speak with her privately.

Kristen ducked underneath the canvas material that had been stretched over the cooking area. She reached for the steaming kettle of coffee to pour herself a cup. No matter how warm the temperature was outside, every time it rained, she always took a slight chill. She stood staring off into the rain-soaked woods, breathing deeply of the clean scent the rain always brought with it. She didn't notice Timothy who came to stand behind her.

He leaned down over her shoulder and spoke.

"Enjoying your coffee?"

His words caused her to jump, spilling the hot liquid all over herself and him.

"Timothy! Good grief, what are you doing sneaking up on people like that?" Her irritation at him evident as she wiped at the spilled, hot, liquid all over her shirt front.

"Sorry, Kristen. Why are you so jumpy?" He smiled at her, but she didn't return one.

"Oh, I don't know, Timothy. Let me see, new place, on a mission, not sure who, or what, could walk up on us at any minute. Not to mention I thought I was alone." She rattled off, blowing at the burning skin of her right forearm. She stuck it out from underneath the canopy to allow the coolness of the rain to ease her burning skin.

"Here, let me see your arm." Tim took it in his hands and pulled it out of the rain, examining the red skin.

Kristin unsuccessfully tried to pull her arm away from his grasp. "It will be fine, just let it cool down in the rain." She began to feel uncomfortable as it felt like the heat was creeping up her chest and neck to her face at the touch of his hand on her arm. She was still attracted to him regardless of her feelings for Sean. She had never had a man as good-looking as Timothy interested in her before. He was extremely confident as well, and this alone made her nervous enough.

She watched as he held her arm up and leaned over, blowing on the redness of it. Kristen swallowed hard at the sensation it made upon her skin.

Timothy looked up at her face, smiling ever so slightly at the look in her eyes. He knew he was having an effect on her. *Good*, he thought.

Kristen straightened her stance and cleared her throat before speaking. Not wishing to let on as to the effect he was having on her.

"You can let go of my arm now, thanks." She managed to pull it free from his hesitant grasp. "Um…it looks like I spilled some of the hot coffee on you as well." She pointed to his shirt front which was now stained with the dark liquid.

"Oh, so you did," he said looking down at his shirt. "No matter, it's just a shirt." He gazed down into her eyes.

Kristen began to back up slightly at the discomfort of his nearness.

"Surely it burns like my arm does?"

"No. Actually, I don't feel a thing. Just the sensation of water on my skin. My gift is armored skin, remember?"

"I don't understand how that works. If you can't feel pain and nothing can pierce your skin, how does that affect how you feel everything else?"

"I don't understand it either, but I *can* feel everything else. The rain on my skin, the wind, the heat, and the sun's rays." He took Kristen's hand in his and placed her open, flat, palm against his chest, holding her hand there with his own. "Someone's touch."

Kristen's breath caught in her throat as their eyes locked.

"Kristen," Timothy barely breathed, "I really like you, and I want to see if we could manage having a relationship."

"I...can't, Tim. Not now." She abruptly pulled her hand away and crossed her arms against her chest, suddenly feeling the burning sensation in her arm again.

"Why, Kristen? I know you have feelings for me. I can see it in your eyes."

"Yes, I do. I'm just unsure what those feelings are. And, until I know, I'm not jumping into a relationship with you or anyone else." Kristen turned from him and ran out into the now pouring rain to her tent, disappearing inside and zipping it closed.

Tim watched her go, unsatisfied with how the conversation went. He usually got what he wanted, and right now, that was Kristen. He would eventually wear her down, he knew he would. He grinned ever so slightly to himself, knowing he had some effect on her. He was certain that it wouldn't be much longer before he could sway her in his direction.

Sean stood beneath the minimal cover of the tree canopy, watching the scene between Timothy and Kristen unfold. It was all he could do not to march over and punch Timothy in the face, but it wasn't his right. Kristen and he were not in a relationship and she was free to do as she wished. It was a bit hard to see through the now pouring rain, but he was encouraged by her pulling away, and he thought he saw her shake her head no to something just before she ran to her tent. All he could do was pray that God would give them both a clear answer as to what to do. He knew she struggled with having a relationship with Timothy, but he didn't know why. A few weeks back on Reader's Island it had appeared that she had been very interested in the man. What had changed since then to make her so hesitant now? He shrugged the rain from his jacket, pulled the hood further down over his face, and turned toward his own tent to mull things over in his mind. He needed to figure out what was going on, just for his own peace of mind, and he prayed it would be soon.

Kristen changed out of her wet clothing as her mind reeled. Confusion returning to her tumultuous feelings that tore her between Timothy and Sean. Even though Sean had yet to express any feelings other than friendship for her, she couldn't deny she had feelings for him. Both men were vastly different people in every way, yet both attracted her. She had to admit that she preferred Sean to Timothy, but Sean just didn't seem to feel that way about her. Timothy obviously did and didn't mind telling her so. Kristen curled up in her sleeping bag and began to pray that God would lead her in the right direction, even if it meant that neither man was the one for her. She soon drifted off to sleep as she prayed.

Back at the large central meeting tent most everyone else was still hanging out inside, gingerly chatting with each other. Down time with nothing to do wasn't something they got much of, so most everyone was taking advantage of it.

Odessa sat and watched Alec laugh and converse with some of the others. Since their argument back on Reader's Island he had hardly spoken two words to her, or from what she could tell, even looked her way. He had never before been so upset with her like he was now, and the lack of communication was tearing at her heart. Alec had been her best friend for the last eight years and now she couldn't even talk to him about what the problem was because *she was* the problem. She would need to speak to him soon to set things right. He couldn't keep avoiding her all the time. It was easy to do right now with all the extra people to take their attentions, but they would have to settle things soon. Odessa needed her best friend back, but she wasn't at all sure that Alec was willing to fill that role anymore. She had hurt him deeply with her rejection of his exclamations of love for her. She loved Alec; she just wasn't sure that what she felt was romantic love.

Nadia had noticed there was a problem between the avid friends, Alec Chevalier, and Odessa Megalos. They were usually inseparable but now did not speak at all. Odessa was sitting alone in a corner of the tent watching Alec. She appeared to need a friend, so Nadia walked over to speak with her.

"Odessa, are you all right? You seem a bit forlorn." Nadia took a seat next to her.

"Yes, just dealing with some personal things that crept up recently."

"You mean between Alec and yourself?"

Odessa blanched at her question. "Is it that obvious?"

"Well, I'm not sure it is to everyone, just myself and Dominic." She grinned slightly at the woman. "We are both very perceptive people. We pay attention to things that happen all around us. Perhaps it is our artistic natures that afford us this perception."

"If only I had some of that perception then perhaps this awkward situation could have been avoided?"

"I don't believe that would have been possible. How do you avoid someone falling in love with you?"

"My goodness, you are perceptive!" Odessa said with surprise.

"You do not love him in return?"

"I do love Alec, I'm just not sure I am *in* love with him."

"Then perhaps this time apart from each other would allow you to sort through your feelings for him. Perhaps give him some time to heal, unless your answer to his question is favorable to him. I am certain he is still hurting from your rejection. But perhaps you should tell him that you need time to make sure about your feelings, just so he does not think that you are avoiding him completely."

"How did you become such a wise person, Nadia?" Odessa grinned at the woman's advice.

"Experience. My life has afforded me with much experience." Nadia grinned at the woman, patted her hand, and stood to leave the large tent for the privacy of her own. Sometimes talking to others about their problems would allow memories from her past to surface. She could handle it most days, but on rare occasions the memories became too much and she needed alone time to deal with them. God had granted her peace long ago, but the memories never fully disappeared.

Odessa watched her go, realizing for the first time that there was a sadness that lay beneath Nadia's jovial exterior. She was a quiet person, never said much but always seemed joyful. She wondered about Nadia's "experience" as she had called it. Perhaps one day Odessa could give her the same kindness that Nadia had given her. Someone to simply talk to and listen. Odessa grinned and stood, making her way toward Alec.

"Alec, can I speak with you?"

He turned to her almost unwillingly. "Certainly." His answer was short as he turned, crossing his arms across his chest.

"Privately, Alec," she insisted.

Alec excused himself from the conversation he was having with some of the others.

"All right. Where would you like to go?" he asked, as they walked away.

"How about I pour you a cup of coffee?"

"After you." Alec motioned her ahead of him out of the tent into the still pouring rain. When they reached the cover of the cooking area's canopy, they both shook the rain from their hair and clothing. Odessa grabbed two of the metal cups, poured them coffee and added cream and sugar to both. She had spent enough time around Alec to know almost everything about him. She handed him the cup and without looking at her he added a quick, "Thank you."

"Alec," she began, "this has to stop. You are my best friend in the entire world and for us that is saying a lot. I'm sorry if I hurt you, but you have to give me time. This is a big decision, one that will affect both of us forever, regardless of the outcome. I'm not willing to lose your friendship if a loving relationship doesn't work out. Please, just give me time to sort out my feelings. You know you're the most important person in the world to me."

"Yes, I know. But that could one day change, Dee. I have been patient for eight years. Seeing the others together has made me realize that I have wasted very many of those days. I don't wish to waste any more. But I will give you the time for which you ask. Just know that I won't wait forever for someone who has no desire to be with me. I only hope you can sort your feelings out quickly. I am a fiercely loyal person, Dee. You know this. Understand that I do not give my love easily, but when I do it is forever and unbreakable." Alec drained his cup, placed it on the table and looked her in the eyes. Before she knew what hit her, he had reached up behind her head and pulled her to him, planting a gentle but passionate kiss on her lips that relayed to her the love and truth of what he spoke. He slowly let her go and looked at her. "That should give you something to think on." He then turned from the canopy and left.

Odessa stood there; shock written across her features. Alec had never been that forceful with her before. Not in the way he spoke to her and he had never dared to kiss her before. Odessa brushed her lips with her fingertips, the sensation of his lips on hers still fresh. She wasn't sure how she felt about that kiss, but it certainly stirred feelings in her she didn't know existed. However, she wasn't sure if they were for Alec or the fact that it had been *way* to long since she *had* been kissed. She sighed, leaned against the large tree trunk that hung down against the forest floor, sipped her coffee, and listened to the sound of the rain falling against the different textures of the forest and their tents, lost in thought as she tried to make sense of it all.

The end of a matter is better than its beginning,
and patience is better than pride.

Ecclesiastes 7:8

Chapter 13

The rain continued to drizzle well into the midnight hour before it finally stopped. When everyone awoke the next morning, the ground was still very wet as it was early, and the lack of sunlight prohibited the drying of the forest floor. The thick tree canopy also forbade what little sunlight that was trying to penetrate through.

Seth and Zeke took turns last night watching and observing the camp for any unusual happenings. Neither one saw anything out of the ordinary, but they did nail down who was sleeping where. The three tents in question were one women's tent, and they already knew who was in there. One men's tent which held Uriah, Zeke, and Timothy. The other was Nick and Sean, the two of them sharing one tent along with most of the camping supplies that needed to stay dry. So, their suspects were Uriah, Timothy, Sean, Kristin, and Bridget. And this was only based on the strange, late-night nightlight, which could be absolutely nothing at all.

Last night, during downtime, the leaders got together and discussed what it might have meant. Zaccai had asked if whoever it was could have been examining the key, or maybe someone had taken the book it belonged to as well and had opened it. That was quickly squelched by Simon who told them the books were safe and sound in a hideaway on Reader's Island. They may have been looking at the key, but why risk being caught just for that? Was there something else that was of interest that the betrayer needed to hide? They formed a plan, deciding when everyone went to town today two of the leaders would stay behind in camp to search through everyone's things for the key.

Zeke heard Zaccai volunteer to stay behind and he quickly followed suit. He had wanted a chance to get to talk to her more and this was the perfect opportunity.

Just after breakfast everyone saddled their horses, packed a few necessary items into their shoulder bags, strapped on their weapons and was ready to mount up. Timothy noticed that Zaccai was traveling rather light. Actually, she appeared to be lagging behind the rest of them.

"Zaccai, why aren't you ready to go?" he asked her.

"Ezekial and I are staying behind to watch over camp. We can't leave all of our equipment unattended. Thieves could come in and take everything."

"Too bad you won't get to explore the town."

"I saw it yesterday, remember? Not a big deal to miss out today." She grinned at him.

"See you later then." He mounted his steed as she acknowledged him with a nod.

Zeke and Zaccai waited for an hour after everyone had ridden out before beginning their search. They didn't want anyone returning unexpectedly to find them rifling through their belongings.

"I feel a little guilty going through our friends' things like this," Zeke stated as they walked toward the three tents in question.

"Yes, I know, but it is necessary. You take the men's tents and I will search the women's. If we come up empty handed, then we will search the other tents as well. We will look through everything if we have to. We certainly have plenty of time."

"True. Simon did say that they would be gone most of the day didn't he."

The two of them split up and entered the tents in search of a particular key, and anything else that may lead them to the betrayer.

Everyone split up into groups of four, each taking separate parts of the village. Uriah, Nadia, Bridget, and Dominic ventured through the open-air markets that ran through the village's interior and was scattered from one end of town to the other.

Gabriele, Wade, Safra, and Nick took to the harvest fields around the outskirts to talk to the local farmers and their families.

Timothy, Sean, Sofia, and Kristen visited the local pubs where the town drunks and storytellers who wax on about the glory days of old generally pass the day away. Ready to regale anyone who is willing to listen to their tales of fantastical deeds, or the heroics of others that they once witnessed.

Seth, Caroline, Alec, and Dee explored the local shops and businesses to chat up the merchants about their wares and local legends, while Simon, Oz, and Jason headed to the sea-cave's western entrance where they exited yesterday. They had no desire to be questioned by the castle guards by returning to the same entrance. They would just have to backtrack to exit upon leaving. While still in the cover of the trees and underbrush the groups began splitting up and taking separate paths into town.

As Gabriele's group broke through the heavy foliage of the forest into the bright early morning sunlight, she strummed her ukulele and sang like a beautiful canary perched upon the saddle of her horse as they rode past the fields of wheat blowing in the slight breeze. She had a wonderful singing voice and it usually attracted the attention of whomever was near. That was the plan anyway. People were more apt to speak to someone who captured their attentions in a pleasing manner.

It seemed to be working as bent bodies and heads began popping up from beneath the tops of the golden wheat shafts where they were gathering their harvests. The younger members of the families would walk behind to gather the chaff which had fallen to the wayside. Gabby's playing and singing had truly captured their attention as children laid down their bundles on the ground and ran to the field's edge to better see and hear the strangely beautiful and different looking girl riding along the town's roadway with the other strangers. The parents stopped their own work to see what had taken their children from their chores.

They watched the strangers ride by easily and slowly. Gabriele had prepared for her minstrel role well. She had worn the traditional, colorful, detailed silken robes of her ancestors, knowing that people's natural curiosity would draw them to such a foreigner in their lands.

The children ran along the roadside, giggling, waving, and pointing at the small band of travelers. Gabby smiled back at them. She loved children and their sweet innocence. Her small group pulled up to a stop just at the edge of the harvester's village houses and she finished her song while the others dismounted; all the children's eyes still fixated upon her.

She handed her ukulele to Wade, while Nick made a show of helping Safra down from her horse. Safra had also dressed the part as well in her traditional native robes of vivid colors and beauty from Morocco. He then turned to Gabby to assist her as well, with her playing the part as a frail, proper Asian doll, whose sole purpose in life was to entertain and be beautiful.

Nick turned to the small crowd of gathering farmers and their families and introduced their small group.

"Good morning good people of Tintagel. We are minstrels from far-away lands, here to learn from you and to write new stories to sing."

Gabriele stepped up and introduced herself in her native Japanese tongue then spoke to the children in English.

"Hello. I am what is called a lyricist." She noticed some confused looks among the children and explained. "A musician who makes lyrics from old legends. Do you have any such legends here of heroes or heroines past or present?"

Several suggestions were made to her, but none mentioned the famed Arthur, Knights of the Round Table, or the wizard Merlin. Gabby made a few limericks of several suggestions and her band of riders moved on to the next field, prepared to play the same game.

Sean watched Timothy quickly place himself between Kristen and himself, then placed his hand on her back, which she quickly stepped away from, and escorted her into the dark, musty, yeasty-smelling pub. Sean's lip tightened into a thin line as his jaw twitched at the possessiveness that Timothy was exhibiting toward Kristen. He caught the heavy wooden door that Timothy let go behind him and held the door open for Sofia to enter the building ahead of himself. *So much for chivalry not being dead,* he thought. Timothy may act like he is all polite manners, but it was all show and Sean knew it. He used it only for his benefit. At least Sofia didn't seem to pay much attention to his neglectful behavior.

It took a few minutes for his eyes to adjust to the darkness of the room, but once they did, he noticed only a handful of people sitting around. They quickly chatted amongst themselves and decided to split up and find someone to talk with.

Kristen and Sofia each took a place at the bar a few seats apart. Kristen chatted with the barmaid while Sofia chatted up an elderly gentleman who didn't appear to be too far into his ale yet. Sean and Timothy each took a seat at an empty table next to a few men who were seated a table over, so conversation would be possible.

Kristen ordered a glass of water, and the barmaid eyed her suspiciously. Sofia quickly ordered.

"Goodness, it's awfully hot out already. I'm needing a glass of water myself." She eyed the barmaid and then cautiously winked at Kristen.

"Yes," Kristen replied. "I lost my water bladder somewhere. You wouldn't happen to know where I can purchase another?" she asked.

"No, sorry, I'm not from around these parts. Just passing through," Sofia answered.

The barmaid turned back with their water glasses and set them on the counter. "There's a miller just on the other side a town that sews pig bladders. He might have what ya need."

"Thanks," Kristen said, taking a long drink from her glass.

Sofia spoke next, to no one in particular, when she said, "Did any of you hear about that incident outside of town yesterday? Seems some giant of a man took down a charging bull. It would have run over a little girl had he not stopped it. Pretty brave man to take on a large bull like that."

"Can't say as I heard about that," the barmaid stated. "What about you Earl? You hear a' any such story?"

"Sure haven't," the elderly man stated without hardly moving a muscle.

"Hmm. I thought maybe he was some sort of local hero or legend. Seemed to be a knight of some sort." Sofia kept the story going.

"Don't really have any local legends round these parts," the barmaid stated.

They quietly finished drinking their waters, asking for another glass while the men tried speaking to the other tavern flies.

"Well now, love. What'll you be havin' ta drink?" the tavern waitress swooned as she leaned on the table, flirtatiously waiting on Tim's order.

Tim smiled at the woman, charming her with his perfect teeth.

"I'll have an ale, ma'am."

"Sure thing, love. What about your friend?" she said, not taking her eyes off of Timothy.

"He'll have an ale as well, thanks."

The waitress slowly stood up and sauntered back to the bar, throwing appreciative glances back at Tim. Sean used to grab the attention of women that way, but next to Tim he was just your average Joe. Not that he really wanted the waitress's attention. She wasn't exactly bragging material with her dingy, torn, clothing, half falling off her bare shoulder, her dirty sandaled feet, and her messy hair that looked as though it hadn't seen a brush, or water, in months, and half her teeth were stained brown with several of them missing. The thing is, she really didn't appear to be that old, maybe in her early thirties. Sean was grateful for the life he was able to lead. This poor woman probably had no other options than to prostitute herself to make a living.

When she returned with their drinks, she placed them on the table, again raking her eyes over Timothy. Sean rolled his eyes but being polite told her thank you.

"Oh, a gent'lman eh? Ain't seen one a yer kind in a long time," she said, finally turning to Sean. "Kinda' cute as well. If you two "gents" need anythin' further, you just ask fer Mags, all right? I'll take *real* good care a' ya." She grinned toothily before taking payment for the drinks and walked over to another table. Sean and Tim watched her go and noticed a man at a corner table watching them.

Timothy and Sean took a long drink of the cool liquid. Sean noticed that Timothy seemed to relish the taste, or coolness of the drink. As they drank their ale, Mags continued to eye Timothy. It wasn't long before the large burly man in the corner stood up and walked over to them.

"What business you two fellas got here?"

Tim seemed to become a bit perturbed by the man's obviously, unfriendly question.

"What business is it of yours?" Tim asked, not moving from his seat, calmly taking another sip of his ale.

"Mags is my business, and if the two a' you think your gonna' have yer way with her, then you'd be wrong."

"Sir," Tim stated calmly, "I have no interest in your wench."

That seemed to calm the man down a bit, and he turned to glare at Sean.

"Me neither." Sean quickly threw his hands in the air as a sign of a truce. "We just came in to get a cold drink. That's all."

"Darrell!" Mags screeched across the bar as she came stomping to stand in front of him. "What do ya' mean by hasselin' my customers?" She glared up at the man who was at least twice her size.

"I told you, Mags. I don't like you workin' here!" he belted back.

"Then you know what ya' need to do then don't ya'?"

"Now, Mags, we done had this conversation. You know I can't afford ta marry ya'."

"Then stay out a' my business. A girl's got a right to support herself any way she can!" With that threat, Mags walked around Darrell, grabbed Timothy by the shirt front and planted a kiss directly on his lips. He couldn't stand up fast enough to get away from her and all but pushed her to the floor.

Before he knew what hit him, the large burly man grabbed him by the shirt front and laid a punch on him that turned his head and flung him over the table. Sean barely had time to move before Tim could take him to the floor with him. Timothy jumped up, barely feeling the hit. The suddenness of it had taken him by surprise. If he hadn't been thrown off kilter by Mags's sudden kiss, he wouldn't have lost his balance. He laid a punch that knocked the man back against a roof support pole. He shook off the punch and lunged at Timothy, who side stepped making the man trip over a chair. Sean stepped up to the bar with Kristen and Sofia, who were watching the scene unfold. Mags took a cast iron skillet and hit Timothy over the head with it. He felt the blow but was unharmed by it. Mags's eyes grew round with fear and she backed away from Tim, then went to her precious Darrell's side to help him up. He knocked her out of the way and lunged at Timothy again, this time knocking him to the floor and landing a few punches. Timothy kicked the man off, stood up, grabbed him by the shirt front and hit him so hard it knocked him backward and he hit his head on the thick wooden mantle of the stone fireplace, knocking him out cold. Timothy straightened his shirt and hair, threw a few more coins on the bar and the four of them left the tavern.

Timothy, panting a little harder than usual, took a deep breath and turned to Sean. "You could have helped you know."

"Why? You seemed to have the whole thing under control." Sean gave a slight smirk. "Besides, I'm not one to stand between a woman and her desires." He began laughing at the image of Mags kissing Timothy and the look of udder disgust on his face.

"Yeah, the look on your face was pretty funny," Kristen stated, laughing as Sofia joined in.

"Who knew you were so irresistible to the ladies." Sean managed between deep breaths of laughter.

"Ha, ha, ha," Tim replied sarcastically. "Go ahead, laugh it up. Thank God for armored skin or that woman would have cracked my skull open with that pan." He rubbed his head to make absolutely sure there was no bleeding visible. His head or knuckles may not hurt, but his pride sure did. That woman embarrassed him in front of Kristen, and he wasn't so sure he could take that lying down. He didn't take kindly to being made a fool of. He just needed to figure out what to do about it.

"You sure you aren't hurt, Tim?" Kristen asked, concern now written on her face after the quick bout of laughter.

"Yeah, I'm sure. Other than my pride, I'm fine."

"Well, I wouldn't worry too much about your pride," Sofia chimed in, "who knew she would turn on you like that and attack you from behind over the big oaf she had just told off."

"Yeah, who knew." Tim turned to take one last look at the tavern they had just exited. They then walked the streets of Tintagel in search of another tavern in which to chat up the locals. "Next tavern, I'm sticking with Kristen and Sofia. Hopefully that will ward off any new 'interests' by any of the locals."

Bridget smiled at the familiarity of the open-air markets. She wouldn't exactly say she missed her old life from 1580s England, but there was something oddly comforting about being back in this era and lifestyle. The fresh fruits, vegetables, and the aroma of the salty dried meats brought back several old memories. Some of her father from her younger years. Her face took on a look of longing, one that got Dominic's attention.

Dominic had never seen Bridget look sad and it shook him just a bit to know that someone like her, who always seemed so bubbly and happy, could have something happen in her life that would make her sad.

"Bridget, are you all right?"

She turned to him; sadness replaced with a genuine smile for the young man's concern.

"Yes, thank you. Just remembering my childhood and my father. I still really miss him at times."

"Yeah, I know what you mean. I still miss my family too. Even though my older brothers were loud and always tormenting me, it was meant in fun."

"Brothers? That must have been awfully fun? I never had any siblings; it was always just me and my father. That is, until he passed away when I was fourteen."

Dominic looked at Bridget. "So, what about your mother?"

"Haven't you heard all the rumors about my family?"

"Only that your dad had something to do with the disappearances years ago."

"Well, my mother died when I was very little. My father was a Dragoman who fell in love with a normal person. When he tried to bring her through a portal, she died. He got angry and staged a coup apparently and several people died or disappeared. He then disappeared through a portal with me. Father wasn't a particularly happy person. He seemed rather sad mostly, but he wasn't mean or abusive to me in any way. That's why it shook me so to find out that he did those horrible things that everyone says he did. He may seem like a monster to them, but he was just father to me."

"So, who took care of you after he died? You couldn't have had any family in a place that you peregrinated to, could you?"

"No, we knew no one except the people we met there. I lived alone and took care of myself, until Caroline appeared one day after a major earthquake. Six weeks later we peregrinated and met Oz."

Dominic was beginning to have a new appreciation for Bridget. How could someone be so happy, having experienced so much pain and loss? She was truly an enigma to him. One he seemed to be curious to unravel. He had to admit, he did want to get to know more about Bridget now that he had talked with her and gotten to know her a bit better.

"Hey, you two. Quit dawdling behind and keep up. We have a lot of people to talk with here," Uriah scolded them.

"Dominic, you and Bridget take the right side of the street while Nadia and I work the other side."

Dominic nodded to Uriah and they all split up, Dominic and Bridget staying together while Uriah and Nadia went their separate ways on the opposite side of the street-market.

As they all chatted with the people none of them seemed to notice the hooded figure that watched them from the shadows of a side street.

Seth, Alec, Caroline, and Odessa entered the small shop filled with trinkets and local items made by a skilled craftsman and jeweler. Caroline and Odessa decided to take turns pretending to be writers from London, researching for a book of stories on lore and legend of villages surrounding the outer banks of the larger cities. Most people being very willing to talk to them in hopes of getting their names written in a book.

Still with all the eagerness of those willing to share, there was no mention of King Arthur, Merlin, or any Knights of the Round Table. Caroline had even gone so far as to mention Arthur's name and still received nothing about them in return.

They had spent the better part of the morning moving between the shops with no success, so, Seth decided it was time for a break.

"I say we take lunch now. How about you, Sweetness, are you hungry?" He smiled down at Caroline while grabbing her for a quick kiss.

She smiled back at him. "Yes, actually, I am starving."

"What about you two?" Seth asked, looking between Alec and Odessa.

"I could definitely eat." Alec smiled.

"Me too," Odessa stated, rubbing her now growling stomach.

"I think I remember a place that we passed not too far back. Let's head that way." Seth took Caroline by the hand and walked back up the street from where they had come.

Alec looked at Dee and waved her in front of him in a gentlemanly manner, still longing to take her by the hand the way Seth did Caroline.

Simon, Malachai, Jason, and Oz searched the cavern with no luck, and decided to call it a day and head into town to grab a bite to eat. Fortunately, they ran into Nick, Safra, Gabby, and Wade doing the same at a small eatery on the edge of town. As they chatted, they discovered that Nick had also ran into some of the others earlier on and they all reported the same thing. No one had mentioned Arthurian legend of any kind.

"Well then," Simon said while they waited on their food to be delivered, "I say we head back to camp, pack up and try a later time period. I would assume that, even if Arthur had lived further back, the people would still know his name. His legend was such a great one and almost every household in the future, even to the latest time period, still knows of him."

Everyone agreed, and after lunch they all split up planning to search for the others and head back to camp. Nick's group found Uriah and the others, while Simon's group ran into Seth's shortly after leaving the eatery.

They all made their way back to camp; unfortunately, failing to notice the hooded figure that followed them from a safe distance into the woods and all the way to their camp. The hooded figure patiently watched from among the trees as the strangers milled about the camp, packing up their belongings.

Jason approached Zeke and Zaccai who had stayed behind to search for the missing key.

"You two find anything?"

"Not a thing, Jason," Zeke answered.

"Especially nothing resembling the description of the key that Seth and Sofia gave us," Zaccai stated.

"Then the betrayer either has it on their person, or they already disposed of it. Let's hope and pray that they still have it but are guarding it very closely. Just keep your eyes open. Watch everyone."

They nodded their consent and went about helping the others with packing.

The hair on the back of Jason's neck stood straight up and he got the odd sense that they were being watched. He looked all around the edges of camp, trying to see anything out of the ordinary, but spotted nothing. This feeling usually meant a demon was close by, but if that were so then why wasn't it attacking? Have they become smarter, and more cautious than in the past? If that were the case, they could all be in more danger than ever before. One of the biggest benefits of dealing with the demons was the fact that they were usually stupid, brash, and noisy. If they had grown wiser, then their jobs had just become much harder and more perilous. He would have to talk with Simon about this new idea and see what he had to say about it. He shook off the feeling and went about packing up as well, still stealing glances around the camp's perimeter, just for good measure.

Show proper respect to everyone, love the
family of believers, fear God,
honor the emperor.

1 Peter 2:17 NIV

Chapter 14

Tintagel, England. 1035 AD

Packing up camp just to walk through a portal a few hundred years later was quite a chore, but it was a necessary part of the lifestyle and unavoidable. At least now with the Portgens they didn't have to waste time waiting on a storm to pass for traveling.

Jason checked the radar for future geographical markings, to make sure the town hadn't grown exponentially to the point where they might open a portal in the middle of it. The Portgen's screen still showed a fair amount of wooded area available for them to peregrinate to without fear of discovery. At least, that's what he thought anyway.

They waited until nightfall to open the portal. Deciding to make quicker work of all the travelers passing through, they chose to open four portals to the same coordinates to get everyone through quickly.

Unfortunately, when they entered the woods in the exact same spot, but two-hundred years later, they were met by a young man who happened to be camping in the same spot as well.

The young man was startled, to say the least, upon seeing the four brightly glowing lights, and twenty-two people emerge from them. He dropped his plate of food upon the ground, and literally ran screaming from his campfire. Several of the Peregrines took off after him, but Alec being able to teleport himself was the one to catch up to him before he got too far away.

"Wait, please. We won't hurt you!" Alec quickly told the terrified young man, catching him by grabbing the collar of his coat. He held up his hands in front of the young man to assure him he meant no harm.

Luckily the young man had not seen Alec teleport or there would be even further explanation. The poor fellow just stood there stock still, his arms pinned to his sides, apparently terrified to move any further.

"Are you a w-w-wizard, or a d-demon?" he stuttered, almost afraid to look at Alec.

"Neither, just a traveler."

"I've n-never seen a traveler like you o-or the others back there? Wh-where did you all c-come from? One minute there was no-nothing but trees, and next four bright lights appeared out of nowhere and out walked a small army of people!"

"We are just travelers, that's all. Just come back to camp with me and we will explain everything to you, okay?" Alec pleaded calmly.

The man took a few deep breaths, turned to look back at his camp he had just fled from, looked back at Alec sizing him up and noting the weapons he carried, and slowly but reluctantly shook his head yes.

Alec gestured the man ahead of himself and watched as he turned to look at Alec every so often, apparently still unsure of this stranger who appeared out of thin air.

"What is your name?" Alec asked him.

There was a slight hesitation on the man's part. "Thomas, sir."

"My name is Alec, Thomas. I am sorry my companions and I frightened you, but I assure you we are as normal as you are. We will explain everything in just a bit, all right?"

Thomas shook his head yes and watched everyone carefully as they approached the camp, now riddled with people of all shapes, sizes and ages. Thomas nearly jumped back again when he walked into the camp and looked at Oz and Seth. Both men were head and shoulders taller than most of the others.

"A-are those two giants?" Thomas stuttered to Alec, not removing his eyes from the two men.

"Not really. Just very large men, neither of whom will harm you." Alec tried to reassure the young man and get him settled back onto the log where he had been sitting, before they so rudely interrupted his meal.

"Thomas," Alec continued, "are you alone out here?"

Thomas seemed reluctant to answer. "Yes. I-I was traveling to the next village for work and stopped here to camp for the night."

"I see. Are you headed to Tintagel or away from it?"

"Away from it. Look, who are you people and how did you just appear out of thin air?" He almost shrieked the last part as the pitch of his voice grew in excitement. As he spoke, he wildly looked about the camp as everyone watched him.

Alec held his hand up again to show him they meant no harm. He looked at Simon for guidance on how much to tell the man.

Simon stepped forward to speak to Thomas and sat down across from him to offer an explanation.

"Thomas, my name is Simon. We are a group of traveling performers. What you witnessed earlier was only a trick of the mind, nothing more. You see, I am a magician and I am working on a new trick that makes people believe that I can move things between places. It's really all just a simple trick."

"That didn't look like a trick to me. How did you all just appear out of thin air like that?"

"We didn't really. You see, it's dark, correct? What you saw was a trick with lights and mirrors. You only think we just appeared, but we were walking through the forest when we saw your fire and decided to be as quiet as possible upon our approach. A few of the others got a little excited at the smell of your delicious meal and moved in too quickly. The lights you saw were a new device that

Jason here has been working on to provide light without the use of fire."

"I don't believe you," Thomas said, not falling for the story Simon was telling him.

"What other explanation could there be?" Simon smiled and slightly chuckled.

"There's been lots of people lately accused of witchcraft in the area and the King has been trying to rid the lands of it. I think you're all witches and wizards and that will lead to a lot of trouble for anyone who comes in contact with you. The King needs to know about you all," Thomas said, as he began to stand and back away from them.

"I'm sorry, Thomas. I really didn't want to have to do this to you, but we can't have you going around causing trouble for us."

Before Thomas could utter another word, Simon had chanted something and waved his staff in front of him and he soon stood motionless, as if frozen in time.

"Simon, what did you do?" Seth questioned, amazed and a little frightened by what he just witnessed.

"I just made time stand still just for Thomas here. We will move on and I will reset his memory for just before we arrived. He won't remember a thing."

"Will that harm him in any way?" Caroline asked, almost unable to take her eyes off the statuesque man.

"No, not at all, but it isn't something I like doing. I don't believe in messing with people's memories or experiences. It's my belief that things happen for a reason. But, still, we can't have him drawing unnecessary attention to us while we are here. Everyone move on eastward while I erase the last ten minutes from young Thomas' head."

Everyone began moving out as they stole glances over their shoulders at what Simon was doing. He was standing in front of Thomas, his staff raised between them as he whispered something.

When Simon appeared a few minutes behind them at their new camp site, Dominic questioned him.

"Simon, what will happen to Thomas' memories?"

"Thomas will only forget what he saw and heard for the last ten minutes. He won't lose anything else; I assure you."

"But how do you manipulate people's memories like that?"

"Magic, my boy, pure and simple. Like I said earlier, it isn't something I like doing."

"How many times have you had to do something like that?"

"Only a few times in the past."

"To whom?" Uriah questioned.

"No one any of you know. Why all the questions?"

"Just wondering if you've ever done something like that to any of us?" Uriah asked, uneasy about the idea that someone could mess with his very own thoughts and memories.

"Of course not! What sort of question is that?"

"I just didn't realize that was possible."

"This is exactly why I normally don't perform such spells. Whether you believe me or not, I don't like doing them and only use it when it is absolutely necessary. I tried to talk to the man, but he wouldn't believe what I was saying."

"We could have just told him the truth," Dominic stated.

"Do you really think he would have believed us? He didn't believe the whole performer story; do you really think he would have believed we were time travelers and warriors called by God to fight demons and find important people and artifacts?" Simon argued. "Besides, like I said, it didn't harm him a bit. It will appear to him like he just zoned out for a moment. Haven't any of you ever experienced losing a small bit of time, or not realizing how you got from one place to another?"

Everyone shrugged their shoulders and shook their heads yes.

"That is what the memory spell is like."

"Well, I'll have to make sure I'm never alone with you. No telling what you might *erase* from *my* memory," Uriah spat.

Uriah's accusation fueled Odessa's anger. "Simon would never do such a thing and I'll have it out with any of you who says otherwise!"

"I agree, Uriah," Jason spoke up. "No need in going around creating unrest over nothing."

"Of course, you're all loyal to your Dragoman! I was too long ago, remember. It didn't get me very far now did it?" Uriah said, glancing in Bridget's direction.

The young girl curled her arms around herself in sadness.

Dominic noticed her discomfort and went to stand next to her, supportively putting his arm around her shoulders. She weakly smiled at him.

Safra who watched the scene play out in front of her spoke up in Simon's defense.

"That is enough!" Safra's harsh tone grabbed everyone's attention. The tiny woman was generally quiet and demure. None of them had ever seen this forceful side.

"Firstly, Uriah, there are also concoctions of herbs that can have the same effect as a memory spell. It isn't like this is all new to the world. Second, why would any of you question Simon's loyalty just because he *saved* us all from dangerous questions using the gift that *God* gave him? This bickering amongst us is exactly the sort of division the evil one wants. I suggest we all forget this squabbling and tend to the tasks at hand."

Everyone seemed to take Safra's chiding them to heart and backed off with the questioning.

Simon looked at Safra with an appreciative glance.

"You heard the lady," Seth answered, "you all know what to do."

Seth trusted Simon more than almost anyone else and believed what he said to be true. It just made him uneasy to know that some people had the ability to freeze time and make you forget things. Whether by using a potion or magic. It appeared by the mood in camp that he wasn't the only one uncomfortable with the possibility either. Or everyone was feeling rather ridiculous for letting their imaginations get the better of them and letting someone else's insecurities plant distrust in their own hearts as well. Seth silently applauded Odessa for speaking up and for her loyalty to Simon. Jason as well. He only wished he had displayed such loyalty. But man's deceitfulness was a hard one for him to get over since his father had abandoned him and his mother when he was younger. He was over it of course, but it still left its mark on his life. Especially where trust was an issue, except with Caroline. Even though he had learned to trust his new Peregrine and Dragoman friends, he guessed when it came to convincing arguments by someone else, the seed of doubt could be planted. Strength and discernment were something he would have to work on and pray about.

By the time camp was set up it was late into the night and everyone went to bed. Zaccai and Sofia had leaders watch duty that night, and camp was very quiet with hardly any sound or movement at all except for the camp sentries who changed out every four hours. The leaders did try to position their tents where whoever was on duty that night could see the tents in question from behind their supposedly *closed* tent flap.

The mood the next morning was back to normal and most everyone was their regular, jovial, selves, ready to tackle the mission ahead. They were returning to the same village at Tintagel Castle's border but two hundred years into the future. Many were excited to see what differences and what similarities existed, if any. But mostly whether or not King Arthur was present yet, or ever had been. They still weren't certain if he was an actual person or just myth and legend.

All the teams from yesterday remained the same except for Zeke and Zaccai trading places with Nick and Sofia, explaining what all they dug through yesterday. Even though the camp was thoroughly searched they decided to do it again just in case anything might have been missed. Besides, Sofia had actually seen the key before and could easily recognize it.

The large group rode out, realizing they were an hour closer to town than they were yesterday. They soon realized that the town had actually grown large enough to expand two miles south in the two-hundred-year period. It was bustling with activity and appeared to be prospering. Many new establishments were visible, some businesses and outlying farms were now gone, replaced by more homes, or upgraded buildings.

Simon was curious to see if Tintagel Castle had changed at all. The outer wall seemed to be taller and more fortified with rock. The courtyard doors seemed to have been upgraded to a newer thicker wood, fortified with larger iron hinges and strapping. He wondered if it were due to wars that possibly took place over the years or just the new king's orders.

Now that he had seen what he wanted, they rode back toward the western side of the coastline and entered the cave on the more hidden side of Tintagel.

Simon, Malachai, Jason, and Oz left the horses tied at the cave entrance and walked slowly through the damp cavern while Simon worked his magic trying to find any hidden passages.

Oz decided to take a break and lean against an obliging rock. When he placed his full weight against the bulging stone, it suddenly gave way causing the far side of the cavern wall to rumble.

As everyone turned in anticipation to the area where the rumbling was coming from, at the top of the cavern wall, the side of the wall began to open up as the rock slid away into the wall itself. As it did, a smooth pathway up to the opening appeared.

The three men turned to each other and smiled.

"Good job, Oz," Simon stated, beginning the short climb up the pathway.

"Simon," Jason asked, "why didn't your magic reveal the doorway?"

"The magic which concealed it must have been very strong indeed for it to block my revealing spell. Possibly cast by Merlin himself." Simon grinned broadly at the thought.

"Sounds like we may 'ave found what, or who, we were lookin' fer." Oz grinned.

"Yes, I think you are right about that, my friend." Simon turned away, taking the first steps into the dark, hidden passage.

While inquiring around town the others did indeed discover that the people of Tintagel all spoke of a King who once was so great, honest, and fair that his vision for the kingdom had changed the outlook of all Tintagel's residence, and most of those who came in contact with the village and its people. This king's name was Arthur Pendragon, and he had been gone for more than one-hundred and thirty years.

Odessa, Alec, Seth, and Caroline stood in the street just outside the store they had just left, discussing what to do next.

"Well, at least we know we are finally on the right path, and that King Arthur's legend was true. Although some of it could have been embellished like most legends over the years. But where do we go from here?" Odessa questioned her friends.

"I am not certain. Perhaps we should go to Merlin's cave to see if Simon and the others have had any luck?" Alec suggested.

"Sounds good to me," Seth stated.

"Shouldn't we find the others first?" Caroline asked.

"I don't think we need to. They can all figure out their next move themselves. Besides, if they've all had the same response to the questions that we have, they may have already headed to the cave," Seth replied.

"How about some lunch first?" Odessa chimed in. "I am starving. Breakfast wore off hours ago."

"Good idea, we have no idea how long we'll be out at the cave," Seth answered.

"There is a tavern and eatery just around the corner back that way," Alec stated, pointing down the street they had just walked up earlier.

The four of them led their horses through the crowded streets, tied them off at the hitching post and went inside the dark, cool, tavern. The place was rather packed with people and finding a table for four was a bit tough, so they found four seats at the bar and sat down.

A woman behind the counter strode over to them to take their order, her eyes never leaving Alec's face. Odessa noticed the focus of the woman's attention.

Alec of course did not notice as he had been talking to Seth about something.

"Hello," the woman said, directing her greeting toward Alec, but making a sweep to the others with her eyes. "Anything I can get you?" she asked stopping in front of Alec and smiling brightly at him.

Alec smiled back in his usual friendly way, making the young woman positively beam and become rather chatty with him. He was apparently unaware of her attraction to him.

Odessa felt an odd sense of unrest at the exchange. Surely she wasn't jealous? No, no way. It was probably just aggravation at being so hungry that it was beginning to make her a bit cranky.

Caroline quietly sat and watched the looks of exasperation that were flitting across Odessa's face as she watched the exchange between Alec and the barmaid. It made her very curious about what was going on inside Odessa's head at the moment. Caroline almost giggled when Odessa rolled her eyes at the barmaid's obvious flirtation with Alec. If she didn't know any better, she would say Odessa had romantic feelings for Alec. She may just have to ask her friend about this later in private.

Odessa's hunger and frustration at being ignored was boiling over.

"Excuse me, Abigail is it? Can we order our food, please? We've had a long day and I'm very hungry," Odessa stated rather rudely, catching her friends off guard. Alec looked at her from the corner of his eye as the now embarrassed Abigail quickly took their orders and smiled at Alec once more before leaving them.

"What was that all about, Dee?" Alec turned to look her in the eyes this time.

"What?" she asked defensively, knowing full well what he meant.

"You were uncommonly rude to Abigail."

"I was not. Besides, her job is to take our food order. Not stand around flirting with everyone who comes in the door."

"Yes, you were. And she was not flirting with everyone. Just me," Alec said, a grin on his lips at the unusual attention. He had to admit, it was nice to have someone interested in him. It had been a very long time since he captured someone's attention.

"Yes. And you were lapping it up like a thirsty dog at water," she said, rolling her eyes at him.

"So what. What is wrong with that?" They both turned in their bar stools and faced each other.

Seth and Caroline sat quietly watching the two go at each other. If things began to escalate out of control Seth would step in, but this argument was a long time coming and things needed to be said.

"Nothing, except for the fact that you are leading the poor girl on. You do realize you're playing a very dangerous game, don't you?" Odessa squinted at him in disbelief.

"I am merely chatting with a very attractive young woman. IF, I choose to pursue more than conversation with her than that is my business. We will not live this life forever, Dee. The Twelve have been chosen, we are searching for the Armor of God, and I truly feel that we will not be at this much longer than a few more years." Alec seethed as quietly as possible to avoid prying ears.

"So, what? She's just going to wait around on you for years until you return?"

"Why not? You think I am not worthy for someone to wait for? Memnah has committed to Jason to wait for as long as it takes!"

"I did not say that Alec! Memnah knows of our ways. Are you planning on telling this…girl, what you do for a living?"

"No, but apparently it is what you think. Besides, Dee, I can come back to this period any day I choose. And after we free the earth, hopefully I will be free to live wherever and with whomever I wish."

Odessa looked at Alec. He was really serious about finding someone to spend his life with. Fine. If this medieval wench was what he chose then that was, as he stated, his business. She turned back to the bar, grabbed her cup, and took a long drink to calm her nerves. Alec had chosen her first, but had she hurt him too badly for him to even consider her now? Did she even want to be in the running for Alec Chevalier's heart? If she said yes, then it would be forever, and Dee had seen far too much pain in relationships growing up. The way men in her culture would just cast the women away when they were done with them, or brand them as property was a stark memory. Something owned but not loved. Sure, the world was a different place now, and she knew Alec would never do such a thing to the woman with whom he chose to spend his life. But did she really want a loving relationship with the man who had been her best friend for the last eight years? And being as damaged as she was emotionally, it wouldn't be fair to him if she couldn't love him back the way he deserved.

She ate her meal in silence with her thoughts, while Seth, Caroline and Alec chatted amiably. After their lunch was complete, Abigail gave Alec some more of her attention, chatting with him across the bar before they exited the tavern. Dee didn't wait around to see more but stepped outside into the bright mid-day sunlight. She and the others mounted their horses, waiting on Alec who was the last one to exit the building. She couldn't help but notice the small smile on his lips when he mounted his horse. She spurred her horse on as fast as she could go without running anyone over and headed quickly out of town toward the western entrance of the cave. They did indeed meet up with Zeke who now traveled with Gabby, Safra, and Wade as they rode through the forest just outside of town. The men glancing back over their shoulders to make sure that none of the locals were interested in them or where they were headed.

Seth had noticed some of the local men inside the tavern and outside on the street stealing glances at Caroline and Odessa. Abruptly turning away when Seth, in all of his massiveness, warned them with a foreboding look. Even though the women could handle themselves quite well, men sometimes became stupid when their desires outweighed their common sense. Seth didn't want to have to get into any fights with the locals. He only hoped that whatever was going on between Alec and Odessa got straightened out soon. You could almost cut the tension between them with a knife. He watched Odessa's straight stiff back and decided he would talk with her later. He and Odessa had become close friends since their trip to Reader's Island with Simon when they found the underground temple and books. It pained him to see her so unhappy and decided that maybe she just needed a friendly chat.

Uriah watched Bridget and Dominic roam the street market once again chatting with the locals in an animated manner. *Oh, to be so young and trusting* he thought. He barely remembered those days so long ago. He watched Bridget giggle at something and the childlike innocence that ran across her face. He felt badly for giving Bridget that accusatory look last night. She pretty much shied away from him now. His intentions were to get to know her better, she was after all the daughter of the man he once called friend, but he wasn't sure that would be possible now. He remembered playing with her when she was a young child, before Hiram whisked her away from this way of life. Uriah had watched as Hiram, who had been one of the most powerful and confident Dragoman he had ever known, turn into someone completely cut off from everyone with the loss of Mary. He had become an introvert who trusted and communicated with no one. Not even Uriah, who had been his best friend.

He caught up to Nadia, satisfied with what they discovered about the man for whom they were looking. Plenty of people were willing to tell stories of the famed King Arthur. It was time to break for lunch, so he and Nadia called to Dominic and Bridget to cross the street and meet them. They each picked something from the market to eat, then found an obliging corner bench at which to sit and enjoy their lunch. After eating and some friendly chatter, Nadia took the trash and left to find a receptacle in which to dispose of it.

Uriah saw his chance to speak with Bridget semi-privately.

"Bridget, I owe you an apology for last night. I know it isn't your fault, what happened with your father, I mean."

"That's all right, Uriah. I know my father hurt a lot of people and I am sorry if he caused you undue pain."

"Only in the fact that he was my best friend and he just up and left, with no explanation."

"You and my father were very close?"

"Yes. I even used to play with you when you were just a baby." He watched as a smile broke out on her face, just before it turned serious once again.

"Did you know my mother, Mary?"

"Not very well I'm afraid. Hiram spoke of her often, but I only met her briefly a few times."

"How is that possible?" Dominic questioned Uriah. "She couldn't peregrinate. So how or where would you have met her?"

Uriah realized his mistake too late. He had never told anyone else that he had ventured to Zanchier with Hiram a few times. Of course, he didn't know then that it would become the final resting place or prison for so many of the others when Hiram went dark.

"I actually traveled with Hiram to Zanchier many years ago, before Bridget was even born. We never knew that it was a place that was untraceable that dwelt between dimensions."

Uriah turned his attention back to Bridget. "If you ever want to know anything about your father, you know, what he was like before all that happened, you can ask me. I'd be willing to talk with you about him."

"Thank you, Uriah. I would like that very much." Bridget grinned at the man.

Nadia soon returned with them deciding to call it a day and head back to camp early. There wasn't anything else for which they needed to search, and Uriah figured everyone else had done the same. They mounted their horses and left the bustling village headed for their encampment a short thirty-minute ride south.

What, then, shall we say in response to these things?
If God is for us, who can be against us?

Romans 8:31 NIV

Chapter 15

The hidden passage located inside Merlin's Cave was dark and dry. Simon, Malachai, Jason, and Oz all pulled out their flashlights and walked for a good five minutes with nothing unusual happening. They soon came to a spiral, stone staircase that went upward beneath the cliffside. They carefully climbed the staircase for another five minutes before coming to stop before a large oak and iron hewn door. Oz gave the door a push and it only slightly gave way, as though something were blocking it from the inside. He turned off his flashlight.

"Jason, give me a hand here, would ya'? We need to push harder."

Jason handed his flashlight over to Simon, and he and Oz pushed with all their might as the door moved little by little with each strained shove. Although the door never fully opened, it did lend enough room for the men to squeeze through the opening.

"Let me go in first, Simon," Oz instructed. "Jus' in case there be somthin' dangerous on the other side." Oz took out his flashlight and shined the beam through the opening into the darkness beyond.

"It appears ta be another passageway. Looks like there might a' been a cave-in b'fore. Lots a' rocks layin' against the door here." He stepped over some larger rocks that had rolled into the path.

Simon and Malachai entered the passage, looking about. "Perhaps, but it may have intentionally been sealed off. I would think that if the passage collapsed there would be rock strewn everywhere, but the majority of the fallen rock appears to be in front of the door. Hmm…curious."

"You're right, Simon," Jason chimed in, "it does look as though only that area has rock. Why do you think someone would have sealed just this area? Why not the first door inside the cave?"

"I really don't know. Unless we passed another hidden passage somewhere along the way without knowing it. Oh well, we've gotten into this one. Let's finish exploring where it goes, shall we?" Simon's boyish smile graced his features.

Oz and Jason grinned at each other, knowing that Simon was having the time of his life. Going on missions was a rarity for him these days and finding anything that had to do with the fabled Merlin was the ultimate archeological find for him.

The passage broke off into three different directions and the men stopped to decide which way was the best one to take.

"We could split up. Oz and I will each take one tunnel, while you and Malachai take the other," Jason offered.

"I'm not so sure that would be a good idea." Simon replied.

"Maybe not, but we're all grown men 'ere. It would cover a lot more ground th'n jus' all a' us goin' in the same d'rection. 'Sides, we all have skills, don't we?"

"Yes, of course. You're right. Let's split up, but *be* careful, will you? We don't want to have to come and rescue you two fellows." Simon grinned, chiding his friends, knowing full well that if anyone would need rescuing it would most likely be him and Malachai.

The men all went in separate directions. Simon said out loud to no one in particular, "All right Lord, lead me to wherever it is we're supposed to go. If Merlin has been here, then show me where. Or where to find the Breastplates of Righteousness." As Simon and Malachai moved deeper into the tunnel that still seemed to be moving at an upwards slant, they began to see what they thought was a light coming from somewhere further up. Simon turned the flashlight away and waited just a few seconds for his eyes to adjust.

Sure enough, what appeared to be thirty feet ahead was a dim light at the base of what he assumed was the passage wall.

He turned his flashlight back in front of him and moved toward where he had seen the light. When they reached what they discovered was another oak door, Simon turned off the flashlight and placed his ear against the wood, listening for any signs of noise coming from the opposite side. He stilled his excited breathing and tried to concentrate. It sounded like shuffling on the other side and it seemed to be getting louder. He also saw a shadow of movement that broke off bits of light underneath the door. There was definitely someone on the other side. Simon backed away from the door, put his flashlight into his bag, and was beginning to do a revealing spell when the heavy wooden door opened. Standing on the inside was a man of considerable age, with a long white beard which reached his waist. His long, grayish-white hair framed a thin face with high cheekbones, a thin, pointed nose, and barely visible lips beneath his long mustache. Gray bushy eyebrows that shaded dull, gray-blue eyes, and a weathered face full of age lines from years of worry finished off his aging yet friendly face. His demeanor was one of complacency from years of learning to go with the flow of life. He wore a long, thick, deep-colored purple cloak over a navy-blue floor-length tunic. His shoes were slightly pointed at the toes and gray in color, and the tops were made of a clothlike material.

"Hello, Simon. I've been waiting for you to show up," the stranger said.

Simon blinked at the way the stranger addressed him, then turned to look at Malachai. He turned back to the stranger and said, 'Err...have we met before, Sir?"

"Not exactly, but I have heard of you in certain circles. Just as you have heard of me. Come in, please," he said stepping aside to allow them to enter the room. "I'm sorry. I have forgotten my manners. I'm Merlin," he said holding out his hand to shake Simon's and Malachai's.

Simon grinned from ear to ear, exuberantly shaking the man's hand. "Hello, Merlin. This is *quite* a pleasure to meet you!"

"As you are for me, and I assure you, the pleasure is mine," Merlin offered graciously.

"Surely whatever you say you've heard about me is nothing compared to what legend says about you, Sir. Historians weren't even sure that you really existed." Simon grinned at the man as he and Malachai sat in the seats that Merlin was gesturing for them to take. "You said you were expecting me. How did you know I would be here?"

"Well, I have protection spells on all the entrances to my little hide-away here. When you and your friends found the cave entrance the spell alerted me to your presence."

"Ah yes, my friends. Will they be all right?"

"Yes, the other passages lead to rooms inside the castle just a few floors above our heads. When we finish our discussion here, we'll go and find them." Merlin groaned slightly upon taking a seat across from them.

"I'm still unsure as to how you know who I am. I could have been anyone coming through that door."

"Well, you see, I've seen you two and all the others before. Two-hundred years ago about five miles outside of Tintagel, I followed a group of riders into the forest and watched from afar as you all packed up your belongings. Now for you that could have just been days ago, I'm certain. Depending on how you traveled here."

"Jason mentioned he felt someone watching us. How could that have possibly been you? You would have to be hundreds of years old."

"You're not, are you?" Merlin smiled at Simon.

"Are you telling me that you are a Dragoman or Peregrine?" Malachai asked astonished.

"Yes, one of the very first. A Dragoman to be exact. But back when I was involved with all of that they called us Readers. We actually discovered an island somewhere in the middle of the ocean."

"Yes! Reader's Island! That was you? The one who discovered it?" Simon asked, amazed.

"No, but it was a friend of mine. A Dragoman turned Monk who swore to protect the Armor of God, but the island of Patmos in Greece was raided by pirates so many times over the years that the pieces were stolen and separated. We are unsure where they all ended up, but I am assuming, since you were led here that you are searching for the Breastplates?"

"Well, yes, we are. But, if you are a Dragoman, then why is there no mention of you in the archive books? And why do you not still practice that way of life?"

"We are mentioned in one particular archive book. It was placed in a temple far beneath Reader's Island for protection. There were many during our time that tried to stop what we were called to do. They chose to honor the dark side instead of the light. We secretly created the temple and placed the books inside. The keys were all separated and given to brothers and sisters of the Light. Those who served God. They were all charged with hiding the key given to them in a safe, secure place. I am assuming since you are looking for the armor then the final battle is soon to be fought?"

"Yes." Simon was amazed and over-joyed to know that Merlin was one of his very own. "We found the books but have still been unable to open one of them. The key, once found, has been stolen by someone among us."

"Ah yes, treachery. It never seems to lose its grip on the human soul. No matter how hard we try we always seem to stray from the light," Merlin said, anguish evident across his tired face. "As for why I do not still serve, I was called to another purpose. To lead Arthur through his reign as king. To bring about the morals and values that have, and will, shape the world at large."

"My goodness," Simon sighed, "so much we still don't know about the very life we lead. Since you know of the Breastplates, do you know where they are located?"

"Yes, or, I did once." Merlin smiled. "Last I actually saw them was when the Knights of the Round Table used them as part of their own armor. After Arthur's reign ended and the Knights all retired from duty, I gathered the Breastplates and gave them to some of the most trusted and agile men to ever exist. The Knights Templar. Last I heard, they took the Breastplates to their fortress on Cyprus Island. You should find them there."

"That would explain the white tunic and red cross that was in Odessa's dream," Malachai offered.

"Yes. It certainly does," Simon answered.

"Now, let's go gather the other two who are with you before they get themselves into trouble, shall we?" Merlin stood and walked to another door on the opposite side of the room.

Simon and Malachai stood and followed Merlin up some wooden stairs, in what appeared to be the inside of the castle. Simon marveled at the paintings and ornate tapestries that adorned the castle walls. Beautiful antiques settees, and large, intricately carved buffet tables stood in front of them. The buffet tables were adorned with silver bowls filled with fruits. Silver candelabras fitted with unlit, partially melted candles sat on both sides. A long-handled silver snuffer sat in the middle upon a large, oblong silver platter.

The stair railings were thick spindled wood, sanded and smoothed to the touch. The large bolsters at the end were intricately carved with lions sitting upon their haunches, front paws up and roaring, demanding respect. The people roaming the castle were sparse, but the few there looked at Simon and Malachai curiously but did not question Merlin. They only bowed their heads in greeting and walked on about their business.

Merlin led them to a room where a small, five-foot-high door, hidden amongst the wall-paper pattern soon opened, and out walked—almost crawling—one Wendal Ozer Osmond. He stopped briefly in his hunched over position, looking between Simon and the other men.

"Er…I suppose I came out at the right spot," Oz awkwardly said, climbing his way through.

"Yes. We were expecting you," Merlin stated.

Oz walked up to Simon and whispered, "So, is this him?"

"Yes, it is." Simon grinned up at his old friend like a schoolboy.

"Now, we go to retrieve the other gentleman who was with you. This way." Merlin motioned for them to follow him.

"Er…Simon," Oz said, "What about the horses? We left 'em tied outside the cave. The tide should be comin' up soon."

"Not to worry. Oz is it?" Merlin interjected. "I've sent some of the stable boys to retrieve the animals."

"But how did ya' know they were there?" Oz questioned, surprised.

"The same way I knew *you* were here. Magic." Merlin continued to walk without turning to look at whom he was addressing.

Oz looked at Simon with a look of acceptance and a shrug of his massive shoulders.

They soon came upon Jason, who was in another room, already out of the secret passageway. He stood at the massively wide and tall windows, looking out over the scene below. He jumped slightly, automatically grabbing for his sword when he saw them appear in the doorway. He quickly recognized Simon, Malachai, and Oz.

"I'm hoping you are Merlin." Jason held out his hand to shake the strangers.

"You would be right, Sir. And you are?"

"Jason Marshal. Wow, you're like meeting a celebrity. Especially since no one knew for sure if you were even real."

"So I've heard." Merlin turned to look at Simon. "The stable boys should be back soon with your steeds. Are you all hungry? It is well past lunchtime and I am certain that you missed it."

"I could eat," Oz said with a grin.

"I'm sure you could eat us out of house and home." Merlin smiled at the large man. "Come, right this way." He motioned to them. "The kitchen is just a small walk across the castle."

As they reached the center of the castle, the doorman walked over to whisper something in Merlin's ear, becoming very animated as he glanced at Oz cautiously. Merlin turned to Simon with a questioning look.

"Were you expecting others to show up?"

"It is possible. We travel with a very large group, as you know."

"The stable boys were happened upon by four other people when they went to fetch your horses. They were mistaken as horse thieves and almost gutted, apparently by some giant they say."

"That would be Seth." Simon grinned.

"Where are they now?" Merlin asked the doorman.

"At the stables, my Lord. One of the boys ran ahead to inform me of the situation."

"Order the horses to be fed and watered, and our guests to be brought to the kitchen when they arrive at the castle," Merlin instructed the man who bowed and walked out the massive castle doors to speak with a young boy standing outside. The boy's eyes widened, and he grinned and sped off.

Simon watched and looked at everything, taking it all in. Was this castle the fabled Camelot? He had so many questions but wondered if he would have the time to inquire of Merlin as to the answers. He only wished Safra could be here to witness this moment. She would have loved it. Perhaps he could convince Merlin to travel with them to the camp to meet her and the others.

While they were seated at a large table waiting for lunch to be served, Seth, Caroline, Odessa, and Alec arrived. Introductions were made, excited greetings went around the table and they were also seated. Although they politely declined lunch as they had eaten before arriving. They all quietly watched Merlin speak and it seemed as though every one of them hung onto every word that Merlin uttered. He did agree to Simon's request to meet the rest of the Peregrines as soon as lunch had finished.

The mood at camp was one of relief and joy at finding the information they wanted. Arthur Pendragon was in fact an actual person, and everyone hoped that since Simon and the others weren't back just yet, that Simon had found either the breastplates or Merlin. It was early afternoon, and everyone sat around enjoying the free time. Dominic sat with his sketch pad and pencils drawing the scene before him. Bridget, Wade, and Gabby played charades. Sean and Kristin set conversing and just enjoying each other's company. Timothy, visible through the open tent-flap, sat sipping on a bottle of liquor that he had purchased in Tintagel in a tavern, watching the interaction between Sean and Kristin. Nadia and Nick sat talking, also watching the interaction and activities amongst the younger people. Sofia, Zeke, and Zaccai were spending time grooming and watering the horses. Safra was wild-crafting local herbs on the outskirts of camp to replenish her supplies.

Uriah sipped from his coffee cup as he sat on a log and watched curiously as Timothy took swig after swig on the liquor bottle, his anger fueled more with each drink. He noticed that Timothy watched Sean and Kristen laughing and talking and wondered what it was about the two of them that seemed to anger Tim so much. Just then young Bridget joined him on the obliging log. She sheepishly sat at first, saying nothing, apparently feeling a bit awkward. Uriah had to admit, he wasn't the most approachable person. He sat quietly, giving her time to get around to whatever it was she wanted to discuss.

"Uriah," Bridget finally spoke fidgeting in her seat, "can you tell me something about my father? Something not horrible, please." She looked at him with such a longing that it made his heart ache for her. He could only imagine how she had been feeling since coming to

Reader's Island. Most of the older crowd had been less than welcoming, but it hadn't taken her very long to win everyone over. Her personality was hard to ignore or dislike. She was a ray of sunshine in their otherwise dark world. Yes, she even managed to make *him* smile on occasion, although he would never let any of the others witness it.

"Well, let's see." Uriah thought for a moment, careful to pick a happy memory for her. "Your father, Hiram, was one of the most gifted magi that I have ever seen. When we first met, I was sort of a hard man to get through to. I couldn't verbally communicate with anyone, I was confused, angry, and didn't know what they were trying to tell me about where I was or how I had gotten here. When I was having a particularly bad day your father would make these paper animals and then animate them with magic. They would move, dance, fly, jump, hop…whatever it was, it came alive. It always calmed me down, mesmerized me to the point that I forgot my troubles momentarily. It was a way to communicate without words. I knew that he was a kind man by this gesture alone. He really led me and guided me through this lifestyle for several years. He was truly my mentor in so many ways."

Bridget smiled from ear to ear, as she sat listening to him speak. She could imagine her father doing what Uriah said. She remembered days in Dover that were some of the best she could ever remember. Her father had some very dark days as well, but mostly he was just sad. She always tried to remember and dwell on the good ones. Until she came to peregrinate and hear the stories of her father's past actions, she never knew what had made him so unhappy. Now, she was beginning to understand why her father behaved the way he did all her life. He must have loved her mother very much indeed.

Several hours later, Simon and the others returned to camp with Merlin. Most everyone was completely enamored with meeting the man. After building the fire and starting their dinner meal, they all spent the next several hours bombarding him with questions about the legends that had surrounded his life. So much so, that no one had noticed the thick fog that was beginning to roll into camp as the sun began to set in the evening sky.

Jason noticed Caroline shiver in the cool night air as Seth stepped closer to her, leaning over her from behind and wrapping his large frame around hers. Jason swallowed hard, a sense of longing stirring in his very soul as memories of his desert princess came rushing into his mind. He suddenly became disinterested in Merlin's stories and memoirs and decided to take a walk. He had been watching all the *would-be couples* that seem to be forming in their Peregrine groups as of late. Jason realized that he would never have that unless he chose someone from amongst his peers. But he only ever wanted Memnah.

He hadn't gotten very far from camp when a thought came to mind. No one would notice if he decided to take a little trip back to Timna Valley, Israel to see her. He could sneak away tonight after everyone else went to bed. With the Portgens he could make very easy work of it. He could see Memnah and be back in no time at all. No one would be any the wiser. It had only been about three days since they had to part ways, but it felt like a lifetime to him. Why wait until everyone goes to sleep when he could go now? He'll just walk out somewhere where the Portgen's light won't be visible. No one will miss him since they're all focused on Merlin. Jason ventured further out into the thick, now very foggy woods, set the coordinates close to Memnah's village and stepped through.

The hour was beginning to grow late, and they had another long day tomorrow of packing up camp and traveling to the Greek island of Cyprus, in the Mediterranean Sea, in the year 1295. For this journey, Simon decided, since it was such an unknown area of the world for them, they would buy passage for their group aboard a ship. They didn't need another event like the one yesterday evening to happen.

"Merlin, you're welcome to bunk with us in our tent instead of heading back at this late hour," Simon offered.

"No need, I can manage rather easily from here." Merlin gave a knowing smile. But before he could say his goodbyes the corralled horses all began to become very agitated and dance around wildly. Suddenly chaos erupted around the camp's borders as demons began descending upon them from every direction. They were hard to see through the thick fog that had rolled in and it was hard to make out how many there were. Everyone, totally unprepared for the attack, scrambled for their weapons, many running into the woods for some kind of cover.

Merlin and Simon sprang into action using magic to light up the darkness, giving everyone the ability to see better what they were fighting against. Merlin cast a clearing spell to rid the area of the fog while Simon battled a demon.

Bridget, Dominic, and Wade all ran the same direction, told early on by Alec, their weapons teacher, to try and stick together in battle situations and watch out for each other. Dominic did have some fighting skills after all, and Bridget and Wade had become pretty good shots with the guns Alec had given them.

The battle within and around the camp was intense, with everyone doing what they could to overcome. Several people were injured in the battle, but no one was able to find Jason for him to heal them. They had to fight through their injuries as best they could.

Bridget and Dominic had gotten separated from Wade somehow and were hunkered down behind a large tree stump trying to keep as still as possible. They could hear someone or something approaching, but then the noise suddenly stopped. Bridget could feel her legs beginning to cramp with how she was sitting. She tried to adjust her position as quietly as possible, but fell over in the process, making some noise. Whoever it was, began moving in their direction, and she and Dominic jumped up and took off running. Just then, the skies dropped its load of rain, and lightning and thunder boomed over-head streaking the forest with temporary light.

Back at camp, after fifteen minutes of intense battle, things began to quieten down, and those left inside the camp's perimeter began looking for the others who had taken to the woods.

They found Timothy, unharmed of course, passed out inside his tent, an empty liquor bottle in his hand. Uriah, Caroline, Nadia, and Sean had all sustained slight injuries. Safra and Nick busied themselves applying her poultices and herbal medicines to their injuries. No one had found the teenagers just yet. Gabby, Zeke, Oz, Kristin, and Sofia all took to the surrounding woods in opposite directions to look for them. And Seth, Alec, and Odessa all went in different directions as well in search of Jason, Seth fearing the worst, for he hadn't seen him since before the battle began.

Back in the woods the lightning gave Wade the ability to barely make out Dominic and Bridget about sixty feet away, running through the forest with several demons in hot pursuit. He pointed his pistol in the direction of the demons and pulled the trigger, unsure whether the bullet had found its mark. The only light available was the temporary streaks provided by the lightning overhead.

Oz, Zeke, and Gabby all heard the shot, unsure whether it was from the lightning or a gun but decided to follow the sound as best they could.

As Dominic and Bridget ran, a storm portal began to open in front of them about fifty-feet away. It glowed brighter than any Bridget had yet to see, pulsing with electricity. They continued to run as their pursuers continued to chase, arrows whizzing by them.

"Dominic, what should we do?" Bridget asked frantically, looking back over her shoulder at the quickly approaching demons, trying to speak between running and the thunder drowning out her speech.

"We either fight demons or we time-jump to escape," he yelled back, still running toward the open portal.

"I say we take our chances with the portal!" Bridget yelled in a panic. She and Dominic ran into the portal with one last arrow following them through.

Wade heard what he thought were gunshots for sure as the sky lit up once more, enabling him to make out who he thought to be Oz and Zeke. They had found the demons and were trying to shoot them but were unsuccessful. The demons had made it into the portal, about twenty-seconds behind the kids. Wade ran up to them shouting their names so they would know it was him.

"Wade," Oz said, "have ya' seen Bridget and Dom'nic?"

"Yes sir. They ran into the storm portal to escape the demons." Wade's near breathless answer came between gulps of air.

"Let's pray those two had their Portgens on them, and that they found somewhere on the other side to get away from the other two," Zeke said, worry evident in his voice.

"Well, if they don't have the Portgens, at least we should be able to track them with the chips, right?" Wade asked.

"Let's hope so, boy. All depends on where those two end up, an' wheth'r er not they got away." Uncertainty tinging Oz's words. "Let's get back ta' camp an' see if'n they found Jason yet." They turned and headed back toward camp coming across Gabby along the way.

Seth had just rounded a massive oak tree whose roots went down a steep incline. As he worked his way down to the bottom, he saw a light appear somewhere around the corner and suddenly Jason stepped out into Seth's light beam.

"Jason, thank heavens, where have you been? We need you back at camp, several of the others have been hurt."

"Hurt? How did that happen?"

Seth stopped and looked at his friend. "Jason, camp was just attacked by demons. A lot of them. Where have you been, man?"

Jason hung his head, truly upset with himself now. He had let down his friends for a few minutes with Memnah. Even though his guilt ate at him, he still relished the small thirty-minute visit with her.

"Anybody dead?" Jason asked concerned, stalking past Seth toward camp.

"Not that I know of. Some of the kids are missing though. Well...?" Seth asked, knowing Jason knew what *well* meant.

"I went to see Memnah."

"You *what*? Surely you're joking!" Seth said, following his friend.

"No, Seth, I'm not," Jason bit back.

"You put everyone in jeopardy for a little fling?"

"No, Seth, I left for thirty minutes! I doubt whether or not I had been there would have made much difference one way or the other, besides, Merlin was there. And Memnah is not a fling! She is the only woman I have ever loved. Someone who, no matter how hard I try, I cannot seem to forget!"

"Don't you remember all the lectures you gave me about losing Caroline when I first arrived. All the *wise* advice about moving on and accepting that I would *never* see her again?" Seth yelled back.

"Yes, Seth, I do! But you now have Caroline, don't you?" Jason stopped walking and turned to look his friend square in the eyes. "I don't know why God gave me these feelings for Memnah. Someone I apparently can never have. The temptation to see her, knowing it only takes the push of a button, was just too great. You know, it's been really tough watching you and Caroline get to have what all of the rest of us desire. It isn't fair, Seth. I know that fairness doesn't play into our lives, but I *will* not feel sorry for taking *thirty minutes* for myself and Memnah."

"Jason, I understand what you're saying. But if you remember correctly, I had given up hope of ever being with Caroline again. I stopped looking for ways to find her, even though the hope was still alive in me, I stopped for the good of my friends, and our missions, and I chose to follow God whole-heartedly. It isn't either of our faults that God chose to bring us back together."

"Good for you, Seth. I'll give you credit for that. You're a much stronger man than I am when it comes to matters of the heart." Jason turned and walked away. Seth watched his friend go, shook his head, and followed behind as they made the walk back to camp in silence.

Fortunately, by the time they arrived back at camp the rain had stopped, and the thunder and lightning could be seen and heard in the distance. Entering into the mess and chaos that was once the campsite, Jason heard Simon call out. "Praise the Lord, you're unharmed!" He walked over to Jason, hugged the man, and slapped him on the back. "Although I wish I could say the same for some of the others, but you can fix them up. What on earth happened to you, my boy?"

Jason looked at Simon. He could never lie to Simon, but telling him where he had been, in front of the others, wouldn't do.

"He was out searching for the teenagers as well. He said he saw them running into the woods, but never found where they went," Seth said, stepping in to aid his friend in his time of need. Seth may not agree with what Jason did, but he was his friend after all, and he did understand how Jason felt. If he had had the opportunity to do what Jason did when he first arrived here, he probably would have never come back. Jason did come back and deserved his respect for that alone.

Jason looked at Seth giving him a slight, almost undetectable nod of appreciation.

"Did anyone find them yet?" Jason asked.

"Not yet I'm afraid." Simon led Jason to the four who had sustained injuries. Jason bent down to heal the wounds of the injured, but when he got to Sean, he refused Jason's healing touch.

"No thanks, Jason. Safra's herbs have taken the sting out, and frankly the scar will make for an interesting story in my old age." He grinned broadly at Jason.

"All right, Sean. If you're sure." Jason grinned back.

"I am. Besides, battle wounds remind me that I survived, and I am still alive to fight another day."

Jason was learning to appreciate the courage and outlook of the young man whom he once thought was brash and irresponsible, briefly recalling the incident at Solomon's Copper Mines. He stood, patted Sean on the shoulder, and walked off to help the others clean up camp. Thank goodness for the campfire and the many flashlights and camping lanterns they had or clean up would be near impossible in the dark.

Oz and the others returned to camp with the news that Bridget and Dominic had vanished into a storm portal followed by two demons. Simon, and several others all tried searching for their location with the updates that Ryan had made to the Portgens, but the signals were random and sketchy; possibly due to the amount of electricity that still lingered in the air. At least Simon hoped that was all it was.

Merlin was curious as to what the Portgen was, so Simon spent several minutes explaining it to him and showing him how it worked.

"Simon, may I suggest that you all come back to the Castle with me to spend the night?"

"Thank you, Merlin but I am afraid I must decline. I would have rather enjoyed that, but we need to stay here just in case the two missing kids show up."

"I understand. Well, it appears you all have things well in hand here. I think it's time for me to head back before they send a search party out to find me." With that being said, Merlin, with a swish of his arm, vanished into thin air.

"Now if only I could do that!" Simon smiled with admiration, shaking his head in respect for the living legend whom he had always greatly admired.

Sofia came walking into camp and finding Simon, headed straight for him.

"Simon, can I talk to you privately?"

"Sure, let's just step inside my tent here."

She followed him inside, making certain that no one watched them.

"I was walking through the woods looking for the teens. When I circled back toward camp, I found this lying on the ground." She held out her hand and there was an odd-looking shaped item.

"Is this what I think it is?" Simon asked, incredulously.

"Yes, it's the stolen key."

"How ever did you find it?"

"Something flashed in my light beam. When I bent down to see what it was, I couldn't believe it. The jewel in it must have reflected the beam when I passed over it."

"Well, at least we found it," Simon said smiling. "And we know the betrayer is definitely someone here in camp. Now let's go finish helping the others clean up, shall we?"

Simon decided he would inform the leaders about the found key in the morning. They already had enough to deal with tonight, and everyone could do with a good night's rest. They would deal with everything else in the morning. He just prayed that Dominic and Bridget were safe no matter where they had ended up.

For the Spirit God gave us does not make us timid,
but gives us power, love and self-discipline.

2 Timothy 1:7

Chapter 16

Storm Valley, Bakrashan, Zanchier

Bridget and Dominic exited the storm portal into a very dark, very stormy night unsure as to where, until Bridget realized where they had landed.

"Dominic," she yelled against the torrential wind and rain, "follow me, quickly." She grasped the sleeve of his jacket and pulled him into the tree line at the edge of Storm Valley. She knew this place well, and she hoped she would find Oz's tree house in good shape. Zanchier may not be the safest place to land, but at least she was very familiar with it, and she had some old friends here she wanted to see.

Dominic slowly drug up behind her and she wondered why in the world he was moving so slowly. They made it to the cover of the trees, when the sky lit up once more just as the two demons, now in their true grotesque forms, stepped out of the portal into Storm Valley. Thank goodness they didn't know where she and Dominic were. She doubted they would be any match for two demons by themselves. She turned to speak with Dominic when she noticed the arrow sticking out of the back of his shoulder.

"Oh my, you're hurt. I'm sorry, I didn't know. Can you make it further?"

"I think so, it hurts really bad though." Dominic squeaked out.

"Please Dominic, you must try. I know where we are, and I know where I can take care of you, but you must walk. I will try to find a cave close by or one of Oz's hideouts. Here, put your arm around my shoulder and lean on me." Bridget grabbed him around the waist and hoisted his weight onto her small frame. They walked about half a mile further into the woods through the torrential rains toward Oz's tree house, with Bridget constantly glancing back over her shoulder to make sure they weren't being followed. Dominic collapsed about a mile from Oz's tree house, pulling them both to the cold, wet, slippery ground beneath.

The thunder cracked overhead streaking lightning across the sky. Bridget closed her eyes and telepathically called out to Han for help. She called over and over, willing him to find her as she threw herself over Dominic's shivering form, trying to keep him warm somehow. She soon heard it; the small crying call Han often used when he was looking for her. She felt his powerful presence as he landed in the trees that encircled them, finding a way to make it down to ground level where she was.

Bridget looked up into the large golden eyes of Han, who happily rubbed his beak against her face and hair. She hugged the bird around his enormous beak and looked up into his large golden eye.

"Han, my friend is hurt! I need you to carry us to Oz's tree house on the lowest platform you can reach." Bridget stood and climbed upon Han's back, instructing him on how to pick up the lifeless body of Dominic. With his large front talons, he grasped the boy, then hopped through the large, lower tree branches upward, to find a place from which to take flight.

Ten minutes later, Han had deposited them on the lowest platform of the tree house, squawked at Bridget, then flew away. Bridget ran inside, grabbed one of the blankets from her and Caroline's bedroom, ran back up the stairs, and wrapped Dominic in the blanket so she could drag his body down to the closest room in the house. But before she could do that, she had to remove the arrow from his shoulder. She had no choice but to pull it back out the same way it went in. She prayed God would give her strength, grabbed the arrow with both hands, then braced Dominic's body to the platform with her knees.

"I'm sorry Dominic but this will most likely hurt." She exhaled and yanked with all her strength. Dominic screamed in pain and passed out once again.

"Well at least I know you're still alive."

She wrapped the blanket as tightly as possible and dragged him into the bedroom, about twenty steps down into the tree house. Bridget's body protested with each movement she made, but she had no choice but to keep going. She undressed Dominic down to his underwear and wrapped him in even more blankets to get his body temperature up. She threw off her own waterlogged coat as she ran downstairs into the kitchen to start a fire, grab some clean water from the barrel in Oz's kitchen, clean towels, and some herbs Oz used medicinally. Once the fire was going, she ran back up and tended to Dominic's wound. She just couldn't understand why an arrow wound could make him so sickly and lethargic until she lit the candle, turned him over, and had a good look. Apparently, the arrow with which he was hit was laced with some kind of poison. Purplish black streaks threaded out from the wound across his body in all directions.

"Good Lord! What do I do now? Please God, show me what to do?" Bridget prayed as she worked to clean the wound and pack it with a drawing salve that Oz made from the root of a plant that grew here in the mountains of Xantifal. She temporarily bandaged the wound and went to check on the hot water. She knew hot water, although it burned, would draw out poison. She grabbed the kettle, hauled it to the room, soaked the rag in the water and placed it on the open wound. Dominic moaned slightly from the contact. She continued in this manner, rinsing the rag in cold water after each time. When the water had cooled too much to be of any benefit, she repacked the wound with the drawing salve, bandaged it well before tucking the blankets tightly around Dominic's now shivering body, and sat helplessly looking at her very sick friend. She prayed fervently for their safety and for God to spare Dominic's life before she fell asleep, completely worn out, still sitting in the bedside chair with her torso lying across her friends' stomach.

Tintagel, England, 1035 AD

Simon had a very sleepless night as did most of the others. Everyone was worried about Bridget and Dominic and most had stayed up praying through the night. Many urged to do so by a feeling that something wasn't right. Simon was one of those urged to pray. Safra had risen earlier and got the campfire going for coffee, drawing the images she was given during the night as she prayed for the two lost Keepers.

"Good morning, Simon," Safra greeted him rather solemnly as he appeared from his tent. "Coffee?" she asked holding out a cup to him.

"Yes, thank you, Safra."

"God gave me a vision last night. It is a strange range of mountains and open plains that I have never before seen."

"Well, we will show them to everyone later when they wake to see if anyone recognizes the area. Either way, I am unsure as to whether we should continue on or wait here for Bridget and Dominic. With Merlin's visit last night and then the demon attack, we were lax in giving everyone the new destination. They have no idea where we are headed next."

"Have you tried to communicate with them via the Portgen? Did not Ryan install vocal communications abilities?"

"He did, yes. We haven't tried that yet. I guess we all forgot about that new feature. I will go get my Portgen and see if that will work."

Simon, with coffee cup in hand, returned to his tent. As he was walking in, Jason and Oz were up and had already began to prepare for the day ahead.

"Good morning, Gents," Simon greeted them, sipping from his mug. "Before I forget to mention it, spread the word to the other leaders that the mysteriously vanishing key has made an even more mysterious re-appearance."

"How's that?" Oz exclaimed.

"Apparently after the demon chase last night, Sofia came across the item in her flashlight beam while walking back to camp after looking for Bridget and Dominic."

"That seems a bit fortuitous, don't you think?" Jason asked skeptically.

"What do you mean, Jason?"

"Well, the key goes missing from *her* room on Reader's Island. We searched for two days through everyone's things and found nothing. Now, she just *happens* to find it lying on the forest floor. Am I the only one who finds that suspicious?"

"No. The thought crossed my mind as well, but if she did take it, then why give it back now?"

"She knew we were searching hard for it and would eventually find it," Jason said assured.

"Perhaps, but unlikely. Oz, do you think she is capable of betrayal?" Simon addressed him.

"I wouldn't a' thought so. She was always one a' the good' 'uns back in the day. But she was trapped on Zanchier like me, only she endured a *whole* lot worse for *much* longer 'an I did. Sometimes people just change, even if they don't wanna'. If she did take it, th'n she's a might better actress than I fig'red her for. She sure has me fooled."

"Well, anyhow, let's not jump to conclusions. It could have fallen from anyone's pocket, pack or whatever during last night's battle. But, still, let's keep an eye open, shall we?" Simon concluded. "Now, let's go see if we can find our two lost lambs."

Oz and Jason followed Simon back to the campfire and the steaming pot of coffee, each pouring themselves a cup. The rest of the campers were already stirring about in search of coffee themselves.

Simon noticed from the open front of Timothy's tent that he was moving very slowly this morning.

"Excuse me, fellas, I have some unsavory business to tend to. Jason, you and the others see if you can find a signal to contact the missing two with the Portgens." With that, Simon turned and headed in the direction of Timothy's tent.

"Timothy," Simon addressed the man as he entered his tent. "May I ask what in the world you're doing with an empty bottle of whiskey?"

"Isn't it obvious?" he said matter-of-factly, not bothering to look at Simon, his eyes closed against the brightness of the early morning light.

"Yes, painfully so. Why, I'm still unsure. Do you know we had a demon attack in the camp last night?"

Timothy sat up a little, daring to slightly open his eyes, fearing the painful headache it would bring on.

"No, I...I didn't. Is everyone all right?" Tim stammered.

"Some sustained a few injuries, and then there are the two that are missing," Simon said sharply.

"Who's missing?" Tim quickly sat up; concern actually present in his voice. The sudden movement shot pain through his head and nausea through his stomach.

"Bridget and Dominic. I suggest you get up and go get some food. Safra may have a remedy for your hangover. But first, let me make myself perfectly clear, Laddie. I'm not against an occasional drink, but letting yourself lose all sense of self preservation, putting the others in danger because of your selfishness, or forgetting the importance of what you are called to do here is a *grave* mistake. It will not happen again. Do I make myself perfectly clear?" Simon spoke gruffly to him. "If it does, I will restrict you to camp from then on for every mission." With that, Simon left the tent to rejoin the others.

Timothy didn't look up, just cleared his throat, and saluted as he replied, "Sir, yes sir, Mr. Simon, sir," in a cocky yet somewhat serious tone. For he knew Simon meant it and was a man of his word.

Tim raked his hands across his face and through his hair trying to wake himself up a bit and will some of the grogginess away. He pushed himself up, decided to change clothing since he wore the same ones from yesterday and they wreaked of liquor. After cleaning up some, he went in search of Safra before trying to eat or interact with anyone else. He could truly kick himself for letting things get so out of control last night. He needed to get a handle on his feelings and emotions, or he may end up falling back into alcoholism. It isn't a place he wished to revisit again. He only hoped that his mistake at the pub yesterday with the taste of the ale, and the stress of the Kristin situation didn't drive him back to it. He looked heavenward and uttered a prayer.

"Lord, give me strength."

Tim found Safra, and she did indeed have a tonic that he could take to help with the side-effects of his over drinking yesterday afternoon. It wasn't pleasant tasting at all, but she assured him it would work in about thirty minutes.

Simon took a minute to watch the people mill about camp. Most seemed lost in their own thoughts this morning. The spiritual trials seemed to be hitting everyone relatively hard today. Jason was moody and distant as of late, surely missing Memnah. His and Seth's relationship seemed to be a bit strained as well lately for unknown reasons. There was something happening between Sean, Kristin, and Timothy that he was unclear on. Timothy had taken to getting drunk, which from what Simon knew of him was oddly out of character. Bridget seemed to be dealing with her father's past as mention of it seemed to creep up. Uriah appears to have grown even more distrusting, if that were at all possible. Alec and Odessa were strangely at odds, barely talking at all these days. Nick always seemed to have a dark cloud over his head, but that wasn't new. Simon would have to pray very hard indeed for his people if they were to come out on the other side of this for the better and not the worse.

"Anyone have any luck contacting Bridget or Dominic?"

"Not yet, Simon, but we aren't going to give up," Jason stated.

"Simon," Caroline asked, "you said before that the chips didn't work when Seth was in Zanchier. Do you think that may be where they were transported to?"

"Hmm…it is a very real possibility. That may explain why we can't seem to reach them."

"Can't we go after them?" Zeke asked.

"The problem there is we aren't exactly sure how to get there ourselves. It isn't a marked or plotted plane. Ryan hasn't even been able to find it with all of his technological know-how."

"Still, there must be some way to communicate with them?" Zaccai stated.

"We can try mental telepathy?" Caroline suggested. "Perhaps if we all tried at the same time, it might cross the necessary boundaries?"

"I don't have that ability," Zeke stated.

"Neither do I," said Sean.

"Me either," Kristin confirmed as everyone chimed in with the same answer.

"You mean to tell me you can communicate with Bridget using just your mind?" Uriah stated, aggravated that yet again, he seemed to be left out of something. "Can you read minds?" he looked at her pointedly.

"Not exactly, I've never really tried other than when communicating with Bridget and Oz," Caroline replied.

Uriah and the others looked at Oz. "You're telepathic as well?" Uriah asked stunned.

"Yeah," Oz stated with a shrug of his shoulders.

Uriah seemed to stew over his answer. "Can you tell what I am thinking right now?" he said rather harshly.

"No," Oz stated, "But I fig're I can guess if I think 'bout it," Oz growled back at the man, who exchanged an irritated look with him.

"Who else has this ability?" Simon inquired of the group.

Sofia raised her hand, but no one else.

Jason spoke up, "It's odd that Sofia can as well. Do you think it might have something to do with those that have been on Zanchier?"

"Well, if none of the others are, then perhaps so. Seth has been there." Simon looked at Seth. "Have you ever had an experience with telepathy, Seth?"

"No. I don't believe so. But I can't say that I've ever tried."

Alec interjected, "I can move objects and myself with my mind, but I've never tried to communicate with another person." He was now curious to know if it were a possibility.

"It's possible that I can as well," Odessa stated, "especially since my gift is premonitions."

"Why don't we all try a little experiment," Simon said, looking at everyone in turn. "All of you gather around the fire here in a circle. Clear your minds and think of another person in this circle and try to mentally communicate with them. More of you may have the ability, but since it was never brought up, we just never tried."

People got up and moved their seat positions, doing as Simon asked. There was complete silence other than the noises of the forest in the early morning hour.

"Now, I want you all to concentrate. If any of you feel someone else communicating with you then raise your hand, but do not speak so as not to break the other's concentration."

A minute passed with only Alec and Odessa raising their hands, Odessa wiggling excitedly in her seat at the realization of another ability. Simon smiled at her zest for life and excitability over most anything related to the peregrination lifestyle.

"All right, everyone, open your eyes." Everyone looked around noticing that Alec and Odessa did indeed have the ability.

"Now, just because you didn't hear someone today, doesn't mean the ability isn't there. It could show up at any given time. I suggest everyone take some time to exercise your minds to accept the possibility that you may one day receive this gift as well."

Oz spoke up. "Alec, Odessa, I suggest the two a' ya' spend some time with Sofie, Caroline, and me ta get it under control. It may take a while ta learn ta tune other's thoughts out, an' ta keep people out a' yer own head."

"We still need to try and reach Bridget," Caroline said.

"Yes, you three more experienced ones try that out, will you?" Simon stated. "Before you all leave to pack camp, Safra has some pictures for all of you to look at to see if you recognize anything from them."

Uriah glanced about the camp, especially at those who seemed to have so much, most of who were relatively new to peregrinating. He looked over at Timothy who was sitting next to him, drinking coffee, and nibbling on a biscuit.

"Why do you think *they* all get so much over the rest of us?" Uriah said, motioning with his head toward Caroline, Odessa, Alec, and Seth."

"I don't know, Uriah. Right now, I really don't care." Tim's reply was barely audible.

Zaccai, standing just behind Uriah, overheard the question he posed to Timothy.

"Perhaps, Uriah, it has to do with the ability to *handle* added responsibility," she said walking up next to him. "It is not ours to question why God gives to others and not us, but to accept our place, and do as He instructs us." She looked pointedly at him, then at Timothy, threw the remainder of her coffee into the fire, and then walked away.

Uriah stood and walked to his tent to begin the packing process. Not wishing to be near anyone else just now.

Tim, still seated, looked around the camp watching everyone busy themselves. He watched Kristin and Sean working together to load the extra equipment that was kept in Nick and Sean's tent. Since there was only the two of them in one tent, the things that needed to be kept dry was stored in the extra space. Sean and Kristen seemed to get along very well. They worked together in a way that Timothy and she did not. He didn't know what had changed in their relationship in a few short weeks, but something certainly had, and Tim wanted to know how he could get Kristin's attention the way Sean did. He finished up his coffee and food and went to pack like everyone else.

"Simon," Oz stated, pointing at the picture Safra held. "them moun'ains there look like the ones back on Zanchier. Looks like that might be where the two a' them may 'ave ended up."

"Is that good news or bad?" Simon peered over his glasses at his friend.

"Depends," Oz said with a shrug of his shoulders. "Bridget knows the area, perty well, but there's still all sorts a' dangers there. At least she'll have the animals ta' protect her."

"What good could a few animals do?" Simon questioned.

"Ya' ain't seen the like a' these animals b'fore," Oz said assuredly. "'Sides, she knows how an' where ta go ta leave Zanchier."

"Which brings us back to our first problem. Do we stay here, or do we press on?"

"Well, if they do come back here, she can find us on the Portgen. She did take care a' herself fer two years after Hiram passed."

"All right then, we shall move on and assign some people to keep trying to reach them."

"Me an' Caroline 'll take care a' that," Oz offered.

"I'll also leave word with Merlin. Perhaps he could keep an eye out here for them as well."

The mid-morning sun lit the forest with light as the busy travelers packed and readied themselves for the long voyage across the ocean to the island of Cyprus, Greece, in the year 1295. There they would continue the search for the Breastplates, hoping for a successful mission.

Zanchier

Bridget awoke four hours later; her body numb in spots and her neck and back ached from the uncomfortable position in which she had slept. Dominic was still unconscious, but he was breathing. She rolled his body forward so that she could check his wound. She removed the bandages to have a look. The area around the hole in his skin was now pink instead of red, and the black veining poison lessened, meaning it was drawing back out of his body. *The salve was working, thank you, God,* Bridget thought, offering a prayer of thanks to her heavenly Father. She went downstairs, stoked the slowly burning embers in the fireplace, and grabbed a clean bowl of water and towels to clean the wound again before applying a fresh round of drawing salve and bandages.

When she went back upstairs, Dominic was awake but groggy.

"I am certainly glad to see that you're going to be all right," she said with a slight grin.

"I feel awful. What happened to me?" He tried to push up into a sitting position, but found he lacked the strength.

"Just lie still. One of the demon's arrows hit you in the shoulder when we time jumped. It was poisoned. I need to clean it again and reapply the salve. It may hurt, but it is working to draw the poison out, so, you'll have to bear it."

He shook his head weakly in agreement as Bridget shifted his weight onto his side once more.

Dominic winced in pain as she used the hot water to clean the wound. "Where are we?" he asked, glancing around the room moving only his eyes.

"We are in Oz's tree house on the plane, or planet, or, whatever it is, in Zanchier. This was mine and Caroline's room when we were here."

"Is there anyone else here?"

"No. It is just us."

"Will we be safe here?"

"Yes, for now we are fine. Now, stop asking so many questions. We can discuss all of this when you get better," she fondly scolded him as she rolled him onto his back again.

Dominic looked at Bridget. Her hair was a sight, her clothes a wrinkled mess and she had dirt all over her. He realized that she must have been taking care of him and neglecting herself.

"Thank you, Bridget. For saving my life," he weakly breathed before closing his eyes and falling back into a deep, restorative sleep.

Bridget noticed Dominic's eyes rake over her appearance. She knew she must look a sight. After tucking the covers around him once more, she cleaned up the medicine supplies and went in search of something clean to wear after she took a shower. Oz's tree house fortunately had running water from a rain catch basin he had fashioned. Unfortunately, it would be very cold water, but a shower none the less. She found a clean shirt to dry off with and went into the bathroom.

As she stood there, letting the water run over her mostly bare skin, she thought about her friends and how worried they must all be about the two of them. She also wondered if everyone else fared well in the demon attack. Wade had gotten separated from them somewhere along the way. She only hoped he wasn't lost in a portal somewhere as well, all alone and frightened. Neither Wade nor Bridget were much as far as warriors went. The only one out of the three of them that knew how to fight was Dominic and look what had happened to him. Goodness how was she ever going to do this on her own. Zanchier was a treacherous place to navigate alone. Dominic knew nothing of this world. She only had herself and God to rely on, and the animals of course. How grateful she was to Han for answering her call for help. She would have to give him proper attention in the morning when he came around to visit. She knew he would, and she would call Paxton and Mother as well. She had missed them so much. She was glad about being back here, just to be able to see them again. As soon as Dominic was well enough to travel, they would go to the dustbowl and leave here once again.

After her chilling shower, she found another of Oz's large shirts he had left behind, changed, and then headed back upstairs. She looked at the sleeping Dominic one last time before climbing into the other empty bed in the room. With her body still exhausted from the trials of yesterday evening and the long night's watch over her sick friend, she instantly fell into a deep sleep.

When morning's light broke through the window into the small room of the tree house, Bridget stirred awake. She opened her eyes to Dominic who was lying quietly, just watching her. She tilted her head up at him and he smiled brightly at her.

"You're awake," she said in her chipper lilt, though it sounded more like a question. "Why didn't you wake me? You must be starving after last night. I know I certainly am." She sat up and pushed the covers away, swinging her legs over the bed's edge.

"You looked so peaceful I didn't want to wake you." Dominic smiled back.

"You certainly appear to be feeling better." She stood and walked across the room, hands on her hips looking down at him.

He looked over her appearance and grinned.

Bridget looked down at the shirt she was wearing and giggled at what she must look like. It was huge and the hem nearly touched the floor. The sleeves were so long that she had to roll them up many times and they still nearly fell to her wrists.

She looked back up at Dominic and giggled. "This is one of Oz's shirts that I found in his room. He really is a very large man, isn't he?" She smiled, holding her arms out to her side and swinging her body back and forth as the two of them laughed at the material spinning around her.

"I'm going to find something suitably sized and clean to wear, then, I will scrounge us up some food."

"I can help, Bridget."

"No, you cannot!" She abruptly stopped his ascent from his bed. "You have got to get well enough for us to leave. Leaving Zanchier isn't like other places. There is a lot more involved than either of us will like, so stay in bed and rest. I shall return shortly."

She found something to wear that had belonged to Sofia and left the room to change, grabbed Oz's bow and arrows and went in search of something to eat. When she returned, she would wash hers and Dominic's clothing and hang them to dry. Then she would call her animal friends and have a proper reunion.

S.G. BOUDREAUX

Pride goes before destruction and a
haughty spirit before stumbling.

Proverbs 16:18

Chapter 17

Tintagel, England

Caroline and Oz took turns every hour trying to telepathically reach Bridget as their band of riders traveled by horseback to the seashore. There they could buy passage across the strip of Atlantic Ocean that separated England and France. Some of the others had packed Bridget and Dominic's belongings and were pulling their horses behind the rest of the group.

Simon gave Merlin the coordinates for Cyprus Island, Greece, to hand over to Bridget should they return to Tintagel. Simon knew that Bridget and Dominic were smart, resourceful kids. If they came back and everyone was gone, they would head to Reader's Island where Ryan could show them where they needed to go next.

The trip from Tintagel, England, to France would take them approximately half a day. Then they would travel by land until Ryan could give him a good, unpopulated area, close to the southern-most tip of Turkey into which they could Peregrinate. If they made the entire trip over land by horseback it would take them two months. Once in Turkey, they would take another day to boat across the Mediterranean to Cyprus Island.

Merlin had given Simon a letter marked with a special seal with which he communicated with the Knights Templar. That way, they would know Simon to be who he claimed, a man sent by Merlin to take the breastplates off their hands.

The ride through the forest was peaceful, but the mid-morning sun was beginning to heat things up a bit. Fortunately, it didn't take them but a few hours to reach a seaside port, where they could find a ship large enough to not only carry all of them and their equipment, but also all twenty-two horses plus the two pack animals.

Seth looked over the boat as they boarded, smiling, and breathing deeply of the salty air. It had been a while since he had put out to sea; past the harbor of San Francisco Bay anyway. He had missed the water and the open ocean, traveling from port to port on the next big adventure. Of course, his life was definitely full of adventure now, and the best part about it was the fact that he got to live those adventures with Caroline.

"I see that smile on your face, Seth Jager," Caroline teased as she came to stand beside him at the railing, joining him to watch the animals and equipment being loaded by the sailors.

"Hello, beautiful," he greeted her with a smile and a kiss. "I have to admit, I do miss the sea some, but I get to travel with you all over the world in ways I could have never imagined. I'm certainly not complaining."

She leaned her back against the railing, propping her elbow on top and locking her fingers together across her abdomen. She grinned also, taking in the scene before them.

"I know what you mean. I've lived most of my life inside the San Francisco library, always reading about adventures others had taken. I never dreamed I would be doing something like this myself. God really threw us for a loop, didn't He?" She chuckled.

"Yeah. But what a loop!" Seth grinned again. "Even with the deaths, injuries, and near-death experiences, almost constant and usually unexpected demon battles, the traveling, training, and the fact that you and I really don't get much privacy, I have to say I'm pretty happy."

"Me too." She grinned at him, then her brow furrowed with worry. "I just hope we can find Bridget soon. I'm worried about her Seth. She's become like a younger sister to me."

"I know. I'm sure we'll find them soon. Have you had any luck contacting her telepathically?"

"No. Not at all. Oz either. We've never been this far apart since we learned of our abilities, so I'm not certain how far it transcends. But apparently, not to wherever she is now."

"So. Can you read minds?" he asked her curiously.

"I don't think so."

"Let's try an experiment. Can you read *my* mind right now?" He grinned, turning to face her, their noses almost touching.

Caroline laughed at the look on his face. "I don't need mind reading abilities to know what you're thinking right now, Seth Mitchel Jager."

He wrapped his arms around her, planted a kiss on the tip of her nose, and the two of them turned back to continue watching the loading of the boat. Grinning at the antics of some of the other Peregrines and some rather clumsy sailors. The mood amongst everyone seemed to be a happy one, even though just underneath the surface, everyone was either worried about Bridget and Dominic, or still dealing with their own insecurities, emotions, and spiritual trials.

Odessa walked up to Simon who was standing midway on the boat, watching the organized chaos while chatting with Safra.

"Simon, can I speak with you a moment?" she asked, nodding to Safra as the woman turned and walked away.

"What is it, Odessa? You look a little bothered by something."

"I just wanted to say that I'm sorry for not sensing the demon attack last night before it happened. What good is the gift of premonition if you don't pay attention to the urgings," she stated flatly.

"There was a lot to distract all of us last night, not just you," he said understandingly. "You can't expect to know when everything will happen you know."

"I know. But I've been very distracted lately and focused on my own problems. I haven't really been giving God or my gift much thought."

"Well, it happens to all of us, Lass. Don't be so hard on yourself." Simon grinned at her in his usual way.

Odessa grinned at him and walked away to roam the ship and have a good look around, then maybe find a quiet place and spend some time in prayer. She had a lot to think about and needed some answers to why she was so upset over Alec flirting with the waitress back at Tintagel, and whether or not those feelings had anything to do with how she truly might feel about him.

On another part of the ship, Sean found Nick standing at one of the railings on the boat's port side watching the seagulls bellowing their morning cries into the wind and glancing down nervously at the water below.

"What are you thinking about Nick?" Sean asked his friend, curious about the look on his face.

"Hey, Sean. I didn't hear you approach." Nick breathed deeply as he turned to his friend.

"I noticed. Is something bothering you?" Sean watched him closely. He didn't think he had ever seen Nick look anxious about anything before.

"Just nervous around this much water. I'm not a great swimmer." He looked down at his prosthetic leg.

"You didn't look like you had much trouble on the dive back at Jog falls when we went looking for that key."

"That was just a little river basin where I could touch bottom in most areas. Plus, I had a scuba tank. This," he said looking out across the expanse of ocean, "is a whole lot more water than I am used to." Nick glanced back at him.

Sean grinned and slapped him on the shoulder. "Don't worry, man. If anything happens, I promise to keep an eye out for you and be your very own personal hero." He finished with a large grin, puffing out his chest and flexing his biceps in a comical manner.

Nick looked at him and grinned. "Thanks, buddy." Nick cleared his throat and asked Sean a question. "So, where's Kristin this morning?"

"She's around somewhere, why?" Sean asked, getting a little nervous about where the conversation was leading.

"Oh, just wondering. You two seem pretty inseparable since Israel. Just curious if anything is going on?" Nick gave a small, crooked grin.

Sean was now the one clearing his throat, as he puffed out his chest a bit with a long exhale of breath. "No, why do you ask?"

"Because it appears that you two have a budding relationship forming. I'm not the only one who sees it you know."

"We *are* peregrination partners. There isn't anything unusual about us spending time together."

"No, you're right. But I see the way you look at her, and the way she looks at you when she thinks no one is watching."

Sean looked at his friend. "I'll admit, I do have feelings for Kristin. Surprising as that may sound with our history. But I'm pretty sure she and *Timothy* have a thing going."

"I wouldn't be too sure about that, Sean. I've watched her with you, and, yeah, I've even watched her with Tim. She doesn't seem to be as comfortable around him as she is with you."

"That doesn't really mean anything. Besides, I don't want to be someone else's second choice. You either like me or you don't. If I have to work too hard at getting your attention, then is it really worth it?"

"Well what if she feels the same way? Have you told her yet how you feel?"

"Well, no. Our lives aren't exactly optimal right now for a relationship anyway."

"Seth and Caroline make it work." Nick glanced at them.

Sean looked at them too. He often wondered if he could make things work the way they did.

"Yeah, but they were already married when they became Peregrines."

"So what?" Nick said.

"Well what about you, Nick? Isn't there a woman amongst our lovely co-travelers that has caught your eye?" Sean teased him.

"Nope. Not interested in a relationship."

"Why not? You're not old, Nick," Sean stated flatly.

"I know I'm not *old*," he defended, "It has nothing to do with my age."

"Well what's stopping you then?"

"I have a past. I'm not…good with relationships." Nick looked at him sideways.

"We've known each other for five years. Why have you never mentioned anything before?"

"Maybe I'll tell you about it someday," Nick said leaning against the railing again.

"I plan to hold you to it." Sean nodded. The two of them stood there in companionable silence watching the waves lap against the side of the boat. He thought about what Nick had said, and he had made some very valid points. If he didn't tell Kristin how he felt, how was she to know that he liked her. Maybe she was waiting on him to make the first move? Still, he didn't like the idea of having to compete for a woman's attention.

The boat was finally loaded and pushed off for the trek across to France. This was serious downtime for everyone. They all visited amongst themselves, enjoying the cool breeze and salty spray of the waves crashing against the hull as they sliced through the water. The journey took most of the remainder of the day, and it was late into the evening, just shy of nightfall when they pulled into port. The sailors began unloading their equipment, while Simon went in search of a hostel for them to board in for the night. They would sleep and rest up tonight, get up early in the morning, and travel to a remote, woody location from which to peregrinate. After acquiring enough rooms, Simon went in search of a quiet remote place in which to contact Ryan through the Portgen.

"Ryan, my boy. How are things on the island?"

"Fine, Simo.." Came a no-nonsense answer from the other end.

"Can you pinpoint me some coordinates around the southern-most part of coastal Turkey where we can all walk out of a portal without detection?"

"Sure Simon. I'll send them to you as soon as I have them."

"Ryan, I also need you to keep trying to get a chip reading on Bridget and Dominic until they are found."

"Okay, Simon. I will set the program to run a continual search."

"Thank you, Ryan. I'll talk to you later."

Simon went in search of a hot meal to retire to his room with, passing by most of the others in the tavern along the way.

Uriah and Timothy sat at a table finishing an after-dinner cup of coffee. Tim nonchalantly watched Kristen visit and eat with some of the others. He had avoided her all day. He was too embarrassed by his actions last night and really didn't feel like explaining his behavior just yet. She hadn't exactly tried seeking him out either. On board the ship she had spent her time visiting, and taking turns chatting with everyone, including Sean. Of course, he hadn't watched her the whole time, he wasn't that obsessed with her. He had slept on and off and visited with others some as well. Thank goodness Safra's tonic had worked it's magic or the boat ride would have been pure torture for him. He noticed that Sean suddenly appeared and decided to have a seat at the table with Kristin and some of the others.

"I'm going to the room." Tim got up from the table and left the tavern, trying his hardest not to take a bottle of liquor with him.

Uriah silently watched him go, then looked back at the table where Kristen and the others were laughing and enjoying each other's company. Uriah watched Timothy's back disappear out the door into the night, shaking his head at his friend's allowance of his own misery.

Zanchier

Bridget returned from hunting with some sort of mid-sized animal in her hand. Dominic was sitting at the kitchen table when she entered the door.

"Dominic, you stubborn boy, what are you doing out of bed?"

"I was bored. Besides, I am feeling pretty good. I had to do something, so I came down to make sure the fire was ready when you returned," he said in his defense.

"Well, I suppose I understand that." She grinned.

"Bridget, what exactly is that you're carrying?" Dominic's facial expression belaying the question.

"This is called a Tribhon. It's sort of like a cross between a large squirrel and a raccoon back home. Tastes about the same as well. There is plenty of meat on it for the both of us. After this meal, we won't have to hunt for our food anymore. The animals will most likely start to bring it to us."

"What animals? Will things like that just offer themselves up to us?" Dominic pointed to the limp creature in her hand, unsure what she meant by her remark.

"Of course not, silly. I'll show you what I mean after we eat. Since you're up and about you can help me with breakfast. I also found several large eggs. They're in my pack." She slipped it off her shoulder and handed it to him. "I'm going to clean the Tribhon while you look through Oz's flour and sugar stores to make sure they are still good. He's only been gone about a few weeks so everything should still be usable unless something has gotten into them." She pointed to where Dominic needed to look.

Dominic watched her methodically clean the animal, making short work of it.

"How did you learn to do that, Bridget?" He was finding himself constantly surprised by things he was discovering about her.

"Well, Caroline and I did live here for two months. While she and Oz took care of other things, I did the cooking, cleaning, and other small tasks. It took me a bit to figure it out. Oz showed me a few tricks as well. This Tribhon will be our lunch or dinner meal. The eggs should be enough to tied us over until then. I'll also bake a loaf of bread to eat with the Tribhon and gravy. There are some wild herbs that grow close to the tree house that we can go pick after breakfast. I'll use them to season the meat."

Dominic found the flour and sugar to be unspoiled, then removed the almost, football-sized eggs from Bridget's pack.

His eyes grew round with surprise. "Good grief! What did you have to wrestle or climb to get these?"

Bridget giggled at his words. "Nothing. The birds that lay these eggs are non-flight birds. The have wings but can't get off the ground. They are very fast though and quite protective of their ground-level nests. Fortunately, I found these unattended."

She finished cleaning the animal while Dominic cooked the eggs in the large swing-style pan that Oz had fashioned in the fireplace. They ate their meal, both of them hungrier than they expected, then went to the platform to introduce Dominic to Han and Cho, and several of the other forest creatures which recognized Bridget and came to call. Since Dominic was also a Keeper, he could speak with the animals as well, and the two of them spent the next hour or so playing with and getting to know the native beasts.

Bridget needed to start cooking their next meal, so they went outside to gather the herbs needed for seasoning and cooking. While outside amongst the trees, Dominic heard distant rumbling.

"It sounds like a storm is coming," he stated as he watched Bridget to know what plants to collect.

"That's no storm. That is the mountain rumbling. The Shifts are happening somewhere."

"What does that mean?"

"The mountains here sort of disappear then reappear but are sort of turned around when they do. They are called 'Shifts' and can be very dangerous. But don't worry, the Shifts don't happen this high up into the mountains."

"This sure is a strange place."

"There are so many other things I need to tell you about. We can discuss all that while we are making lunch."

The two gathered what was needed and headed back to the safety of the tree house.

French Coast

Waking with dawns early light, the large group of travelers packed up and headed southeast toward Turkey. They would make the twelve-mile journey into a heavily wooded area and open the Portgens to pass through quickly. The light of day should camouflage the Portal's light.

Ryan had given them what he thought to be a heavily secluded location. How he found such places with his technical equipment was an enigma to Simon and the others. The man hardly ever left his computer room or even stepped outside, but he was almost never wrong about a place or idea, and today was no exception. The Portgens showed the closest town to be twenty miles due south toward the coastline. They would most likely reach the coastal town well after dark and would again find a place to sleep for the night before procuring another ship for another twenty-four to forty-eight-hour trip across the Mediterranean Sea, to Cyprus Island.

Jason rode up to Simon to make a suggestion.

"Simon, since the next town is a good distance ride from here, I suggest that since it is close to eleven, we go ahead and take a thirty-minute lunch and bathroom break."

"Good idea, Jason." Simon needed a break. He wasn't used to all of the physical prowess that was needed for these missions anymore. But he reminded himself that he chose to come on this mission, and he would stick it out to the end. When they found the

Breastplates of Righteousness, then he and Safra would return to the island. He figured that she was as exhausted as he was, especially since she was much older than any of the others.

All Jason had to do was pull up to an open spot and dismount. Everyone else followed suit as he announced the immediate plans.

"We have a very long ride ahead of us, so we are going to go ahead and stop to allow for lunch and bathroom breaks. Women to the right and guys to the left."

"That is correct," Zaccai stated loudly, "because women are always right." She smiled broadly as she dismounted.

"Ha, ha, ha." Jason smiled back at her.

Most everyone else chuckled at the chiding remarks between the two.

Sean decided that maybe a twenty-mile horseback ride through the forest might be a good time to have a heart to heart with Kristin. That is, if he could get her to himself long enough to have it. Sean watched Timothy as he occasionally chanced a look in Kristen's direction every minute or so. He knew that Timothy must be feeling pretty foolish after his drunken display the other night, because he was pretty much staying away from Kristen, which was totally out of character for him. But Sean also knew that it wouldn't last long. He had had the perfect opportunity over the last twenty-eight-hour period to speak with her, and yet he still hadn't gotten up the courage to do so. He wasn't afraid of her, but maybe at how she would react, not to mention the fact that something was going on between her and Timothy. Sean just wasn't sure how serious they were. But, if she had *any* feelings for Timothy, could she really have feelings for him as well? Nick seemed to think so, but he was, by his own admission, not good with relationships.

"All right, Lord. If this is the right time to speak to her, then show me," Sean said audibly, but not where anyone else could hear him. Sean made his way over to where she happened to be sitting alone on the side of a fallen, moss laden tree trunk.

"Hey, Kristen." He nervously approached her.

"Hey Sean." She returned. They were so used to each other she didn't think anything about him plopping down beside her.

"Hey," he said again, turning to her.

"You just said that." She looked at him confused.

"I know, just trying to start a conversation is all," he replied, a bit exasperated.

"Okay, so start one." She turned to look at him like he was crazy.

"I just wanted to know if you would mind riding the tail end of the procession line with me. There's something I want to talk to you about, in private."

"Sure. Is everything all right?" she asked, a bit unsure what all the secrecy was about.

"Yeah," he said animatedly, his nerves getting the best of him.

"Sean, are you okay? You're acting a bit weird." She watched as he fidgeted in his seat, fiddling with all manner of forest debris.

"Yes," he breathed out heavily, "I'm fine."

"Sean, you should drop that." She pointed at the leafy stick he was picking at.

"Why?"

"Because it's poison oak." She smiled as he quickly threw down the stick, wiping his hands on his pants.

"I'm just gonna' go wash my hands now. So, I'll catch you later when we mount up to leave." He hopped up from the log.

"Yep." She shook her head in unison; a tight-lipped grin on her face.

"Okay, I'm gonna' go now." He awkwardly backed away, almost tripping over a large branch lying on the forest floor.

Kristin's eyebrows raised in question to his strange behavior. *What in the world has gotten into him*, she wondered? She finished her meal and went in search of an obliging bush to relieve herself.

Thirty minutes later, everyone had finished eating and taking care of business. They mounted their horses and fell back in line like before. Normally riding in groups of two, side-by-side. On occasion someone's horse would lag behind a bit. Sean waited until everyone else passed, and he took up the rear with Kristen as the last two.

"All right, Sean. What's the big secret?" She grinned at him.

"It isn't exactly a secret per-say, I just wanted to talk to you about something. Something that concerns just the two of us," he started nervously.

Kristen waited for him to say more but he didn't, he just nervously fidgeted with his reins and the horn of his saddle.

"Sean," she said abruptly, "any day now would be nice. The suspense is killing me." She threw in, trying to lighten the mood.

Sean cleared his throat and started again. "Sorry, just trying to think how to start this. Kristen, when we first met, we didn't exactly get along well, right?"

"That's an understatement. We couldn't *stand* each other." She smiled at him.

"Right. But things have changed a lot over the last three or four months, right?" he asked, wanting to make sure they were both on the same page.

"Yeah. I'd say that we've become very close friends."

Friends. Sean thought, *Is friendship all she feels?*

"Sean?" She coerced him to continue.

"Sorry." He hadn't realized he had drifted off into his own thoughts again. "Anyway, I just wanted to let you know that I like you, Kristen."

"Well, I like you too, Sean."

She was still looking at him like he had two heads or something.

"No, Kristen. I *really* like you. I have for a while now. I just have been lax at telling you because, well, for one, our lifestyle makes it hard to have a relationship, and two, I know that something is going on between you and Timothy, and if that is what you want then I don't want to stand in the way."

Kristen sat there with her mouth hanging open at his declaration. He wasn't sure what was going through her mind, but by the sheer look of surprise on her face, and the fact that she seemed to be struck dumb and unable to answer, made him assume that her feelings were not in line with his.

"Look, Kristen, just forget I said anything. This isn't the time to bring this up right now anyway."

"Sean, no…I'm just surprised is all," she stammered.

"No, no, it's okay. Really, don't worry about it. We probably would fight to much anyway, you know. End up taking each other's heads off or something."

"Sean…can I explain, please?" She was trying to get him to shut up and let her speak.

"Hey you two. Looks like some serious conversation goin' on back here. Mind if I join in?" Timothy said as his horse waited for them on the path.

Kristen was taken by surprise at his rudeness. "Actually, Tim, Sean and I were in the middle of something private."

"Don't worry about it, Kristen. I think I got my answer." Sean said, riding off ahead of them, glaring at Timothy as he passed him.

Kristen's horse slowed almost to a stop at her loss for words. Her anger at Sean for not letting her speak, and at Timothy for not letting her be for more than a day, was boiling to the surface.

"Tim, what's wrong with you?" She turned to him in her saddle.

"Whatever do you mean, dear Kristen?" He played the fool.

"You know exactly what I mean. What right do you have to interrupt a private conversation?"

"What was so private about it?"

"That is none of your business, Tim!" She seethed.

"Let me guess, shall I? Sean has declared that his feelings for you are more than that of just friends?" Tim's agitation now growing that Sean had made his intentions known.

"What of it? It doesn't concern you?"

"Really, Kristen," he said in disbelief. "I made my intentions known quite a while back. How is it that him having feelings for you is none of my business?"

"Because I never encouraged your intentions. I told you I needed time to think and that I was in no way ready for a relationship at this time. *What* I do, and *who* I talk to is my business, and I do *not* appreciate you butting in where you don't belong. You want an answer, Tim. Well here ya' go. I do not like you in a romantic way, so back off." Kristen was about to spur her horse on when Tim reached out and grabbed her reins, holding her back. He took his other hand and placed it on her arm.

"Kristen, I'm sorry, please forgive my intrusion. But you can't seriously be thinking about a relationship with *Sean*? You know that you and he don't have the chemistry that we do." He brushed a stray hair back behind her ear.

She pulled her head away from his hand. "Maybe our so-called chemistry might turn out poorly when mixed. It might cause an explosion."

"Wouldn't that be something?" Tim grinned from ear to ear.

"I don't mean the good kind!" She breathed between clenched teeth. She yanked the reins out of his hands and spurred her horse forward into the group.

Timothy grinned as she rode off, his thoughts and temperament quickly growing serious. Sean had posed a real problem today. He just upped the game and Timothy would have to rethink his strategy now. He watched his fellow Peregrines in the line ahead of him when his eyes landed on Zaccai.

Timothy decided to seek counsel with her about the situation. She was after all a woman and maybe could offer him some advice on how to win over Kristin. He sped up his horse until it fell in sync with hers.

"Zaccai, may I speak with you a moment. I have a question to ask you concerning women," Tim asked, a little embarrassed. He had never had to ask anyone for advice on this subject in his previous life before peregrinating.

Zaccai looked at him, eyebrow raised with a small smile forming on her lips at his obvious discomfort. "Certainly. I will try to answer you the best that I can."

"It's concerning Kristin. I really like her, and I can't seem to quite get her where I want her to be. She is... reluctant." He wasn't about to tell her that Sean was a large part of the problem.

"Where *you* want her to be?" Zaccai looked at him in disbelief. "You cannot make a woman be where you wish her, she must want it also. I have watched you with her a few times. She is at unrest around you. You make her nervous, which is not good for any relationship."

"That's just the chemistry between us." He grinned at the memory of how she shook the last time they spoke in private back at Tintagel.

Zaccai sighed. "Ever since you discovered your armor-like skin, you have grown even more cocky and self-assured."

"What's wrong with being a confident person?" He defended.

"Nothing, as long as it isn't pushy, rude, or cocky," she offered, looking at him.

"It always worked for me before," he stated with a crooked grin.

"Perhaps, but you are now dealing with a different type of woman than what I am certain you are used to."

"Women are all pretty much the same. They all desire the same things. What could be so different about Kristen?"

Zaccai's back straightened at his remark. She smirked at him.

"You my friend, have a lot to learn about women. Especially Christian women. Your added cockiness at not being able to receive physical, bodily harm on the outside has added no benefit to your personality I'm afraid. Because of this, what you believe and practice in thought and actions, can rot you from the inside out. You need to take extra precautions with what is beneath the skin, within your heart, lest you risk your very soul in the process." She looked at him with a cautionary glance, then spurred her horse on to distance herself from him, stopping when she caught up to Zeke.

Timothy rode along thinking about what she said. Surely Zaccai didn't know what she was talking about? Maybe he should have consulted with one of the men instead, suddenly remembering his earlier conversation with Zeke and Zeke telling him almost the same thing. No matter, he'd win her over eventually, how could he not? He knew the effect he had on Kristin. It was just a matter of time.

Watch and pray so that you will not fall into temptation.
The spirit is willing, but the flesh is weak.

Matthew 26:41

Chapter 18

French countryside

The trip through the forest was long and hot. The end of summer was nearing but the weather was still very warm and humid. Most everyone rode in silence now that the heat was overtaking them and talking was beginning to become a chore. Zeke's ability to create cloud cover was a possibility, but the tree canopy already covered them from the sun's rays. The ability to control the humidity was the issue. Simon had informed them that it would be better to just deal with the temporary discomforts of the heat than to risk being seen using their gifts by anyone who might be in the woods. Having Nadia make snow flurries from the humidity in the air to cool things off would definitely draw unwanted attention should they be seen.

Simon's mind once again returned to his concern for Bridget and Dominic, wondering how the demon attack the other night happened so unexpectedly. It had proved that most everyone's demon detection was off for whatever reasons. Simon wondered about this for a moment. Odessa had explained why she did not foresee the attack, but Jason usually felt attacks before they happened. Simon wondered why he had not mentioned to him about sensing the danger of demons nearby. He supposed that Jason too was preoccupied by his own personal torments, and as Odessa said, *hadn't paid attention to the urgings.* No matter, except for still missing Bridget and Dominic things were all right. At least, once they made it to the island, they would still be able to locate the

Breastplates since neither of them were one of 'The Twelve'. Still Simon worried about them. If they were where they could use the Portgens, they should have already tried to return. Perhaps they were injured or had been captured by the demons who followed them through the portal? Simon turned to his friend riding next to him.

"Oz, have you or Caroline had any luck reaching Bridget?"

"Nope. Neither a' us has felt a thing, which concerns me jus' a bit. I'm a wonderin' why they ain't used their Portgens?"

"Yes, those are my concerns as well."

"It keeps soundin' more an' more like they might a' ended up back on Zanchier."

"Yes, or they were captured by the demons who followed them through. Or worse, killed."

"Nah, I don't believe that fer a minute, Simon. Both a' them kids are smart ones. Surely God has protected 'em."

"I pray you're right my friend." Simon sighed heavily.

Seth and Caroline road along in silence like everyone else. Seth watched her demeanor and could tell something was bothering her.

"Hey, you look like you have the weight of the world on your shoulders. What's wrong?"

Caroline sighed. "I do, Seth. As do we all, remember? You know, fighting to save humankind and all. There is a lot to be concerned about. Finding Bridget is the biggest one right now," she snapped at him.

"Well you don't have to take it out on me. I was just asking what's wrong?"

"That's just it, Seth. You should know what's wrong."

"Then just don't think about it for a while."

"Unfortunately, Seth, women don't have the pleasure of turning our brains and emotions off anytime we feel the need," she said, aggravated.

"All right, sorry! Just trying to help!"

"Well you're not, so stop trying. You're only making it worse."

"Fine, sorry for asking," he said forcefully.

She looked at him with agitation before turning back to concentrate on the path ahead.

The trek through the woods to the small seaside Turkish town finally ended at the edge of sunset. Simon procured them all rooms once again at a local hostel for the night and inquired of the innkeeper.

"Could you also tell me where I might find a captain to book passage on a ship for tomorrow morning?"

The tall, thin, man looked at Simon. "There is a tavern just down the street where most of the sailors frequent when they're in town. You might have some luck there."

"Thank you kindly, sir," Simon replied, turning to hand out room keys.

"All right everyone, listen up. Same room assignments as before. I am heading to the local tavern to speak with someone about passage for tomorrow. Would anyone like to come along?"

"I'll come with you Simon," Jason offered.

"So will I. I need to unwind," Seth spoke up. Caroline's eyebrows shot up, knowing his comment was about their small argument earlier. It appeared they might be in for another one later on tonight.

A few of the others, such as Sean, Gabby, Kristen, Nick, Oz, Uriah, Zeke, and Zaccai all stated they were coming along as well.

Simon glanced at Timothy with a look of warning. Tim received the look with irritation but knew better than to argue. He didn't need the temptation anyway.

Everyone else feigned exhaustion, and after grabbing a bite to eat, all headed to their rooms.

Caroline paced the small bedroom for half an hour, waiting on Seth to appear. She then decided to head to the tavern herself to have a nightcap as well. She needed to unwind and sitting in this small room by herself with literally the weight of the world on her shoulders, and the worry for her young missing friend pestering her, was not doing her any good.

The tavern was full to capacity when she entered the building. It wreaked of spilt beer and tobacco, and the noise was almost deafening. She felt as though she was being watched and glanced around the crowded establishment. She spotted Seth's back across the room at the bar with several of the others. As she began making her way through the crowded room, someone grabbed her arm.

"Well now, who do we have here?" a man's slurred speech told her he was not going to be easy to negotiate with.

"Kindly release my arm, sir," Caroline said, looking him square in the eyes.

"What for little lady, we were just going to have some fun. Why don't you join us?" He laughed rakishly.

"I asked nicely once. Now, if you do not remove your hands from my person, I will be forced to make you," she warned, her voice steady and confident.

All the men that were gathered around them laughed heartily at the little woman's threat.

"Is that so?" The man smiled wickedly. "Just what do you think little ole you could do to me?"

Caroline back fisted the man in the face, breaking his grip on her arm. She then leaned forward, lifted her leg, and back kicked, landing a foot across his chest, sending him sprawling back across the tables and chairs.

All the men laughed at the other drunkard's expense. Another man yelled, "We have a feisty one here, boys!"

The chaos garnered the attention of everyone in the bar, especially Caroline's friends, and of course, Seth.

Zaccai was the closest to the scene and walked up first, stepping next to Caroline. "You want feisty do you boys? What she did to him, will pale in comparison to what I shall do to you if you do not back away."

"Caroline?" Seth questioned, taking in the scene, and putting two and two together. Seth stalked across the room toward his wife, along with the rest of the Peregrines. Simon kept his seat at the bar and just watched, waiting to see if his services would even be needed, which he doubted.

"Gentlemen, I suggest you leave the ladies alone." Seth stepped in between them.

All the men looked at the looming figure between them and the women. "What's it to you, fella'?" one daringly asked, not willing to back down.

"That one," he said gesturing over his shoulder at Caroline, "is my wife. And the other, a good friend. Now, are we going to continue with this or are we going to part ways amicably?" Seth crossed his large forearms across his chest as the rest of their friends fell in behind Caroline and Zaccai.

The men looked at his foreboding stature, noticing the other people all gathered around ready to defend their friends. They took one last look, shook their heads in agreement and everyone parted ways to go back to their night of debauchery.

Seth turned to Caroline. "Are you all right?"

"Yes, Seth. I'm fine. I did have it under control."

"Sure you did. The entire room full of men were about to jump you," he grated between his teeth.

"I know, Seth. I'm also unscathed by the event. I am a trained warrior, trained by God's chosen. You don't have to act like I'm some China doll who is going to get broken at any minute." Her aggravation growing with his obvious anger toward her.

"I know, sorry. I'm just protective over you. You are my wife after all, and I don't like the idea of other men trying to take advantage of you."

"I know, and I appreciate the fact that you want to protect me. But do you now understand how I feel about Bridget?"

Seth sighed. "Yes, I see your point, and I'm sorry about making light of your feelings earlier. If there was anything more we could do to find her, you know I would be the first to go? Anyway, what are you doing out here? I thought you went to the room?"

"I was agitated and couldn't rest so I decided to come down to calm my nerves as well."

Seth turned her to look at him. "I'm sorry sweetheart, can we just put this argument behind us?"

"Yes, I would very much like that." She grinned at him, sighing heavily as some of the tension left her body. They stepped up to the counter to order a few drinks and hopefully enjoy the rest of their night.

Gabriele watched Sean sit at the counter and sulk. He wasn't his usually chipper-self tonight and she wondered why. She decided to go ask.

Kristen was on her way over to talk with Sean just as Gabby sat down beside him. When she saw Gabby sit, she made a detour for the doorway. She decided to go back to the room instead of waiting around for another chance. Everyone seemed to be dominating Sean's attentions tonight. First Nick, now Gabby. She thought that maybe, after the almost bar brawl earlier, she would get a chance to speak to him, but still no luck. She would have to wait to speak with him on board the ship tomorrow. With one last look at Sean's defeated form sitting at the counter, she stepped out the door into the night and headed for the hostel.

Gabriele waited a moment before plowing into Sean's personal business.

"Well, are you going to tell me what seems to have you all depressed this evening?" she asked, leaning forward to look up at his forlorn face.

"What makes you think I'm depressed?" He asked without looking at her. He knew she could tell something was wrong. Gabby had a keen sense of observation.

"I'm not stupid. And I know you're not normally a depressed type of person." She grinned at him. "I'm willing to just listen or offer advice. Whichever you prefer." She sat patiently, waiting for him to speak.

Sean took a deep breath, and without looking at her, started his story. "I told Kristen how I felt about her today and she pretty much was struck dumb."

"Ouch," Gabby replied.

"Yeah. Then, *Timothy* interrupted and that was the end of the conversation. They're both probably having a good laugh at my expense."

"I doubt that Sean. We both know Kristen to be a much kinder person than that. I don't think she's laughing at all. As a matter of fact, she's been sitting in the corner with a few of the others all night looking miserable herself. I even saw her watching you a few times."

"Sure she was, probably trying to figure out how to tell me she isn't interested."

"Maybe, but at least she isn't laughing at you. You shouldn't make assumptions about how she feels, Sean. You are a really great guy, and any woman would be fortunate to have a guy like you interested in them. I know I would." She stopped, waiting for him to catch on.

Sean caught the hint all right and turned to her. "Gabby, I am really flattered. You know I am. If I didn't feel like I do about Kristen I wouldn't mind exploring a relationship with you, but it isn't fair to you to try with the way I feel about her."

"I know. But that's just another reason that attracts me to you. You are an honest, straight-forward, guy who doesn't play around with a girl's heart."

Sean smiled slightly at her honesty and understanding. "Thanks, Gabriele. Your friendship means a lot and I appreciate your honesty. And one day, some guy will be worthy of your heart." Sean finished off his drink, smiled at her, and decided to call it a night. He stood up from the counter and excused himself.

"I'll see you in the morning, Gabby. Be careful staying here. These fellows have already proven they're a rough crowd."

"It won't be long before I leave myself," she said. "You know what, I think I'll just walk back with you now." She stood up, and they left the tavern, looking over their shoulders as they did.

Kristen stood at the opened, second-story, window of her room which looked out over the street below. She sat there, staring up at the stars, praying and talking to God about her predicament when motion on the street caught her attention. Walking back to the hostel together was Sean and Gabby. Kristen swallowed past the lump that was forming in her throat. Sean and Gabby got along really well. She only hoped she had a chance to talk with him before anything more could happen between the two of them. Maybe she could catch Sean before he went to his room? She grabbed her robe, throwing it around her body and tied it closed, she slipped on her sandals and carefully opened the bedroom door. Sean and Gabby were standing just across the hall. Kristen quickly closed the door, leaving it open just enough for her to peer out of a small slit. She couldn't make out what they were saying very well, but Sean had his hand on her upper arm, and when she opened her door to her room, Sean stopped her, said something, then leaned in to give her a hug. Kristen swallowed hard again past the lump in her throat that was growing. If he would have just let her answer him today. He had taken her completely by surprise. Now she only hoped that his feelings for her still remained and that he hadn't transferred them to Gabriele. She watched as Sean turned away and walked back to his room with Gabby watching him the entire time.

Kristen closed her door, slid down the frame to the floor as silent tears rolled down her cheeks. Sean was such an amazing guy. One she had come to depend on more than she had realized. Timothy had really put a thorn in their relationship now. Not only could she possibly lose her chance with Sean, but their friendship would probably forever be changed. Kristin sat and prayed until she heard the others coming down the street from the tavern. She dried her face, removed her robe, extinguished the light, and climbed into bed.

She had no desire to explain to anyone what was wrong with her, especially not until she had a chance to speak with Sean.

Zanchier

Bridget and Dominic had spent the last two days gathering food, spending time with the animals, and learning all there was to know about the dangers of Zanchier.

Bridget explained about the Shifts and the Scaithers, and that the only way to leave was by the Dustbowl. They tried using the Portgens but couldn't get a reading at all. Dominic was moving around pretty well, and Bridget figured that he should be well enough to travel in another day or two.

Bridget was her usual chatty self and even though Dominic did understand her better now, it still didn't aid him in dealing with Bridget's propensity to over talk.

On day three, Bridget was having a particularly verbal morning. Dominic tried to keep his patience with her but was beginning to fail miserably. He missed his sketch pads terribly. He would often escape into his drawings to tune people out, but unfortunately their packs were in their tents when the demon attack happened, and they had only what was on their persons when they arrived in Zanchier. It was too bad too, because he would have loved to have drawn Zanchier in all its beauty. The mountains, animals, Oz's giant tree house, even Storm Valley with its multiple storms almost daily. He only hoped he would remember well enough when they left this place.

He was feeling a bit on edge and was growing tired of hearing Bridget go on and on about everything.

"Bridget," Dominic said a bit more forcefully than was his intent. "Stop talking, you're starting to drive me crazy!"

Bridget stopped immediately and looked at him. He could see the hurt on her face. She turned her back to him and said, "I'm sorry, I didn't realize. I'm...I'm going to go for a walk." And with that, she abruptly left.

"Bridget, I'm sorry," Dominic's voice trailed after her out of the massive oak door and through the underbelly of the tree.

She could hear him calling to her to come back, but she just couldn't return. Not just yet anyway. She needed some time to be alone with her feelings.

She broke through the outer edge of the root system, and just kept walking. She was crying so much that she didn't really pay attention to which direction she was going. She wasn't afraid of getting lost nor did she fear any of the animals on the mountain side, but if she traveled too far away from the tree in the wrong direction, she could be moved further away by a shift, that is if she survived it. She didn't care at the moment; all she knew was that she was hurt by her friends' words and tone of voice.

Bridget had grown tired of walking and found a place to sit and rest for a while. As she sat there, her mind wandered to her friends Caroline and Oz, and she wondered if she had driven them, or any of the others mad as well? She sat there for the better part of an hour before her stomach began to growl from hunger. It was almost dinner time and she had missed lunch. She wasn't even sure where she was exactly.

"That's what you get for letting your emotions get the better of you, Bridget," she scolded herself.

She closed her eyes and called to Paxton. She knew he would come to her aid; she just didn't know how long it would take him. Paxton and Mother's den was down the mountain halfway to Catamount Gorge. She would have to keep calling to him for him to be able to find her. How foolish she had been to not pay attention to where she was going. That was one of the first things Oz had taught her and Caroline. To always pay attention to which direction you're going because it is easy to get lost in the woods since everything looked the same.

"Goodness, Bridget, what a ninny you are for getting yourself into a situation like this." She was beginning to grow a bit cold. She had run from the tree house so quickly she hadn't grabbed her cloak either.

"Well, well, look who we have here?"

Bridget heard a voice behind her, and she spun around searching the tree line for who it belonged to. Fear began to grip her soul. *Hurry Paxton, I need you!* Bridget called over and over telepathically as she continued to scan the trees.

"Now what are you doin' out here all by your little lonesome, girl?" Bridget soon realized who the voice belonged to as Marnor stepped out from behind a large tree trunk.

Oh No! Bridget couldn't believe she had put herself in this situation. But the Scaithers had never come this far up the mountain before. Especially since the larger animals lived up here and took shelter in the large trees and underbrush.

"Pagorinx got your tongue, girl?" Marnor cajoled Bridget as he moved ever closer to where she stood, frozen in fear. "Oh wait, you're the little one who can talk to the animals aren't you? I'm pretty sure you were riding a Pagorinx in camp the night Riglan's new girl disappeared. I've really been wantin' to talk to you, yes I have." Marnor grinned menacingly, making Bridget's skin crawl.

Marnor began walking toward Bridget, edging closer and closer as she began to back away in fear. She turned to run, where she didn't know, but she knew she couldn't get caught. Bridget ran through the trees as fast as she could go. She could hear Marner stomping through the forest floor behind her, getting closer with each step.

Suddenly the smaller trees and brush parted and out stepped Paxton, growling fiercely at Marnor, stepping between them. Marnor stopped so quickly that he slid on the rotting debris of the forest floor falling onto his back. His hands flew to his face, palms raised up trying to show the animal he gave up.

Bridget stopped running and turned at the growl.

"Paxton!" She yelled, turning to run back to him. She grabbed the animal around the front leg and hugged him tightly.

She realized he was still growling fiercely, warning the intruder to beware.

"Paxton, no. You cannot eat the awful man. Even though he may very well deserve it," Bridget said, looking at Marnor who watched the exchange between the large cat and the small girl with utter amazement.

"How are you doing that?" He dared ask.

"It is a gift, from God. Someone you really ought to get to know. He can save your blackened soul." Bridget climbed on the back of the now squatting Paxton, who still lowly growled and watched Marnor.

Marnor lay there on the ground, waiting on the cat to tear him to shreds, regardless of what the girl who now sat on his back instructed of him. Paxton walked up to him, leaning down over top of him, his hot breath blowing against his body, ruffling his hair and clothing with each pant and guttural growl. Marnor closed his eyes, his body stiffened and his heartbeat pounded in his ears, as he waited for death to take him.

As moments passed, he realized he no longer felt the hot breath of the juvenile Pagorinx. He slowly opened one eye, careful to move as little as possible. When he realized he was alone, he rolled over onto his stomach searching the surrounding forest for any sign of the cat and the girl. He fell back against the ground, relief washing over him to still be alive.

Why didn't the cat kill him? No one he ever knew survived an encounter with any of the large beasts of Zanchier. Did it really obey the girl riding on its back? Why did she instruct the cat to spare him? He wouldn't have spared her unless she was of some benefit to him. Marnor lay there on the ground thinking over the last several minutes. He finally stood and made his way back down the mountain. He had been searching for the girl who rode the animals and the one who she had rescued months back. Now that he knew they were still here for sure; he would venture a trip back up to the ridgeline. They had to be living up here somewhere, but next time, he wouldn't be as careless. She and the Pagorinx may have spared his life this time but may choose differently if they crossed paths again.

Turkish Coast

The Peregrines had to board the ship very early in the morning due to the captain's schedule. They met at the docks at four in the morning to load up and be ready to set sail at dawn's first light. Everyone was quiet this morning, most still half asleep as they found a place aboard the ship to curl up and maybe get a few more hours of rest.

The ride across the Mediterranean would take them approximately eight hours before reaching Cyprus Island, which should put them there around two or three in the afternoon. Then, hopefully, it would be a short ride to find the Knights Templar castle and possibly they would be back on Reader's Island by nightfall.

It was lunchtime before everyone had an opportunity to fully wake and get their sea-legs beneath them again. Lunch consisted of whatever snack foods they had in their packs along with their water bladders and canteens.

Kristen avoided Timothy like the plague, and still had not found the right time to speak with Sean. He and Gabriele were as thick as thieves this morning which was a major discouragement to her.

Uriah, seeing the spirit of defeat and anger beginning to well up again in his younger friend Timothy, decided to try and make light talk with him to take his mind off his situation.

Jason was moody this morning, once again missing Memnah. He stood at the railing of the ship, twisting the jewel handled knife she had given him between his fingers, gazing out over the sea. In the distance he saw storm clouds forming and knew they were sailing straight into it. He sheathed the knife and went in search of the captain.

"Captain," Jason called out, "there appears to be a storm brewing at the bow of the boat."

"I am aware of what is happening at sea, Mr. Marshal. I do not need your direction in this matter. If you are concerned you are welcome to take cover below deck," the captain stated rudely without even acknowledging his presence with so much as a glance in his direction.

Jason looked at the man, turned on his heels and went in search of Simon. He found him at the bow of the ship, watching the impending storm stir in the clouds above. Lightning began to dance between the clouds, shooting ripples of light and sound in every direction.

Simon sensed Jason's presence as he came to stand beside him at the ship's railing.

"What do you think, Jason?" Simon asked nervously. "Do you think this ship can handle something like that?" He motioned with his head.

"The captain seems to think so, but we need to have a plan just in case it can't."

"Let's round up the others and set that in motion in case of an emergency." Simon and Jason went around the ship telling everyone to meet at the ships bow in five minutes and to make sure to pass the word along.

Making sure they weren't missing anyone; Simon began the quick meeting. Everyone turned occasionally to watch the quickly forming storm into which the captain apparently had no qualms about sailing. As far as storms went, this one promised to be something fantastic, and dangerous. On land, it was something with which they could easily deal. In the middle of the ocean with no land in sight, that was a different story all together.

"If the ship starts to go down, *only* if it starts to go down, can you use your Portgens. Set your coordinates to this setting." Simon showed them, passing around the numbers written on a piece of paper.

"What if someone sees us peregrinate?" Wade asked.

"If they do, they more than likely won't survive the storm anyway if the ship sinks," Simon said honestly.

"Can't we help them somehow?" The soft-hearted young man questioned.

"I don't see how, Wade. They can't peregrinate. If it is God's timing for them or any of us to go, then it isn't our place to judge. We are here only to do God's bidding. And right now, that is finding the Breastplates. Do you understand?"

"Yes sir." Wade hung his head in fear for the ship's crew and the animals stowed below deck, and the bleak future they may all soon face.

Simon spoke again. "All right, everyone, I want you all to stay close to one another. No one strays far from where we are right now on this ship. We certainly don't need to lose anyone. Everyone find something to hold on to and pray that God brings us all through this storm."

Ten minutes later the storm was upon the ship. Lightning surrounded the vessel as the clouds let forth their load upon the ship and its occupants. The wind blew ferociously, slicing through the rigging of the ship sending things not yet tied down flying across the deck.

The ship rocked violently in the turbulent waters, tossing them back and forth from one side to the other.

Jason had to grab hold of Nadia to keep her from rolling across the deck.

"Hold tightly to the mast's ropes," he instructed her, yelling against the wind as it nearly stole his words.

Jason stumbled away to right someone else as Nadia shook her head in understanding, trying desperately to grip tightly to the ropes.

Nick noticed her struggling to keep her grasp as her hands continually slipped on the thick, rough, surface. He scooted up behind her, wrapping his arms around her back and gripping tightly to the mast, looping the rope around his wrists.

Everyone was huddled up together trying to keep from being thrown overboard in the torrential wind and rain. The waves were so large it felt as though the ship were standing on end at times.

Sean looked around frantically for Kristen, finding her grasping onto the railing at the ships port side of the bow, struggling to keep hold. He carefully and quickly crawled toward her, reaching her, and holding tightly to her as she pressed back into the safety of his arms, wrapping one arm around his waist and the other around the ship's railing.

A large wave hit the ships port side, tearing Sean from Kristen's grasp, and sending him flying across the deck and over the starboard side of the ship into the turbulent waters below.

"Sean!!" Kristen screamed over and over, catching Simon and Jason's attention. They saw her trying to stand, then run as best she could to the starboard side of the ship. She screamed his name over and over, searching the waters below for him.

Sean was tossed back and forth in the cold water, being pulled beneath the surface more times than he cared. Once when he was pulled under, he saw what appeared to be an under-water portal opening up several hundred feet away. He looked at it before swimming to the surface to catch a much-needed breath. Then he suddenly remembered he had the power to manipulate water. Could he get himself out of the turbulent ocean and back on board the ship? Sean prayed that God would find favor with him and allow this to work.

On board the ship, his friends were frantically searching the water for any signs of him.

"If I could find him, I might could get him back on board," Simon yelled to Jason.

Kristen continued to search the water as she clung desperately to the railing, screaming Sean's name over and over again, willing him to survive this somehow.

Sean concentrated on moving the water that was directly surrounding him up and over the ship. As he concentrated and moved his hands upward, the water, from what he could tell, cooperated at his command, lifting him up and over the bow of the ship, like one big wave washing him back on board.

Sean's body slammed into the deck beneath him as his friends began calling to Simon, Jason, and Kristen that Sean was on the boat. He spat and puked up water as he tried to find something else to hold on to.

Simon, Jason, and Kristen, shocked at what they saw, clumsily ran to his side to see if he was all right. Kristen threw herself into his arms, grasping the rope at his back to hold him down, knocking him back against the deck again. She clung to him, crying, as he tried to answer Simon and Jason who bombarded him with barely audible questions, him shaking his head that he was fine.

The storm raged on for another fifteen minutes before the sun dared to part the gloomy sky, bathing the ship in broken beams of light. The ship's crew frantically ran around setting the deck and rigging to rights and checking to make sure everyone was accounted for.

Sean and Kristen still clung to each other, as did most of the others, as the seas began to calm, and the rain began to stop. Kristen and Sean didn't speak at all, just sat and held each other. Kristen's grip on Sean was so tight he wasn't sure his lungs were working at full capacity.

"Kristen, I'm okay. You can let go now," Sean hesitantly said, reveling in the feel of her arms around him.

"I thought you were going to die." She began to weep again, stammering between deep breaths. "You were... thrown overboard,

Sean. I s...saw it. H...how did you end up back on board the sh...ship?"

"I prayed, Kristen. I prayed God would allow my water manipulation ability to put me back on board. I can't believe it actually worked though."

"Thank God it d...did. I thought I l...lost you for good." She buried her face in his shirt again and breathed deeply, trying to calm herself and her stammering speech.

"I'm not going anywhere for a very long time if I can help it." He turned her face up to his and wiped at the tears streaming down her cheeks. "Now, let's go see if we can get into some warm, dry, clothes."

Sean stood up and pulled Kristen to her feet. They followed the rest of the Peregrines below deck, all like-minded to do the same.

Timothy watched the two of them go below deck, knowing he had lost the fight for Kristen's heart.

He gives strength to the weary and increases
the power of the weak.

Isaiah 40:29

Chapter 19

Cyprus Island, Greece, 1295

The remaining few hours on board ship was smooth sailing, with everyone bombarding Sean with questions about how he got back onboard after being washed over. He also explained to them about seeing an underwater portal where there was none above water.

Kristen still didn't have the chance to speak with him, but she was pretty sure he knew how she felt now. But the next private moment they had she would lay it all out for him.

They soon docked at Cyprus Island. The horses, who had all but gone wild with fear during the storm, were extremely skittish and full of pent-up energy as they whinnied and kicked to let their owners know that they were down-right put out at being aboard the ship.

Wade tried to calm the animals as best as he could, but he was currently the only Keeper available, and trying to communicate with twenty-two horses plus two more pack animals was quite a chore. Several had already calmed down while onboard ship shortly after the storm had ended, but the majority were just being downright stubborn.

Several other Peregrines helped him to walk the animals in circles by the reins, allowing them to burn off the fear and energy created by the tossing of the ship. Several of the ship's men, watched in amusement at the seemingly crazy young man who talked to the animals.

Soon, though, the animals began to listen as Wade walked to each one and spoke softly, stroking their necks and heads to calm them.

The men on board the ship stood there in shock. They had never seen any beast take to a person the way all those excited horses did to Wade. He seemed to quickly soothe them with a few words and a soft touch.

They also watched the one called Sean as well. A few of them were certain they had seen him get washed overboard and the others searching the turbulent water for him, but a minute later he was at the bow of the boat. All they could figure was he got washed around deck and tossed between some of the coiled rope at the bow.

Soon the Peregrines were saddled up and ready to head inland to search for the Knights Templar's castle. Merlin had instructed Simon where he could find it, but that the Templars were a careful lot of highly trained warriors and trusted few people since their downfall and flight to the island years before.

They headed out, with Simon in the lead. They rode about an hour before they could see the tall spires and the tips of the tall stone walls of the Templar's castle. It sat off in the distance amongst the sparsely wooded patches of trees that graced the edges of the large grassy field that stretched out before them. They would have to proceed with caution. Simon knew that if they saw such a large group of people riding up to the castle, they may take it as a threat.

Simon halted his horse as he turned to speak with Jason, Seth, Malachai, and Zaccai, the leaders nearest to him.

"All right, this is far enough for our group right now. Zaccai, why don't you have everyone take a few hours break while I, Malachai, Jason, and Seth ride up to the castle."

"All right, Simon," Zaccai said. "I shall instruct everyone here as to the plans." She then turned to ride back to inform the others.

"I'll just go and tell Caroline," Seth said, as he rode off to let her know the plans, returning shortly.

"All right, lads, off we go." Simon kicked his horse onward for the mile or so left to reach the castle gates.

Zaccai rode up motioning and calling for everyone to gather around her.

"Listen up, everyone. We have a few hours down time here until Simon, and the others return." She dismounted from her horse and threw the reins over an obliging tree branch.

Zeke came up to sit beside her underneath the shade of the tree. It had been a while since he'd had the chance just to talk with her about anything other than mission related stuff.

"Mind if I join you?" He asked, waiting for her reply.

"Not at all, have a seat," she said, looking up at him.

Zeke stooped down, sitting upon the ground next to her.

"So, what's the plan?" He motioned toward the castle.

"Simon didn't want them to think we were here for a fight." She looked in the direction of the castle herself.

"Good plan. I'm a bit weary of fighting and travel at the present moment." His exasperation evident.

Zaccai grinned broadly at his statement. "I too understand your feelings very well. The storm earlier was enough to wear me out for several days." There was a comfortable pause of silence for a few seconds.

"Zaccai, I've been meaning to ask you a question."

"All right. Go on." She noted the serious tone of his voice.

"There are a lot of eligible men that travel with us. Is there anyone in particular that you are interested in or with who you are already in a relationship?"

"There are none with whom I am in an active relationship. But there *is* one man with which I may be interested in pursuing one." She gave him a tight-lipped grin as she looked him in the eyes.

Zeke grinned toothily at her response, taking it to mean that he was the object of her attention. That was very good news for him indeed.

"Am I correct in assuming that I am that man?"

"You are." She toothily grinned back.

"Well then, it seems that we are of one accord."

They grinned at each other, growing comfortably silent once again. The silence was short lived, because a ruckus was stirring on the other side of the knoll where they were taking shelter from the sun. The horses began to prance and neigh in agitation.

They jumped to their feet as several of the other Peregrines came running, announcing that demons were here.

"Ugghhh." Zaccai moaned drawing her sword with Zeke following suit.

"So much for a quiet afternoon chat." Zeke braced for the impending war.

"Yeah, and we are down four of our warriors."

The clash of steel on steel rang out across the valley, echoing off the nearby trees. Simon, Malachai, Jason, and Seth all heard the ringing and wondered where it was coming from. Realizing that their group was under attack, they rode off at full speed, back in the direction from which they had come.

The castle guards watched in curiosity of the four men who were just a few hundred feet from the castle gate, suddenly turn and take off upon hearing the battle which suddenly was taking place across the field.

The guards positioned at the top of the castle wall called down to the guards at ground level.

"Captain, I think we're under attack, sir!"

"Why is that?" He yelled back up.

"Four men approached and then turned back upon hearing a battle in the direction from which they had ridden.

"Let's go check it out, men," the captain instructed, mounting his horse.

"Lower the gate!" He shouted, his horse prancing in anxiousness.

The ground guards grabbed their armor and weapons, mounted their horses, and followed their captain who had already ridden through the gate. Thirty armed men rode out of the castle toward the sounds of the battle.

Simon, Malachai, Seth, and Jason rode as hard as they could toward the battle ahead. They weren't sure who their friends were fighting against, but something was certainly happening.

As they got closer to the fight, they realized it was another demon attack. They hadn't even bothered with changing to human form this time. There appeared to be about forty demons in all, battling against their small group of Peregrines. It was currently more than two to one.

Simon glanced back over his shoulder, noticing a large group of riders headed their way at full speed. This could be a problem if they had to battle the Knights Templar as well. Simon yelled to the others, motioning behind him. Seth and Jason glanced over their shoulders, looked at each other, and pushed the horses harder.

As the war waged on, Zeke and Zaccai were fighting about five demons between the two of them, trying to keep their backs to one another. Zaccai used her plant manipulation to grab and hold one of them, enabling one of Alec's arrows to find it's mark from far across the knoll. Another demon appeared and struck out at Zaccai, hitting the strap to her Portgen, freeing it from its holder. The demon's curiosity at the fallen object caused it to pick up the Portgen. It turned the device over and over in its hand while Zeke and Zaccai were steadily battling three other demons. It began curiously pushing buttons on the device, causing a portal to open next to where Zaccai was standing.

Zeke and Zaccai had been separated during the fight and were several feet apart. Zeke noticed the portal at Zaccai's back and yelled across to her to try and get her attention. The demon was pushing her backward toward the portal. Zeke, now anxious for what was about to happen, struck a fatal blow against the creature he battled and ran toward Zaccai. Just as she stepped inside the portal, Zeke got close enough to follow her through before the curious demon accidentally closed it, then fell dead upon the ground from another of Alec's arrows.

The battle at the other end of the knoll was still in full swing with the Peregrines battling fiercely. They were exhausted, hungry, and short on help. Simon, Malachai, Jason, and Seth finally arrived on scene and took to fighting, evening out the odds just a bit. It wasn't long before they were joined by the Knights Templar who also fought along-side them to battle the obvious evil that was present. Not a word was spoken by anyone until the last demon was vanquished.

The captain of the Templars approached Simon and Seth, recognizing them as two of the men who were approaching the castle walls earlier.

He saluted them with an arm across his chest and his fist upon his heart, bowing ever-so-slightly.

"I'm Captain Bartholome' of the Knights Templars."

Simon bowed in return. "I'm Simon Lane and this is Seth Jager."

"We saw your approach to our castle and then your hasty retreat. One of my men saw a battle up here and we rode out to see if you were friend or foe. Imagine my surprise at seeing the legions of demons in plain view. I can only assume that we were fighting on the correct side." He grinned, extending his hand to Simon, who shook it gladly.

"I and my warriors are eternally grateful to you and your men."

"What exactly is the nature of your visit here to the Templar Castle?"

"Merlin sent me." Simon's answer garnered a surprised look from the captain.

"There's a name I haven't heard in a few years. Why exactly did Merlin send you here?"

"We've come for the Breastplates of Righteousness." Simon motioned to his group of travelers.

"That isn't exactly something that we just readily give away. We were sworn to protect them by Merlin himself."

"Yes. He told me as much. He also gave me this letter to give to you should you need further convincing." Simon pulled the letter from his pocket and handed it to the captain.

Bartholome' took the letter, and recognizing the seal on the outside, instructed his knights to help their visitors gather their things and take them to the castle.

"Simon," Alec yelled as he quickly approached them. "I think something happened to Zaccai and Ezekial. I found one of their Portgens on the ground on the other side of the trees. They were battling several demons over there. I managed to take a few out, but I turned away to battle some others and when I looked back, they were gone. After the battle ended, I went to search the area and found this on the ground." Alec handed the Portgen over to Simon.

"It appears we may have two more Peregrines lost somewhere. Let's get to the castle with the captain and try to sort this mess out."

The Peregrines mounted up and followed the captain and his men to the Templar's castle. At least the Breastplates had been found, and if Merlin's letter would be of any assistance, they should soon have them in their possession.

Now, however, two more Peregrines were missing without a clue as to where. Once they got to the castle, they would try locating Zaccai and Zeke. Surely, they too would not prove undetectable.

Moshi, Africa

Zaccai glanced around at their surroundings.

"Could it be?" she stated in surprise, recognizing where she was.

"Could what be?" Zeke asked, noticing the look on her face. "Zaccai, do you know where we are?"

"Yes. Yes, I do. I am home," she said, still shocked.

"As in home, do you mean home as in your Dragoman's safe-house location?"

"No. I mean home." She smiled widely at the realization as tears stung the back of her eyes. Zaccai reached for her Portgen, realizing that it was gone. The leather strap that held it to her side, severed clean by the demon's blade.

"Zeke, do you still have your Portgen?"

"Yes, that's why I followed you here. I saw the demon playing with yours when the portal open, and I didn't want you to be stuck here alone."

"Thank you, Zeke. But they could have located me with the chipping device." She tapped the side of her neck, grinning at him.

"Well, now they won't have to. We can just set my Portgen to return us to Cyprus Island right away."

"No," she said hurriedly. "Please, wait, just for a moment. In what year does your Portgen say we are?"

"1785, why?" Zeke was unsure of what she was thinking.

"I might could see my father again." Zaccai took off across the jungle floor headed in the direction of the Kilimanjaro Mountains.

"Zaccai! Wait, where are you going?" Zeke took off after her.

Zanchier

Bridget thanked Paxton for finding her and saving her from the Scaither before she sent him home. She ran into the tree house ready to forgive Dominic for his hurtful words and tell him all about her encounter with the local bandit.

"Dominic, I'm back. I'm sorry for leaving you alone for so long, but I got lost, see..." Bridget realized she was alone. "Dominic? Where are you?" Still no answer. Maybe he was up top on one of the upper tree platforms. She ran up the steps, calling his name as she went.

"Dominic!" she yelled, cupping her hands around her mouth. *Where could he be?* she wondered.

"Oh no! Surely he didn't go looking for me?" She panicked, thinking about her friend all alone in the Xantifal Mountains searching for her. "What have I done?" She then called Han telepathically.

Han made short time coming to the call of Bridget. He found her mid-way up the tree and landed on the platform she occupied.

"Han, we need to find Dominic, quickly now. It's almost dark. He'll never survive out there alone at night." Bridget climbed onto the back of the Kabihanxu and the pair flew off to scan the mountains for him. Bridget also called to Cho, Mother, and Paxton to join in the search for the young man that the animals had just met days ago.

Cyprus Island, Greece

The Templars welcomed the Peregrines into the castle grounds as the stable hands took the horses reins to care for them. Simon and the others were led to a large meeting hall and offered drinks while they waited until Captain Bartholome' returned with whomever was in charge of the castle business. While they waited, they used the Portgens to track Zeke and Zaccai's chipping signals.

"It shows they are somewhere near the base of the Kilimanjaro mountains in the year 1785," Simon stated unaffected.

"Simon," Uriah stepped up, "that could be a real problem."

"Why is that Uriah?" Simon asked quizzically.

"Because that is where Zaccai grew up, that time date is just ten years after her disappearance as a Peregrine."

"Oh my," Simon stated troubled.

"What if someone recognizes her?" Nadia asked.

"The bigger question here is, if they are where they can return then why haven't they?" Nick added.

Uriah looked around the room. "If any of you had the chance to go back and see those you left behind one more time, wouldn't you take it? Especially since she wasn't the one responsible for making it happen."

Seth and Jason exchanged a quick look between them, then Jason momentarily looked somewhat uncomfortable, but not before Simon caught the exchange. He filed that memory away for a later discussion with the both of them.

"I see your point, Uriah. Fortunately, Zeke is with her and should be able to keep her from any real danger. Zaccai has been a Peregrine for longer than any of you. She knows to be very careful with time-traveling." Simon finished his speech just before the large doors to the room opened and in walked the captain of the guard with someone else.

"Simon Lane, this is Lord Rowthorn, High Regent of the Knights Templar." Captain Bartholome' introduced them as Simon extended his hand in greeting, the man shook it happily.

"Pleasure to meet you, Lord Rowthorn."

"Likewise. I understand you have a letter with Merlin's personal seal upon it. It has been many years since we have heard from Merlin. This was unexpected to be sure." Lord Rowthorn looked at Simon and started again. "This letter states who you all are, but I'm afraid I will need further proof. Legend states that someone would arrive here one day with The Twelve. Each one of The Twelve will be marked with a symbol for one of the tribes of Israel. I have a list of the markings that are acceptable to receive the Breastplate of Righteousness. I must first compare the markings on my scroll to those that your Peregrines bear, before I can give you the Breastplates of Righteousness."

"We may have a bit of a problem there. You see, we were just attacked by demons and two of my marked Peregrines disappeared into a time-portal, and they have yet to return."

"I see. Well unless they are present, I cannot release the armor. But until then, we can compare the scroll against the marks of those who are present."

"All right everyone, line up and be prepared to show Lord Rowthorn your marks," Simon instructed, hoping that Zeke and Zaccai would return soon.

Lord Rowthorn unrolled a scroll as each Peregrine who was supposedly marked as one of The Twelve stepped forward. Seth, Jason, Caroline, Odessa, Alec, Oz, Sean, Nicholas, Uriah, and Timothy all stepped forward to have their marks checked. Lord Rowthorn stepped back to privately speak with Captain Bartholome' for a moment, then called Simon to step forward for a private conversation.

"Simon, I am afraid you have more than two missing from The Twelve. Are you certain these are the only people with marks?"

"I believe so, why? I and the other Dragoman have personally seen the marks that each of these bear. We had a prophecy ourselves that Judah, which was Seth, would be the last of The Twelve. How can they not all be present, other than Zeke and Zaccai; and they represent Benjamin and Manasseh?" Simon was very confused now.

Lord Rowthorn showed Simon the scroll with The Twelve represented. Simon scanned the list, mentally comparing it with the one he and the other Dragoman had made of The Twelve. Every tribe was listed except for two, Ephraim and Dan.

"How can this be?" Simon stated in disbelief. "There are still twelve tribes represented, but according to scripture the two that you claim are not accepted, were also listed amongst the tribes."

"Yes, but in the book of Revelations, these two tribes, Ephraim and Dan, are replaced by Joseph and Levi. The tribes of Ephraim and Dan strayed from God, defiling themselves in worldly ways and refused to repent. God then set them aside replacing Ephraim with

Joseph, and Dan with Levi. Unless you have two more people who are marked for Joseph and Levi, I'm afraid you aren't prepared to accept the Breastplates."

Simon returned to the group of people who were anxiously awaiting an answer to whatever trouble was brewing.

"Apparently, according to the Bible, two tribes that we had listed as part of The Twelve are not listed on the scroll. Two more of you must bear marks for two more tribes of Israel. I want those of you who think you have no mark to follow me." Sofia, Nadia, Kristen, and Gabriele all stepped forward. "Caroline would you and Odessa take the rest of the women to the bathroom and check them over. We are looking for marks that look like olive branches or trees, and a breastplate but not like armor; umm, more like four rows of four squares."

"Do you mean like this, Simon?" Gabriele lifted her shirt at the small of her back. Just above the waistline, intricately inked into her skin was exactly that. Four rows of four jewels with scrolled marks extending from the four corners. The marking was approximately a three inch by three-inch image.

"How did we miss that?" Simon asked surprised. "How long have you had this Gabriele?"

"I'm not certain. I think I was born with a birthmark that resembled the image. When my mother saw the mark, she told me I was destined for something great, but she never said what it was. When I became older, she took me to an ancient man in the village who inked into my skin the image he said the creator gave to him. When I peregrinated, I took that as the destiny in which my mother saw for me."

"Well, that's one down, the rest of you go with the ladies and let them check you over." Simon took Gabriele to Lord Rowthorn for a mark comparison. Gabriele's mark was approved as one of The Twelve and she went back to sit with the others, waiting on the rest to make an appearance.

Several of the others began questioning Simon about what two marks were not approved and who had them.

"We will discuss that back on Reader's Island later, after I've had the opportunity to speak with the other Dragoman about this new development." Simon didn't want to have this discussion here and now. He wanted to make sure they researched what Lord Rowthorn was telling him and make sure the information was correct.

Caroline and Odessa checked the women over carefully, looking for anything that might resemble a tree or olive branch. They finished checking Nadia and Sofia when Caroline began examining Kristen's backside. There was nothing on her back or shoulders or anywhere around her hip area. When Caroline reached Kristen's calf muscle of the right leg, just to the inside from the back, there was a faded mark that appeared to look like a leafy branch, but it was so dull it was hard to see exactly.

"Kristen, do you know what this mark is on your calf muscle?"

"Umm, yeah. I think I remember when I was about eight years old, my dad and I were on a camping trip. I was being particularly stubborn that day and not listening to my dad very well when I fell into a burning log. It was a small one, but it still had a small branch with burning leaves on it. It laid into my skin pretty well and left a scar for a long time. I think it stretched from growth and faded so much that it's almost gone now. I'm surprised you can still see it."

"It is a bit hard to see, but with your description of what happened and what we are supposed to be looking for, I would say this is it. What about you Odessa?"

"I would say so. I mean that story is hardly a coincidence and what I can make out, it certainly looks like a tree branch with a few leaves still on it. I think we've found our girl." Odessa smiled brightly.

"Let's go inform Simon and see what Lord Rowthorn says about it." Caroline and the others returned to the room, explained to Simon about Kristen's story and had it examined and compared.

All of The Twelve were now accounted for except for Zaccai and Zeke, and Simon wondered what on earth could be keeping them.

Moshi, Africa

Zaccai hadn't run this quickly in years, nor had she been this excited. She only wanted to make certain that her father had survived the brush fire that had taken her from her home and family eighteen years ago.

She crept up on the village that lay just at the base of the Kilimanjaro Mountains in Moshi. She only wanted to catch a glimpse of her father. As carefully and quietly as possible, she inched her way forward to get a clearer view of the people milling about below. Zeke was a bit clumsier in his approach.

"Shhh…" Zaccai turned to him with her finger at her lips.

"Sorry," he silently mouthed back.

Zaccai turned back to the scene below her, scanning the people for her father.

"Zaccai," Zeke whispered to her, as she absently waved at him to be quiet.

"Zaccai?" came the sound of another voice she didn't recognize as Zeke's. She turned around to find Zeke standing with his arms in the air and a spear at his chest.

Zaccai stood up, surprising the man standing there holding the spear. "Hello Viho."

"Zaccai?" he asked, shocked to see her there. "How can this be? I saw you die in that brush fire ten years ago. Are you a ghost?"

"No Viho, I am as real as you. There is much to explain and little time to do so. Is my father still alive?"

"Yes. He is fine," Viho answered her, still in shock that she stood before him.

"Can you please bring him here to me, and do not tell another soul that you have seen me? Not even my father. I shall explain when he comes." She told her old friend and one-time fiancée.

"I shall bring him straight away, but I too wish an explanation, Zaccai." Viho stared at her momentarily, then turned and ran down the mountain.

Zeke watched as Zaccai sat upon an obliging rock, waiting for her father to arrive. He decided to try and make small talk.

"So, Viho. Is he a brother, cousin, friend?" Zeke pried, his curiosity getting the better of him.

Zaccai grinned at his questioning. "He was my betrothed when we were both very young. We were from neighboring Chaga tribes. He is a chieftain's son and I a chieftain's daughter. Our union would have meant great prosperity and strength to both of our tribes."

"So, the two of you never got the chance to marry?"

"No. On the eve of my eighteenth birthday and the day before our wedding, I peregrinated during an intense brush fire."

Zeke was unsure what more to say to her, when to his relief, they heard someone coming back up the slope. He only hoped it was who they were expecting.

Breaking through the lush greenery was an elderly gentleman as tall and lean as Zaccai.

"My daughter? How can this be?" he exclaimed, walking forward slowly and cautiously, as though afraid she would vanish into thin air once more.

"Father." Zaccai walked to him and embraced him.

"How? We thought you dead. We could find no trace of your body after the fire died out. We just assumed that it burned so hot it turned you to ash."

"No father, it is very hard to explain, and I have very little time, but I was chosen by God to travel through time doing his bidding. For you and Viho, I disappeared ten years ago. But for me it has been eighteen years, Father."

"Eighteen years?" Her father turned to Zeke for clarification that what she said was true. "So, you do this time traveling as well?"

"Yes sir, I do."

"You are not African?" Her father observed Zeke's accent.

"No sir. I come from Australia, in a much later time period."

He turned back to his daughter. "I do not understand how this is all possible. But the Creator's ways are not our own. I have learned this. You look well my daughter. This life suits you?"

"I *am* well father, and It does. It is a great mission for which we are selected. It is for the good of all mankind. I miss you terribly, but we all have given up our lives and loved ones to live the life God has set before us." She looked at Zeke as a reference, then back to her father.

"My dear Zaccai," her father said, tearing up as he stroked her hair. "I am so happy to know you are alive, and so very proud to know the Creator has chosen you for a life of greatness and sacrifice." He hugged her tightly, sensing the urgency of her having to leave.

"Thank you, Father. I miss you and think of you often." She kissed the leathery cheek of her father one last time.

"Zaccai," Viho stepped forward.

"I must go, Viho. I have no choice; it is my destiny such as yours is here." She stood still, looking at him.

"I understand. Live well, Zaccai."

"Live well, Viho."

With that last farewell, and a wave to her father one last time, Zeke opened a portal and they walked through, back to where they had left during the demon battle.

"Zaccai, are you all right?"

"I am well, Zeke. I am very well." A large grin spread across her face.

"Good," he said, looking around. "I would assume the others made their way to the castle since there doesn't appear to be a single living soul anywhere around us."

"I believe you are right. Shall we walk then?"

"Seems like the only choice we have. All the horses are gone as well."

The two set out for the mile-long walk to the castle gate. They reached the gate in record time seeing as how they jogged most of the way. The guards had been instructed to watch for two people fitting their description, and to escort them into the castle should they arrive. Simon and the others were overjoyed to see them, and their marks were compared with those listed upon the scroll. With all Peregrines now present and accounted for, the Knights Templar handed over the Breastplates of Righteousness and the group soon left, collected their horses, and opened a portal to return to Reader's Island. There they would wait for the next message from God showing them where to locate the next piece of armor. They also hoped to possibly find Bridget and Dominic waiting for them on the island but knew that was unlikely.

So in everything, do to others what you would
have them do for you for this sums
up the Law and the Prophets.

Matthew 7:12

Chapter 20

Bakrashan, Zanchier

Bridget searched frantically all over the mountainside for Dominic, but she nor any of the animals had any luck finding him. She prayed that he found adequate shelter. She knew he could also communicate with the creatures here on Zanchier and hoped that he remembered that ability. Any of the creatures could bring him back here if he couldn't remember the way himself.

Bridget knelt beside the fireplace and prayed. "Lord, please protect Dominic. I can only assume he went in search of me when I didn't soon return, and I know it is my fault he's lost. I was behaving like a ninny and let my emotions control me. Forgive me Lord, and bring him back safely, amen."

Bridget climbed the stairs to use the telescope to continue the search for Dominic the only way she knew how. There was nothing more she could do until morning, but she would watch and pray throughout the night.

Dominic stumbled through the underbrush of the mountain, wondering where he could be. He thought the tree house was in this direction. Boy did he really screw things up this time. He went to find Bridget when she didn't return after a couple of hours. He thought something may have happened to her. If she was somewhere hurt, he had only himself to blame. He needed to learn to control his tongue. He didn't have a temper exactly, but he also didn't mind telling people what he thought. Even at the expense of their feelings.

Bridget was one of the sweetest people he had ever met. And after she had saved his life, that was how he repaid her! By losing his patience with her. He should have just told her in a better way how he was feeling. So she liked to talk. It wasn't like she repeated herself. Everything she said was useful, funny, quirky, or kind. And yet he had been very unkind to her. Now, they could both be in very real danger.

Dominic's body ached. He wasn't completely well yet from the arrow and he could feel the wound pound with the blood circulating through it. He found a small cave tucked back beneath a large rock-face that seemed to be free of any animal dens. He climbed inside the cave, curled into a ball against the back wall and fell asleep.

When he awoke, it was early morning and Dominic thought he could hear water running somewhere nearby. He stood up, feeling much better this morning and went in search of the sound. He walked about half a mile before stumbling upon a rapidly running river. Could this be the gorge that Bridget had told him about? If it was, then he had traveled much further from the tree house than he expected and was about four hours down the mountainside. And from what Bridget had explained, very close to where the Shifts began.

He had heard the rumbling as he walked the forest last night. He wasn't sure yet how to tell if it was a storm brewing somewhere or the Shifts changing the mountainside.

He leaned over the ten-foot-high ledge overlooking the rushing water below when he heard the bushes rustling behind him. He turned, hoping that one of the large Pagorinx had found him, but to his dismay it was not them.

Out walked a man, and from what Bridget had told him, none of the men who roamed this mountainside were friendly.

Marnor stopped dead in his tracks.

"Upon my word. Every time I trek this mountain, I seem to run into someone new. Now who might you be?"

Dominic hesitated to answer, unsure what to say or how much he *should* say. "I'm no one important."

"I'll be the judge of that. Where is it you come from…what did you say your name was?"

"I didn't," Dominic answered.

Marnor grinned at the sharp-witted boy. "Are you here alone?"

"Yeah, I got lost. Separated from my family walking from the other side of the mountain. The Shifts planted me here and I'm not sure where my family is." He lied to protect Bridget.

Marnor stood silent for a minute sizing the young man up. "Well then, you can just come back to camp with me and we'll see about locating this *family* of yours. I have people that can help with the search." Marnor's greasy grin made Dominic hesitant about the truth of his statement.

"No thanks. I think I'd like to keep looking for them on my own," Dominic replied confidently.

"I'm not askin', fella," Marnor said, pulling a sword from his side and pointing it at Dominic. "Move." Marnor motioned in which direction with the end of the sword.

Dominic looked down, realizing his gun holster was not on. He must have left it back at the tree house. Boy, his incompetence over the last day or so was really getting him into trouble. He took a deep breath, looked at Marnor and knew he had no choice but to follow the man's orders.

The two of them trailed along the stream's edge until they reached the bottom where the ground level was even with the water. There, near the water's edge was a camp with about four tents and maybe five other people milling about.

Dominic threw up a silent prayer to God to help him out of this mess he had gotten himself into. Marnor pushed at him with the tip of his sword hitting him in the wounded part of his shoulder. Dominic winced in pain catching Marnor's attention.

"Have a seat, boy." Marnor motioned to the stump beside a low burning fire.

Dominic obliged him, unable to do much else.

"What's wrong with your shoulder there," Marnor asked him.

"I fell and hurt it trying to navigate the woods last night in the dark," he lied again. He felt like he should tell this man as little as possible about who he really was.

Marnor watched him closely trying to gauge whether or not he was lying. So far he couldn't tell one way or the other. If the boy was lying, then he hid it well. Marnor figured him for one of those Peregrines that kept popping up over the last several months. If he was, then he might could tell him how to do this time-travel business as well.

Morning came, and as soon as it was bright enough, Bridget called for Han once again. She soared through the skies on the back of Han in search of Dominic. They weren't having any luck locating him around the upper ridgeline, so she decided to try further down the mountain.

Surely he didn't walk all the way to the river? she thought.

"All right, Han. Let's fly to the gorge and see if we can spot him there."

It took about an hour for Han to reach the river. As they flew around, in wide circles, Bridget spotted a camp near the lowest part.

"I believe those might be Scaithers down there. Get a bit lower Han, but not too low. I just want to see who it is."

Han circled the skies, flying lower as instructed. Bridget could make out that there were about seven people below. She had to fly lower to be able to make out who everyone was.

Bridget's breath caught in her throat. "Dominic, oh no!" Marnor had Dominic.

The Scaithers all ducked and ran for cover at the familiar shadow of the large bird that momentarily blocked out the sun. All but Marnor that is. The bird did frighten him, but not enough for him to leave the boy. He gathered that the girl from yesterday was riding the firebird, and this boy here was just who she was searching for. He figured as long as he stayed beside the boy, he'd be safe.

Bridget and Han landed a little way from the camp edge. She dismounted and waited for Marnor to speak.

"Look boys, we have a visitor. First time we've ever had one come willingly." He laughed, as did the others.

"Let him go, Marnor," Bridget called to him.

"Well, now. I don't remember being introduced to you yesterday. It isn't polite for you to know my name and me not know yours." Marnor smiled, enjoying the little game they were playing.

"Why should I tell you anything?"

Marnor's blade rested at Dominic's throat and with her refusal, he grabbed Dominic by the shirt, pulling him closer to the blade. Dominic flinched in fear.

"Wait!" she yelled. "Bridget. My name is Bridget."

Marnor's hold on Dominic weakened slightly, giving the young man cause to sigh. Marnor looked at Bridget silently studying her for a moment. Her age seemed about right, her coloring, and the fact that she traveled with those called Peregrines. Could it really be her?

"Your last name wouldn't happen to be Burke would it?"

Bridget grew nervous again at the mention of her surname. Her father must have made enemies everywhere he went.

She took a deep breath and answered, "Yes, it is."

Marnor couldn't believe what he was seeing. He believed them both to be dead. This was fortuitous indeed!

"Well now, why don't you come over here and have a bit of a chat with me, Bridget. I have some news for you that just might surprise you."

"Let him go first."

"Nah, I don't think so. See, he's the only thing keeping your pet there from roastin' me alive. Send the bird away."

Dominic grew worried at the request. "Bridget, don't listen to him," he yelled.

"Shut up, boy, or I'll skin you alive," Marnor threatened him.

Bridget turned to Han. "Go, Han, but stay close. I will call on you again as soon as I can get Dominic away from Marnor." Han squawked loudly in protest, flapping his wings violently, as he gazed at the evil man just thirty or so feet away. He then took to the skies and sailed out of sight.

"Wise decision, Bridget." Marnor sheathed his weapon but did not step away from Dominic.

"Now, what is it that you could possibly know that you think would be of interest to me?" she asked as she got closer to the camp.

"I just wanted to say, that I knew your father."

"Yes, I've gathered that he knew a lot of people." She sighed.

"Yeah, well, I also knew your mother too," Marnor said, chancing a small step away from Dominic in Bridget's direction.

"How could you possibly have known my mother?" she asked confused.

"'Cause Mary Draiwood was my mother too." Marnor smirked.

Bridget froze in place and exclaimed, "What!?"

"Yeah. That would make you and me brother and sister." Marnor grinned at the look on her face. He had waited so long to get even with Hiram for taking his mother away, now he had his daughter.

"No. It isn't possible," Bridget mumbled, her brain going in so many different directions.

"You might not like it, but you're part Scaither." Marnor's wicked laugh echoed through the trees all around her.

Bridget stood there shaking her head no, unable to process what he was saying to her. She was so shaken by his declaration that she didn't see Marnor's men come up behind her until they had grabbed her.

Dominic tried to warn her but the minute he went to yell, Marnor backhanded him across the face to shut him up.

The Scaithers carried Bridget into camp and deposited her down beside Dominic on the stump.

"Well now, Sis, it seems we have a lot of catching up to do." Marnor grinned broadly as he leaned down over her.

Bridget looked up into the face of Marnor as he spoke. She didn't say a word. He had to be lying to her. There was no way she could be related to this evil man. But then her father had been considered an evil man as well. Good Lord! She didn't know how much more she could take when it came to her family history!

"Let's all head inside my tent over here and have us a little chat, shall we?" He bowed at the waist while he gestured for her and Dominic to lead, mocking her.

Bridget and Dominic stood up and walked the short distance to Marnor's tent. As she entered, she heard him give orders to the other five men to stay outside and to round up some lunch. Then he stepped into the rather large tent, containing a cot for his bed, a table and two chairs, and a chest which probably held a few changes of clothing.

She watched as he stepped inside and pulled out a chair from the table to sit on, watching her the whole time as he did. Dominic stepped between her and Marnor acting as her protector, unsure what Marnor's intentions toward Bridget were. Marnor found his actions quite amusing and began to laugh at the young man.

"Boy, what do you think you could do to me if I did want to hurt her? From what I've seen so far, she has way more power than you'll ever have." He leaned back in his chair and crossed his ankles, throwing both arms behind his head clasping his fingers together. When Dominic didn't move, Marnor asked another question.

"What, are you two a couple? A bit young don't you think?"

"No, we are not." Bridget placed her hand on Dominic's arm, giving him a grateful look as she stepped in front of him. "He is a loyal friend."

"Well isn't that sweet," Marnor mocked.

"What exactly is it that you want with us, Marnor?" Bridget asked boldly.

"There are a few things. Especially now that I know exactly who you are. One, I want to know how to time-jump or whatever it is your kind calls it. Two, I want to know where mother and Hiram got to. And three, I want to know how you can control the deadliest beast known to everyone around here." Marnor's gaze suddenly turned very serious.

"All right. First, we are chosen by God to time-jump. It isn't something just anyone can do."

"How did Mary do it then?" He quickly leaned forward waiting for her answer.

"She didn't. She died, just on the other side of the portal."

Marnor's face suddenly flashed with emotion, but she couldn't tell exactly what it was. "Then how come you survived, and she didn't?"

"I don't know exactly. Except that God chose me for it."

"Where's that backstabbing leach you call a father now?"

Bridget's face grew sad. "He's gone. Died several years ago."

Marnor sat mulling something over in his head for a second. "All right, next question. What about the animals."

"I'm not exactly a Peregrine like the others. I am a Beast Keeper. My God given gift is communicating with them. I understand them and they me."

"So, you just speak to them and they do whatever you want?"

"Sort of. But they still have their own will, I can't control everything they do. They just respect me enough to usually cooperate."

"This could be very useful to me." Marnor stroked his beard as the wheels of his mind turned.

"I will not use the animals for your wicked gain," Bridget said boldly.

"You won't have a choice, girl!" Marnor threatened, as he stood and towered over her small frame.

"When I am afraid, I put my trust in you. In God, whose word I praise - in God I trust and am not afraid. What can mere mortals do to me?" Bridget quoted from Psalm 56:3-4.

"What are you talking about? Who is this God you keep speaking of, and trust enough to not fear me?" He leaned even closer to her.

"He is the creator of all things, in all worlds. It is because of him that you and I even exist." She stared up into his hard face.

"We exist because of our mother, and whatever man she decided to take up with next. Not because of some…God."

"You're wrong, Marnor. Yes, mother had us, but God created us first."

Marnor laughed at her now. "Where in the world did you ever come up with such nonsense?" He stepped away from her.

"The Bible. It's a book divinely written by God himself."

"A book? You're basing your whole life and belief about a God on what a book says?" Marnor laughed at her, actually doubling over with laughter.

Bridget's heart ached for the man's ignorance.

"One day, Marnor, you'll stand before God in judgment and you won't laugh then."

"Enough!" He yelled, his laughter suddenly halting. Anger streaked his face again. "Don't *you* tell me that some *God* is going to judge me. I make my own future!" He stood, almost nose to nose with her again. Marnor turned away, grabbed some rope, and tied each of their hands together. Then he put them back-to-back and tied the rope around their bodies. "This ought to keep the two of you where I want you until I can decide what *I want* to do with you." His threatening glare made Bridget's heart beat faster with fear.

After Marnor left the tent, Dominic spoke. "Bridget, I'm sorry, this is all my fault."

"No, Dominic it is mine. If I hadn't run off like a silly little girl, you wouldn't have gone looking for me."

"If I hadn't been so rude to you, you wouldn't have run off. I'm truly sorry, Bridget. I didn't mean to hurt your feelings."

"I understand, Dominic. I do tend to chatter away at times. In the future, you are free to tell me to stop."

"Okay. But I promise to not be so horrible about how I do it. That is, if we make it out of here alive."

"I don't think he'll harm us, at least not kill us. If he wanted to do that, I believe he would have already done so."

It grew quiet for a moment before Dominic asked. "Bridget, do you really think he's telling you the truth about being your brother?"

"I don't know. I'm not even certain how I feel about it. I was an orphan for so long, alone for years before Caroline showed up. As much as she is like an older sister to me and Oz a grandfatherly type, I am still alone. No family to even wonder if they are all right, or how they are doing. I know none of us really have our family with us, but to find out that I may have a brother, well, it's kind of... nice. Even if he is a complete cad."

Marnor stood outside the tent, listening to their conversation, hoping they would say something or admit something that would be useful to him. He never expected to hear Bridget actually say that she was a little happy at finding him. Over the years, he had encountered plenty of these people called Peregrines, and most of them were very different than anyone else he had ever met. He thought it was just some sort of defense mechanism, or training that they all possessed. Bridget didn't appear to be trained, just sincere in her crazy beliefs. Still, he was angry. With, Hiram, Bridget, and most of all his mother, Mary. She had chosen Hiram and the new life he offered her over her own fourteen-year-old son. He had thought all these years that she had left him and was living somewhere with Hiram and their new baby girl, in the lap of luxury. Far away from the dismal existence of the Scaithers here in Zanchier. He shook the reverie from his head and stalked away from the tent into the woods. He needed to distance himself from the girl in his tent. His sister. Like her he had thought he was alone in the world. As far as he was concerned, he was. She and her father had taken everything from him. And it wasn't something he was ever willing to forget or forgive.

Dominic and Bridget used each-others weight to slide to the floor so that they could at least sit down. As they sat there in the quiet, hot, tent, she suddenly had a thought. When she had lived here before, she had seen a beaver type animal whose teeth appeared to be razor sharp, which lived near the river. If she could call to one telepathically, she might be able to get it to chew through the ropes. She closed her eyes and concentrated on the animal she wanted to contact. At least ten minutes had past when they heard scurrying outside the tent.

"Bridget, I think he's coming back," Dominic said nervously.

Bridget kept her head down, giving cautious instructions.

Dominic grew anxious at the rustling sound at the front of the tent flaps. He watched, his nerves growing tight when suddenly the tent flap moved ever so slightly and in scurried a medium sized animal. It was so furry that it almost looked like a ball of fuzz rolling around on the floor. As it got closer, Dominic noticed a protruding pinkish-white nose. He couldn't see the creature's eyes at all as it approached them. And, although Dominic was a keeper, he wasn't sure of the animal's intentions.

"Hey, you, what are you doing?" he nervously asked the fuzz-ball as he began to wiggle, trying to avoid the animal's approach.

"Dominic, it's all right. I called it to chew the ropes."

"Whew…I wasn't sure what that thing was here to do. How did you know it could do that?" Dominic watched the furry creature lean its front paws against the rope tied around Bridget's hands and began chewing.

"I remembered it from when I lived here before. Caroline and I got lost down here as well and separated by the river. This camp is close to where I first met Paxton and discovered I could talk with the animals. While Paxton and I searched for Caroline, I saw all manner of creatures that dwell here near the river. This furry little thing I noticed building a dam further down-stream where the river splits in different directions."

"Let's hope it can chew through these ropes."

"I believe it can. I've called for Paxton and Mother. They should be here soon."

"Why do you think Marnor left us alone knowing you could call them to help you?"

"He knows that I can speak to the animals, but he doesn't know that I can telepathically communicate with them as well. If he heard me screaming for them, then he could stop me."

"You're a pretty smart girl, Bridget," Dominic said, a smile lacing his voice.

"Thank you, Dominic."

Bridget grinned as the fuzzy creature had finished its job. It then walked to Dominic and began chewing his ropes as Bridget wriggled free of the rope that was tied around their waists. She pulled the ropes off Dominic, patted the little animal thank you, and finished undoing Dominic's hands while the creature scurried out of the tent.

It wasn't long before they heard shouts of fear outside. The men that were still in the camp ran away screaming as Mother and Paxton entered the camp, growling and hissing, calling to Bridget.

Bridget and Dominic ran outside and were climbing upon their backs when Marnor, who had heard the screams of his men, ran back into camp.

"How did you get untied, and how did these animals get here?" he yelled at her as they locked eyes.

"God, Marnor." She then looked away, and she and Dominic rode out quickly, back up into the mountains to the safety of the tree house.

Marnor watched them go, furious they had gotten away. She had been his last chance at possibly leaving Zanchier. He screamed into the sky, kicking at the rocks along the riverbank, his frustration at losing one of these Peregrines again making him lose all sense of control.

Less than a minute later, Faigen and Quenzie, two of Marnor's men, came screaming in fear headed straight for Marnor, yelling for him to protect them, and babbling about how *they* killed the others.

"What are you idiots yelling about now? Who killed who?" Marnor grilled them. But before they could answer, two of the ugliest creatures Marnor had ever seen walked out of the woods. These creatures were not from Zanchier, and if they were new here that means they probably got here the same way the Peregrines did; through the portals. Maybe Marnor could use that to his advantage.

322

Pride goes before destruction and a
haughty spirit before stumbling.

Proverbs 16:18

Chapter 21

Reader's Island

As the large band of travelers returned to Reader's Island with the Breastplates of Righteousness, they were weary indeed. It seemed like an eternity had passed over the last month. So much had happened since they left Reader's Island to search for the first piece of armor.

They had spent three weeks traveling and living in the Timna Valley desert of Israel where they encountered the largest demon war most of them had yet fought. Then, they spent an entire week of non-stop traveling, most of which was in a saddle or onboard a ship where they experienced a massive thunderstorm, almost losing another Peregrine to an angry sea. Amongst all of that was the two demon battles, and the spiritual trials that had weakened their resolve and wounded their spirits. Just recently they discovered that two of them bore tribal marks that were not found to belong to 'The Twelve' by some Lord from the dark ages. And, to top it all off, Bridget and Dominic were still missing.

They were ready for a quiet day or two on the island to rest and recharge. Hopefully God would allow them that small bit of solace before He called them to search for the next armor piece.

The men took wonderful, steaming-hot, showers, while the women indulged in luxurious bubble-baths to ebb away the tired aches from their muscles.

The island chef, Clancy, created a wonderful dinner for them finishing it off with a decadent dessert to sooth and comfort the palette and soul. The nightly Bible study which was held just after dinner was spent in prayer for Bridget and Dominic to be returned to them soon. After which, most everyone retired to the patio area where they sat in the loungers and thickly padded, over-sized chairs, visiting or gazing up at the fantastic star filled sky, and enjoying the cool, salt-tinged breeze from the nearby beaches.

They would also relish in the feel of the overly-large comfortable beds for however long they got to stay here. The old-world hostel beds and tent living was hard on a body after a while, no matter how young you were, or how great your physical prowess was.

Simon took a moment to seek out Seth and Jason for the chat he wanted to have with them about the quiet exchange they had back in Cyprus earlier. The sooner he got the questioning out of the way, the better he and everyone else would sleep.

"Jason, Seth, a word if you please." Simon gestured for them to join him on a quiet and currently unused portion of the patio. "I believe that something is going on with the two of you and I am curious to know what it is exactly? Is there something I need to know about?"

Jason cleared his throat and spoke up. "It's my fault, Simon. Seth has nothing to do with it except for him being a good and loyal friend." Jason nodded at Seth as he spoke. Seth returned a nod of thanks.

"Well, what is it?" Simon stated, waiting for the reluctant Jason to speak.

"I didn't sense the demons back in Tintagel because I wasn't there. I figured no one would miss me for a little while since Merlin had every one's attention, so I went back to Timna Valley to see Memnah."

"Well, that certainly explains a few things."

"I'm sorry, Simon. But the Portgens make it very easy and the temptation was just too great. It's really hard watching Seth and Caroline. And when we are here on the island, Oz and Prisca have each other, as well as most of the island staff. Now, young Sean and Kristen have started a relationship. My soul aches for Memnah in a way I never knew it could."

Simon sighed in understanding. "I do understand, Jason. But missions are no place to be disappearing off to another world and time when the possibility of a demon attack is present, and we seem to be having so many of those lately."

"I know, Simon. I'm sorry, I'll try not to let it happen again." Jason apologized but his words clearly made no guarantees.

"Yes, well, since we are here on the island, I don't see why you can't take off and go to her now, do you?" Simon smiled over his circular, wire-rimmed glasses.

Jason grinned from ear to ear. "Thank you, Simon. I *shouldn't* be gone *too* long." Jason jumped up and ran to his room to grab his Portgen and open a portal to 1840 Israel at Timna Valley.

"Ah, young love." Simon smiled at the exuberance the man displayed for this woman. He only wished there was some way for the two of them to be together. Maybe Ryan could figure something out. He would have to have a chat with the young technical genius about that later.

"Yeah," Seth concurred, "I still feel that way about Caroline." The two men smiled at each other. "Speaking of which, I have my own beauty to go find." Seth stood and left to find his wife and enjoy their possible, uninterrupted, island time.

Simon watched the younger men go, his mind returning to his own life and lost love of so many years ago. How he wished he could go back himself and find his Lily. With the Portgens it was possible, but he looked nothing like he did back then. Especially with the premature aging from creating storms. You could always go back, but never look or be the same again.

Simon watched the interaction of the people as they sat and chatted. His gaze shifted to Sean Doran and Kristen Wright. Jason had mentioned that they seemed to be forming a relationship, and with the way Kristen had clung to the young man when they discovered he did not drown, he would have to say that Jason was very likely correct in his thinking. The two of them were just exiting the house and went to sit in a quiet, somewhat secluded section of the porch.

Kristen and Sean sat in two of the large Adirondack chairs that were nestled beneath the second-floor terrace, and graced with the wonderful scent of the climbing, purple and white Wisteria vines. Kristen breathed deeply of the flower's fragrance, not only enjoying the scent but also trying to steady her nerves. She exhaled, turned toward Sean, and began.

"Sean, I've been trying to talk to you since our last conversation. The one where we were so rudely interrupted by Tim."

"Yeah, I remember." Sean turned and looked out across the veranda at the others. "I also remember the look on your face. I'd say that said it all."

"Sean, you never even gave me the chance to answer you. I'm not sure exactly what you read in my expression, and, honestly, no one can tell what a person is thinking simply by what you read into their facial expressions. No matter what you think you saw, I have to say that you were wrong in your conclusion."

Sean looked at Kristen, hopeful in her meaning.

"Sean, I was so shocked by what you said. Not because I don't feel the same way, but because I *do*. I pretty much settled my feelings on you back in Timna while we were searching through Solomon's Mines"

Sean still wasn't convinced. "What about you and Timothy? I saw the exchange between the two of you back at the Tintagel camp site. He has some kind of effect on you."

"I'll admit that he *did* have an effect on me. I did like him for a while when we were here on the island for that one month. But I hadn't really gotten to know him yet. And after the way he's been behaving lately, that has all passed, I assure you."

"Are you certain about that, Kristen?" Sean leaned forward to look into her eyes. "I don't think my heart could take deception from you. Once I give my heart away, I plan to see it through."

"I'm positive. If the way I acted back on board the ship wasn't any indication, then I'm not sure there is anything else I can do to show you how I feel that would convince you." She stared down at the cement beneath their feet.

Sean reached beneath her chin, bringing her eyes up to look at him. "I'd say that *was pretty* convincing." He grinned broadly.

Kristen grinned sheepishly along with him, giggling a bit in the process. He always knew what to say to make her feel better about herself.

"When I thought you were gone, washed overboard in that storm, I felt like my heart had been ripped out of my chest. Like I would be lost forever if you weren't a part of it."

"Now you know how I felt when you almost fell to your death through that old mine shaft. And every time I saw you with Timothy," he said seriously, gazing into her eyes.

Kristen saw, and felt, the pain in his eyes as he spoke about it all.

"Sean, I'm so sorry. I had no idea how you felt. I thought you just saw me as a friend." She took his hand in hers and laced her fingers through his.

Sean watched her actions and smiled. He and Kristen sat there, hand in hand, well into the night, just talking and enjoying each other's company, knowing that they were finally a couple.

Alec and Odessa also made amends, although still not in the way he wished, but he couldn't stay angry with her forever. They spent the evening pleasantly, talking with Nick, Nadia, Sofia, Gabby, and Wade.

Zeke and Zaccai also sat close to them, joining in occasionally in the group conversation, but also having a private one of their own as they spent some time getting to know one another better.

Clancy and Shannon brought the large decanters of coffee on a cart, along with a mild banana cake and a few platters of cinnamon rolls for everyone to enjoy. They sat outside amongst the stars, and the gently glowing tiki torches that twinkled brightly at the edge of the patio. Some of the lowly burning torches were also mixed in amongst the tropical potted plants scattered all around.

Gabby had brought her ukelele outside after dinner and was strumming and singing as some of the others joined her in song. Oz and Prisca, Seth and Caroline, and Clancy and Shannon, all swayed to the music as the others sang, dancing beneath the stars.

Kristen was surprised to find that Sean actually had a nice singing voice, and knew a lot of the words to Gabby's Christian music. She thought about the last time she had seen them together and silently wondered whether or not they were beginning to be an item. Gabby didn't seem to care that she and Sean were holding hands, but perhaps she couldn't see them? It wasn't something she was going to let bother her. Sean had told her he liked her and that was good enough, for now. They would take their relationship slowly and see how things went. Neither of them were willing to rush anything, not with so much uncertainty facing their futures.

Uriah and Tim sat on the balcony of Uriah's room which overlooked the courtyard patio below and all the others who were enjoying the night. Tim's spirits were a bit low seeing as how he had lost the game for Kristen's affections. Uriah sat and watched his friend wallow in self-pity.

"You've really got to get yourself out of this mood you're in over that girl. Is she really worth all this missery?" Uriah asked.

"I don't know. I just know that I shouldn't have lost her to a guy like Sean Doran. I don't understand what happened." Tim sat, truly befuddled with the loss.

Uriah decided to change the subject. 'Hey, what do you think about the marks? You know, the two that aren't considered acceptable? Who do you think bares those two marks?"

"I'm sure I don't know, Uriah. What difference does it make anyway? The Twelve have to fight in a major war with some un-known opponent. It doesn't sound all that glamorous to me."

"I know. But, The Twelve will also rule over kingdoms afterward, when, and if, the battle is won. Don't you remember the prophecy that Simon read from the *Book of Armor*?"

"Yeah, I do sort of remember that. I guess it would be nice to rule my own kingdom one day. What do you think the rest of those who aren't part of The Twelve will be left with? Do you think they'll rule somewhere?"

"The prophecy didn't say. More than likely they will serve The Twelve somehow." A smile began to form on Uriah's face. "It sure would be nice to Lord over some of those pompous peacocks down there."

"You really don't like some of them, do you?"

"No. I don't"

"You might want to get a handle on your anger, Uriah. It's getting uglier by the day. Besides, what did any of them do to you?"

"That's my business, besides, you're one to talk. You're just as angry as I am at two of the people down there."

Tim didn't like the insinuation that Uriah was making, and he also didn't feel like discussing losing Kristen any more tonight.

"I think I'm done with this conversation. I'm going to bed. See you in the morning." Tim stood up and left Uriah's room for the seclusion of his own.

Zanchier

Bridget and Dominic made it back to the tree house a few hours later realizing that it was time for them to leave.

"Dominic, we need to gather whatever supplies we might need and close up the treehouse. I so love my beautiful Zanchier and all the animals, but we can not stay any longer. Are you feeling all right after all the events of today?"

"Yeah, I think so. I should be fine to travel, Bridget. Besides if that Marnor fellow comes looking for us again, we may not be so fortunate next time."

"Yes, you are right about that. Especially knowing what he does now about who I am. He seemed awfully angry that Hiram was my father."

"Yeah, I don't think he'll extend you the hand of brotherly love anytime soon."

Bridget's heart ached slightly at Dominic's words, knowing he was correct about that.

"All right, Dominic, let's head up to the top Platform and call on Han and Cho. They'll have to fly us to the Dustbowl for our return. Let's make sure Oz's place is shut tightly up and everything is stored properly before we go." Bridget busied herself with cleaning up the kitchen and putting things in their proper place.

"Where exactly should we return to? The others have most likely moved on by now." Dominic joined in the effort to put things in their proper places.

"I suppose we should go to the island. It would be the most likely place to return to. The others there should be able to tell us where everyone else has gone."

"Can you decide where you want to go at the Dustbowl? Isn't it like most other storms? It just spits you out wherever it wants?"

"Yes, then, wherever we end up, we just simply push the home button for the island. We haven't gotten to use that yet," she said with a smile.

Dominic smiled back and they finished cleaning and packing things away. They chose to spend the night in the tree house one last time, not wanting to make the two-hour flight to the dustbowl and then time-jump during the night hours.

The next morning they ate breakfast and cleaned up before calling to the large firebirds. Dominic hadn't yet experienced riding the massive, four-legged birds and the thought excited him immensely.

Bridget mounted Han while Dominic mounted Cho. The four of them took off one last time from the platform of the tree house. Bridget looked back at the home she would miss the most. This place held a special spot in her heart. She thought about yesterday's events, anxious and fearful of what her future might reveal next about her past.

Reader's Island

The next morning on the island, a few people woke early, again enjoying the down time. Only those whose internal clocks wouldn't relent were up with the morning sun.

Simon, of course being one of those few, took his coffee outside to the veranda where Nuncio just happened to be this morning.

"Well, this is fortuitous." Simon sat down beside his friend.

"Oh? Why is that?" Nuncio questioned him with a grin.

"I've been meaning to have a chat with you about The Twelve's marks. It appears that we may have a problem there."

"Really? How so?" Nuncio's brow furrowed in question.

"When we acquired the breastplates from the Knights Templar, their High Regent, someone by the name of Lord Rowthorn, specified that the scroll he read from claimed that two of our Peregrines were not to be of The Twelve."

"How was he to know this? Who is this Lord Regent, anyway? And how do we know we can trust him?"

"Well, Merlin gave me a letter addressed to the man." Simon noticed the look on his face. "Yes, my old friend, Merlin was real, as was Arthur. We didn't meet him but we did get to meet and speak with Merlin. He was a Dragoman of old."

"Really?" Nuncio's face was full of wonder and questions.

"I'll tell you more on him later. Right now we have this problem with The Twelve to figure out."

"What exactly did this Lord Rowthorn say?"

"He said two of the marks were unapproved. Those two marks belong to Uriah and Timothy."

"Well, what about the two approved marks that take their place. Do we know who has them?"

"Yes. Gabriele and Kristen. Gabriele had the mark for Levi and Kristen bares the mark for Joseph."

"Hmm, that does sound familiar. I believe I have read in scripture before about the defilement of certain tribes. They were approved in the old testament, but in Revelations the tribes are listed with Dan and Ephraim being replaced with Levi and Joseph. I just never thought about which of those twelve tribes we would be representing."

"Yes, neither did I. I just assumed that since we had twelve already we had who we needed. I must say, I'm fearful that this turn of events may cause some bitterness in the group. Uriah is already angry and resentful about not being one of the leaders. Especially since most of the others that are in those positions are much less experienced than he is."

"But the leaders weren't chosen based on experience. More on who knew about the missing key."

"We know that, but the others do not." Simon reminded him.

"Oh yes, I see your point. Well, let's pray that this new development does not cause more hard feelings for Uriah."

"Timothy may not take it all that well either. He has had feelings for Kristen and doesn't appear too happy that she has chosen young Doran instead."

"Goodness, plenty of things have certainly transpired over the last month or so haven't they?"

"You don't know the half of it I'm afraid," Simon said, looking at his friend. "Remind me to fill you in later this evening, when we have more uninterupted time to discuss things." Simon finished the sentence just as others began to trickle out on the veranda with their morning breakfast.

"After breakfast, we can go to the archival library and research this further before making an announcement," Nuncio suggested.

"I agree. There's no need to be too hasty with this one." Simon sipped the strong coffee from his mug.

Breakfast was a leisurely affair with people fading in and out throughout the morning.

Simon and the other Dragoman called a brief mid-morning meeting in the main hall with the Peregrine group leaders, having much to discuss.

"First we have found the key that opens the last book, but unfortunately, not the traitor. That is something that must still be uncovered, so you seven must continue to search for this person. On another note, with the finding of the key, we Dragoman will work to make sense of the books and their mysteries while the rest of you are out on missions," Simon said.

"What, no more missions, Simon?" Seth joked with him.

"Not for me, thanks. I've gotten to old for all that running around. Unless God specifically wants me there, I'll stay here on the island." Simon gave him a strained grin and chuckle. "What's more, Merlin has given me some very good information on how to determine the undecipherable language in which the *Book of the Keepers* was written, and a possible way to find the language key that could break the code. Ryan, I would like you to run an extensive search on ancient cultures that vanished unexpectedly throughout history. Also, try to find as much information on those civilizations as possible, especially anything that had to do with ancient languages, cuniforms, and the many forms of heiroglyphics."

"Okay, Simon, I can do that," Ryan said shyly.

"Thank you, my boy." Simon encouraged him.

"Also, we need to call a meeting of only The Twelve. Unfortunately right now there are fourteen people who have been marked and we need to determine which Twelve are the ones that must fight in the end. After lunch, we would like all foruteen to meet back here in the meeting room. Please, Dragoman, pass the word to your Peregrines. Now, everyone is excused and let's see if we can continue the search for Bridget and Dominic."

Zanchier

Marnor quickly dropped to his knees, his hands raised in the air as the hideous beasts grew nearer to them.

"Get down you idiots," he hissed to Quenzie and Faigen who stood rooted in fear. They quickly dropped to their knees, covering the back of their heads with their hands.

Marnor adressed the half man-half beast creatures who stopped at the obvious worship before them.

"Gentlemen," Marnor said coaxingly, "Perhaps we could make a deal. Maybe I can help you some way if you help me." He dared to look up, grinning reverently at the beings before him. The demons grinned menacingly back at him, growling and laughing to each other.

Reader's Island

The noon hour came and went with the fourteen Peregrines gathering together in the meeting hall with their Dragoman leaders, whom Simon had already briefed about the mark mix up.

Simon stood to address the group seated around him.

"You all know there was a small problem concerning two of the marks that represent the twelve tribes of Israel. Two of you were believed to be marked to fight in the final battle. I'm afraid that, according to ancient script, two of you have marks that will not be accepted by God to fight."

"We already know that, Simon. What we don't know is who the two are." Uriah grinned. He couldn't wait to see the look on their faces, whoever it was.

"Yes, that's why we are here, Uriah." Simon was growing weary of delivering the next news. "The two marks that have not been allowed to battle are Dan and Ephraim."

The room grew quiet as it sunk in as to who those two people were.

Uriah looked at Simon and then at his mentor Malachai. "How can this be? You are the one who told me, no, *convinced* me that I was one of The Twelve. And now, even that has been taken from me as well? Why is my mark one that is unacceptable to God when He is the one who gave it to me?" Uriah's temper began to grow.

Timothy sat there silent for a moment just listening to his friend grow angrier, waiting for his chance to speak up.

"Uriah, Hiram is the one who found your mark, not I," Malachai said, "but that doesn't matter. It isn't anyone's fault and certainly not anyone's choice here that you be excluded. It is simply the will of God."

"Shouldn't that little tidbit have been discussed and figured out before you let us believe we were part of The Twelve?" he steamed.

Simon spoke, trying to calm Uriah down. "Uriah, please listen. According to the Book of Revelations, the tribes listed do not include Dan and Ephraim because they had defiled themselves before God and refused to repent. God deemed them unworthy to fight for this reason. I am certain that God has his reasons for this. None of us here know why. There are many things that the Lord does for which we don't have an answer. We just have to trust that His ways are right and good for what He wishes from, and for, us."

Timothy spoke next. "So, who is it that's replacing me and Uriah?" He knew the answer to this already, for they had figured that out back in Cyprus when the two ladies were sent to the High Regent, Lord Rowthorn for approval.

"According to scriptures, Gabriele stands for Levi and replaces Uriah, whereas Kristen represents Joseph and replaces Ephraim."

"Well that figures." Tim looked aggravatedly at Kristen.

"Look, Tim, it isn't my fault this happened. I'm not even sure exactly what it all means. Neither I, nor Gabriele, have been training as one of The Twelve," Kristen said in defense of the look he had given her.

"All right, everyone, let's just settle down, shall we?" Simon raised his hands in the air to get their attention.

The room grew quiet, but the tension was still so thick that it could have been cut with a knife.

"Now there isn't anything that can be done by anyone other than God Himself to change any of this. I suggest you just make your peace with the idea."

Uriah and Timothy were getting ready to argue their points once again when the meeting room door flew open. Petra stepped into the room and said, "Bridget and Dominic are back. They just stepped out of a portal in the front yard."

"Meeting adjourned," Simon quickly announced as everyone ran out of the room to greet the two young people who had been missing for three days now. Everyone that is, except Uriah and Timothy.

Zanchier

Marnor had bartered passage out of Zanchier in exchange for allowing the demons to possess them. This, the demons had told him, was the only way for him to ever leave the place he hated so much. This would also allow the demons to hide their true forms no matter what dimension they traveled into, even the fourth where their hidden forms fell away. What they failed to mention to Marnor, and Faigen was the constant torment that possession would inflict, both mentally and physically. And the fact that they would never give them back over to their own lives and bodies. They would be trapped forever, linked with these beasts for as long as the demons wanted.

Quenzie watched in fear as the demons took possession of Marnor and Faigen, and the horrible pain it caused them. He slunk away in fear, running for his life. He might be a simple minded fellow, but even he was smart enough to not barter with pure evil.

The End.

If you enjoyed reading this third book in the series, please help me out by leaving me a book review at whatever venue from which you purchased your copy. For more information on future books in the series, visit my website at:

www.sgboudreaux.com

www.zanchierpublications.com

Book 4

The Peregrines have acquired two of the pieces of armor and are searching for the third. One of the last demon battles wounded some of the Peregrines and killed some of the desert people who had aided them in the war.

While searching for the armor pieces they heard a rumor that the last piece of armor to find, the Swords of Truth, were destroyed centuries ago by someone or something that knew of their significance. The last unopened book has been unlocked and its secrets are being closely studied. The Dragoman have discovered many clues between the pages of the ancient archival books.

The Swords of Truth must be used in the final battle for the Peregrines to even have a chance at winning. What it is that they are to fight against they still are unsure. The Dragoman are racing against time to decipher the language in the Book of the Keepers, which they have now determined to be Akrotiri. An ancient, Grecian culture that once existed and disappeared from the face of the earth after a large, storm hit the city long ago. Now they must find some way to interpret the book or all could be lost forever.

The End.

If you've enjoyed reading this third book in the Peregrination Series, please help me out by leaving a book review on whatever venue you choose or where you purchased the book. For more information on future titles visit:

www.sgboudreaux.com   or   www.zanchierpublications.com

About the Author

S.G. Boudreaux began writing clean fantasy, fiction, and time-travel in 2017. She felt people needed a clean alternative when reading these genres and believes that what she writes may influence someone else. Because of this, she puts her faith and beliefs into everything she writes. Her love of these genres began with Star Wars when she was young, and her inspiration for clean writing stems from other authors such as C.S Lewis, and J.R.R. Tolkien. She enjoys music, especially playing the drums for church or for special events, writing, creating new creatures for her books, learning new things, gardening, animals, and all things beach related. She and her special needs daughter, youngest of three children, reside in Louisiana.

For more on her life and current events that she is involved in, visit her website at www.sgboudreaux.com or her amazon authors page at amazon.com/author/sgboudreaux

Other Book in the Series

Book 1: Earth

Book 2: Wind

Book 4: Water

Book 5: The Final Battle; Battle of the Beasts

Other books by author

Zanchier Series of Books

Subjugation Book 1

Uprising Book 2

Anarchy Book 3

Search other Nonfiction books by
Shawna Boudreaux

341

342

343